For Nicole and Alexis.

the Fiery Heart

A *Bloodlines* NOVEL

RICHELLE MEAD

PENGUIN BOOKS

PENGUIN BOOKS

Published by the Penguin Group
Penguin Books Ltd, 80 Strand, London WC2R ORL, England
Penguin Group (USA) Inc., 375 Hudson Street, New York, New York 10014, USA
Penguin Group (Canada), 90 Eglinton Avenue East, Suite 700, Toronto,
Ontario, Canada M4P 2Y3 (a division of Pearson Penguin Canada Inc.)
Penguin Ireland, 25 St Stephen's Green, Dublin 2, Ireland (a division of Penguin Books Ltd)
Penguin Group (Australia), 707 Collins Street, Melbourne, Victoria 3008, Australia
(a division of Pearson Australia Group Pty Ltd)
Penguin Books India Pvt Ltd, 11 Community Centre, Panchsheel Park,
New Delhi – 110 017, India
Penguin Group (NZ), 67 Apollo Drive, Rosedale, Auckland 0632, New Zealand
(a division of Pearson New Zealand Ltd)
Penguin Books (South Africa) (Pty) Ltd, Block D, Rosebank Office Park, 181 Jan Smuts
Avenue, Parktown North, Gauteng 2193, South Africa

Penguin Books Ltd, Registered Offices: 80 Strand, London WC2R ORL, England

penguin.com

First published in the USA in Razorbill, a division of Penguin Group (USA) Inc., 2013
First published in Great Britain by Penguin Books 2013
001

Set in Fairfield LT Std
Printed in Great Britain by Clays Ltd, St Ives plc

British Library Cataloguing in Publication Data
A CIP catalogue record for this book is available from the British Library

ISBN: 978-0-141-35008-0

www.greenpenguin.co.uk

MIX
Paper from
responsible sources
FSC
www.fsc.org   FSC™ C018179

Penguin Books is committed to a sustainable
future for our business, our readers and our planet.
This book is made from Forest Stewardship
Council™ certified paper.

CHAPTER 1

ADRIAN

I WON'T LIE. Walking into a room and seeing your girlfriend reading a baby-name book can kind of make your heart stop.

"I'm no expert," I began, choosing my words carefully. "Well—actually, I am. And I'm pretty sure there are certain things we have to do before you need to be reading that."

Sydney Sage, the aforementioned girlfriend and light of my life, didn't even look up, though a hint of a smile played at her lips. "It's for the initiation," she said matter-of-factly, as though she were talking about getting her nails done or picking up groceries instead of joining a coven of witches. "I have to have a 'magical' name they use during their gatherings."

"Right. Magical name, initiation. Just another day in the life, huh?" Not that I was one to talk, seeing as I was a vampire with the fantastic yet complicated abilities to heal and compel people.

This time, I got a full smile, and she lifted her gaze. Afternoon sunlight filtering through my bedroom window

1

caught her eyes and brought out the amber glints within them. They widened in surprise when she noticed the three stacked boxes I was carrying. "What are those?"

"A revolution in music," I declared, reverently setting them on the floor. I opened the top one and unveiled a record player. "I saw a sign that some guy was selling them on campus." I opened a box full of records and lifted out *Rumours* by Fleetwood Mac. "Now I can listen to music in its purest form."

She didn't look impressed; surprising for someone who thought my 1967 Mustang—which she'd named the Ivashkinator—was some sort of holy shrine. "I'm pretty sure digital music is as pure as it gets. That was a waste of money, Adrian. I can fit all the songs in those boxes on my phone."

"Can you fit the other six boxes that are in my car on your phone?"

She blinked in astonishment and then turned wary. "Adrian, how much did you pay for all that?"

I waved off the question. "Hey, I can still make the car payment. Barely." I at least didn't have to pay rent, since the place was prepaid, but I had plenty of other bills. "Besides, I've got a bigger budget for this kind of stuff now that *someone* made me quit smoking and cut back on happy hour."

"More like happy day," she said archly. "I'm looking out for your health."

I sat down beside her on the bed. "Just like I'm looking out for you and your caffeine addiction." It was a deal we'd made, forming our own sort of support group. I'd quit smoking and cut back to one drink a day. She'd ousted her obsessive dieting for a healthy number of calories and was down to only one cup of coffee a day. Surprisingly, she'd had a harder time with that

2

than I'd had with alcohol. In those first few days, I thought I'd have to check her into caffeine rehab.

"It wasn't an addiction," she grumbled, still bitter. "More of a . . . lifestyle choice."

I laughed and drew her face to mine in a kiss, and just like that, the rest of the world vanished. There were no name books, no records, no habits. There was just her and the feel of her lips, the exquisite way they managed to be soft and fierce at the same time. The rest of the world thought she was stiff and cold. Only I knew the truth about the passion and hunger that was locked up within her—well, me and Jill, the girl who could see inside my mind because of a psychic bond we shared.

As I laid Sydney back on the bed, I had that faint, fleeting thought I always had, of how taboo what we were doing was. Humans and Moroi vampires had stopped intermingling when my race hid from the world in the Dark Ages. We'd done it for safety, deciding it was best if humans didn't know of our existence. Now, my people and hers (the ones who knew about Moroi) considered relationships like this wrong and, among some circles, dark and twisted. But I didn't care. I didn't care about anything except her and the way touching her drove me wild, even as her calm and steady presence soothed the storms that raged within me.

That didn't mean we flaunted this, though. In fact, our romance was a tightly guarded secret, one that required a lot of sneaking around and carefully calculated planning. Even now, the clock was ticking. This was our weekday pattern. She had an independent study for her last period of the day at school, one managed by a lenient teacher who let her take off early and race over here. We'd get one precious hour of making out or talking—usually making out, made more frantic by the pressure bearing down on us—and then she was back to her private school, just as her clingy and vampire-hating sister Zoe got out of class.

Somehow, Sydney had an internal clock that told her when time was up. I think it was part of her inherent ability to keep track of a hundred things at once. Not me. In these moments, my thoughts were usually focused on getting her shirt off and whether I'd get past the bra this time. So far, I hadn't.

She sat up, cheeks flushed and golden hair tousled. She was so beautiful that it made my soul ache. I always wished desperately that I could paint her in these moments and immortalize that look in her eyes. There was a softness in them that I rarely saw at other times, a total and complete vulnerability in someone who was normally so guarded and analytical in the rest of her life. But although I was a decent painter, capturing her on canvas was beyond my skill.

She collected her brown blouse and buttoned it up, hiding the brightness of turquoise lace with the conservative attire she liked to armor herself in. She'd done an overhaul of her bras in the last month, and though I was always sad to see them disappear, it made me happy to know they were there, those secret spots of color in her life.

As she walked over to the mirror at my dresser, I summoned some of the spirit magic within me to get a glimpse of her aura, the energy that surrounded all living things. The magic brought a brief surge of pleasure inside me, and then I saw it, that shining light around her. It was its typical self, a scholar's yellow balanced with the richer purple of passion and spirituality. A blink of the eye, and her aura faded away, as did the deadly exhilaration of spirit.

She finished smoothing her hair and looked down. "What's this?"

"Hmm?" I came to stand behind her and wrapped my arms around her waist. Then, I saw what she'd picked up and stiffened: sparkling cuff links set with rubies and diamonds. And just like that, the warmth and joy I'd just felt were replaced by a cold but familiar darkness. "They were a birthday present from Aunt Tatiana a few years ago."

Sydney held one up and studied it with an expert eye. She grinned. "You've got a fortune here. This is platinum. Sell these and you'd have allowance for life. And all the records you want."

"I'd sleep in a cardboard box before I sold those."

She noticed the change in me and turned around, her expression filled with concern. "Hey, I was just joking." Her hand gently touched my face. "It's okay. Everything's okay."

But it wasn't okay. The world was suddenly a cruel, hopeless place, empty with the loss of my aunt, queen of the Moroi and the only relative who hadn't judged me. I felt a lump in my throat, and the walls seemed to close in on me as I remembered the way she'd been stabbed to death and how they'd paraded those bloody pictures around when trying to find her killer. It didn't matter that the killer was locked away and slated for execution. It wouldn't bring Aunt Tatiana back. She was gone, off to places I couldn't follow—at least not yet—and I was here, alone and insignificant and floundering. . . .

"Adrian."

Sydney's voice was calm but firm, and slowly, I dredged myself out of the despair that could come on so quickly and heavily, a darkness that had increased over the years the more

I used spirit. It was the price for that kind of power, and these sudden shifts had become more and more frequent recently. I focused on her eyes, and the light returned to the world. I still ached for my aunt, but Sydney was here, my hope and my anchor. I wasn't alone. I wasn't misunderstood. Swallowing, I nodded and gave her a weak smile as spirit's dark hand released its hold on me. For now.

"I'm okay." Seeing the doubt in her face, I pressed a kiss to her forehead. "Really. You need to go, Sage. You'll make Zoe wonder, and you'll be late for your witch meeting."

She stared at me with concern a few moments longer and then relaxed a little. "Okay. But if you need anything—"

"I know, I know. Call on the Love Phone."

That brought her smile back. We'd recently acquired secret prepaid cell phones that the Alchemists, the organization she worked for, wouldn't be able to track. Not that they regularly tracked her main phone—but they certainly could if they thought something suspicious was happening, and we didn't want a trail of texts and calls.

"And I'll come by tonight," I added.

At that, her features hardened again. "Adrian, no. It's too risky."

Another of spirit's benefits was the ability to visit people in their dreams. It was a handy way to talk since we didn't have a lot of time together in the waking world—and because we didn't spend much time talking in the waking world these days—but like any use of spirit, it was a continual risk to my sanity. It worried her a lot, but I considered it a small thing in order to be with her.

"No arguments," I warned. "I want to know how things go. And I know you'll want to know how things go for me."

"Adrian—"

"I'll keep it short," I promised.

She reluctantly agreed—not looking happy at all—and I walked her out to the door. As we cut through the living room, she paused at a small terrarium sitting near the window. Smiling, she knelt down and tapped the glass. Inside was a dragon.

No, really. Technically, it was called a callistana, but we rarely used that term. We usually called him Hopper. Sydney had summoned him from some demonic realm as a sort of helper. Mostly he seemed to want to help us out by eating all the junk food in my apartment. She and I were tied to him, and to maintain his health, we had to take turns hanging out with him. Since Zoe had moved in, however, my place had become his primary residence. Sydney lifted the lid of the tank and let the small golden-scaled creature scurry into her hand. He gazed up at her adoringly, and I couldn't blame him for that.

"He's been out for a while," she said. "You ready to take a break?" Hopper could exist in this living form or be transformed into a small statue, which helped avoid uncomfortable questions when people came by. Only she could transform him, though.

"Yeah. He keeps trying to eat my paints. And I don't want him to watch me kiss you goodbye."

She gave him a light tickle on the chin and spoke the words that turned him into a statue. Life was certainly easier that way, but again, his health required he come out now and then. That, and the little guy *had* grown on me.

"I'll take him for a while," she said, slipping him into her purse. Even if he was inert, he still benefited from being near her.

Free of his beady little gaze, I gave her a long kiss goodbye, one I was reluctant to let end. I cupped her face in my hands.

"Escape plan number seventeen," I told her. "Run away and open a juice stand in Fresno."

"Why Fresno?"

"Sounds like the kind of place people drink a lot of juice."

She grinned and kissed me again. The "escape plans" were a running joke with us, always far-fetched and numbered in no particular order. I usually made them up on the spot. What was sad, though, was that they were actually more thought out than any real plans we had. Both of us were painfully aware that we were very much living in the now, with a future that was anything but clear.

Breaking that second kiss was difficult too, but she finally managed it, and I watched her walk away. My apartment seemed dimmer in her absence.

I brought in the rest of the boxes from my car and sifted through the treasures within. Most of the albums were from the sixties and seventies, with a little eighties here and there. They weren't organized, but I didn't make any attempts at that. Once Sydney got over her stance that they were a wasteful splurge, she wouldn't be able to help herself and would end up sorting them all by artist or genre or color. For now, I set up the record player in my living room and pulled out an album at random: *Machine Head* by Deep Purple.

I had a few more hours until dinner, so I crouched down in front of an easel, staring up at the blank canvas as I tried to decide how to deal with my current assignment in advanced oil painting: a self-portrait. It didn't have to be an exact likeness. It could be abstract. It could be anything, so long as it was representative of me. And I was stumped. I could've painted anyone else I knew. Maybe I couldn't capture that exact look of rapture Sydney had in my arms, but I could paint her aura or the color of her eyes. I could have painted the wistful, fragile face of my friend Jill Mastrano Dragomir, a young princess of the Moroi. I could have painted flaming roses in tribute to my ex-girlfriend, who'd torn my heart apart yet still managed to make me admire her.

But myself? I didn't know what to do for me. Maybe it was just an artistic block. Maybe I didn't know myself. As I stared at the canvas, my frustration growing, I had to fight off the need to go to my neglected liquor cupboard and pour a drink. Alcohol didn't necessarily make for the best art, but it usually inspired something. I could practically taste the vodka already. I could mix it with orange juice and pretend I was being healthy. My fingers twitched, and my feet nearly carried me to the kitchen—but I resisted. The earnestness in Sydney's eyes burned through my mind, and I focused back on the canvas. I could do this—sober. I'd promised her I'd have only one drink a day, and I'd hold true to that. And for the time being, that one drink was needed for the end of the day, when I was ready for bed. I didn't sleep well. I never had in my entire life, so I had to use whatever help I could get.

My sober resolve didn't result in inspiration, though, and when five o'clock came around, the canvas remained bare. I stood up and stretched out the kinks in my body, feeling a return of that earlier darkness. It was more angry than sad, laced with the frustration of not being able to do this. My art teachers claimed I had talent, but in moments like this, I felt like the slacker most people had always said I was, destined for a lifetime of failure. It was especially depressing when I thought about Sydney, who knew everything about everything and could excel at any career she wanted. Putting aside the vampire-human problem, I had to wonder what I could possibly offer her. I couldn't even pronounce half the things that interested her, let alone discuss them. If we ever managed some normal life together, she'd be out paying the bills while I stayed home and cleaned. And I really wasn't good at that either. If she just wanted to come home at night to eye candy with good hair, I could probably be that reasonably well.

I knew these fears eating at me were being amped up by spirit. Not all of them were real, but they were hard to shake. I left the art behind and stepped outside my door, hoping to find distraction in the night to come. The sun was going down outside, and the Palm Springs winter evening barely required a light jacket. It was a favorite time of the evening for Moroi, when there was still light but not enough to be uncomfortable. We could handle some sunlight, not like Strigoi—the undead vampires who killed for their blood. Sunlight destroyed them, which was a perk for us. We needed all the help we could get in the fight against them.

I drove out to Vista Azul, a suburb only ten minutes away from downtown that housed Amberwood Prep, the private boarding school that Sydney and the rest of our motley crew attended. Sydney was normally the group's designated chauffeur, but that dubious honor had fallen on me tonight while she scurried off to her clandestine meeting with the coven. The gang was all waiting at the curb outside the girls' dorm as I pulled up. Leaning across the passenger seat, I opened up the door. "All aboard," I said.

They piled in. There were five of them now, plus me, bringing us up to a lucky seven, had Sydney been there. When we'd first come to Palm Springs, there'd just been four. Jill, the reason we were all here, scooted in beside me and flashed me a grin.

If Sydney was the main calming force in my life, Jill was the second. She was only fifteen, seven years younger than me, but there was a grace and wisdom that radiated from her already. Sydney might be the love of my life, but Jill understood me in a way no one else could. It was kind of hard not to, with that psychic bond. It had been forged when I used spirit to save her life last year—and when I say "save," I mean it. Jill had technically been dead, only for less than a minute, but dead nonetheless. I'd used spirit's power to perform a miraculous feat of healing and bringing her back before the next world could claim her. That miracle had bonded us with a connection that allowed her to feel and see my thoughts— though not the other way around.

People brought back that way were called "shadow-kissed," and that alone would have been enough to mess up any kid. Jill had the added misfortune of being one of two people left in a dying line of Moroi royalty. This was recent news to her, and her sister, Lissa—the Moroi queen and a good friend of mine—needed Jill alive in order to hold on to her throne. Those who opposed Lissa's liberal rule consequently wanted Jill dead, in order to invoke an ancient family law requiring a monarch to have one other living family member. And so, someone had come up with the questionably brilliant idea to send Jill into hiding in the middle of a human city in the desert. Because seriously, what vampire would want to live here? It was certainly a question I asked myself a lot.

Jill's three bodyguards climbed into the backseat. They were all dhampirs, a race born of mixed vampire and human heritage from the time our races had shared in free love. They were stronger and faster than the rest of us, making ideal warriors in the battle against Strigoi and royal assassins. Eddie Castile was the de facto leader of the group, a dependable rock who'd been with Jill from the beginning. Angeline Dawes, the red-haired spitfire, was slightly less dependable. And by "less dependable," I mean "not at all." She was a scrapper in a fight, though. The newest addition to the group was Neil Raymond, aka Tall, Proper, and Boring. For reasons I didn't understand, Jill and Angeline seemed to think his non-smiling demeanor was a sign of some kind of noble character. The fact that he'd gone to school in England and had picked up a faint British accent especially seemed to fire up their estrogen.

The last member of the party stood outside the car, refusing to get in. Zoe Sage, Sydney's sister.

She leaned forward and met my eyes with brown ones almost like Sydney's, but with less gold. "There's no room," she said. "Your car doesn't have enough seats."

"Not true," I told her. On cue, Jill moved closer to me. "This seat's meant to hold three. Last owner even fitted it with an extra seat belt." While that was safer for modern times, Sydney had nearly had a heart attack over altering the Mustang from its original state. "Besides, we're all family, right?" To give us easy access to one another, we'd made Amberwood believe we were all siblings or cousins. When Neil arrived, however, the Alchemists had finally given up on making him a relative since things were getting kind of ridiculous.

Zoe stared at the empty spot for several seconds. Even though the seat really was long, she'd still be getting cozy with

Jill. Zoe had been at Amberwood for a month but was in full possession of all the hang-ups and prejudices her people had around vampires and dhampirs. I knew them well because Sydney used to have all of them too. It was ironic because the Alchemists' mission was to keep the world of vampires and the supernatural hidden from their fellow humans, who they feared wouldn't be able to handle it. The Alchemists were driven by the belief that members of my kind were twisted parts of nature best ignored and kept separate from humans, lest we taint them with our evil. They helped us grudgingly and were useful in a situation like Jill's, when arrangements with human authorities and school officials needed to occur behind the scenes. Alchemists excelled at making things happen. That was how Sydney had originally been drafted, to smooth the way for Jill and her exile, since the Alchemists didn't want a Moroi civil war. Zoe had been sent recently as an apprentice and had become a huge pain in the ass for hiding our relationship.

"You don't have to go if you're afraid," I said. There was probably nothing else I could've said that would've motivated her more. She was driven to become a super Alchemist, largely to impress the Sage father, who, I'd concluded after many stories, was a major asshole.

Zoe took a deep breath and steeled herself. Without another word, she climbed in beside Jill and slammed the door, huddling as close to it as possible. "Sydney should've left the SUV," she muttered a little while later.

"Where is Sage, anyway? Er, Sage Senior," I amended, pulling out of the school's driveway. "Not that I don't like chauffeuring you guys around. You should've brought me a little black cap, Jailbait." I nudged Jill, who nudged me back. "You could whip up something like that in your sewing club."

"She's off doing some project for Ms. Terwilliger," said Zoe disapprovingly. "She's always doing something for her. I don't get why history research takes up so much time."

Little did Zoe know that said project involved Sydney being initiated into her teacher's coven. Human magic was still a strange and mysterious thing to me—and completely anathema to the Alchemists—but Sydney was apparently a natural. No surprise, seeing as she was a natural at everything. She'd overcome her fears of it, just as she had of me, and was now fully immersed in learning the trade from her zany yet loveable mentor, Jackie Terwilliger. To say the Alchemists wouldn't like that was an understatement. In fact, it was really a toss-up which would piss them off more: learning the arcane arts or making out with a vampire. It would almost be comical, if not for the fact that I worried the hard-core zealots among the Alchemists would do something terrible to Sydney if she was ever caught. It was why Zoe shadowing her had made everything so dangerous lately.

"Because it's Sydney," said Eddie from the backseat. In the rearview mirror, I could see an easy smile on his face, though there was a perpetual sharpness in his eyes as he scanned the world for danger. He and Neil had been trained by the guardians, the dhampir organization of badasses that protected the Moroi. "Giving one hundred percent to a task is slacking for her."

Zoe shook her head, not as amused as the rest of us. "It's just a stupid class. She only needs to pass."

No, I thought. *She needs to learn.* Sydney didn't just eat up knowledge for the sake of her vocation. She did it because she loved it. And what she would've loved more than anything was to lose herself in the academic throes of college, where she could learn anything she wanted. Instead, she'd been born into her family job, jumping when the Alchemists ordered her to new assignments. She'd already graduated from high school but treated this second senior year as seriously as the first, eager to learn whatever she could.

Someday, when this is all over, and Jill is safe, we'll run away from everything. I didn't know where, and I didn't know how, but Sydney would figure out those logistics. She'd escape the Alchemists' hold and become Dr. Sydney Sage, PhD, while I . . . well, did something.

I felt a small hand on my arm and glanced briefly down to see Jill looking sympathetically up at me, her jade-colored eyes shining. She knew what I was thinking, knew about the fantasies I often spun. I gave her a wan smile back.

We drove across town, then to the outskirts of Palm Springs to the home of Clarence Donahue, the only Moroi foolish enough to live in this desert until my friends and I had shown up last fall. Old Clarence was kind of a crackpot, but he was a nice enough one who'd welcomed a ragtag group of Moroi and dhampirs and allowed us to use his feeder/housekeeper. Moroi don't have to kill for blood like Strigoi do, but we do need it at least a couple times a week. Fortunately, there are plenty of humans in the world happy to provide it in exchange for a life spent on the endorphin high brought on by a vampire bite.

We found Clarence in the living room, sitting in his massive leather chair and using a magnifying glass to read some ancient book. He looked up at our entrance, startled. "Here on a Thursday! What a nice surprise."

"It's Friday, Mr. Donahue," said Jill gently, leaning down to kiss his cheek.

He regarded her fondly. "Is it? Weren't you just here yesterday? Well, no matter. Dorothy, I'm sure, will be happy to accommodate you."

Dorothy, his aging housekeeper, looked very accommodating. She'd hit the jackpot when Jill and I arrived in Palm Springs. Older Moroi don't drink as much blood as young ones, and while Clarence could still provide an occasional high, frequent visits from Jill and me provided a near-constant one for her.

Jill hurried over to Dorothy. "Can I go now?" The older woman nodded eagerly, and the two of them left the room for more private accommodations. A look of distaste crossed Zoe's face, though she said nothing. Seeing her expression and the way she sat far away from everyone else was so like Sydney in the old days, I almost smiled.

Angeline was practically bouncing up and down on the couch. "What's for dinner?" She had an unusual southern accent from growing up in a rural mountain community of Moroi, dhampirs, and humans who were the only ones I knew of that freely lived together and intermarried. Everyone else in their respective races regarded them with a kind of mingled horror and fascination. As appealing as that openness was, living with them had never crossed my mind in my fantasies with Sydney. I hated camping.

No one answered. Angeline looked from face to face. "Well? Why isn't there food here?" Dhampirs don't drink blood and can eat the regular kinds of food humans do. Moroi also need that sort of food, though we don't need it in nearly the same quantities. It takes a lot of energy to keep that active dhampir metabolism fired up.

These regular gatherings had become kind of a family dinner affair, not just for blood but also for regular food. It was a nice way to pretend we led normal lives. "There's always food," she pointed out, in case we'd never noticed. "I liked that Indian food we had the other day. That masala or whatever stuff. But I don't know if we should go there any more until they start calling it Native American food. It's not very polite."

"Sydney usually takes care of food," said Eddie, ignoring Angeline's familiar and endearing tendency to stray into tangents.

"Not usually," I corrected. "Always."

Angeline's gaze swiveled to Zoe. "Why didn't you have us pick up something?"

"Because that's not my job!" Zoe lifted her head up high. "We're here to keep Jill's cover and make sure she stays off the radar. It's not my job to feed you guys."

"In which sense?" I asked. I knew perfectly well that was a mean thing to say to her but couldn't resist. It took her a moment to pick up the double meaning. First she paled; then she turned an angry red.

"Neither! I'm not your concierge. Neither is Sydney. I don't know why she always takes care of that stuff for you. She should only be dealing with things that are essential for your survival. Ordering pizza isn't one of them."

I faked a yawn and leaned back into the couch. "Maybe she figures if we're well fed, you two won't look that appetizing."

Zoe was too horrified to respond, and Eddie shot me a

withering look. "Enough. It's not that hard to order pizza. I'll do it."

Jill was back by the time he finished the call, an amused smile on her face. She'd apparently witnessed the exchange. The bond wasn't on all the time, but it appeared to be going strong today. With the food dilemma settled, we actually managed to fall into a surprising camaraderie—well, everyone except Zoe, who just watched and waited. Things were unexpectedly cordial between Angeline and Eddie, despite a recent and disastrous bout of dating. She'd moved on and now pretended to be obsessed with Neil. If Eddie was still hurt, he didn't show it, but that was typical of him. Sydney said he was secretly in love with Jill, something else he was good at hiding.

I could've approved of that, but Jill, like Angeline, kept pretending she was in love with Neil. It was all an act for both girls, but no one—not even Sydney—believed me.

"Are you okay with what we ordered?" Angeline asked him. "You didn't pipe up with any requests."

Neil shook his head, face stoic. He kept his dark hair in a painfully short and efficient haircut. It was the kind of no-nonsense thing the Alchemists would've loved. "I can't waste time quibbling over trivial things like pepperoni and mushrooms. If you'd gone to my school in Devonshire, you'd understand. For one of my sophomore classes, they left us alone on the moors to fend for ourselves and learn survival skills. Spend three days eating twigs and heather, and you'll learn not to argue about any food coming your way."

Angeline and Jill cooed as though that was the most rugged, manly thing they'd ever heard. Eddie wore an expression that reflected what I felt, puzzling over whether this guy was as serious as he seemed or just some genius with swoon-worthy lines.

Zoe's cell phone rang. She looked at the display and jumped up in alarm. "It's Dad." Without a backward glance, she answered and scurried out of the room.

I wasn't one for premonition, but a chill ran down my spine. The Sage dad wasn't the kind of warm and friendly guy who'd call to say hello during business hours, when he knew Zoe was doing her Alchemist thing. If something was up with her, something was up with Sydney. And that worried me.

I barely paid any attention to the rest of the conversation as I counted the moments until Zoe's return. When she did finally come back, her ashen face told me I was right. Something bad had happened.

"What is it?" I demanded. "Is Sydney okay?" Too late I realized I shouldn't have showed any special concern for Sydney. Not even our friends knew about me and her. Fortunately, all attention was on Zoe.

She slowly shook her head, eyes wide and disbelieving. "I . . . I don't know. It's my parents. They're getting divorced."

CHAPTER 2

SYDNEY

I DIDN'T REALLY EXPECT A SECRET INITIATION into a witches' coven to start off with a tea party.

"Would you pass the ladyfingers, dear?"

I quickly grabbed the china plate from the coffee table and handed it over to Maude, one of the senior witches in the group and our hostess for the night. We sat in a circle of folding chairs in her immaculate living room, and my history teacher, Ms. Terwilliger, was beside me munching on a cucumber sandwich. I was too nervous to say anything and simply drank my tea as the others chatted about light topics. Maude was serving herbal tea, so I didn't have to worry about breaking my caffeine deal with Adrian. Not that I would've minded having an excuse if she had been serving black.

There were seven of us gathered, and although they would allow any number of worthy candidates into their group, they all seemed especially pleased to have a prime number. It was lucky, Maude insisted. Occasionally, Hopper would stick his head up and then go scurrying under furniture. Since witches didn't blink an eye at callistanas, I'd let him come out tonight.

Someone brought up the pros and cons of winter versus summer initiations, and I found my mind wandering. I wondered how things were going over at Clarence's. I'd been responsible for transporting Jill to her feedings since September, and it made me feel strange (and a little wistful) to be here while all of them were gathered and having a good time. With a pang, I suddenly realized I hadn't made any arrangements for dinner. Adrian had simply been the driver, so I hadn't thought to say anything. Would Zoe have taken charge? Probably not. I pushed down the motherly instincts within me that worried they'd all starve to death. Surely someone was capable of getting food.

Thinking of Adrian brought back the golden memories of our time together this afternoon. Even hours later, I could still feel where he'd kissed me. I took a deep breath to help me get a grip, fearful that my soon-to-be sisters would realize magic was the last thing on my mind right now. Actually, these days, it seemed like everything except getting half-naked with Adrian was the last thing on my mind. After a lifetime of praising myself for stoically adhering to mind over matter, I was kind of astonished that someone as cerebral as me would take to physical activity as quickly as I had. Sometimes I tried to rationalize it as a natural animal response. But really, I just had to face the truth: My boyfriend was insanely sexy, vampire or not, and I couldn't keep my hands off him.

I realized then that someone had asked me a question. Reluctantly, I blinked away thoughts of Adrian unbuttoning my shirt and tuned in to the speaker. It took me a moment to recall her name. Trina, that was it. She was in her mid-twenties, the youngest person here, aside from me.

"I'm sorry?" I asked.

She smiled. "I said, you do something with vampires, right?"

Oh, I did a lot of things with one vampire in particular, but obviously, that wasn't what she meant.

"More or less," I said evasively.

Ms. Terwilliger chuckled. "The Alchemists are very protective of their secrets."

A couple other witches nodded. Others simply looked on curiously. The magical world of witches didn't cross with the vampiric one. Most of them, on both sides, didn't even know about each other. Learning about Moroi and Strigoi had been a surprise to some here—meaning the Alchemists were doing their job. From what I'd gathered, these witches had encountered enough mystical and supernatural things to accept that blood-drinking magical creatures walked the earth and that there were groups like the Alchemists keeping that knowledge under wraps.

Witches freely accepted the paranormal. The Alchemists were less open. The group that had raised me thought humans needed to stay free of magic for the sanctity of their souls. I had once believed that too, and that creatures like vampires had no business being friendly with us. That was back when I'd also believed the Alchemists were telling me the truth. Now I knew that there were people in the organization who lied to both humans and Moroi and who would go to great extremes to protect their own selfish interests, no matter who it hurt. With my eyes open to the truth, I could no longer answer blindly to the Alchemists, even though I still technically worked for them.

That wasn't to say I was in open rebellion against them either (like my friend Marcus), since some of their original tenets still held merit.

Really, what it all came down to was that I was working for myself now.

"You know who you should talk to—if she'd talk to you? Inez. She's had all sorts of encounters with those beasts—not the living ones. The undead ones." That was Maude again. She'd recognized the golden lily on my cheek right away that identified me (to those who knew what to look for) as an Alchemist. It was made of vampire blood and other components that gave us some of their healing abilities and hardiness, while also being charmed to stop us from discussing supernatural affairs with those not privy to the magical world. Or, well, my tattoo used to do that.

"Who's Inez?" I asked.

That brought some chuckles from the others. "Probably the greatest of our order—at least on this side of the country," said Maude.

"This side of the world," insisted Ms. Terwilliger. "She's almost ninety and has seen and done things most of us can't imagine."

"Why isn't she here?" I asked.

"She's not part of any formal coven," explained another witch, named Alison. "I'm sure she used to be, but she's practiced on her own for . . . well, as long as I've known about her. It's hard for her to get around now, and she mostly just keeps to herself. Lives in this ancient house outside of Escondido and hardly ever leaves."

Clarence popped into my head. "I think I know a guy she'd get along great with."

"She fought a number of Strigoi back in the day," mused Maude. "She's probably got some spells that you'd find useful. And, oh, the stories she can tell about them. She was quite the warrior. I remember her talking about how one tried to drink her blood." She shivered. "But apparently, he couldn't do it, and she was able to take him out."

My hand froze as I lifted my teacup. "What do you mean he couldn't do it?"

Maude shrugged. "I don't remember the details. Maybe she had some sort of protective spell."

I felt my heart speed up as an old, dark memory sucked me in. Last year, I'd been trapped by a Strigoi who'd wanted to drink my blood too. She hadn't been able to do it, allegedly because I "tasted bad." The reason for that was still kind of a mystery, one the Alchemists and Moroi had let fade away when other pressing matters came up. But it hadn't faded for me. It was something that constantly nagged at the back of my mind, the never-ending question of what it was about me that had repelled her.

Ms. Terwilliger, accustomed to my expressions, studied me and guessed some of what I was thinking. "If you'd like to talk to her, I could arrange for you to meet her." Her lips quirked into a smile. "Although, I can't guarantee you'll get anything useful out of her. She's very . . . particular about what she reveals."

Maude scoffed. "That's not the word I'm thinking of, but yours is more polite." She glanced at an ornate grandfather clock and set down her cup. "Well, then. Shall we get started?"

I forgot about Inez and even Adrian as fear settled over me. In less than a year, I'd traveled leagues away from the Alchemist doctrine that had governed my life. I didn't give being close to vampires a second thought anymore, but every once in a while, warnings of the arcane would flit back to me. I had to steel myself and remember that magic was a path I'd firmly committed myself to and that it was only evil if you used it for evil. Members of the Stelle, as this group called itself, were sworn to do no harm with their powers—unless it was in defense of themselves or others.

We held the ritual in Maude's backyard, a sprawling piece of property filled with palm trees and winter flowers. It was about fifty degrees out, balmy compared with late January in other parts of the country, but jacket weather in Palm Springs—or, rather, cloak weather. Ms. Terwilliger had told me it didn't matter what I wore tonight, that I'd be supplied with what I needed. And what I needed turned out to be a cloak composed of six pieces of velvet in different colors. I felt like a peddler in a fairy tale as I flung it over my shoulders.

"This is our gift to you," Ms. Terwilliger explained. "Each of us has sewn and contributed a piece. You'll wear it whenever we have a formal ceremony." The others donned similar cloaks composed of varying numbers of patches, depending on whatever the coven's number had been during their respective initiations.

The sky was stark and clear with stars, the full moon shining like a brilliant pearl against the blackness. It was the best time to work good magic.

I noticed then that the trees in the yard were oriented in a circle. The witches formed another ring within it, in front of a stone altar bedecked with incense and candles. Maude took up a position by the altar and indicated that I should kneel in the center, in front of her. A breeze stirred around us, and although

I tended to think of overgrown, misty, deciduous forests when it came to arcane rituals, something felt right about the towering palms and crisp air.

It had taken me a while to come around to joining, and Ms. Terwilliger had had to assure me a hundred times that I wouldn't be swearing allegiance to some primeval god. "You're swearing yourself to the magic," she had explained. "To the pursuit of its knowledge and using it for good in the world. It's a scholar's vow, really. Seems like something you should be on board with."

It was. And so, I knelt before Maude as she conducted the ritual. She consecrated me to the elements, first walking around me with a candle for fire. Then she sprinkled water on my forehead. Crumbled violet petals spoke for the earth, and a wreath of incense smoke summoned the air. Some traditions used a blade for that element, and I was kind of glad theirs didn't.

The elements were the heart of human magic, just as they were in vampire magic. But like with the Moroi, there was no nod to spirit. It was an only recently rediscovered magic among them, and only a handful of Moroi wielded it. When I'd asked Ms. Terwilliger about it, she hadn't had a good answer. Her best explanation had been that human magic was drawn from the external world, where the physical elements resided. Spirit, tied to the essence of life, burned within us all, so it was already present. At least that had been her best guess. Spirit was a mystery to human and vampire magic users alike, its effects feared and unknown—which was why I often lay sleepless at night, worrying about Adrian's inability to stay away from it.

When Maude finished with the elements, she said, "Swear your vows."

The vows were in Italian, since this particular coven had its origins in the medieval Roman world. Most of what I swore to was in line with what Ms. Terwilliger had said, a promise to use magic wisely and support my coven sisters. I'd memorized them a while ago and spoke flawlessly. As I did, I felt an energy burn through me, a pleasant hum of magic and the life that radiated around us. It was sweet and exhilarating, and I wondered if it was what spirit felt like. When I finished, I looked up, and the world seemed brighter and clear, full of so much more wonder and beauty than ordinary people could understand. I believed then more than ever that there was no evil in magic, unless you brought it upon yourself.

"What is your name among us?" asked Maude.

"Iolanthe," I said promptly. It meant "purple flower" in Greek and had come to me after all the times Adrian talked to me about the sparks of purple in my aura.

She held out her hands to me and helped me up. "Welcome, Iolanthe." Then, to my surprise, she gave me a warm hug. The rest, breaking the circle now that the ritual was over, each gave me one as well, with Ms. Terwilliger being last. She held me longer than the others, and more astonishing than anything else I'd seen tonight were the tears in her eyes.

"You're going to do great things," she told me fiercely. "I'm so proud of you, prouder than I could be of any daughter."

"Even after I burned your house down?" I asked.

Her typical amused expression returned. "Maybe because of that."

I laughed, and the serious mood transformed to one of

celebration. We returned to the living room, where Maude traded tea for spiced wine, now that we were done with the magic. I didn't indulge, but my nervousness had long since disappeared. I felt happy and light . . . and more importantly, as I sat and listened to their stories, I felt like I belonged there—more so than I ever had with the Alchemists.

My phone buzzed in my purse, just as Ms. Terwilliger and I were finally preparing to leave. It was my mom. "I'm sorry," I told them. "I need to take this."

Ms. Terwilliger, who'd drank more wine than anyone else, waved me off and poured another glass. I was her ride, so it wasn't like she had anywhere to go. I answered the phone as I retreated to the kitchen, only a little surprised that my mom would call. We kept in touch, and she knew evenings were a good time to get a hold of me to chat. But when she spoke, there was an urgency in her voice that told me this wasn't a casual call.

"Sydney? Have you talked to Zoe?"

My mental alarms went off. "Not since this afternoon. Is something wrong?"

My mom took a deep breath. "Sydney . . . your father and I are splitting up. We're getting a divorce."

For a moment, the world spun, and I leaned against the kitchen counter for support. I swallowed. "I see."

"I'm so sorry," she said. "I know how hard this will be on you."

I thought about it. "No . . . not exactly. I mean, I guess . . . well, I can't say that I'm surprised."

She'd once told me that my dad had been more easygoing in his youth. It was hard for me to imagine, but obviously, she'd

28

married him for some reason. Over the years, my dad had grown cold and intractable, throwing himself into the Alchemist cause with a devotion that took precedence over all other things in his life, including his daughters. He'd become harsh and single-minded, and I'd long since realized I was more of a tool for the greater good in his eyes than his daughter.

My mom, on the other hand, was warm and funny, always willing to show affection and listen to us when we needed her. She was quick with a smile . . . though she didn't seem to smile so much these days.

"I know it'll be emotionally difficult for you and Carly," she said. "But it won't affect your daily lives that much."

I pondered her word choice. Me and Carly. "But Zoe . . ."

"Zoe's a minor, and even if she's off doing your Alchemist work, she's still legally under the care of her parents. Or parent. Your father intends to file for sole custody so that he can keep her where she is." There was a long pause. "I plan to fight him. And if I win, I'll bring her back to live with me and see if she can live a normal life."

I was stunned, unable to imagine the sort of battle she was proposing. "Does it have to be all or nothing? Can you guys share custody?"

"Sharing might as well be giving it to him. He'll wield the control, and I can't let him have her—mentally, that is. You're an adult. You can make your choices, and even if you're established on your path, you're different from her in the way you go about it. You're you, but she's more like . . ."

She didn't finish, but I already knew. *She's more like him.*

"If I can get custody and bring her home, I'll send her to a regular school and maybe salvage some sort of ordinary teenage existence for her. If it's not too late. You probably hate me for that—for pulling her from your cause."

"No," I said swiftly. "I think . . . I think it's a great idea." *If it's not too late.*

I could hear her choke up a little and wondered if she was fighting tears. "We'll have to go to court. No one's going to bring up the Alchemists, not even me, but there's going to be a lot of discussion of suitability and character analysis. Zoe will testify . . . and so will you and Carly."

And that's when I knew why she said this would be so difficult. "You guys will want us to choose one of you."

"I'll want you to tell the truth," she had said firmly. "I don't know what your father will want."

I did. He would want me to slander my mom, to say she was unfit, just some homemaker who fixed cars on the side and couldn't possibly compare with a serious academic like him, who provided Zoe with all sorts of education and cultural experiences. He'd want me to do it for the good of the Alchemists. He'd want me to do it because he always got his way.

"I love and support whatever you feel is right." The bravery in my mom's voice broke my heart. She was going to have more than family complications to deal with. Alchemist connections extended far and wide. Into the legal system? Very possibly. "I just wanted you to be prepared. I'm sure your father will want to speak to you too."

"Yes," I said grimly. "I'm sure he will. But what about right now? Are you okay?" Stepping away from Zoe, I had to acknowledge how life-altering this was for my mom. Maybe their marriage had become painful, but they'd been together for almost twenty-five years. Leaving something like that was a big adjustment, no matter the circumstances.

I could sense her smiling. "I'm fine. I'm staying with a friend of mine. And I took Cicero with me."

Thinking of her spiriting our cat away made me laugh, in spite of the solemnity of the conversation. "At least you have company."

She laughed as well, but there was a fragile quality to it. "And my friend needs some work done on her car, so we're all happy."

"Well, I'm glad, but if there's anything you need, anything at all, money or—"

"Don't worry about me. Just take care of yourself—and Zoe. That's the most important thing right now." She hesitated. "I haven't spoken to her lately . . . is she okay?"

Was she? I supposed it depended on how you defined "okay." Zoe was thrilled that she was out learning the Alchemist trade at so young an age but arrogant and cold toward my friends— just like anyone else in our organization. That, and she was a constant, looming shadow over my love life.

"She's great," I assured my mom.

"Good," she said, her relief nearly palpable. "I'm glad you're with her. I don't know how she'll take this."

"I'm sure she'll understand where you're coming from."

It was a lie, of course, but there was no way I could tell my mom the truth: Zoe was going to fight her, kicking and screaming, every step of the way.

CHAPTER 3

ADRIAN

WHETHER SHE GOT A PARENTAL PHONE CALL of her own or simply had to deal with Zoe's shock, I knew Sydney would've found out about the divorce by the time I visited her in her sleep.

The few spirit users I knew could all heal pretty well, but none of them could walk dreams as adeptly as I could. It was nice to know I excelled at something, and surprisingly it involved a pretty low level of spirit—just a steady hum, rather than the burst that healing required. The downside was that unlike the person I visited, I wasn't actually asleep—more in a meditative state—so I could end up pretty exhausted if the dream took a while. Seeing as I wasn't that great a sleeper to begin with, I supposed it didn't make much difference.

I pulled Sydney into a dream around midnight, making the two of us materialize in one of her favorite places: the courtyard of the Getty Villa, a museum of ancient history out in Malibu. Immediately, she ran up to me, a frantic look in her eyes.

"Adrian—"

"I know," I said, catching hold of her hands. "I was there when Zoe got the call."

"Did she tell you the ugly details?"

I raised an eyebrow. "There's something uglier than a divorce?"

Sydney then proceeded to tell me about the bloodbath of a custody battle to come. While I could appreciate their mom wanting Zoe to have a semi-normal life, I had to admit to myself that my reasons for hoping their mom would win were pretty selfish. Zoe disappearing from Palm Springs would make things a hell of a lot easier for Sydney and me. But I knew Sydney's immediate concern was her family being torn apart, and my immediate concern was her happiness. One part of her story in particular caught my attention.

"You really think your dad might be able to work some Alchemist coercion with a judge?" I asked. I'd never thought of that, but it wasn't that far-fetched. The Alchemists could create new identities, get a group of dhampirs and Moroi into a private school on no notice, and cover up dead Strigoi in the press.

She shook her head and sat down on the fountain's edge. "I don't know. Maybe it's not needed if Zoe's adamant about wanting to be with Dad. I don't really know how these kinds of hearings work."

"And what are you going to do?" I asked. "What will you say?"

She met my gaze levelly. "I'm not going to slander either of them, that's for sure. But as for what I'll advocate? It's hard to say. I'll have to think about it. I get my mom's view, and I even believe in it. But if I lean that way, Zoe'll hate me forever—not to mention the fallout with my dad and the Alchemists."

A small, bitter smile crossed her lips. "When I got back to our room tonight, Zoe didn't even ask me about my thoughts. She just assumed it was a done deal—that I'd take Dad's side."

"When will it all go down?"

"Not right away. They haven't set a date yet."

She fell silent, and I picked up on the vibe that maybe it was time to switch topics. "How'd the initiation go? Was there any naked dancing or animal sacrifice?"

Her smile warmed up. "Tea and hugs."

She gave me a brief recap, and I couldn't help but laugh at the thought of Jackie loading up on wine. Sydney wouldn't tell me her secret name, though, no matter how much I tried to wheedle it out of her.

"I don't suppose it was Jetta?" I asked hopefully. Whenever I had to take on a fake name, I used Jet Steele because let's face it, that was pretty much as badass as you could get.

"No," she laughed. "Definitely not."

She then wanted to hear about my night, naturally worrying that no one got fed in her absence. We talked for a long time, and although it was hard not to be distracted by her perfect lips and the edge of her shirt's neckline, I found I liked having these dream conversations. I certainly didn't mind our afternoon make-out sessions, but I actually *had* originally fallen for Sydney because of her mind.

As usual, she was the responsible one who noticed the time. "Oh, Adrian. It's time for bed."

I leaned toward her. "Is that an invitation?"

She lightly pushed me away. "You know what I mean. You're never in good shape when you're exhausted." It was a polite way of saying that being worn out made me susceptible to spirit's attacks on my sanity, which I couldn't argue with. I could also tell from the uneasy look in her eyes that she wasn't thrilled about the use of spirit this dream involved either.

"Think you can get away tomorrow?" Weekends were always difficult because Zoe trailed her like a shadow.

"I don't know. I'll see what I can—oh, God."

"What?"

She put a hand to her forehead and groaned. "Hopper. I left him at that witch's house. He was running around during the party, and I was so out of it after Mom called that I just walked right out the door with Ms. Terwilliger."

I took hold of her hand and squeezed it. "Don't worry. He'll be fine. Wild night on the town, staying out with an older woman. Warms my heart."

"So glad you're a proud dad. The problem is getting him home. I might be able to sneak out and see you later tomorrow, but I don't think I've got enough time to get out there. And I think Ms. Terwilliger's busy too."

"Hey," I said, feeling mildly indignant. "You just assume if you and Jackie can't do it, it's a lost cause? I'll go rescue him. If he wants to leave."

She brightened. "That'd be great. But I thought you had your art project."

It was such a small thing I was offering, no effort at all, really, and it warmed my heart to see how much it meant to her. Sydney was so often forced to be the responsible one who had to handle every single detail that I think it was an almost shocking surprise that someone might run an errand for her. "I'll have time afterward. She won't be freaked out about a vampire coming by, will she?"

"No. Just don't elaborate on your parental role." She gave me a light kiss, but I craftily pulled her closer and made it a much, much longer one. When we finally broke away, we were both breathless.

"Good night, Adrian," she said pointedly.

I took the hint, and the dream faded around us.

Back at my apartment, I indulged in my one daily drink, hoping it would send me to a quick slumber. No such luck. In the old days, it usually took at least three before I'd pass out in drunken oblivion. Now, my fingers lingered on the vodka bottle as I teetered on the edge of getting a refill. I missed it. Badly. Aside from the bliss of the buzz, alcohol could numb out spirit for a little while, and although the magic was a pleasant addiction, a reprieve from it was nice. Self-medicating had fended off a lot of spirit's negative effects for years, but this new deal was letting it start to gain ground.

A few more moments passed, and I pulled my hand back, clenching it into a fist. I retired to my bed, throwing myself onto it and burying my face in the pillow. It smelled faintly of jasmine and carnation from a perfume oil I'd recently gotten Sydney. She wasn't a perfume fan in general, claiming the chemicals and alcohol weren't healthy. But she couldn't argue against the pure, all-natural blend I'd found, especially when she'd heard the price. She was too pragmatic to let something like that go to waste.

I closed my eyes and wished she was with me—not even for sex, but just for the comfort of her presence. Considering the danger in our brief afternoons, a night together probably wasn't going to happen anytime soon, which was a damned shame. Surely I'd sleep better if I had her with me. It was frustrating because I really was exhausted in body, but my spinning mind refused to settle down.

I finally fell asleep an hour and a half later, only to be awakened by my alarm four hours after that. I stayed in bed, staring bleary-eyed at the ceiling, wondering if I could possibly cancel the meeting I'd set up with a classmate to work on a project. Seriously, what had I been thinking? Eight on a Saturday? Maybe I was closer to madness than I feared.

At least we were meeting in a coffee shop. Unlike my lovely soul mate, I had no restrictions on caffeine and ordered the biggest cup of drip they could manage. The barista assured me there was more where that came from. Across the room, my partner watched with amusement as I approached her table.

"Well, hey there, sunshine. Nice to see you all bright eyed and ready to start the day."

I held up a warning hand as I sat down. "Stop right there. It's going to take at least another cup of this before you become charming and witty."

She grinned. "Nah, I always am, day or night."

Rowena Clark and I had met on the first day of our mixed media class. I'd sat down at her table and said, "Mind if I join you? Figure the best way to learn about art is to sit with a masterpiece." Maybe I was in love, but I was still Adrian Ivashkov.

Rowena had fixed me with a flat look. "Let's get one thing straight. I can see through bullshit a mile away, and I like girls, not guys, so if you can't handle me telling you what's what, then you'd better take your one-liners and hair gel somewhere else. I don't go to this school to put up with pretty boys like you. I'm here to face dubious employment options with a painting degree and then go get a Guinness after class."

I'd scooted my chair closer to the table. "You and I are going to get along just fine."

And we had, enough so that we'd partnered up for a project on outdoor sculpture. We'd have to head over to campus to work on it soon but first needed to finalize the sketch we'd started in a pub after class earlier this week. I'd given up my bedtime drink to have a beer with her, and while it hadn't had much effect on me, Rowena had proven to be a total lightweight. Our sketch hadn't gotten very far.

"Up late partying?" she asked me now.

I took a long drink of the coffee, feeling only slightly guilty that Sydney would be salivating if she could see me. "Just up late." I yawned. "Where are we at?"

She pulled out our sketch, which was on a bar napkin and read, *Insert sketch here.*

"Hmm," I said. "Promising start."

After an hour of hashing out ideas, we decided to do a model of the monolith from *2001: A Space Odyssey* and then cover it with advertising slogans and internet lingo. I'd actually gotten bored during that movie, but Rowena was going off about how it was a symbol of advanced evolution and how our designs would be an ironic statement of where our society had ended up. Mostly I was on board because I thought it wouldn't involve too much effort. I was serious about my painting, but this was just a general required class.

A good chunk of our day was spent just getting the supplies. Rowena had borrowed a friend's pickup truck, and we went to a building-supply store in hopes of finding a large concrete rectangle for our monolith. We lucked out and even found some smaller blocks to put at the base of it.

"We can make a ring," Rowena explained. She'd recently dyed her hair lavender and absentmindedly tucked wayward locks behind her ears as she spoke. "And then paint the various stages of evolution. Monkey, caveman, all the way up to some hipster texting on his cell phone."

"We didn't evolve from monkeys," I told her as we wrestled the rectangle onto a pallet. "The earliest human ancestor is called *Australopithecus*." I wasn't entirely sure where vampire evolution fit in, but I certainly wasn't bringing that up.

Rowena released the block and stared in amazement. "How the hell do you know that?"

"Because I mentioned the monkey thing the other day, and my girlfriend had a, uh, few things to say about that." A "few" things had actually turned into a one-hour lesson on anthropology.

Rowena laughed and lifted one of the smaller blocks. They were still pretty heavy but didn't require both of us. "I'd really like to meet this mythical girlfriend of yours, if only to see who in the world could put up with you. I could get Cassie, and we could all go out for a drink together."

"She doesn't drink," I said quickly. "And she's eighteen anyway. Well, almost nineteen." With a start, I realized Sydney's birthday was fast approaching at the beginning of next month, February, and I didn't have anything for her. In fact, after my investment in vinyl, I didn't have much money at all until my dad's next deposit came in mid-month.

Rowena smirked. "Younger woman, huh?"

"Hey, it's legal."

"I don't want to know about your sordid sex life." She hoisted another block. "We'll go to Denny's or something. If you don't bring her around soon, I'll think you made her up."

"I couldn't make her up if I tried," I declared grandly. But inside, I couldn't help but feel a little wistful. I would've loved to go out on a double date with Rowena and her girlfriend. I was pretty sure Sydney would hit it off with her, if only to gang up and tease me mercilessly. But public appearances weren't an option, not unless we went for a night on the town with the Keepers.

We took our concrete haul back to Carlton College's campus and began the arduous task of transporting the blocks to a large quadrangle that our class had gotten permission to use. A few of our classmates were working as well, and they helped us carry the centerpiece, which made things a lot easier. Even if it wasn't up to scale with the movie's monolith, it was still a bitch to lift. That left us to bring in the small blocks, and our conversation quieted as we worked. We were both tired and glad to be nearly done for the afternoon. The actual painting would happen tomorrow. It was Rowena's specialty too, and we wanted to be ready and fresh to make the most of our strengths in this project. It was cool out, but the sky was clear, leaving nothing between the sun and me. That was why I'd consented to the early time, sparing me from the worst of the light. I'd be able to rescue Hopper from that witch soon and then go home in the hopes that Sydney could get away.

Once all the blocks were on the quad, Rowena grew obsessed with arranging them perfectly. I didn't care at this point and busied myself texting a message to Sydney on the Love Phone, letting her know that my art was a paltry thing compared to the brilliance of her beauty. She texted back: *This is me rolling my eyes*. To which I replied: *I love you too*.

"We could do this," said Rowena, setting three of the smaller blocks on top of one another. "Mini-monoliths."

"Whatever you want."

She decided against it and started to lift the top one. I'm not entirely sure what happened after that. I think it was just a subtle shift in her hand gone wrong. Whatever it was, the block slipped from her grasp and fell hard—slamming her hand between it and the brick-covered ground below.

Her scream rang through the diag, and I moved with a speed that would've impressed Eddie. I grabbed the block and lifted it, but as I did, I knew it was a little too late. A few tendrils of spirit told me she'd broken some bones in her hand. And in those split seconds of chaos, I acted. It was her right hand, and breaking it was going to put her out of commission with painting for the rest of the semester. She could do intricate, delicate things with watercolors that I could only dream of. No way could I endanger that. I sent a burst of spirit into her hand, drawing from my own life energy to mend the bones. Healing usually felt like a tingle to the recipient, and I could tell from the shock on her face that she had noticed.

"What did you do?" she gasped.

I fixed my eyes and sent out a burst of compulsion. "Nothing," I said. "Except move the block. This is a pretty traumatic and confusing experience for you."

Her eyes glazed over for a brief moment, and then she nodded. I let go of the magic, the sudden emptiness within me the only indication of just how much I'd pulled out for the healing and compulsion. With the tingling gone from her mind, Rowena cradled the afflicted hand as our classmates came running over.

"Holy shit," said one of them. "Are you okay?"

Rowena winced. "I don't know. It doesn't feel . . . I mean, it aches . . . but nothing like when it first hit."

"You need to see a doctor," the same guy insisted. "It might be broken."

Rowena flinched, and I could guess that the same fears I'd felt were running through her head. I knew there was no permanent damage but had to play along because it was the reasonable thing to do.

"Give me your keys," I told her. "The campus clinic's open."

Triage got us in quickly, since having a thirty-pound concrete block fall on you was pretty serious. But after an examination and X-rays, the doctor simply shrugged. "Everything's fine. Maybe it wasn't as heavy as you thought."

"It was pretty heavy," Rowena said, but relief filled her face. I even thought I caught a glimmer of tears in her eyes as she looked at me. "I guess you just got the block off fast enough." There was no sign that she remembered that burst of healing.

"Because I'm manly and brave," I said solemnly.

They discharged her, and as we were leaving, her girlfriend, Cassie, showed up. Rowena was pretty, but Cassie was a knockout. She flung her arms around Rowena, and I shook my head ruefully.

"How in the world did you pull that off?" I asked.

Rowena grinned at me over Cassie's shoulder. "I told you: My wit and charm are always on."

We made arrangements to finish the project tomorrow, and I headed back to my apartment. I hadn't used such an intense amount of spirit in a long time, and the rush was heady. The world was full of life and light, and I practically floated on air when I walked inside. How could spirit be a bad thing when it made me feel like this? I felt glorious. I felt more alive than I had in days.

I picked a random record from one of the boxes. Pink Floyd. Nope, not in my current mood. I swapped it out for the Beatles and then threw myself into my self-portrait with a renewed vigor. Or rather, portraits. Because I couldn't stop. My mind was abuzz with ideas, and it was impossible to pick just one. Color flew fast and furious onto the canvas as I experimented with different concepts. One was an abstract of my aura, the way Sonya and Lissa always said it looked. Another was more accurate, as realistic as I could manage from a picture on my cell phone, save that I painted myself in reds and blues. On it went.

And bit by bit, the energy began to fade. My brush slowed down, and at last, I sank onto the couch, feeling drained and exhausted. I stared around at my handiwork, five different paintings, all drying. My stomach rumbled, and I tried to remember when I'd last eaten. A muffin with Rowena? I was getting as bad as Sydney. I put a pizza in the microwave, and as I watched it cook, my mind began to spin with thoughts of a different nature.

Sydney's birthday. How could I have forgotten it? Well, I hadn't forgotten it. I had the date burned into my mind, February 5. It was the logistics of getting her a gift that had eluded me. Turning toward the haphazard boxes of records, I stared at them with dismay, suddenly hating them for the dent they'd made in my monthly funds. Sydney had been right about how foolish the purchase was. What could I have bought for her instead? I imagined a dozen roses showing up at her dorm anonymously. Maybe two dozen. Or even three. Equally appealing was the thought of a diamond tennis bracelet on her slim wrist. Something subtle and classy, of course. She'd never go for anything too outlandish.

Thinking of diamonds made me remember Aunt Tatiana's cuff links. I ignored the microwave beeping that it was finished and trotted off to my bedroom. The cuff links were still sitting out, a dazzling array of red and white fire that glittered in the overhead light. *Sell these and you'd have allowance for life*, Sydney had joked. Not just allowance or my car payments. I could get her a present. Presents. The roses, the bracelet, a romantic dinner.

No. No dinner, nothing in public. The thought descended heavily on me as I contemplated our future together. Could we have one? What kind of relationship was this, grasping at these stolen moments? She was too reasonable to do this forever. Eventually she'd realize it was time to let it go. Let me go. I put the cuff links back in their box, knowing I could never sell them and that I was in the full throes of a spirit crash.

It happened with these bouts of magic. I'd barely been able to drag myself out of bed when I'd brought Jill back. The toll of wielding so much life was just too great, and the mind crashed from the high. Well, mine did. Lissa didn't have these dramatic ups and downs. Hers was more of a steady darkness that lingered with her for a few days, keeping her moody and melancholy until it lifted. Sonya had a mix of both effects.

My little brooding artist, Aunt Tatiana used to say with a chuckle when I got in these moods. *What's gotten into your head today?* She'd speak fondly, like it was adorable. I could almost hear her voice now, almost see her standing there beside me.

44

With a shaking breath, I closed my eyes and willed the image away. She wasn't here. Shadow-kissed people could actually see the dead. Crazy people only imagined them.

I ate my pizza standing at the counter, telling myself over and over that this mood would pass. I knew it would. It always did. But oh, how the waiting sucked.

When I finished, I returned to the living room and stared at the paintings. What had seemed wonderful and inspired now seemed shallow and stupid. They embarrassed me. I gathered them all up and tossed them into a corner on top of one another, not caring about the torn canvas or wet paint.

Then I hit the liquor cabinet.

I'd made good progress on a bottle of tequila, sprawled on my bed and listening to Pink Floyd, when the bedroom door opened a couple hours later. I smiled when I saw Sydney. I was adrift on the buzz of tequila, which had effectively muted spirit and taken the edge off that terrible, terrible low. That wasn't to say I was bright and peppy either, but I no longer wanted to crawl into a hole. I'd defeated spirit, and seeing Sydney's beautiful face lifted me up even more.

She smiled back and then, in one sharp glance, assessed the situation. The smile vanished. "Oh, Adrian" was all she said.

I held up the bottle. "It's Cinco de Mayo somewhere, Sage."

Her eyes made a quick sweep of the room. "Is Hopper celebrating with you?"

"Hopper? Why would—" My mouth snapped shut for a few moments. "Oh. I, uh, kind of forgot about him."

"I know. Maude sent a message by way of Ms. Terwilliger asking if someone was going to come for him."

"Crap." After everything that had happened with Rowena,

my dragon fosterling had been the last thing on my mind. "I'm sorry, Sage. Totally slipped my mind. I'm sure he's fine, though. It's not like he's a real kid. And like I said, he's probably loving it."

But her expression didn't change, except to grow graver. She walked over and took the tequila from me, then carried it to the window. Too late, I realized what she was doing. She opened the window and dumped the rest of the bottle outside. I sat up with a jolt.

"That's expensive stuff!"

She shut the window and turned to face me. That look drew me up short. It wasn't angry. It wasn't sad. It was . . . disappointed.

"You promised me, Adrian. A social drink isn't a problem. Self-medicating is."

"How do you know it was self-medicating?" I asked, though I didn't contradict her.

"Because I know you, and I know the signs. Also, I sometimes check up on your bottles. You made a big dent in this one tonight—much more than a social drink." I nearly pointed out that technically, she was the one who'd made a big dent in it.

"I couldn't help it," I said, knowing how lame that sounded. It was as bad as Angeline's "it's not my fault" mantra. "Not after what happened."

Sydney put the empty bottle on the dresser and then sat beside me on the bed. "Tell me."

I explained about Rowena and her hand and how the rest of the day's events had unfolded. It was difficult staying on track with the story because I kept wanting to meander and make excuses. I left out the part about despairing over birthday gifts. When I finally finished, Sydney gently rested her hand on my cheek.

"Oh, Adrian," she said again, and this time, her voice was sad.

I rested my hand over hers. "What was I supposed to do?" I whispered. "It was like Jill all over again. Well—not quite as bad. But there she was. She needed me, and I could help— then when she noticed, I had to make sure she forgot. What else was I supposed to do? Should I have let her break her hand?"

Sydney drew me into her arms and was silent for a long time. "I don't know. I mean, I know you couldn't *not* help. It's who you are. But I wish you hadn't. No . . . that's not right. I'm glad you did. Really. I just wish it wasn't so . . . complicated." She shook her head. "I'm not explaining it correctly. I'm no good at this."

"You hate that, don't you? Not knowing what to do." I rested my head against her shoulder, catching the faint scent of her perfume. "And you hate me like this."

"I love you," she said. "But I worry about you. Have you ever thought about . . . I mean, didn't Lissa take antidepressants for a while? Didn't that help her?"

I lifted my head swiftly. "No. I can't do that. I can't cut myself off from the magic like that."

"But she felt better, right?" Sydney pushed.

"She . . . yes. Kind of." I had no problems with "liquid healing," but pills made me squeamish. "She *did* feel better. She didn't get depressed. She didn't cut herself anymore. But she missed the magic, and so she stopped the pills. You don't know what it's like, that rush of spirit. Feeling like you're in tune with every living thing in the world."

"I might understand it better than you think," she said.

"It's more than that, though. She also stopped because she needed the magic back to help Rose. What if I needed it back? What if it was you who was hurt or dying?" I gripped Sydney's shoulders, needing her to understand my desperation and how much she meant to me. "What if you needed me, and I couldn't help you?"

She removed my hands and held them between hers, her face tranquil. "Then we deal. That's what most people do in the world. You take your chances. I'd rather have you stable and happy than risk your sanity on the slim chance a concrete block will fall on me."

"Could you sit by if you had the ability to help someone?"

"No. Which is why I'm trying to help you." But I could see the conflict in her, and I understood her anxiety.

"No pills," I said firmly. "This won't happen again. I'll try harder. I'll be stronger. Have faith that I can do this on my own."

Hesitating, she looked as though she might keep arguing the matter, but at last, she nodded in resignation. She drew me down to the bed and kissed me, even though I knew she didn't like the taste of tequila. The kiss managed to be both tender and intense, and it reinforced that connection between us, that burning sense I always had that she was made for me, and I was made for her. I showered her with kisses, wishing I could do a lot more than that. Surely if I could just drown myself in her, I'd never need alcohol or pills of any kind.

But despite her quickened pulse and the heat in her eyes, things didn't progress much more than they normally did.

And as usual, I didn't pressure her. She might not agree with Alchemist policies, but she'd still held on to a lot of their personal habits. Conservative clothing. No drinking. I didn't actually know where premarital sex fell in there, but since a lot of them tended to be religious, I wouldn't have been surprised if she adhered to that too. It had never come up between us. I figured if she was ready, she'd let me know.

"I have to go," she said at last. "I'm only supposed to be out buying toothpaste. It was a boring enough errand that Zoe wouldn't want to come."

I brushed wayward golden strands away from her face. "Clarence's tomorrow night?"

She nodded. "Wouldn't miss it."

I walked her to the front door. She did a double take at the ruined paintings but didn't say anything and kept her expression neutral.

"I mean it," I told her. "I'll try."

"I know," she said. That earlier look of disappointment in her eyes still haunted me.

"I can be strong," I added.

She smiled and stood on her tiptoes to kiss me goodbye. "You already are," she murmured just before she disappeared into the night.

CHAPTER 4
SYDNEY

THE TEARS DIDN'T START UNTIL I WAS WELL AWAY from Adrian and back in my car. I drove to Amberwood with blurred vision and wet cheeks, feeling more useless than I had in a long time. Forgetting about Hopper wasn't the worst thing in the world, but what about next time? Spirit made its users do crazy things. They hurt themselves. They killed themselves. That was what scared me, and I wanted to control the situation before it controlled us. And that, as Adrian had astutely pointed out, was what really ate at me: my helplessness to come up with an immediate solution. It wasn't a feeling I had very often.

I couldn't stop spirit from ravaging Adrian, and I couldn't condemn him for that gut instinct to help others. It made my heart ache, thinking of that burning kindness within him that so few ever saw. The only thing I could do was be there for him and encourage him to draw upon the strength I knew he possessed. Maybe he couldn't defeat spirit permanently, but I knew he could put up better resistance against falling back on his old habits to cope. There had to be healthier ways to survive, and I believed without a doubt that he had the self-control and willpower to enact them. I just wished he believed that as well.

I parked in Amberwood's garage after diligently seeking a spot between two other properly parked cars. Honestly, how hard was it for people to park between the lines? My Mazda was still shiny and new, and I feared dents and dings. My last car, a brown Subaru named Latte, had been spectacularly blown up by foam, courtesy of an evil witch who'd been after Ms. Terwilliger. After Neil and Zoe had increased our numbers, the Alchemists had ordered that Latte's replacement be a seven seater. This CX-9, dubbed Quicksilver for its paint, was the sexiest SUV crossover I could find. Adrian told me I was one step away from being a suburban mom in a minivan.

I'd calmed down by the time I reached my dorm room but couldn't help a few sniffles in my pillow. Zoe, who I'd thought was asleep, spoke through the darkness.

"Are you upset about Mom and Dad?"

"Yeah," I lied.

"Don't worry," she said. "They won't take me away from him."

I pretended to fall asleep.

I felt back in control when I woke the next morning, particularly because I had a task at hand. Ms. Terwilliger, good to her word as usual, had made midday arrangements for me to visit Inez, the witch that the other Stelle had regarded with a mix of both amusement and nervousness. As far as Zoe was concerned, I was going off on a research trip to a university library in San Diego.

"Why are you always off doing stuff with her?" Zoe asked.

She stood in front of our mirror, brushing her long brown hair into a ponytail.

"She's my teacher, and it's part of my independent study with her." I was sifting through my drawers for something to wear, and my hand lingered on a purple T-shirt that had a silvery Celtic-style heart with flames trailing from it. Adrian had made it for me, sort of as a joke, but it had become one of my most prized possessions. "Besides, I've pretty much already taken every other subject with Dad. This is my only interesting class."

"I suppose." She sounded unconvinced and then abruptly brightened. "You'll tell them that, right? In court? About how thorough Dad's education was? That'll go a long way."

"I'm sure it will." I smiled stiffly as I shut the T-shirt drawer and moved to my closet for something more formal. I didn't know much about Inez, but if she was some venerable elder, maybe I should show extra respect. I opted for a black pencil skirt and long-sleeved white shirt covered in black dots. A small wooden cross with morning glories painted on it, courtesy of Adrian, was my only accessory.

Zoe frowned. "You're wearing that to a library?"

"It's a prestigious one," I said evasively. "I should be back in time to go with you guys to Clarence's, but if not, Eddie will take you. Ms. Terwilliger's driving me, so you can have Quicksilver."

"Thank God," she said with a shudder. "You can't imagine what it was like in Adrian's car. I had to sit *right next* to Jill."

After rooming with Zoe for a month, I'd grown surprisingly immune to her commentary and found it was easier on everyone if I just didn't react, even when her comments were extreme by Alchemist standards. "And don't forget to stop and pick up dinner this time."

"It's not our job to remind them," she protested.

"Our job is to make sure Jill gets to Clarence's and that life runs smoothly for everyone. Those 'family dinners' are a nice way for everyone to destress and get along. It's not a big deal to grab something to go. You should do Chinese," I added decisively. "They haven't had it in a while." Also, Adrian had mentioned a craving for kung pao chicken the other day.

"Do you ever wish we had a cooler car?" Zoe asked unexpectedly.

I started laughing. "Yes, but the mission trumps our car choices right now. I didn't know you thought about that kind of stuff."

She sat down on her bed, and a mischievous smile played at her lips. "Hey, I grew up in the same place as you. Do you remember when Mom worked on that Jaguar at our house? *That* was a cool car."

"Of course I do." A surge of affection welled up in me as I regarded her. "But you were . . . what? Eight? Nine?"

"Old enough to wish I could drive it. I used to sneak into the garage at night and sit in it. I thought I was being stealthy, but I think Mom knew the whole time." That fledgling smile bloomed on her face, and I caught my breath. My dad *didn't* have complete control over her. Was there a chance she hadn't tossed our mom aside? Was there a chance the custody hearing might work out amicably?

And was there a chance that Zoe might ever come around to thinking of Moroi and dhampirs as real people? Until this moment, seeing these glimmers of the sister I remembered and loved, it had never occurred to me that it might be possible to sway her thinking—on a lot of issues. Since her arrival, I'd been tiptoeing around her, nodding and reciting party lines. Was there a way that I might actually be able to influence her? It was more than I dared hope, and I knew better than to tip my hand too soon, lest it ruin this unguarded moment. I simply filed it away for later and put on my poker face.

Ms. Terwilliger picked me up in her red Volkswagen Beetle soon thereafter, wearing sunglasses with leopard-print frames. After five minutes on the road, she pulled off at a coffee shop. "Are you still doing your ridiculous abstaining?" she asked.

"Yes, but I haven't had my cup today." I'd held off for this very reason, knowing she'd make a stop. Holding out this long was making my hands twitch.

She shifted the car into park and nodded toward the shop's door. "Good thing."

I follow her gaze and gaped as Adrian straightened up from where he was leaning against the outside of the building, a cup in each hand. He grinned at us and sauntered toward the car. "That's Adrian," I said stupidly.

"Yes, I'm aware," Ms. Terwilliger said. "He called this morning and asked if he could join us. Inez is no stranger to Moroi, so I didn't see it being a problem. In fact, it might throw her off a little, which would be to our advantage. Thank you, dear." That was to Adrian, as she accepted her coffee through the driver's side window.

He slid into the backseat and handed me my cup. A flutter of emotions stirred inside my chest. Last night's encounter had left me unsettled, but seeing him now in the light of day, clear-eyed with that devil-may-care smile, I dared to hope that he really would make good on all that he'd said. How could he not? He radiated confidence, full of the charm and good looks that had drawn me in before I'd even known it was happening. There was no drunkenness or despair. He looked like he could do anything, and just then, I needed to believe he could. There were so many things weighing me down, so many things— including our future together—that seemed impossible. Having this invincible Adrian by my side filled me with a joy I rarely allowed myself. Our fingertips brushed as I took the cup, sending a jolt of electricity through me. I held his gaze for several long moments, and as his cocky smile softened into something more serious, I knew he could hear all the things I couldn't give voice to.

"Weren't you supposed to be painting your monolith?" I asked once we were back on the road.

"Rowena rescheduled. It gave me time to go get you a present," he told me.

"I know. I'm drinking it right—ah!"

A glittering, scaly form scurried up my leg and curled into a ball on my lap. Carefully holding the coffee in one hand, I used the other to give Hopper a pat on the head as I ran a few mental calculations.

"You must have been up at the crack of dawn to get him and be back," I said. "How much sleep did you get?" My shiny vision of Adrian began to falter a little. Lack of sleep was his enemy.

"More than enough for this escapade. Isn't there a giant Muffler Man statue in Escondido? Do we have time for a photo op?"

"We've barely got enough time for this," I said, thinking back on Zoe's disappointment. But Adrian's chatter and enthusiasm cast a cheer on the drive, and I could tell that even

Ms. Terwilliger liked having him along, though worry lines appeared on her face the closer we got to our destination.

"Like I said before, I don't know how helpful Inez will be," she explained. "She's very eccentric and controlled by her whims. If she likes you, she might tell you something. If she doesn't, well . . ." Ms. Terwilliger shrugged. "Then maybe we'll have time for photo ops."

"Score," said Adrian. When I shot him a look, he added quickly, "But of course she'll like you."

When we reached the outskirts of the city, Ms. Terwilliger made a stop not for coffee, but for a bouquet of burgundy roses that she thrust into my lap when she returned to the car, much to Hopper's dismay. "Hang on to these," she told me. I did without question and used the opportunity to transform Hopper back into his statue form. He'd had more than enough out time these past few days.

A recluse witch made me think of Clarence, so I was surprised when we pulled up at a very modern Spanish-style house that was pretty much the opposite of an old Gothic manor. It was made weirder still by an El Camino with a flat tire sitting out on the driveway. I'd expected something outlandish and eccentric from what the other witches had said, so this nod to normality was almost a disappointment.

Then we stepped inside the door.

It was like being in a shrine . . . to roses and doilies. Every surface in the place was covered. In that way it wasn't unlike Ms. Terwilliger's house; despite having her former home and possessions recently destroyed, she had somehow managed to fill up a new house with junk in less than a month. But whereas her items were tossed haphazardly around because she didn't feel like putting them away, all the clutter here seemed to be by design. There were vases of silk roses carefully centered on crocheted doilies, figurines of puppies carrying roses in their mouths on lace doilies, and delicate rose-covered tea sets placed on paper doilies. And that was just the start of it. It all had a really old feel to it as well, like I'd been transported back to the 1890s.

Adrian stood behind us, just outside the door, and I was pretty sure I heard him mutter, "Needs more rabbits."

"Well, hello, Inez," Ms. Terwilliger said to our hostess. With a start, I realized I couldn't ever recall my teacher acting so nervous around anyone. "You look as lovely as ever."

Inez Garcia was a tiny waif of a woman, like some fairy from the hollow hills. Her white hair was pulled into a long braid down her back, and she wore her glasses around her neck on a long blue-beaded chain. Her jeans had an impossibly high waist and were paired with, unsurprisingly, a rose-printed shirt. The lines of her ninety years showed on her face, but there was a sharpness in her dark eyes that explained Ms. Terwilliger's unease.

"Don't you start up with me, Jaclyn Terwilliger! I know why you're here. You want something. It's the only reason anyone comes by these days. There's no pleasantries, no tea. Just want, want, want."

Ms. Terwilliger gulped and pushed me forward. "Inez, this is Sydney Melrose. Look what she's brought for you."

It took me a moment to remember the roses, and I held them out with a forced smile. Inez took them warily and sniffed each of them before giving a small grunt of approval. "Come in." We entered further into the foyer, and that's when she noticed Adrian. "Well, well, look what you dragged up. You could've saved yourself the money on the flowers and just brought me *him*. Been a while since I entertained a handsome young Moroi."

"It's been a while since I've met a woman who appreciates roses as much as I do," said Adrian, ever quick on his feet. "Not that my experience has always been great with them. I've got to say, though, I've never seen such excellent decorating taste. You go for pink too, huh? I told them that when they got the flowers, but would they listen to me? No. They insisted on burgundy."

Inez narrowed her eyes as she gave Ms. Terwilliger a once-over. "What are you playing at, bringing one of them here? Their kind almost never come to us for help."

"This isn't about him," explained Ms. Terwilliger. "It's Sydney. My apprentice."

Inez pondered this as she put the roses in a vase (which had roses painted on it) and allowed us to sit in her mauve parlor. The scent of roses was cloying, and I counted at least three plug-in air fresheners responsible for the oppressive atmosphere. Inez settled back into a velvet padded armchair that I almost thought was rose-free until I saw more of them carved into the wood.

"So." Inez scrutinized me as I gingerly sat down beside Ms. Terwilliger on the sofa. Adrian made himself comfortable on a thronelike chair. "An apprentice, huh? And here I thought you just spent your free time advocating chia seeds in natural-foods forums." The old woman's eyes suddenly widened, and I realized she'd caught sight of my left cheek. She chuckled softly to herself. "This gets stranger by the minute. You're braver than I thought, taking on one of them."

"She's very strong," said Ms. Terwilliger almost defensively.

Inez tsked and picked up a teacup. It smelled like Earl Grey, and I hoped she'd offer us some. "Do you think I don't know that? I could tell as soon as I opened the door. How'd you manage that? Aren't you worried about consorting with the devil, girl? Or whatever it is you Alchemists believe?" She glanced over at Adrian. "But then, you must've overcome a few of your hang-ups about the supernatural if you rode in the same car as Jaclyn's pool boy."

I'd known Inez was familiar with the vampiric world. It was why we were here, after all, to learn about her history of fighting Strigoi. I also knew from being with the coven that vampires were just business as usual to some witches. Nonetheless, it was a completely new and baffling experience to be with an outsider who was so at ease with Moroi.

"These hands don't do manual labor," Adrian told her.

"Be quiet, boy," she snapped. "Before you become less endearing."

I cleared my throat. "I don't do any consorting with the devil, ma'am." Just an insolent yet irritatingly attractive vampire. "Mostly I've been translating spells and learning to defend myself."

"Her training has made her an excellent scholar," insisted Ms. Terwilliger.

"Scholar, pah." Inez made a dismissive wave of her hand. "Just looks like some flighty teenage girl to me, one who probably thinks she's being a rebel by tinkering with magic. Doesn't matter how strong she is if she can't focus and get serious about the craft. Do you have a boyfriend, girl? Yes, of course you do. That just makes things worse. There's no getting through to them when all they've got is the backseat of a car on their mind. We didn't have those problems in my day. They'd send us off to our mentors and lock us away. No boys. No temptation. Lose your virginity, girl, and you lose half your magic. Something you might have thought about, Jaclyn." She finally paused to catch her breath and drink more tea. I made a point of studying her teacup because I knew if I looked at Adrian, I was going to start laughing. "No, there's no use bothering with kids these days, not with all their texting and reality TV and power drinks. She's a snappy dresser, I'll give you that, but that's not enough to get me to waste my time with some young girl."

"You don't even know what I want," I blurted out. "And I'm not *that* young. I'll be nineteen in about two weeks."

Inez rolled her eyes. "Aquarius? Worse and worse."

Ms. Terwilliger had regained some of her confidence and met Inez's shrewd gaze with a level look. "She's extremely disciplined and extremely advanced. She takes this very seriously and has already joined the Stelle."

That, at least, came as a surprise, and Inez glanced at me with new consideration—though still not approval. "I suppose that's something."

"It's just the warm-up," said Adrian.

I gave him a warning look, not wanting him to "help" my case. "Please, ma'am. I need your guidance. I heard you've had lots of encounters with Strigoi. That you've fought some. I want to know more about it."

She didn't look impressed in the least. "Hmphf. That's all? I figured someone like you would know more than me."

"Not the magical side," I said. "How did you fight them?"

"The same way anyone does. Stakes, fire, or decapitation.

Not that the Moroi give us many stakes. But I've lit up a few Strigoi in my day. Just takes a good fireball spell."

That wasn't a huge revelation. "Yeah . . . I know a lot about that spell."

Inez gave Ms. Terwilliger a quizzical look. "Didn't your house burn down recently? Good grief, you guys weren't experimenting with fireballs indoors, were you?"

My teacher shifted uncomfortably. "No. You'll have to get that story from Alicia DeGraw." There was a slight catch in her voice. "Veronica's apprentice."

"The one who went rogue," said Inez.

"Yes. Sydney defeated her and saved my life."

Inez studied me in a way that said I might not be a complete waste of time, and I took advantage of it. "Please, ma'am. Please help me. You seem like someone who really appreciates knowledge and learning, and I'd be so grateful if you'd share just a little of your wisdom."

"Why should I help?" she asked. I could tell she was intrigued, though. Flattery really could get you places. "You don't have any superior knowledge to offer me."

"Because I'm superior in other things. Help me, and I'll . . . I'll fix your car out front. I'll change the tire."

That threw her off. "You're in a skirt."

"I'm offering you what I can. Manual labor in exchange for wisdom."

"I don't believe you can do it," she said after several long moments.

I crossed my arms. "It's an eyesore."

"You have fifteen minutes," she snapped.

"I only need ten."

Naturally, Adrian felt the need to "supervise" my work. "Are you going to get mad if I tell you how hot this is?" he asked, kneeling near me, though careful not to get his own clothes dirty.

I had no time for such niceties as I sized up the spare tire, which seemed to be in only slightly better shape than the flat. "I assume you mean the temperature." I was starting to sweat, which wasn't helping matters.

"You really think this car is important enough to her that she'd help? Something tells me that the last time she drove anything, it was a horse-drawn carriage."

I opened up a toolbox that had been in the back of Ms. Terwilliger's car, pleased that it was well stocked and compatible. "It's not really about the car. This is a test to prove I'm not some 'flighty girl.' I think she gets a kick out of seeing others jump through hoops. That'll hopefully buy me credit."

He fell silent and watched me work for another minute or so. "Was that true what she said? About virginity affecting magic?"

"For some spells," I said. "For others, not so much. Some of the witches in the Stelle are married, and Ms. Terwilliger's still pretty formidable."

He didn't say anything, and I could guess his thoughts. He was wondering if that would influence my own views about sex. In truth, it was only one of the many factors I was juggling when it came to going to the next level with him. His being a vampire was one of my smaller concerns. But other things—vague ones, like simply reaching a milestone, and specific ones, like knowing Jill was watching—certainly weighed on me. Magic played into it as well, but to a lesser extent.

One of the biggest influences was just an overwhelming

desire to be cautious. Even engaging in our relationship was a reckless thing, and some part of me needed to compensate by holding back on other aspects. That wasn't to say I didn't want to have sex. I did . . . enough that I was carrying a secret that not even Adrian knew about: I'd actually started taking birth control pills. Was it because I had a definitive sexual plan? No, not yet. But I had that definitive cautious nature of mine that felt it was best to be prepared. I wasn't sure how he'd react if he knew.

He helped me up when I finished in nine minutes and made sure I knew that he thought my dirty, sweaty state was adorable. We went back inside and found Inez and Ms. Terwilliger sitting comfortably in the air-conditioned mauve living room. I hesitated to sit on the couch again and instead settled on the floor in front of Inez.

"Took you long enough," she said. She looked me over and nodded. "Go ahead, then. Ask your questions."

I knew better than to waste this chance. "I heard that you were attacked by Strigoi, ma'am—that they tried to drink from you but couldn't. How? What happened?"

"Oh, there was no 'try' about it," Inez said. She touched the side of her throat. "Right there that monster bit me—but you're right. He didn't get very much before the taste got to him. When he realized he couldn't eat me, he got enraged and tried to snap my neck—but then I got a fireball out on him." There was a gleam in her eye as she spoke, as though she were seeing the battle play out in front of her. "Odd things, vampire bites. In some ways, they're exquisite. Exquisite, but lethal."

"Yes, I know," I told her, once more surprising her. "A Strigoi tried to drink from me too but couldn't."

Inez nodded. "It's our magic. It leaves a residue on the blood when you use it. Hasn't Jaclyn taught you that?"

"Er, yes . . ." I began. "But how would that matter to a Strigoi?"

"Magic is life. Strigoi have none, so when they're struck with it—like with a Moroi charmed stake—it goes against their essence. A stake through the heart kills them. A witch's blood is simply unpleasant."

"But I hadn't—" I stopped, realizing that even though I hadn't been working great spells before that Strigoi attack, I'd begun the preparation of some at Ms. Terwilliger's behest. They'd required low-level, unconscious magic—apparently enough to leave a mark that had saved my life. Accepting this, I moved on. "But if magic blood can harm them, how come they can drink from the Moroi? Seems like Moroi would be even more potent because their magic is already within them, not like us."

Inez seemed pleased by my questions. "Exactly because the magic is intrinsic. It's woven into the blood and doesn't have the same shock to a Strigoi system. Our magic . . ." She groped for the words. "It coats our blood because we pull it from the outside world into us. A similar thing occurs with a charmed stake. Magic is forced into it, becoming a more tangible weapon against the undead."

I could just barely follow along. "A lot of nuances here, dealing with internal and external magic."

"To say the least." Inez almost gave me a genuine smile. "And it gets more complicated when you compare Moroi and human magic. Sometimes they behave similarly, sometimes completely differently. And of course, there's the whole other issue of them contradicting each other."

"Contradicting each other?" Something in those words pricked my inner alarms.

Inez put her hands into fists and slammed them together. "External, internal. Two sides of the magical coin. Sometimes they clash. Your tattoo there. The Alchemists get vampire blood to infuse it with compulsion, right?"

I nodded slowly. "Yes. To stop us from discussing supernatural matters with outsiders." And to stop us from doing other things.

"Well, not for you. I guarantee your tattoo stopped working when you first dabbled in magic."

The world came to a halt as the full impact of her words hit me. "No . . . that's not possible. I mean, I guess it is, but I swear, there wasn't any difference in me. Not then." Things had certainly progressed afterward.

Inez's gaze pinned me to the floor. "Did you ever try to do anything? Try to talk about vampires to ordinary people?"

"No . . ."

"Then how do you know?"

"I don't, but I figured the tattoo's magic was still going strong until—"

"Until what?" she asked. Even Ms. Terwilliger was looking at me now.

Last month, I'd run into a former Alchemist named Marcus Finch who'd rebelled and run away from them. Like me, he believed the Alchemists were too harsh on vampires, but he even went as far as to say there were some Alchemist factions actually working with vampire hunters. Marcus claimed to have discovered a way to undo the magic in our tattoos, freeing us of the compulsion magic that enforced Alchemist loyalty and made us keep supernatural affairs secret. I'd undergone the first part of the two-step process to negate the tattoo: receiving injections of new ink that contained "broken" vampire elemental magic. That allegedly had freed me of the initial compulsion. The second step was to get the golden lily tattooed over with a sort of indigo ink Marcus had to acquire in Mexico. He said without that step, the Alchemists could just eventually reinstate the compulsion. I'd declined Marcus's offer to go to Mexico, however, saying I'd take my chances without the indigo seal. I couldn't bring myself to leave Adrian, Jill, and the others, seeing as there'd be no returning to my life in Palm Springs after open rebellion.

I chose my next words very carefully as I touched my cheek. "This tattoo is infused with elements made by vampire magic. If the two magics conflict, what would happen if elements derived from human magic were also put into this tattoo? Which magic would dominate?"

That clearly wasn't the question either of them had expected. Inez frowned. "In you? The human magic, for sure. Like speaks to like, at least in this case. Your own humanness would strengthen what was there."

"So . . . whatever charms or spells were worked into the ink with vampire magic would be undone by new ink powered with human magic."

"Yes."

The world was moving again, but I was barely aware of it. I was on the edge of something so, so big. I could tell. I just needed to grasp it. My fingertips could practically feel it.

"To hold Moroi magic in the body, you need a physical component," I began. "In this case, ink made from their blood. To hold human magic in the body, you'd need a physical ink too . . . would that require human blood?"

"No," said Inez swiftly. Her wrinkled brow frowned. "Blood is a good medium for a charm made of theirs because their magic is so tied to their bodies. Since we have to take our magic from the world around us, you'd be better off stabilizing it with some sort of physical compound. Something from nature."

"Like what?"

She looked over at Ms. Terwilliger in what I suspected was a rare show of deference. "It's hard to say. Something plant derived?"

Ms. Terwilliger pursed her lips as she mulled it over. "I'd say rock or mineral based."

My heart raced. "A blue one?"

"I don't think that the color matters so much in this case," she said. "Certain substances hold certain kinds of magic better than others. Honestly? You'd have to get into the nitty-gritty of geology. Look at crystalline structure, and see what types would form the best charm with what you're wanting to do. It's dull and dreary work. You'd probably love it."

"Where would I find this out?" I exclaimed.

"There are books and books on it," said Inez, in a voice that suggested I should've already known that. She took a deep breath, and for the first time in our meeting, she looked uncertain. Finally, resolve filled her face. "If you can be trusted not to do something stupid with them, I *might* lend you some of my books."

I clasped my hands together. "That would be . . . wow. Thank you. Thank you so much."

"Stop babbling," she snapped. "I said 'might.' I haven't given them to you yet. These are quality books, passed down through my family. I'm not some upstart witch. My magical lineage goes back generations."

"Yes, ma'am," I said.

She hesitated a few moments more. "If you can get them, you can borrow them. They're in the attic." She jerked her head toward a ceiling trapdoor on the far side of the room.

I immediately stood up, and Adrian started to join me.

"Not you, pretty boy," she warned. "I want her to do this on her own. They're in a box labeled 'Charm Mechanics.'"

He gave me a sympathetic look, but I shook my head. "No problem." I'd at least only worn half-heeled shoes. Surely I could maneuver in an attic.

And I did . . . but not easily. The place was filled with dust and insulation, and the "Charm Mechanics" box was underneath five other heavy boxes. When I finally hauled my treasure down the attic ladder a half hour later, Adrian's and Ms. Terwilliger's amused expressions told me exactly how I must look. Inez nodded in approval.

"I think I like you," she said thoughtfully. "You should visit again. You're interesting."

Later, when we were on the highway to Palm Springs, Ms. Terwilliger was full of mirth and incredulity. "Do you realize what you accomplished here? You not only got her to lend your books—which she *never* gives out, by the way—you also got the closest to a personal invitation I've ever heard her give." She shook her head and laughed. "You never cease to amaze me, Sydney. Do you want to store the books at my house?" That was where most of my growing collection of magical supplies were. They couldn't be trusted to my dorm room anymore, not with Zoe around.

"I'll keep them at Adrian's," I said automatically. She didn't comment, and I wondered if I'd made a mistake. Ms. Terwilliger asked few questions about my personal life, romantic or Alchemist, but she was neither stupid nor oblivious. Maybe witches took vampires in stride, but I wondered if she suspected—and judged—the full extent of my relationship with Adrian.

Adrian leaned forward from the backseat. "That was a lot of work you did for some books. I assume you have some genius plan?"

I dragged my attention from my disheveled skirt and allowed myself to rekindle the excitement I'd felt earlier when Inez's words had set off a lightbulb in my head. "I'm not sure if it's genius or not," I said. "But I think . . . well, I think I can replicate Marcus's ink."

CHAPTER 5
ADRIAN

SYDNEY SPENT A LOT OF TIME ON MY BED THESE DAYS. Unfortunately, it wasn't with me.

I didn't entirely follow how all that back-and-forthing with Inez had given Sydney the idea to make anti-Alchemist ink, but I'd never claimed I could keep up with her mind. Once she took up the quest, make-out hour had become research hour. She couldn't work on it around Zoe, and although Jackie pretty much let Sydney do whatever she wanted, their time was limited too. And so, our romantic interludes were reallocated.

I'd be lying if I said I didn't miss the old system, but I wanted her to pursue the ink. As much as I'd disliked Marcus Finch, I had supported his goals to thwart the Alchemists' influence and attempts at mind control. Sydney had chosen not to go with him to finish the process because she wasn't ready to embrace his drifter way of life; plus she believed she could accomplish more by staying connected to the Alchemists. Those were noble reasons, but I knew full well that another one—perhaps the greatest—was that she hadn't wanted to leave me.

And who was I kidding? I didn't want her to leave me either. At the same time, there'd always been a pang of guilt that I was responsible for leaving her vulnerable to being re-inked. I also knew every stolen moment we had together put her at a terrible risk to face the Alchemists' wrath. Even though Inez had claimed that Sydney was already immune to future tattooing because of her magic use, both of us wanted that golden lily sealed, just in case the worst happened. But it wasn't just about herself. She knew that if she could discover an easily reproducible ink capable of negating the Alchemist tattoos, she'd hold a lot of power in her hands.

These research afternoons weren't so bad. I dragged my supplies into the bedroom and worked on that goddamned self-portrait while she sat cross-legged on my bed, surrounded by books and her laptop. She was so engrossed that she didn't notice how often I got distracted and watched her. Maybe it was crazy, but there was something incredibly sexy to me about seeing that thoughtful expression juxtaposed with her casual posture as she shifted her legs and leaned forward to read some arcane text. Moroi shied from sunlight, but as I watched the way it illuminated her, I knew without a doubt that humans had been made for the sun.

"It's boleite," she said abruptly one day.

I turned from my canvas, which so far had one green line on it. "Like an Indian musical?"

"Boleite, not Bollywood." She tapped her laptop screen. "It's this deep blue mineral that has large deposits in Mexico. I've been reading all about the mechanics of charm making in

Inez's books, and there's almost a scientific aspect to it. The composition of different minerals and plants in nature affect the kind of elemental spell components they can hold for charms. Boleite's cubic crystals and isometric system would make it an excellent medium to suspend the four elements in a way that could be held in the skin and negate any added Moroi magic. Its specific gravity and perfect cleavage go a long way too."

The only part of that I understood was "perfect cleavage," but I had a feeling we weren't thinking of the same thing. "So, uh, what's the summary?"

She leaned back, eyes enraptured. "It's not the mineral alone. Marcus thinks he goes to Mexico to get some material that fights the gold ink in and of itself. But it's more than that. I'll bet you anything his tattooist is a magic user who charms the boleite before mixing it into the ink. The rebel Alchemists are using human magic and don't even realize it."

That was a little more on my level. I set down my paintbrush and picked up a nearby glass of water. "So can you do the same thing? Charm that mineral and make ink out of it to seal your tattoo?"

"I'm not sure. I'd need help from Ms. Terwilliger to figure out that kind of spell. There's no recorded one that I can use, and we'd have to create our own. I've never done anything like that." She frowned. "Even bigger than that is getting enough boleite to work with. Pretty sure it's not something lying around in Palm Springs. I could probably order some off the Web . . . or maybe find a more common substitute. Something else in the halide family might have similar properties."

"And you'd be doubly protected." That was the most important part here to me, not all the geological jargon.

"If I can do it, yeah. And if Inez's right that I'm already protected." Inspiration lit her features. "*And* I could save Marcus a lot of trouble. He loses time on his Mexico trips. If I could replicate the ink, he'd have a domestic supply and could help more people. Let's just hope he surfaces someday so that I can actually share this with him."

I shrugged. "Why wait? We'll find him in a dream. Not that I really enjoy spending nights with him, but it'll be passable if you're there."

Her features instantly hardened. "No. No unnecessary dreams."

"It's necessary. You just said what a huge breakthrough this could be, and no matter how much I hate his hair, Robin Hood Finch is your contact in the underground. You need to run this by him."

"And I will," she said obstinately. "The next time I see him. He always comes back. You don't need to waste spirit on this."

"It's not a waste. A dream is cake, Sage."

"And it's exactly what I was saying before. You can't help yourself from doing this kind of stuff—and it's why I love you. But it's a risk."

"Yeah? Some people—not me, of course—might argue that you taking on this whole ink-making mission is an incredible risk. You think insubordination pisses the Alchemists off? What if they found out it was being fueled by magic? And that's not even considering what they'd do if they found out about me." I waved the water glass at her for emphasis. "You're risking a lot, my love. If the Alchemists found out about even one of these things . . ."

"Then what?" she asked warily. "You think I should stop?"

"No, of course not," I said with more confidence than I felt. Part of me wished there was a way she'd never be in any danger, but that wasn't reality. At least not our reality. "Because I know you can't. It's what you do. And spirit dreams? Those are what I do." I nodded to her laptop and books. "I can't do all that sleuthing and magical spell work, but let me do something little like this. Let me feel like I'm contributing something to us."

Her eyes went wide. "Oh, Adrian. You contribute plenty. You . . . you have no idea what you do. You're the greatest joy in my life. The greatest joy I've ever had."

"Then it's settled," I said. "We'll do a dream conference call."

That love and rapture faltered. "Wait. How is it settled? How did we go from me declaring my love for you to me being okay with a dream?"

"It's Adrian Ivashkov logic. Don't try to understand it. Just roll with it."

"That's easier said than done."

I nodded solemnly. "That's just because you aren't used to living the kind of spontaneous and unpredictable life I do. The unexpected is par for the course with me. Nothing surprises me anymore."

A sly look appeared in her eyes. "Oh, I don't know. I bet I could totally tell you something you never saw coming."

"You're welcome to try."

"If I surprise you, will you not do the dream?"

"Let's hear what you've got."

She hesitated a few seconds, and although there was still a mischievous glint in her eyes, I detected a little nervousness too. "Well . . . I'm on birth control."

I was drinking the water again and choked on it. It took several moments of coughing before I could gasp out, "*What*?"

She shrugged, unbelievably casual, as though the suggestion of having sex wasn't a big deal. And yeah, there was no question about it. I was surprised. Very surprised. I should've known better than to doubt her abilities. "It takes a while for it to start working, so I figured I should be prepared, just in case."

"Just in case," I repeated, still dumbfounded.

Whatever nervousness she'd had was turning to delight at my discomfort. "Come on, are you saying you don't think about it?"

"Oh, believe me, I think about it all the time. I just never knew you did. I mean, I figured when it came to sex, the Alchemists had all these principles about purity and marriage and sin . . . and stuff."

"Most do," she agreed. "Me? My principles are about love and doing it because there's meaning and commitment. A piece of paper doesn't always signal that. If there's any sin involved, it's doing it in a . . . I don't know. Cheap way. With people you don't care about. When it's meaningless."

I couldn't muster a comment on that because the majority of sex in my life had pretty much been the cheap kind. I couldn't remember the names of half the girls I'd been with. Sydney was fully aware of this, but she made no condemnation and shifted to a topic that was more expected of her personality.

"And, of course, doing it responsibly is huge too. There are a million pills on the market, so I had to compile all the data." Then, incredibly, she pulled out a chart from her messenger bag entitled *Oral-Contraceptive Comparison*. It was hand drawn, but you'd never guess it from the perfect lines and neat writing.

There was lots of color coding, as well as columns filled with unintelligible terms like *estradiol* and *androgenicity*.

I stared, slack jawed, even though this was completely in line with the Sydney I knew and loved. "You've been working on this?"

"I actually made it a while ago. Didn't take that long." She regarded it with a sigh. "There are lots of side effects for all of them. I mean, plenty of people have no problems at all, but there are things that sometimes happen that you have to take into consideration. Tons of these are linked to weight gain."

I studied her very carefully, realizing what a big concession that was. No matter her new healthy habits, I knew her figure was a constant source of worry, which was ridiculous considering how great she looked. "I'm surprised you'd take the chance. There are plenty of other safe sex options, you know. Ones that don't involve pills."

"I know." She set the chart down. "But we don't have to worry about disease, and this is one of the most effective methods—and it lets me control it. My doctor gave me the one with the lowest incidence of weight gain, so we'll see."

I stood up and sat beside her on the bed. "Promise me if you notice anything happening, you just stop taking it. I don't want you trying to compensate with some crazy diet."

She met my eyes. "You think I'd do that?"

"I'd rather not risk it and find out."

"And risk not having sex?"

"I'm not having sex right now and am doing just fine," I said nobly. "Although . . . uh, just out of academic curiosity, at what point are you thinking about . . ."

Sydney laughed and brushed a kiss against my lips. "I don't

know. Whenever I'm ready." Abruptly, she sobered. "And there's Jill . . ."

"Ah," I said, because it was all I could say.

Jill. Jill, who could see inside my world and the things I did—including the things I did with Sydney. I knew it bothered Sydney—and I couldn't blame her. Having a reluctant witness to our most intimate activities wasn't something I liked either, especially when that witness was sweet and innocent Jill. Not that she was probably that sweet and innocent after living in my head. Jill, more than anything, was what I suspected had slowed down my physical relationship with Sydney. There were some things she could grudgingly accept Jill knowing about. There were others she couldn't.

And I had no argument or conciliatory words to offer. I didn't know how to get around this, and no way would I pressure Sydney into something she was so uncomfortable with. The only thing I could hope for was that Jill and I could develop the self-control to block each other out. My ex, Rose, had been bound to Lissa, and they'd eventually developed that ability . . . though it had taken a couple years. Was I willing to wait that long for Sydney? Studying her as I held her hand, I knew the answer immediately. Yes. Yes, I would.

I gave her what I hoped was an encouraging smile. "Then we'll just have to see what happens. If it works, great. If not, you stop taking it. It's a pill, not a lifelong commitment. Besides, there are lots of ways to keep busy in the meantime."

That brought her smile back, and my heart lightened. "I'm guessing whatever 'ways' you have in mind aren't Jill-appropriate either."

"Put your books away, and I'll show you."

Jill was still on my mind after Sydney left, largely because I had plans to have dinner with her that night. It was something I tried to do once in a while. Maybe Jill knew all about my life, but I wanted to keep in touch with hers. Besides, despite all our group dinners, it was nice just to have the two of us hang out. Well, almost two of us. Occasionally, Jill might leave the school with Sydney, but everyone preferred that a dhampir go along. I knew Jill found it oppressive sometimes, but this was one instance of stiff rules I could support. I'd been there when the assassins had attacked her. I'd seen the blood and her chest grow still. Those images woke me out of sleep all the time, and I'd be damned if there'd ever be a repeat of those events.

And so, Eddie tagged along for these dinners, which I didn't mind that much. He was a good guy, one who'd seen his own fair share of trauma and heartache. It was a part of him, one he'd used to strengthen himself and carry on. He was real, and I appreciated that.

Except it wasn't Eddie waiting at the curb with Jill.

"Damn it," I muttered.

A wry look flashed across Jill's face as she read my reaction. Although she was respectful of my thoughts and feelings, this was one matter that she stood firmly opposed to me in.

"Hi, Adrian," she said cheerily, getting into the car. "Neil decided to come along with us tonight."

"So I see." He slid into the backseat, giving me a curt nod of greeting in the rearview mirror. "Does Castile have a hot date?"

"No, but we just thought it'd be fun for Neil to get out." What she actually meant, of course, was that she thought it'd be fun for her to get out with Neil. I didn't need a bond to know that.

"Plus, I've had one more year of experience than Eddie,"

added Neil. "So really, I should be the one who always goes out in public with Her Highness."

Jill normally chafed at her title, but whenever Neil used it, he seemed to act like some ye olde knight that set her heart aflutter.

"Castile's faced a few tough situations," I said. "How many Strigoi and assassins have you run up against?" I watched him in the rearview mirror, and although he had that tough-guy look on his face, I saw him shift uneasily.

"I was once part of a large regiment of guardians protecting a royal family when two Strigoi decided to attack," he said.

"Two Strigoi against a whole group of guardians, huh? Wow. That's pretty hard core."

I saw Jill shoot me an angry look in my periphery. "Neil's done and seen a lot of things. His training is excellent."

In a great act of generosity, I decided to give up on tormenting her fake crush . . . for now. My attention soon turned to fighting for a parking spot downtown amid all the other evening diners. One opened up just as I was driving in front of the Greek restaurant I'd picked for dinner. "Adrian Ivashkov wins again," I declared.

There was only a short wait inside, and as the hostess led us to our table, we passed the dessert case. "Fresh baklava," observed Jill, face perfectly innocent.

"Looks that way," I said, just as sweetly. "Maybe we can get some to go." Baklava was one of Sydney's favorites. It may or may not have played a role in my decision to come here.

I passed wistfully on the ouzo and asked Jill about her swimming team. All Amberwood students needed to participate in a sport outside of classes, and swimming was the perfect choice for her since most meets were indoors and because her elemental specialty was water. Personally, I wasn't a huge sports fan, though I did like Super Bowl parties, especially if I didn't have to watch the game. I had gone to a few of Jill's swim meets and found it was worth enduring the overexcited parents to see her excel.

Even now, there was happiness on her face as she described achieving a new personal best, and it was a pleasant distraction from the storms continually brewing in my mind. She'd had a lot of difficulties adjusting to Amberwood, and I was glad to see something going her way. The interlude was ruined when she turned to Neil with shining eyes.

"Neil's on the wrestling team. He's really amazing. The best one. He wins all his matches."

I leaned back in the chair, feeling no more qualms about going after him if she insisted on bringing him up. "Well, of course he does. Any dhampir is going to dominate over a human. It's nature."

Neil thought this over as he chewed his souvlaki. "I suppose so," he said at last.

"Hardly seems fair," I continued. "I mean, they make adjustments for weight class, but there's no regulating something like that. You're playing with people who can in no way keep up with you."

Jill shot me a warning look. "Well, there's nothing he can do, seeing as Amberwood doesn't sort by human and dhampir teams."

"You could always throw the matches," I told Neil.

He blanched. "Throw a match? I couldn't do that! It'd go against my personal code of ethics."

"Where does taking out people who can in no way defeat you fit into your ethics?" I asked. "If you ask me, that's the real moral transgression." I wished Sydney were here because I think she would've appreciated my use of *transgression*. "But I mean, it's your life. I don't judge, and honestly . . ." I gave a light laugh. "I tend to always err a little too much on the side of morality. It's one of my few flaws."

Even Neil wasn't oblivious enough to buy that. He narrowed his eyes. "I somehow must have missed that. Tell me more about your views on morality."

I waved him off. "Oh, we don't have that kind of time. But you know who you should talk it over with? Castile. There's a guy who understands the right thing to do. He faked spraining his ankle to get out of most of the basketball season so he wouldn't have to deal with the, uh, ethics of competing with humans. Now that's someone who really walks the line."

While I still couldn't gauge Neil's interest in Jill, I knew beyond a doubt he regarded Eddie as a rival in life. Eddie wasn't quite as bad, but he had a competitive streak as well. I guess there could only be one alpha dhampir at Amberwood.

"Lying isn't exactly honorable either," said Neil hotly.

"No, but humility is." I sighed as dreamily for Eddie as Jill often did for Neil. "He'd rather face the humiliation of being out of the game than reap glory he doesn't deserve."

That might have been going too far, judging from the anger flaring in Neil's eyes. "Neil," Jill said quickly. "Will you go up to the counter and order me some baklava to go? Walnut. And pistachio."

Jill was truly becoming my pupil. Pistachio wasn't one of this place's common types, so they didn't usually keep it on display. Making Neil wait while they hunted some down would buy us time.

"You're so mean," she told me once Neil was gone. He didn't take his eyes off us as he waited, but at least he was out of earshot.

"You can do better, Princess Jailbait." I enunciated each word with my fork. "Besides, Big Ben over there's married to his duty. You'll never get him. Find some Moroi prince and give up on dhampirs altogether. They're nothing but trouble." Didn't I know it. "Besides, you may have everyone else fooled, but I know you're not into him."

"Yeah? You have a psychic bond now?"

"Don't need one." I tapped my head. "I have aura vision. That, and I just know you. What are you playing at? Why are you trying to pretend you're interested in him?"

She sighed. "Because I hope I *will* be interested in him."

"Like, if you do a good enough act, you'll convince yourself?"

"Something like that."

"That's nonsensical. And coming from me, that's a serious accusation."

She kicked me under the table. "If I can fall in love with Neil, then maybe I'll stop . . ." Her voice faltered a moment. "Maybe I'll stop thinking about Eddie."

I deleted the snarky comments I'd been mentally accruing. "I don't think it works that way. Actually, I know for a fact it doesn't."

"I have to do something, Adrian. I wish I'd realized how I felt about Eddie sooner . . . I was so stupid and missed my chance. Now Sydney says he's all caught up in honor and duty and thinks no princess could lower herself to him."

"That sounds like something he'd say," I agreed. I'd never

actually heard the tale directly from Eddie, but Sydney had had a heart-to-heart with him and gotten the scoop. He'd once had a crush on Jill that he staunchly denied. Neither of us knew if it had survived his Angeline days, but something told me if it had, his views on chivalry hadn't changed.

"Maybe instead of trying to trick yourself into falling for another guy, you should just go confront Eddie and get it all out," I suggested.

"Like you did with Sydney?" asked Jill archly. "That didn't go so well."

"Not at the time." To describe Sydney's reaction to my initial declaration of love as "not going well" was a kindness. "But look at me now, lounging in the lap of love."

Jill's earlier grin returned. "You should make Sydney dinner. For her birthday."

It was one of those times when it was nice having someone who was already up to speed on my life. It saved me a lot of explaining what had been weighing on me. I also realized this abrupt topic change was Jill's subtle way of saying she didn't want to talk about her own love life anymore. "That's not a real gift. She deserves more."

"Diamonds and roses?" Jill shook her head. "You should know her better than that. She's not a material person, and you don't need to make some big expensive gesture. A homemade dinner's romantic."

"Also disastrous. You know better than anyone else that I can't cook."

"And that's why she'll love it even more. She's into personal effort—and learning. Figure out how to make a simple dish, and it'll go a long way. Imperfection is endearing."

Jill had a point, but it was a tough one for me to swallow. Most of my courtship with girls—even the one-night stands—had involved those "big expensive gestures." Flowers and more flowers. Seven-course meals with wine pairings. Cooking boxed spaghetti didn't measure up.

"I'll think about it," I conceded.

That perked Jill up. "Maybe if the atmosphere's romantic enough, you guys can—"

"No, Jailbait." I held up a hand. "Don't go there."

"But you want to," Jill insisted. "And she does too, or she wouldn't have made that chart."

"I don't know about that. That chart's the kind of thing she'd do in her free time for fun. Anyway. She and I don't agree on everything, but you not being involved with our sex life is one point we're in perfect harmony on, so there's no point in discussing this."

She propped her elbow on the table and rested her chin in her hand, causing her wavy, light brown hair to fall forward and frame her face like a veil. It would've made a powerful pose for a painting.

"I feel terrible. It's all my fault that your love life is ruined. If it wasn't for the bond—"

"You'd be dead," I said flatly. "And there's no debate about that whatsoever. I say this with absolute seriousness: I'd rather be celibate for the rest of my life than not have you in this world."

Jill swallowed, and I could tell she was fighting back tears.

"Careful," I teased. "Start crying, and London Bridge'll think I've been mean to you. He'll rough me up outside."

She sniffed but managed a smile. "No, he wouldn't, but

he's finishing up over there. Maybe I could drink or something if you and Sydney—you know. It'd numb the bond on my end."

"No," I said firmly. Neil began walking toward us. "Absolutely not. One recovering alcoholic in this bond is bad enough. Don't worry about it for now. We'll figure it out."

"How?" she asked.

"I have a plan."

Jill knew me too well and gave me a knowing look. "Liar."

CHAPTER 6
SYDNEY

I DIDN'T KNOW HOW LONG I'D BEEN ASLEEP when the spirit dream drew me in. The Getty Villa's columned courtyard materialized around me, and sunshine sparkled on the enormous fountain. Here in these dreams, the sun didn't affect Adrian. I scanned around and found him leaning against a pillar, hands in his pockets as he watched me with that roguish smile of his. For a moment, I was dazzled by him and the way the sunlight lit up his cheekbones and hair. He was breathtaking. He could've been one of the villa's classic works of art.

Then, I remembered he wasn't supposed to be here.

I strolled over and caught hold of the front of his shirt, tugging him toward me. "Hey! What's going on? I thought we agreed to no more dreams."

"You agreed to that. I never actually took you up on that surprise bargain."

"But I—" I stopped and replayed our earlier conversation, when I'd delivered the bombshell about the birth control pills.

He actually *hadn't* said he'd skip the dream if I surprised him. "You tricked me."

"There was no trick involved. If anything, I'm the victim here, after you dropped that tantalizing pill info. How am I supposed to get anything done now?" He gave me a long kiss before going on. "Did Jailbait deliver the baklava?"

"Yes, but don't think that'll get you off the hook for this dream."

He drew me into another kiss. "I already am."

We finally managed to drag our lips away from each other, though Adrian kept his arm around my waist. The sunlight brought out the chestnut glints in his brown hair, and that fair skin that had once marked something frightening and otherworldly was now stunning in my eyes. His features hardened into resolve.

"Ready to summon Robin Hood?" he asked.

The mention of Marcus snapped me away from carnal thoughts and reminded me of the breakthrough I was teetering on the edge of—and the dangerous situation we were in. Adrian was a master at distracting me from those things.

"You shouldn't be doing this," I warned.

"I'm already doing it," he said cheerfully. "So let's get it over with."

He released me and focused off in the distance, green eyes full of concentration as he tried to reach out to Marcus in the dream world. There was a very strong probability it wouldn't work. Marcus could be awake. Or maybe Adrian didn't know Marcus well enough. Adrian was the best dream walker of the spirit users we knew, but some things were beyond even him.

And yet, after almost a minute of tense silence, I saw a

glimmer of something across the courtyard. Slowly, it expanded into a man's figure, and Marcus suddenly stood before us. He looked the same as ever, with his shoulder-length blond hair and the bright indigo tattoo latticed over his now-fading Alchemist lily. There was a confusion written all over him that I could understand. I'd thought I was in a normal dream the first time Adrian had summoned me, and then, gradually, I'd gotten the sense that there was something off about it.

"Nice to see you again, Marcus," I told him.

He frowned and examined his hands, touching them together as though he expected them to have no substance. "Is this real?"

"Real enough," said Adrian.

"You're in a spirit dream," I explained.

Marcus looked disbelieving for a moment, and then wonder filled his eyes. "Wow." He glanced around. "Where are we?"

"Malibu," I said, earning more surprise. "Where are you? Mexico?"

He dragged his gaze from the buildings around us. "Yeah, but we're heading back soon. Amelia and Wade got their tattoos, and I got a tip about some rebels who need me in Arizona. We're just waiting on a guy who's going to help us get over the border. Always a lot harder getting back in."

Marcus was on the Alchemists' most-wanted list. Any Alchemist who slipped out of their grasp was bad enough, let alone one actively recruiting others. With their many connections, he had to be extra careful in his movements, especially at high-security places like a border. It seemed to occur to him then that this wasn't a social call.

"What's going on? Are you okay?" He almost seemed to

expect that I wasn't okay. For all his quirkiness, he'd been legitimately worried about me staying behind.

"Surprisingly, yes. I've got something that might help you." I allowed a dramatic pause that was straight out of his playbook. "I might be able to make the ink that you use to seal the tattoos."

He went slack jawed. "That . . . that's impossible."

Adrian scoffed. "Is it? She broke into a high-security Alchemist stronghold and hunted you down. You think she can't replicate what some random guy you dug up can do?"

Marcus had no counter for that and fixed his gaze back on me. "You've got indigo ink?"

"Not exactly. I can't get the mineral I'm pretty sure your guy uses, but I think I know a couple others that'll do the trick."

"You 'think,'" he repeated.

"The mineral's not what matters. Well, it does a little. It's the process of creating the ink that matters, and I know how to do that." That wasn't entirely true. I understood the principles but had yet to test them out. I hoped Marcus wouldn't push me for details, because while he was on board with a lot of far-out stuff, I wasn't sure where me being involved with magic would fall.

He mulled things over for several long moments and then gave a rueful smile. "If anyone could pull off something like that, it'd be you."

"Think what it means," I said, excited that I'd made progress. "If we could mass-produce the ink, you could reach more people. You also wouldn't have to travel. You'd save a lot of time and be able to do more."

Adrian, careful to keep his distance from me, laughed. "I

don't think Marcus minds the traveling. Beaches and margaritas, right?"

Marcus glared. "It's not all about that. And you're one to talk."

Hostile tension suddenly filled the space between them. They'd actually gotten in a physical fight once, following a misunderstanding when Marcus had accidentally hit me. Adrian hadn't taken that very well, and although he'd eventually accepted that it was a mistake, I knew the incident weighed heavily upon him.

"Focus, you guys," I snapped. "There's no time for this."

Their eyes stayed locked for several more agonizing seconds, and then Marcus turned back to me, unclenching hands I hadn't realized were in fists. "So when will you know if you can pull this off?"

Excellent question. I'd learned a lot in my brief research but still needed to figure out a few more things. That, and I'd need a long stretch of time away from Zoe to work on it. Although I could still keep claiming I had to go off on projects with Ms. Terwilliger, I knew Zoe was starting to think the outings were too frequent. Maybe she didn't have arcane suspicions, but there was always the chance she might tell my dad I was more focused on my fake education than the task at hand.

"A week. Maybe two." I spoke more confidently than I felt.

Marcus frowned and then gave a slow nod. "I think we'll be back near then. I need to get more information from my contact. Can you check in next week and let me know how it's going?"

I hesitated. "It'd be better if you could manage a phone call—"

"No problem," said Adrian, ignoring my sharp look. "As long as you're asleep around this time and not too busy with ocean villa parties."

He knew as well as I did that Marcus was usually forced to stay in hovels. "Great," I said. "We'll be in touch."

Adrian took that as a dismissal and sent Marcus away. "Always a delight."

"You shouldn't have done that . . . but, well, thank you. It helps a lot," I admitted.

Alone again, Adrian wrapped me in his arms. "Anything for you, Sage. Come over tomorrow, and I'll consider it a debt well paid."

Thrills ran through me, both at the suggestion and the way his hand slid up my hip and played with the edge of my shirt. Things felt real in these dreams. Very real.

"I can't," I admitted. "I've got to use that time to get some help from Ms. Terwilliger."

The disappointment in his eyes was so fleeting, I could almost believe I'd imagined it. The smug smile he put on made it seem as though nothing in the world was wrong. That was how he operated and why so few knew of the inner turmoil that raged within him.

"Well, then, I suppose that'll just give you more time to fantasize about me," he declared. "Because of course that's what you'll secretly be doing instead of working."

"Of course," I laughed. After long kisses goodbye, I faded off to true sleep.

When I showed up for Ms. Terwilliger's independent study the next day, she was waiting with her coat and keys. "Spencer's first," she said curtly. "It's been one of those days."

"We don't have that much time," I protested. That, and going to my favorite coffee shop was pretty torturous these days.

"We can talk along the way," she said.

She was true to her word as we drove over, explaining some of the more pragmatic aspects both of charm making and manipulating the elements. "It's a tricky art, working with them in their purest form," she mused. "Simultaneously simple yet infinitely complex." It sounded like my relationship with Adrian.

When we walked into Spencer's, I half hoped to see my friend Trey Juarez working the counter. I remembered moments later that we were still technically in school hours and not everyone got to take off early like I did. Between Adrian and Zoe, I hadn't had much time to talk to Trey. The new semester had rearranged our schedules, so we no longer shared any classes. I didn't know if avoiding him was a good or bad thing. He had a lot of complex issues going on in his life, issues that overlapped with my own life—because Trey had been born into a group of vampire hunters.

Calling themselves the Warriors of Light, they claimed their focus was on destroying Strigoi, but much like the Alchemists, the Warriors didn't have that high of an opinion of Moroi and dhampirs either. Trey was currently on the outs with the Warriors, after inadvertently helping me disband a crazy killing ritual of theirs. For a while, being ostracized had tormented him, especially because of his dad's pressure. Then, something had changed.

Trey had fallen for Angeline.

Out of all the outlandish things she was involved in, that one had caught me by surprise more than anything. The drama had grown increasingly complex because she had technically been dating Eddie at the time, who had rebounded to her after deciding his love for Jill was futile, since he'd never be worthy of her. Eddie and Angeline's relationship had ended abruptly when we'd discovered that her tutoring sessions with Trey had become make-out sessions.

Hooking up with a human wasn't such an odd concept for Angeline, having grown up with the Keepers. Trey had taken it harder when he realized how many of the Warriors' tenets he was violating; plus he'd felt guilty over Eddie. I was pretty sure Trey still harbored feelings for her. As for Angeline, it was hard to say. Like Jill, she seemed to have joined Neil's fan club. Adrian claimed both girls were faking their feelings for him, and I couldn't even begin to sort that out.

To say my friends were living a soap opera was an understatement. They almost made my dangerous relationship with Adrian look boring.

The only bright side was that everyone seemed to be in a holding pattern. Trey's conflicted principles kept him away from Angeline. Eddie's resolve kept him away from everyone, as did Neil's. And so long as Neil held true to that stance, Jill and Angeline would have nothing to act on. Maybe it would have been nice for everyone to have some sort of happy ending, but I selfishly had to admit that my life was a lot easier when the drama dial was kept on low.

Trey might not have been behind the counter today, but another barista I knew well was. His name was Brayden, and he and I had briefly dated. Even at the time, it had seemed a little cool and unreal, and now, alive with the thrill of Adrian, I couldn't even fathom how I'd thought what Brayden and I had was a relationship. There'd been no passion with Brayden, no moments that took my breath away, and certainly no touches that could set me ablaze. In retrospect, the highlight of dating him had been free coffee and a particularly compelling discussion on the fall of the Roman Empire.

"Hi, Sydney," he said. We'd encountered each other here before, and things were pretty civil, especially since Trey told me Brayden had a new girlfriend. "Almost as smart as you," Trey had said. "But not nearly as cute."

I smiled back. "How's it going?"

"Good, good. Just got out of class and found out my essay on the psychosocial implications of Pavlov's associative experiments won me a scholarship." He picked up a cup. "Skinny vanilla latte?"

I looked at the cup mournfully. "Mint tea."

"There, there," said Ms. Terwilliger, after she'd cruelly ordered her triple cappuccino. "You couldn't have had any caffeine anyway." It was true, seeing as I'd likely be experimenting with magic later. "Stay strong."

"That's right," a voice behind me said. "Nothing builds character like a test of self-control."

I spun around, thoroughly unprepared for who had joined us in line. "Wolfe?" I gasped. "You . . . you leave your house?"

Malachi Wolfe, instructor and proprietor of the Wolfe School of Defense, gave me a withering look from his one eye. "Of course I do. How else do you think I get supplies?"

"I . . . I don't know. I figured you ordered them in."

"I do for some stuff," he agreed. "But I've got to come here in person to get whole-bean French roast. The dogs love it."

While I supposed it was reasonable that he'd get out of the compound he called a home, showing up at a hip coffee shop just wasn't what I'd imagined. Adrian and I had taken a self-defense course with Wolfe a couple months ago, and despite how bizarre it had all been, we'd picked up some useful tips. Wolfe himself was quite a sight to behold, with his long grizzled hair and eye patch.

"Ahem," said Ms. Terwilliger. "Aren't you going to introduce us, Sydney?"

"Huh?" I was still floored by the fact that Wolfe was in jeans rather than his usual Bermuda shorts. "Oh. This is Malachi Wolfe. He's the man Adrian and I took a self-defense class with. Wolfe, this is my history teacher, Ms.—er, Jaclyn Terwilliger."

"It's a pleasure," she said.

Ms. Terwilliger extended her hand to shake his, and instead, he bowed grandly and kissed the top of hers. "No, no, believe me. The pleasure is all mine."

To my complete and utter horror, she didn't withdraw her hand when he continued to hold it. "You're a teacher too, eh?" she asked. "I thought I sensed a kindred spirit when I first saw you."

He nodded solemnly. "There's no loftier goal than educating and shaping young minds for greatness."

I thought that was a stretch, considering at least fifty percent of his teaching methods involved regaling us with stories of how he'd escaped from pirates in New Zealand or fought off a pack of hook-fanged ravens. (When I'd pointed out no such bird existed, he insisted the government was covering them up). Adrian and I were currently trying to put together a time line of Wolfe's alleged adventures because we were pretty sure there was no way they could've happened the way he claimed.

"What brings you ladies out today?" asked Wolfe. He glanced around. "And where's your boy?"

"Who? Oh, you mean Adrian?" I asked casually. "He's probably still in class. He's an art student at Carlton."

Wolfe's eyebrows rose. "Art? I always thought he was a little flighty, but I had no idea he was that far gone."

"Hey, he's very talented! He just got a lot of acclaim for a mixed-media project he worked on."

"What was it?" Wolfe didn't sound convinced.

"A piece using the monolith from *2001* as a symbol of mankind's evolution to a world of advertising and social media."

Wolfe's contemptuous snort told me what he thought of that. "Goddamned idealistic college kids."

"It's brilliant," I insisted.

"Sydney," said Ms. Terwilliger. "It *is* a little over the top."

I couldn't even formulate a response to her traitorous words. Wolfe, however, wasted no opportunity. "You want to see art? You should go see this exhibit down by the San Diego shipyard. They re-created a Civil War battle scene completely out of Bowie knives."

I opened my mouth to respond, couldn't think of anything to say, and shut it.

Ms. Terwilliger's eyes lit up. "That sounds fascinating."

"You want to come see it with me?" he asked. "I'm going again this weekend. Fifth time."

As they exchanged phone numbers, I glanced over at Brayden, who was staring openmouthed, holding our drinks. At least I wasn't alone in my reaction. I took out the Love Phone and texted Adrian.

Ran into Wolfe. He asked Ms. T out.

Adrian's response was about what I expected: . . .

I then delivered the coup de grâce: *SHE ACCEPTED*.

Adrian was still unable to get past symbols: *?!?*

I was at a loss for words on the way back to Amberwood, made worse by Ms. Terwilliger's dreamy expression. "Ma'am," I said at last. "Do you think going out with someone like him is a good idea? At last count, he had eleven Chihuahuas."

"Miss Melbourne," she said, reverting to her old nickname for me, "I offer no critique on your dubiously sound romantic choices. Don't question mine."

Flirting with Wolfe had eaten into more of our time today, but to her credit, she didn't delay in making use of our remaining twenty minutes. We pulled some desks together and huddled over one of Inez's books, along with a small bowl of dirt. She pointed to a diagram in the book that depicted a palm with four small clumps of dirt arranged in a diamond.

"There's no real incantation for this," she said, sprinkling the dirt on my palm in the appropriate pattern. "It's one of those that's more meditative. Only you aren't trying to accomplish any concrete result so much as connect with the dirt's essence. What do you think of when you think of dirt?"

"To not wear white."

Her lips twitched, but she stayed on track. "Shift yourself into a casting trance and think of all that earth is in the world and even the role it plays in the spells you know."

I was familiar with casting trances, but simply using it to commune with a substance was a bit more difficult. Nonetheless, I closed my eyes and focused my breathing, entering an odd state where my mind felt both clear and concentrated. The dirt was cool in my hand, and I envisioned damp, mist-covered forests, like one of the redwood parks up north, where trees anchored themselves in the earth and the smell of wet dirt hung everywhere. Dirt itself wasn't always present in spells, but many things that hid within it were: jewels and plants and—

"Open your eyes," said Ms. Terwilliger softly.

I did and saw a faint luminescence surrounding my hand holding the dirt.

"Try to put it in your other hand and hold it."

The light had no substance, and I had to contain it with my mind. I tipped my hand, and it poured into my other one. The glow began to slip out between my fingers, dissipating into the air as it did. I closed my hand, trying to grasp those last shreds of light.

The door to her classroom opened, and I jumped, losing all mental hold of the remaining light. It vanished.

"Sydney?" Zoe stuck her head in.

"Come in, Miss Ardmore," said Ms. Terwilliger coolly, shutting the book without looking down. "Although, please, next time, do us the courtesy of knocking."

Zoe flushed at the rebuke. "I'm very sorry, ma'am. I was just excited to see Sydney." She wasn't offended so much as embarrassed. Like me, she'd been raised with very strict rules of etiquette and politeness. Her eyes lighted on the desktop. Ms. Terwilliger had made sure the book's unmarked back cover faced upward, but my dirty hands were right there in the open. "What are you doing?"

Ms. Terwilliger scooped up the book and bowl and walked over to her desk, as I wiped my hands together. "Being silly and sentimental. I collected some dirt outside the Parthenon on my trip to Greece last summer and saved it as a souvenir.

I was enchanted with the idea of holding on to something that had been present throughout the advancement of a great civilization."

It was far-fetched but a lot less weird than using the dirt to extract the magic of earth's essence. I swallowed and tried to run with the story. "Yeah, and you know how I want to go to Greece, Zo. I wondered if maybe touching it would give me some connection to history." My laugh was brittle. "But it just felt like dirt."

Ms. Terwilliger joined me with a chuckle of her own. "You and I are both given to romantic flights of fancy, Miss Melrose. Someday you'll just have to visit for yourself. For now, this will simply return to my collection." She reverently set the bowl on her filing cabinet. I'd seen her fill it with dirt from one of Amberwood's flower beds when we'd come inside earlier.

Zoe had a frown on her face, but she finally nodded because really, what else was she going to do? "Okay . . . well. Since school's over, I wondered if you wanted to go run errands with me. We haven't been able to hang out much, and I need new shoes for PE. The ones I brought are worn out. No one else needs us tonight." The subtext was clear to me. There were no feedings at Clarence's, and Jill was staying at the school, safely ensconced.

I could sense Ms. Terwilliger watching me, waiting for my cue. If I claimed I had to do some project for her, she'd agree. But Zoe was right about one thing: We hadn't spent much time together. Not only was that making my time away suspicious, it was also hurting my relationship with Zoe. She was still my sister, after all, and I loved her. I wanted to have a good relationship with her. I wanted things to be like they used to be, though that seemed to become increasingly unlikely with each passing day. At least a trip to the mall seemed normal and sisterly on the surface, even if it didn't feel that way in my gut.

"You're lucky," Zoe said as we neared the mall. The car's blind-spot detection had just chimed. "It always tells you when there's a car there. In driver's training, we always had to check blind spots ourselves. Those cars were junk."

I couldn't help a laugh. "You should always check, whether you're driving junk or not. I usually see the other cars before it warns me."

She gave a mournful sigh. "I wish I could drive. I just got my permit back in Utah."

"You can't drive without a parent there or in California," I reminded her.

"Yeah." She slouched into her seat, looking very much like an ordinary girl, not one part of an ancient and world-spanning organization that covered up the supernatural. "Maybe someone could mess with the paperwork and get you legal guardian status. I mean, how else am I supposed to get a license? Unless someone just makes 'Zoe Ardmore' a fake one. I'm a good enough driver."

"You'll have to ask Dad," I said, feeling a pang of guilt. It actually wouldn't be that difficult to work some Alchemist connections to make that kind of thing happen. If we did it without checking with our dad first, we'd probably be chastised, and if we did ask . . . well, something told me he'd probably think it was superfluous. "If he hasn't brought it up, then he probably just wants you to focus on learning other stuff. Our job takes priority."

She couldn't argue against that. After a long moment of

staring out at other cars, she said, "Speaking of priorities . . . have you ever thought that maybe what you're doing with Ms. Terwilliger isn't appropriate?"

I flinched, even though I knew she couldn't possibly be talking about magic. "What do you mean?"

"I don't know exactly. It's just, you've already finished high school. You're here to do Alchemist business, but you seem really into your classes—especially that thing with her. It seems personal too, like you're just hanging out as friends. I mean, talking about her vacation? It wouldn't be a big deal if it was just inside class hours, but you're always doing work for her that doesn't seem like work. Nothing wrong with wanting friends or social time . . . but you can't do it at the cost of the assignment. What would Dad say?"

I kept myself very still and thought for long moments before my answer. "You're right. I do have to be careful. It's just hard when we talk about Greece, when I want to go there so badly. I love her stories. Still, that's no excuse. I guess I just forget that when everything's so quiet with Jill and the others. I've got to do something to pass the time, and I certainly can't spend it with them."

"You could spend it with me," she said hopefully.

I glanced at her long enough to give her a smile. "I will. We'll do more things—not just talking about the assignment. Getting out like this is good. I'll try to make it happen more often—though I don't want to act *too* uninterested in my classes. I can't risk getting in trouble for slacking off." In truth, my teachers thought so highly of me, I could probably skip the rest of the semester.

My story was good enough for Zoe, though, who looked

delighted at more sisterly bonding. Most importantly, she didn't mention our dad again. Like her, he wouldn't suspect magic, but he also wouldn't like me having any sort of personal life. I sealed the deal when I told her, "We should stop for ice cream after we get the shoes. See if we can find some praline pecan."

She grinned at the reference to an old restaurant near where we'd grown up. The menu had always said, "Ask about our daily ice cream special." But every day, it was always praline pecan. When my dad had pointed this out to the elderly owner, she'd shrugged and said, "I can't find anything more special. Why change it?" It had become a joke with the rest of us and even a sort of family tradition.

To my amazement, the ice cream at this place was almost as good, and we took our cones out to sit on the curb. As we ate, an idea suddenly came to me. "Are you serious about driving?" I asked her.

The light in her eyes answered before she did. "Yes! Will you try to get me a license?"

I munched on a pecan, my thoughts spinning. "Well, you know, the whole point of a permit is so you can practice before the license."

"But I don't need to—"

I gave her a stern older-sister look. "Rules are rules, and there's a good reason for them. I can't expedite the license, but if you want to practice, you could do it on private property— parking lots and things. With a licensed driver," I added.

She wrestled with the idea and then nodded eagerly. "Okay, I'll do it. We'll have fun."

"Well," I said delicately. "I may not be able to always practice with you—I'm still tied up with things at school. But we can find someone else."

"Who?"

Moment of truth. I had two licensed drivers at my disposal: Eddie and Neil. Girls seemed to find Neil's accent charming, but I wasn't looking for someone to charm Zoe. I was looking for someone approachable and friendly who'd show her not all dhampirs were evil creatures of the night.

"Eddie," I said.

Her eyes bugged out. "Eddie? But he's . . ."

"I know, but he's a good driver. I mean, if you just want to wait until I have time . . ." I let a meaningful pause settle between us. "I understand. You won't get as much practice that way, but it's not like we're going anywhere for a while."

Silence fell, and I finished off my cone. My performance had been flawless; I knew that. She had no clue my offer was anything but sisterly concern. Now it was time to see if I was as clever as I thought I was.

I'd been thinking about this for a while, how I might get her to start seeing dhampirs and Moroi in a different light. Her walls were strong, and I knew I couldn't force her into doing—or rather, believing—something she didn't want to. But driving? That was something she wanted, and if she could enter into this thinking it had been her own decision, then *maybe* there was a chance of cracking those rigid rules she'd been instilled with. It was a small, fleeting hope, but I had to try. After all, that was how it happened to me: a series of events that forced me to work with Moroi and dhampirs and truly get to understand them. That, and I liked to think my ability to think for myself played a role.

"Okay," Zoe said at last. "I'll do it. But you *will* try to be there most of the time?"

I nodded solemnly. "You bet."

She relaxed a little and twirled the remains of the cone in her hand. "I guess it's a good thing he's dhampir. They look human, at least."

"Yes," I said, trying to hide a smile. I'd told myself the same thing when I'd been forced to travel with Rose Hathaway in Russia. Maybe this plan was crazy enough to work. "They certainly do."

CHAPTER 7

ADRIAN

I WAS WORKING ON THAT STUPID SELF-PORTRAIT AGAIN.

My latest attempt was about to be discarded, not because of any spirit-induced pessimism, but because it just wasn't any good. I mean, it was passable, and I probably could've come up with some plausible crap story about symbolism for my teacher. She would've bought it, and I could've gotten a decent grade. But I'd know the truth. This one was no good.

My mood *was* a little touchy today, mostly because I hadn't slept well. I'd tossed and turned, unable to find deep sleep. Things had been made worse because Sydney wasn't coming over today. She'd decided to stick around so that she and Zoe could do something immediately after classes ended. I understood the logic of keeping Sage Junior pacified, but that didn't ease the ache of missing Sydney. At least we were scheduled for Friday dinner at Clarence's tonight, but it was never the same when others were around.

The phone rang, jolting me out of my maudlin moment. I

had to go on a mad search to find where it had slipped between the couch cushions and just barely managed to catch it before voice mail picked up. The caller was a total surprise.

"Your Majesty," I said grandly.

"Hello, Adrian." I could tell Lissa was already smiling. "How's it going?"

"Oh, you know. The glam life of southern California. Palm trees and movie stars." I slipped into my flippant mask easily, concealing what was really going on. Lissa wouldn't have bought it if she were here in person, but over the phone, I was protected.

"Well, I hope you can drag yourself away from it because I have a . . . task for you."

"Task?" Her word choice and change in tone tipped me off that something big was coming.

"There was another Strigoi restoration."

Wow, the surprises just kept rolling in. "Who was it? And who the hell did it? You?"

"No—a different spirit user. One we didn't know about. Her name is Nina Sinclair, and she just restored her sister. Olive."

"Nina. Olive. Got it. Go on."

Even I knew this was serious. The only thing even remotely as incredible as bringing someone back from the dead with spirit was restoring them from being a Strigoi. It was pretty difficult to do because it wasn't just a matter of wielding a lot of spirit. You actually had to make sure the Strigoi was subdued. Then, the spirit user had to stake the Strigoi while working the magic. We directly knew of only three people this had happened to. We also didn't know very many spirit users, so the discovery of a new one was a big deal.

"I need you to drop everything and go to them," Lissa said. It wasn't exactly her throne-room voice, but it was definitely the kind that didn't expect an argument. "We need to find out if we can see anything in a newly saved person that might help us understand why they can't be turned again. Sonya's in Europe, and I can't leave Court. You're the only spirit user who can go and investigate on short notice."

Now I understood the importance. Strigoi were made by two methods. One was if a Strigoi drained a victim and then gave blood back to him or her. Moroi could also turn by choice if they drained the person they were feeding from. We'd recently discovered that Strigoi who had been restored couldn't be turned again. No one knew for sure if it was unique to them or if there was some way to use spirit to spread that ability to others. We couldn't stop a Strigoi from killing someone through other means, but if there was a way to create magical protection to save others from being forced into that undead state, it could revolutionize our world. Sonya and I had worked for almost two months, running all sorts of tests and examinations to see if we could manipulate spirit into whatever it had done for the restored. No luck.

"Drop everything, huh?" I couldn't help a little bitterness. Even though she knew I was in college, it could apparently be sidelined at a moment's notice.

She sighed. "I know you've got things going on. I wouldn't ask you to do this if it wasn't crucial. She's very recently restored—very recently. Less than twenty-four hours. If there's some residual sign of what exactly happened in the process, we can't waste a moment. We can get you on a flight to Dallas in a few hours. Rose and Dimitri are on their way there now."

"Really?" At this point, there was really nothing I shouldn't expect. Spending the weekend with my ex and her Russian warlord was probably just the warm-up for more shenanigans. "Well, at least he'll have a chance to stock up on his Western wear."

I could hear a hint of laughter in her voice. "You know why he has to go."

I did. Dimitri Belikov was one of the lucky three—well, four now—who'd been restored. He didn't have the ability to see spirit, but he did have the inside track on what it was like to suddenly "wake up" and realize you'd been a bloodthirsty monster who'd subsisted on the lives of innocents. Even I could appreciate how messed up that would make you. A little counseling from someone who'd gone through it would be useful, to say the least.

"I understand. And of course I'll go, Your Majesty."

"Don't call me that. And don't tell me you're doing this just because you're my subject. I hope you'll do it because you're my friend—and because it's the right thing to do." There was a plaintive note in her voice. It must be hard, I thought, when people saw you more as a queen than an actual person.

My next words were true. "I'm doing it for all of those reasons, cousin."

"You haven't called me that in a while," she said fondly. We weren't actually cousins, but it was a term of endearment the royal families often used with one another.

"I haven't seen you in a while."

"Yeah." Her voice grew wistful, and I again spared a thought for what it must be like to be a controversial eighteen-year-old queen with the weight of a nation thrust on your shoulders.

"There wasn't much time to talk at the wedding. How are you, Adrian? I mean, how are you *really*? With Jill . . . and everything . . ."

"You know how it is." No flippancy. "Some days are better than others. What about you?"

There was a long silence. "The same. I didn't realize how much Rose was helping me until our bond went away. She was shouldering so much of that darkness. Now it's all on me. Which is for the best," she added quickly. "But it's still hard."

"I know." I fully understood the burden of spirit and could only imagine how that would compound the stress of her position. "At least Jill and I haven't reached that point. She's safe."

"For now," said Lissa. "It took a little while before the darkness started seeping into Rose. If you guys can work on blocking each other, that'll help out a lot."

In more ways than one, I thought.

"Yeah, we're working on that. Not much luck."

We fell into another moment of silence, but it was comfortable. Even through the phone, there was a warmth and understanding between the two of us about spirit that no one—except Sonya and this Nina girl—could truly ever grasp. Spirit's price was powerful.

"Queen or not, I'm always here," Lissa said, her voice soft. "If you ever need to talk about anything, I'll understand."

I was glad once again that we were on the phone because I was pretty sure all the strife and emotional turmoil over Sydney would've come spilling out. And no matter what Lissa kindheartedly said, I seriously didn't think she'd understand *that*.

"Same here, cousin," I said as gallantly as I could. "Tell me when and where to go, and I'll be there with bells on."

"We'll have the flight info sent to—oh. I nearly forgot. You need to bring one of the dhampirs with you."

"Did you get a free companion fare or something?"

"No," she said, laughing. "It's just safer. If Olive had any connections to other Strigoi—well, you never know if they might come sniffing around. We're taking precautions. But if it helps, you can pick which one to take."

That wasn't even a choice. I was on the verge of saying Eddie when a moment of inspiration struck. "Neil."

"Neil?" Lissa sounded surprised but didn't question it. "Okay. We'll make it happen."

Maybe getting Mr. Buckingham Palace away from Palm Springs for a couple days would snap some sense into Jill and even Angeline. Sure, Jill would give me grief, but she'd thank me later when she realized she needed to give up on Neil as a distraction and just lay it all out on the line with Eddie.

As soon as I was off the phone with Lissa, I texted Sydney on the Love Phone: *Can you talk?* Classes weren't over yet, so I was hoping she'd be Zoe-free. Sure enough, I got a call back a minute later.

"What's up?" she asked, making no effort to hide her worry. "Are you okay?"

"Aside from the fact that that my world is a cold and lonely place when you aren't around? Yeah, I'm okay. But I'm about to take an unexpected vacation." I gave her a quick rundown of Nina and Olive.

"Wow," she said when I finished. "Where are you going?"

"Guess. 'The stars at night are big and bright . . .'"

There was silence.

"You don't know that song?" I asked.

110

"No."

"I'm going to Texas. Dallas. Maybe I can find a cute cowgirl outfit to bring back to you. Leather fringe, short skirt—"

"Just bring yourself back," she said. But there was amusement in her voice. The line between exasperation and adoration was pretty thin with us sometimes. "When do you leave?"

"Lissa made it sound like a few hours, which probably means I'll need to actually get to the airport soon. She's still got to send me the information and have someone get in touch with Neil." I was certain he wouldn't warrant a personal royal call. Not like some people.

"Well, be careful . . . but wow, what an opportunity." I could hear her shifting into intellectual mode. Well, she was always in that mode, but some moments were stronger than others. "I'd kind of given up on being able to find any way to prevent people turning."

"It's not a done deal," I reminded her. "There may not be anything to see. Or I may not be able to find it." The gravity of what was being placed on my shoulders began to settle in. This mystery had consumed some of the best and brightest minds over the last few months. Now, we had a huge lead . . . and it was up to *me* to examine it? Who was I to unlock spirit's secrets? Sonya was better suited to this.

"If it can be done, you can do it," Sydney said, guessing my insecurity. "I believe in you."

"You have to say that because you're my girlfriend."

"I have to say it because it's the truth."

Later, as I packed a hasty overnight bag, I almost wished Sydney hadn't called. Actually speaking to her just made our parting more bittersweet. Never—not even when I was obsessed with Rose—had I thought I'd be so far gone for a girl. A couple days away, and I plunged into despair. It was ironic since there'd been girls in the past that I kind of wished would stay away for a couple of days. Okay, a lot of days. It all seemed crazy, but then, I was crazy for Sydney.

Lissa sent along my travel info, and I took a taxi over to the airport. Sydney would've killed me if I left the Ivashkinator in the long-term parking garage. I was supposed to meet Neil at our airline's desk and spotted him right away, with his height and rigid posture. And, to my surprise, a shorter blond figure stood beside him. Sydney turned at my approach, a cool Alchemist expression on her face.

"Why, Sage Senior," I said, hoping I didn't sound like I wanted to throw her up against a wall and kiss her. "Did they draft you for this crazy adventure too?"

"Sydney was nice enough to give me a ride," said Neil obliviously.

"That was nice of you," I agreed, trying to sound as condescending as possible. "Figured you and your sister would be off doing top secret color coding. Or whatever it is you guys do for fun."

Sydney crossed her arms and put on a stern look. "We rescheduled it so that I could make sure you guys got on your flight. I had to come in and see for myself that you showed up. This is serious, you know."

I shrugged. "If you say so."

She managed to look like a perfect, pissed-off Alchemist. Now I wanted to kiss her more than ever.

"We don't have time for you guys to argue," said Neil. "And this *is* serious." He glanced over at a monitor, and in that brief moment, Sydney met my eyes. A hint of a smile curved at her lips, vanishing just as Neil faced us again. "Time to go. We need to check in."

She nodded, just as businesslike as him. "Safe travels, and good luck."

"We make our own luck, Sage."

That nearly broke her act. It was an old joke between us, and I was glad Neil was too distracted to notice any interpersonal cues or body language. She and I were standing a healthy distance apart, but I was fully conscious of every inch between us and every detail of her body. To anyone else passing by, it was probably completely obvious that we were seconds away from ripping each other's clothes off.

She bid us farewell and left without a backward glance, but as I got in line to check in, my phone buzzed with a text: *I love you.*

On such short notice, we had to fly coach. Keeping me away from the temptation of complimentary liquor was probably just as well, since I'd need a clear head to tune in to spirit. Neil, mercifully, was a quiet companion, and I tried to distract myself by reading *The Great Gatsby*. Sydney had been horrified to discover my home library consisted of a bartending dictionary and an old copy of *Esquire*, and at her pleading, I'd promised to read something more substantial. I was trying to think deep thoughts as I read *Gatsby*, but mostly I wanted to throw some parties.

Nina and Olive were being kept at a safe house on the far outskirts of Dallas, with few neighbors to notice the odd sight of guardians patrolling the property. We parked our rental car in the driveway, and through the window, I recognized a familiar figure sitting on the porch's chair swing, her feet up propped up on the railing. A prickle of anxiety ran through me.

"Here goes nothing," I muttered.

Rose stood up as we stepped onto the porch. For a moment, I was transported to our first meeting over a year ago, also on a porch. That one had been covered in snow, attached to a posh ski resort. Her beauty had taken my breath away then, and now, after all this time, I still wasn't unaffected. Her long, dark hair spilled over her shoulders, and there was a fire in her brown eyes that was both dangerous and alluring. That same mix radiated from her body, even in a casual pose and wearing jeans.

And yet, though I admired her, I didn't feel the old attraction or even pain. Sure, there was always going to be a sting from the insensitive way she'd botched up our brief relationship, but my heart no longer raced at the sight of her. I didn't feel the devastation of having the love of my life ripped away. I didn't even hate her anymore. Mostly, I found myself thinking of Sydney, with her lithe legs crossed underneath her as she studied books on my bed, the golden sunlight illuminating her face when she looked up to give me a knowing smile.

"You made good time," I said by way of greeting. "Did Belikov bend the rules of time and space to get here so fast? He can do that, right?" The Moroi Royal Court was in Pennsylvania, making for a much longer trip than mine had been.

Rose smiled at that, though I could sense a little wariness in her as well. She wasn't sure what to expect from me and was afraid I might do something that would cause a scene. I couldn't blame her. It was probably why she was receiving me here before letting me into the volatile situation inside.

"No need to today. We got really, really lucky and got on a

114

flight the instant we heard about this. And we only just got here about an hour ago." She shook Neil's hand. "I'm Rose."

"Neil," he said, with a formal bow of his head. "It's a great honor to meet you. Your heroics with Dimitri Belikov are legendary."

"Um, thanks," she said. It was nice to see one woman finally immune to that accent. That wasn't to say Rose wasn't a sucker for accents. She just preferred hers from the other side of Europe. "He's inside if you want to meet him."

Neil lit up. "That'd be wonderful." He cast an uncertain look at me, and I waved him off.

"Go, go. I'll be fine. Besides, this is Rose's not-so-subtle way of saying she wants to talk to me alone. Go do some hero worship."

Neil didn't need to be told twice. She watched him with amusement and then turned back to me, sobering a little. "I also figured you'd want a cigarette. Must have been rough going, what, three hours?" she teased.

"Three hours? Hell, Rose. I'm going on about six weeks."

The complete shock on her face was one of the best things I'd seen all day. To be fair, her surprise wasn't entirely unwarranted. I'd kind of quit while dating her, though I'd cracked a few times and then completely relapsed afterward. "You . . . quit?"

I put my hands in my coat pockets and leaned against the railing. "It's a bad habit."

"Wow . . . well, good for you." She overcame her amazement and apparently decided to further assess my new respectability. "And I heard you're in college too?"

"Yup. Taking some art classes. Just finished a project examining the symbolic evolution from the *Australopithecus* age

115

to the one of superficial media obsession." The words rolled easily off my tongue, and I wondered how many hot points that would've scored me if Sydney were here.

"Wow," Rose said again, her eyes widening.

I played it cool. "Just a little something I threw together. But let's focus on business. What am I going to find inside?"

She snapped instantly back to attention. "About what I saw in Lexington when Robert Doru saved Sonya. An exhausted spirit user and a confused patient. Dimitri's been talking to Olive, which seems to have helped already, and I'm sure Nina will feel better having you around."

It was a nice setup for making some joke about how all women loved having me around, but I decided to withhold my stunning wit until I'd seen things with my own eyes. "How'd you find out about this?"

"A guardian called us. I guess Nina had been looking for her sister for a long time and used a guardian friend to create this whole elaborate trap to restore Olive." Rose's face turned sympathetic. "But Nina wasn't prepared for the physical and mental toll it took on both of them. That's when the guardian called for help. It all happened less than twenty-four hours ago."

"Explaining the urgency," I murmured. Everyone really had acted quickly. "Well, we'll see what I can find. Spirit's fickle."

"Yeah, believe me, I know. I miss that connection with Lissa, but I don't miss living with spirit." She tilted her head to study me. "How are things with Jill?"

I gave her the same answer I had given Lissa. "The same. Not much of the nasty side effects getting to her, but we also haven't learned to put barriers between us. So she still gets to experience the awesome adventures of Adrian Ivashkov firsthand."

"I'm a little worried about how 'awesome' they are." Her dubious look transformed to one of horror. "Oh, God, Adrian. You aren't working your way through every Moroi girl in southern California, are you?"

"Of course not," I said. "I'm much more discriminating."

She groaned. "Even one is too much. You should be ashamed of yourself, exposing Jill to your sex life. Isn't it possible for you to abstain from your cheap flings for just a little while? For Jill's sake?"

Some part of me wanted to defend the magnitude of my relationship with Sydney. The rest of me knew that if the world thought I was rampantly having one-night stands with Moroi girls, they'd never suspect I was devoted to a human one.

I gave Rose a cocky grin. "Hey, I've gotta live, don't I?"

She shook her head in disgust and headed for the door. "I guess some things can't change."

It was an older house but still in good condition, and I wondered where they'd dug it up. According to Lissa, it didn't belong to either of the sisters and had been set up by the guardians to provide a safe haven. As we stepped into the front room, a Moroi girl close to my age stood waiting for us. Her hair was a tangle of dark curls, and she had a blanket draped around her like a cloak.

Rose's disposition immediately softened. "Nina, you should get back to bed."

The girl shook her head and glanced between us with wide, gray eyes. "I want to know what's going on. Why are new people here? What are you going to do with Olive? Are you going to experiment on her like some sort of lab animal?" The girl began to tremble, her face full of fear and outrage, and my heart went out to her.

"Everything's going to be fine," I said, sending out a trickle of compulsion to soothe her. "There's no need to worry."

Her features started to relax, and then she suddenly blinked and fixed me with a glare. "Don't try that on *me*."

Worn out or not, Nina Sinclair was still a savvy spirit user. I chuckled and held up my hands in a placating gesture. "Just trying to help."

"Everything really will be okay," Rose told her. "This is Adrian. He just needs to talk to her. You can come along."

Nina gave me a long, suspicious look but said nothing else as she followed us farther into the house. We reached a spacious bedroom with peeling wallpaper and a quilt-covered bed. A dhampir girl sat upright in it. I hid how much that surprised me. No one had mentioned it, and I'd just assumed the sisters were both Moroi. Although they shared black hair, they were complete opposites in other features. Olive's skin was a coppery brown, making me think of Native American heritage, and her eyes were large and dark. She had the athletic build most dhampirs had, contrasting with her sister's tall, slim frame. Only a similarity in their facial shape and high cheekbones suggested they shared a parent, probably their father, seeing as Moroi men liked to have dhampir women on the side. It gave me a new regard for Nina, since dhampir half siblings weren't always acknowledged. Nina had risked her life for hers.

Along with Rose, Dimitri, and Neil, there were three other guardians in the room, creating an almost comical scene, considering how docile Olive looked at the moment. In fact,

Dimitri was making this very argument to one of the unknown guardians, telling him, "There's no Strigoi part of her left, trust me. You don't need this much security. She's safe."

The other guardian didn't seem certain. "We have our orders."

Dimitri raked a hand through his chin-length hair in frustration, knowing better than anyone else that restored Strigoi possessed no more of that undead state. Everyone technically knew it, but fear still ran high in some people. Seeing me, he let his argument go and gave me a smile that was genuine. He and I had recently had to spend a lot of time together, and although it was hard to shake that he was the one Rose had left me for, I couldn't help but feel a grudging respect for him.

"Adrian," he said. "I'm glad you could be here. We're hoping that acting so quickly might get us somewhere the experiments didn't."

He kept talking, but my attention was all on Olive. I summoned spirit to view her aura, which was a mix of what I'd expect from a dhampir and what I would not expect: the brilliant flares of gold seen in a spirit user. Even as I watched, that gold was fading ever so slightly. I drew on more spirit and heard Nina catch her breath. She might be too drained to produce much of her own, but it would be obvious to her how much I was using. I focused on Olive again, trying to look past her aura, more deeply into her very essence. I'd never done it before, and it was much more difficult than I'd expected. I didn't even know if it would accomplish anything. I was simply playing a hunch.

I gritted my teeth and concentrated harder. There—it was hard to see. In fact, it was more of a sense than actual vision.

But every part of Olive was infused with that same golden glow. I couldn't see at a cellular level or anything, but I suddenly knew that all of her being was wrapped in spirit. And like the aura, it was fading with each breath she took. There was still plenty there, but connecting what I saw now with how long ago she'd been saved, I had a feeling it would all dissipate within hours. I blinked, and the spirit burning within me went out. Olive looked normal again.

The room was silent. I dragged my eyes from her and looked at everyone else. They were all staring back expectantly. I swallowed, and for the briefest of moments, my earlier anxiety swelled inside my chest. The magnitude of what I faced slammed into me. We were on the verge of one of the biggest breakthroughs in our race's history, and everyone was looking to me to figure it out. Me! What were they thinking? I was no genius like Sydney. I was just a slacker guy who fought the temptation of his liquor cabinet every day and couldn't finish *The Great Gatsby*. Who was I to do this?

An image of Sydney's face appeared in my mind's eye, calm and lovely. *I believe in you.*

My anxiety faded. I took a deep breath and met the gazes of all those watching me in the room. Who was I to do this?

I was Adrian Ivashkov. And I was about to kick some ass.

"If you want any chance of learning how to save others, you need to do exactly as I say. And you need to do it now."

CHAPTER 8

SYDNEY

ADRIAN'S TRIP SHOULDN'T HAVE BOTHERED ME as much as it did. After all, it wasn't like I would've gotten to spend much time with him anyway this weekend. But the thought of the physical distance between us hit me acutely. Even when we weren't together, I always had a sense of him being nearby—even if "nearby" meant across town at Carlton. In Palm Springs, I felt in control, like I could measure the steps between us or imagine strands of light connecting us no matter where we were. But Texas was out of my reach, out of my control. Adrian had left our safe haven—such as it was—and was out in the world, adrift.

At least I hadn't had to lie to Zoe about canceling our outing together. Neil had needed a ride to the airport, and figuring out how to prevent Strigoi turning was a huge priority among the Alchemists, one we certainly wanted to help the Moroi with. When Zoe asked why Neil couldn't have just taken a taxi, I gave her the same excuse I'd given him and Adrian: that I needed to see them off in person. Since Zoe believed most Moroi and dhampirs were sketchy and unreliable, this story worked.

It also gave me a little free time to stop at a New Age store on the way back and procure a few potential rocks and crystals to attempt elemental binding in. Although I had a lot of theoretical ideas about what might replace the boleite, I wasn't having much luck with anything yet. There was still time before Marcus surfaced, but I worried I wouldn't be able to deliver on my promises to him if I couldn't figure this out.

I stopped by Ms. Terwilliger's classroom with my purchases and found her grading tests at her desk. She gave me a brief glance and returned to her paperwork, not even needing to ask why I was there. I shut the door—after first putting on the KNOCK, PLEASE sign she'd made—and set to work.

Earth and fire were my two best elements so far, but for these trials, I stuck to the former. It was easier to brush dirt off my hands if anyone showed up than it was to cover up the smell of smoke. I worked on my first stone, zircon, and although I felt the transfer of magic into it, something seemed a little off. I took it to Ms. Terwilliger for confirmation since she was more adept than I was at sensing magic within objects and people. She held up the zircon to the light and studied it for several long moments before shaking her head.

"There's some in there, but not nearly as much as I sensed you summoning over there. It didn't all make it in." She handed the stone back. "It might be sufficient for your needs, but I'm guessing you'd probably want as much as you can get."

I nodded. I hadn't explained my purpose, and she hadn't asked. She mostly seemed content that I was independently studying the arts. I returned to my workstation and continued on with the last two stones, achieving equally disappointing results. One didn't absorb magic at all. The other held it briefly, and then the magic bled out. I slouched back in the desk, defeated.

"I'm running out of easily accessible options," I said, more to myself than her. "A halide like boleite's my best bet, but it isn't really lying around. I'm going to have to start ordering from rock dealers on the internet."

Ms. Terwilliger didn't have a chance to respond to my geological ramblings because someone knocked on the door. I slipped the rocks into my pocket and tried to look studious as she called a welcome. I figured Zoe had tracked me down, but surprisingly, Angeline walked in.

"Did you know," she said, "that it's a lot harder to put organs back in the body than it is to get them out?"

I closed my eyes and silently counted to five before opening them again. "Please tell me you haven't eviscerated someone."

She shook her head. "No, no. I left my biology homework in Miss Wentworth's room, but when I went back to get it, she'd already left and locked the door. But it's due tomorrow, and I'm already in trouble in there, so I *had* to get it. So, I went around outside, and her window lock wasn't that hard to open, and I—"

"Wait," I interrupted. "You broke into a classroom?"

"Yeah, but that's not the problem."

Behind me, I heard a choking laugh from Ms. Terwilliger's desk.

"Go on," I said wearily.

"Well, when I climbed through, I didn't realize there was a bunch of stuff in the way, and I crashed into those plastic models of the human body she has. You know, the life-size ones

123

with all the parts inside? And bam!" Angeline held up her arms for effect. "Organs everywhere." She paused and looked at me expectantly. "So what are we going to do? I can't get in trouble with her."

"We?" I exclaimed.

"Here," said Ms. Terwilliger. I turned around, and she tossed me a set of keys. From the look on her face, it was taking every ounce of self-control not to burst out laughing. "That square one's a master. I know for a fact she has yoga and won't be back for the rest of the day. I imagine you can repair the damage—and retrieve the homework—before anyone's the wiser."

I knew that the "you" in "you can repair" meant me. With a sigh, I stood up and packed up my things. "Thanks," I said.

As Angeline and I walked down to the science wing, I told her, "You know, the next time you've got a problem, maybe come to me before it becomes an even bigger problem."

"Oh no," she said nobly. "I didn't want to be an inconvenience."

Her description of the scene was pretty accurate: organs everywhere. Miss Wentworth had two models, male and female, with carved out torsos that cleverly held removable parts of the body that could be examined in greater detail. I had a pretty good sense of anatomy but still opened up a textbook for reference as I began sorting the mess. Angeline, realizing her uselessness here, perched on a far counter and swung her legs as she watched me. I'd started reassembling the male when I heard a voice behind me.

"Melbourne, I always knew you'd need to learn about this kind of thing. I'd just kind of hoped you'd learn it from a real guy."

I glanced back at Trey as he leaned in the doorway with a smug expression. "Ha, ha. If you were a real friend, you'd come help me." I pointed at the female model. "Let's see some of your alleged expertise in action."

"Alleged?" He sounded indignant but strolled in anyway.

I hadn't really thought much about asking him for help. Mostly I was thinking this was taking much longer than it should, and I had more important things to do with my time. It was only when he came to a sudden halt that I realized my mistake.

"Oh," he said, seeing Angeline. "Hi."

Her swinging feet stopped, and her eyes were as wide as his. "Um, hi."

The tension ramped up from zero to sixty in a matter of seconds, and I tried not to groan. After all, their situation wasn't all that different from mine. How would I feel if Adrian and I suddenly ended our relationship because of the taboos ingrained in our races? Trey and Angeline had split up because of outside pressures, not anything between them. And as I studied the longing in her eyes, I knew that the show she put on for Neil was exactly that: a show.

Everyone seemed at a loss for words. Angeline jerked her head toward the models and blurted out, "I had an accident."

That seemed to snap Trey from his daze, and a smile curved his lips. Whereas Angeline's antics made me want to pull out my hair sometimes, he found them endearing.

"That seems to happen a lot," he said.

"It wasn't my fault," she insisted.

"It never is."

"I just have bad luck."

"Or you're just trouble."

"You got a problem with that?"

"No problem at all," he said in a low voice.

"Oh my God," I exclaimed. "Are you going to help or not?"

Somehow, the awkward tension had become sexual tension, and I was about ready to bolt. Trey, after one more long, heated look at her, turned away and threw himself into reassembling the female model. I hadn't put much stock in his bragging, but to my surprise, he finished pretty quickly.

"Told you I'm an expert," he said, with a sidelong glance at Angeline.

They both seemed to have forgotten me again and were going all dreamy-eyed. I cleared my throat. "Angeline, it's almost time for dinner. Do you need to go change?"

"Huh? Oh. Yeah." She had enough presence of mind to fetch the homework that had started all of this. "Thanks for helping," she told Trey, as though I hadn't even done anything.

He gave a nonchalant shrug, like he did this every day. "No problem."

After he'd swaggered out the door, Angeline gave a mournful sigh. "Oh, Sydney. Why does he have to be one of those stupid Warriors?"

I locked up the classroom. "Well, he's not technically one right now."

"But he could be again," she said, trudging beside me as we headed out to catch the shuttle to our dorm. "And if he does, he'll never overcome all that stuff about mixing with dhampirs. One of these days, he'll start dating a human again, and since we're here, I won't be able to do anything about it."

"What exactly do you mean?" I asked cautiously.

She brightened a little. "Well, if we were back home, I could just keep challenging his new girlfriends to duels."

"Well, let's just hope he stays single, then."

I left her to her fantasies when we reached the dorm, each of us off to our own room. Zoe was waiting in mine, looking mournfully at a beat-up paperback. "Where have you been?" she asked. "Not at the airport the whole time?" She regarded me thoughtfully. "With Ms. Terwilliger?"

"Angeline, actually. I had to help her with a, um, problem in her biology class."

"There you go again, doing things you don't need to."

Angeline and Trey's plight had me thinking of my own, and I didn't have much patience for Zoe's Alchemist rhetoric. "I do need to do it. I need Angeline here at Amberwood, and that means making sure she stays in her teachers' good graces." I sat down backward in my desk chair, resting my chin on its back. "You want to be an Alchemist so badly? Don't wait to react to the immediate problem. Plan ahead, look at the big picture, and you won't ever have to deal with that problem. Better to save yourself from a major catastrophe than drag your feet over a bunch of little inconveniences."

"Okay, okay," she said, looking hurt at my chastisement. "I get it. You don't have to lecture."

"Sorry," I said, feeling only slightly so. "You came here to learn. I'm just trying to help."

She gave me a small smile. "I know. I'm here for professional reasons. It's just hard to forget sometimes that you're my sister. You're pretty good at it, though . . . treating me like I'm just another Alchemist. I'll have to try harder to be as good."

I flinched. She meant it as a compliment, that I could

put aside what was between us and wholeheartedly focus on Alchemist mandates. I didn't feel so proud of that, though. In fact, it made me distinctly uncomfortable, and I nodded toward her book. "What are you reading?"

That got her out of business mode, though it also brought a scowl. "I don't know. Some Shakespeare play for my English class. We have to pick one by tomorrow, and I thought this one would be good since it's so short." She held it up. *Richard III*. "But I'm not really getting it."

"Yikes," I said.

"Bad play?" she guessed.

"Great play, but maybe not the best match for you. See if you can hunt down a copy of *A Midsummer Night's Dream*. Might be easier on you." Thinking of my friends' romantic woes, I couldn't help a small, sad smile. "And you're practically living in the middle of it." I laughed when she didn't get the reference. "I forget that wasn't part of Dad's standard curriculum. I did most of my literature research on my own."

She nodded, and suddenly her eyes went wide. "Oh! I nearly forgot to tell you. He's coming here. Dad."

I sat bolt upright in the chair. "When?"

"Next week." I tried to relax, knowing my shock was a bit beyond ordinary surprise. I certainly couldn't let her know I was afraid. "He wants to talk to us about Mom and the hearing. They've set a date for next month."

That was news to me, but then I shouldn't have been surprised at being out of the loop. After all, Zoe had proved a much more eager daughter than I had. It was only natural he'd tell her first.

"He's going to help prepare us," she continued. "So that we can be ready to fight for him."

"Ah," I said.

Zoe flounced back on the bed and stared morosely at the ceiling. "I wish it were over already. No, I wish I was eighteen like you and could just be free."

While I could think of many adjectives to describe myself, "free" wasn't usually one that came to mind.

"Oh, Sydney," Zoe lamented. "Why is she doing this?"

"Because she loves you," I said quietly.

"That's not love."

I was glad Zoe didn't elaborate because I was pretty sure I wouldn't have been able to keep my cool in the face of whatever shallow definitions of love she would've undoubtedly come up with.

"Mom's not going to be able to match all of Dad's educational and cultural talk," I observed. "All she'll have is anecdotal stuff to go on. Like that time you broke your foot."

"It was my whole leg," Zoe said quietly. I didn't say anything else. I didn't have to, judging from the faraway look in her eyes. When Zoe was little, she'd wanted to take gymnastics, so our mom had made it happen. An accident at a meet had broken Zoe's leg, and she'd had to spend the night in the hospital, which was devastating since it was the same night as her team's victory party. Mom had made arrangements to bring the team and the party to the hospital room, much to the staff's astonishment. Zoe, craving social contact back then, had loved it. Our dad had thought the incident was proof of how worthless the class was.

When I drove the gang to Clarence's later that evening, I heard a text come in on the Love Phone in my purse. Strict principles against texting and driving kept me away from it, but it wasn't easy. That, and I tried not to get the phone out when others were around. As soon as we were walking up Clarence's driveway, however, I pulled it out and read Adrian's message: *Escape plan #5: Open an alpaca ranch in Texas, one that requires all blond-haired, brown-eyed, brainy girls to wear sexy cowgirl outfits.* I reread the words and smiled before deleting it, just like I did all of his messages. Jill caught my eye as she passed and smiled back at me. Sometimes her inner knowledge was creepy. Sometimes, it was like a comforting diary, having someone who knew about my romance. I really didn't like a life of secrets, even if I'd been raised to live one.

None of us were great company tonight. I was down over Adrian, Jill over her Neil/Eddie dilemma, Angeline over Trey, and Zoe over our parents. Only Eddie and Clarence seemed to be having a good time—well, and Dorothy, once she was swimming on the high of having given Jill her blood. Clarence was in one of his more coherent moments and was regaling us with some of his tales of traveling, back when he was younger and hadn't withdrawn from the Moroi world. One of his stories mentioned visiting a small exclusively dhampir training academy in Italy that had an excellent reputation. Eddie hung on every detail that Clarence could muster up.

"Deadly on the inside, beautiful on the outside. The entire roof of the building was a viewing deck, and students often spent their evenings—after training, of course—sitting out with espresso and watching the views of Lake Garda." He frowned. "Can't recall its Italian name."

"Lago di Garda," I said automatically.

"Ah, yes. That was it. And it wasn't too far from Verona, either. You could get a little Shakespearean insight." He chuckled.

Zoe looked up from the remnants of her pizza and made a rare show of engaging Clarence. "Don't mention him."

"Why ever not? He's a great writer. And I thought you were such a literature fan too."

Zoe nodded toward me. "That's her. I have to write about one of his plays and don't have a book. I can't believe she's making us e-mail her our choice tomorrow. On a Saturday! I'll have to hunt down an online version on my laptop when we get home."

"I see." Clarence smiled magnanimously. "Well, why don't you just borrow one of mine?"

For a minute, I thought Clarence meant she could borrow a laptop, which would be mind-blowing since, last I checked, the microwave was the most high-tech item in the house. Then, thinking of how every room contained shelves of books, I understood. "You've got some of his plays?" I asked.

"All of them. They're in the extra storage in the garage. You're welcome to go browse."

"Do you have . . ." Zoe glanced at me questioningly. "What was it, *A Midsummer Night's Dream*?"

"Of course," said Clarence. "A great piece on love."

I scoffed. "I don't know about that. It's mostly a series of zany hijinks set against a magical backdrop."

"Didn't you say we were practically living it?" Zoe asked.

"Love, in my experience," began Clarence, "generally *is* a series of zany hijinks."

"Love is . . ." An old memory with Adrian came back to me, and some of the turbulent emotion I always carried within me these days welled up in my chest. It was stupid, feeling so lovesick when he'd been gone less than a day, but I couldn't get him or the ways he described love out of my head. ". . . a flame in the dark. A breath of warmth on a winter's night. A star that guides you home." When I realized everyone was staring at me, I quickly tried to redirect. "I read those in a book. You should check out Clarence's library, Zoe. If you don't get *Midsummer*, there might still be something else you'll like."

As soon as I saw her go pale, I knew I'd succeeded in my distraction. Everyone turned from me to her, though Eddie took the longest. I could immediately guess what she was thinking. Exploring a vampire's garage was akin to going into a crypt, in her eyes. She probably expected to find coffins. I smiled.

"Want me to go with you?" I was kind of curious to see what his "extra storage" contained.

"Would you?" she asked, her head bobbing up and down.

"Of course." I felt a small surge of warmth at doing this seemingly miniscule thing for her. I hadn't forgotten her earlier comments about whether we were sisters or colleagues, and comforting her in a scary place was something I used to do when she was little.

As it turned out, though, Clarence's garage was a complete and total contrast to the Gothic stateliness of the rest of his home. His little-used Porsche was parked inside it, making Zoe gape. There were gardening tools and home-improvement tools, a water heater, a workbench, and a whole area dedicated to boxed books. I cringed a little at that last one. Palm Springs might not be as damp as other places, but it was still an unnecessary risk to the books. I helped Zoe find the box of Shakespeare and then left her to make her own choice, warning her to read the backs and not go by length. Glancing at some of Clarence's other books, I saw a collection of poetry that I pulled out and tucked under my arm for Adrian.

As Zoe continued searching, I found a seat on a stool and made a comfortable footrest out of a bag of gravel. Certain Zoe was engrossed in her task, I covertly took out my cell phone in case I'd missed any messages from Adrian. I hadn't. I jotted out: *Got you a book of poetry. Maybe shorter pieces will be easier than Gatsby.* Clinging to hope, I stared at the screen and willed a response to come. Nothing came, and I had to remind myself he was away on business and probably enmeshed in the spirit case.

I shifted my feet, and a few small rocks fell out of the gravel bag. Except, when I took a closer look, I realized it was a bag of rock salt used for de-icing. Judging from the dirt and grime covering the bag, it didn't see much use around here. Clarence still got points for preparedness, though. I jumped down and knelt to pick up the pieces that had fallen out. As I held some of the crystals in my hand, revelation hit me like a slap in the face.

Rock salt. Sodium chloride. The most common halide out there, with a cubic crystal system—just like boleite. It was so common, in fact, that it had never even crossed my mind as a candidate for the renegade ink experiments. I'd been focusing on the more exotic. I held up a piece of the salt, watching the way the light sparkled off it. My mind ran down which of its properties I could recall, conducting more comparisons to boleite. Could the answer really be right in front of me? Could my search have such an easy answer?

My heart began to pound as I dared a look at Zoe. She was engrossed in her task and appeared to be leafing through *As You Like It*. It was stupid and foolhardy to experiment here, but suddenly, I had to know. Retreating to the far side of the garage, I took up a position that gave me a good vantage of Zoe but kept her back to me. Getting dirt on my hands from the grungy floor was easy, and after one more nervous look in her direction, I summoned up earth's essence.

I'd done it so much by now, it was almost second nature. A glow filled my hand, and I quickly covered my other hand, which held a salt crystal, transferring the light. The salt gleamed briefly, then all light faded. Had it worked? Was this crystal infused? Everything had felt right, but I couldn't say for sure. Ms. Terwilliger could tell me tomorrow, but once again, my urgency got the best of me.

I returned to my stool, like nothing had happened, and texted my teacher: *Any chance you could swing by my dorm tonight to collect an assignment?* If she couldn't, I could find an excuse to leave and go to her, but that would elicit questions from Zoe. Fortunately, the response I received was: *Yes, I'll stop by after my date with MW.* It took me a minute to remember MW was Malachi Wolfe. Ugh.

Zoe stood up and stretched, then waved a copy of *A Midsummer Night's Dream.* "I think I'm set. I hope this works."

"Me too," I said, pocketing the crystal.

It was easy stepping out of my dorm room later, when Ms. Terwilliger got in touch to say she was in the lobby. I met her near the door and tried not to let my jaw drop when I saw her. Not only was she wearing makeup, she was also in an amazingly cute shift dress that didn't look like a Woodstock leftover.

"Wow . . . you look great, ma'am."

She beamed as she smoothed the skirt. "You think so? I haven't worn this in years. Malachi said this shade of pink makes me look like a Botticelli angel."

"He said what?"

"It's not important. Just pillow talk." My jaw *did* drop then. "Now. What was it you needed?"

I swallowed and tried to remember. "Oh, I just wanted to give this back."

I handed her a history book I'd grabbed at random and slipped the salt into her hand at the same time. All trace of lovesickness vanished. Her features grew sharp as she carefully rested the salt on the book. I clenched my hands so tightly my fingers hurt.

"Well, well, well," she said, voice soft. "Look at that."

"Yes?"

She lifted her eyes and smiled at me. "Congratulations, Sydney. You've made a flawless elemental charm."

CHAPTER 9

ADRIAN

I WAS BEING AN ASSHOLE AND DIDN'T CARE.

The thing was, no one else seemed to care either. Maybe they already understood what was at stake. Maybe they could just sense my urgency. Whatever it was, time was slipping away before my eyes, and I'd be damned if I was going to let anyone here screw this up.

"Get a doctor here," I ordered. "Or a nurse. Hell, anyone who can safely draw blood." I didn't need to specify a Moroi doctor. That was understood, and it was a wild card. Moroi sometimes clung together in isolated communities. Some tried to hide from Strigoi by mixing in heavily populated human areas. The key would be finding someone in the latter category with medical training—who was relatively close by.

Dimitri immediately walked out of the room, already dialing on his cell phone, and for once, I appreciated his do-gooder efficiency.

Nina and Olive exchanged startled looks. "What's going on?" Nina demanded. "Why are you taking her blood?"

"Because you'd better have a good reason," snapped Olive, coming to life. "Or I'm going to walk right out of here." She shuddered. "I've seen enough blood for a lifetime these last three months."

I smiled, and a little of my tension faded. There was a fire in both sisters that I liked, and I was also amused at Olive's certainty that she could walk out. Aside from the fact that restoration took a huge physical toll, she'd never get past even one of the guardians.

"Your blood may save lives." I reconsidered my word choice. A Strigoi, discovering he or she couldn't turn a victim, might simply kill. "Or, well, souls. No Strigoi can ever turn you again."

Some of Olive's bravado wavered. "Really . . . you mean it? Because . . . I really would rather be dead than go through that again." She squeezed her eyes shut, but it didn't stop the tears from leaking out. "It was awful . . ."

"I know," I said, watching as Nina sat down and gathered Olive into a hug. I actually didn't know, of course. I had no clue what that hell must have been like. "But you're immune now. And we're trying to see if we can use what Nina did to you to help others."

Nina lifted her head from her sister's chest. "Can I do something to help you now?"

"I think your part's over, though another spirit user's input can't hurt. When you're able to grasp it again," I added.

Those unusual gray eyes met mine. "I grasped enough to see how much you were wielding earlier. I couldn't use that much."

I brushed her comment off and ignored the curious look Rose gave me. "Not true. Saving her would've required at least that much."

Dimitri returned a few moments later. "There's a nurse on her way. It'll probably be an hour." For the first time in our acquaintance, he looked at me deferentially. "Is that enough time?"

"It has to be," I said, tuning back in to the spirit radiating around Olive. We'd lose some of it, but I was pretty sure we'd still have a little left.

Meanwhile, I had to plan ahead. Sonya had always hoped that by studying the magic in the blood, we might be able to replicate that spell. I didn't know if that was possible. Looking at the way it shone around Olive now, I couldn't see anything definable about it that would've allowed me to cast it in the same way. Maybe I didn't have the skill. I wondered if perhaps it was as straightforward as Nina casting spirit in the same way she had to restore Olive. If that was the key, we had a few problems. One was that the spell required a silver stake through the heart. The other was that even doing it once wiped out a spirit user. We were hardly in a position to mass-produce some magical vaccine.

Speaking of vaccines . . . I wondered if it was as simple as that. Could we just inject her blood into someone else? Or tattoo it? The biology side of this wasn't my thing. That required someone like Sydney.

Thinking of her made me wish she were here. I checked my cell phone and found a message about poetry that made me smile. I tried to think of something witty to send back and ended up going with the naked truth: *I need you. In all senses of the word.*

It was true. Crises like these were her specialty, not mine. I slipped the phone back into my pocket and tried to ignore the pang of her absence. If she were here, she'd stick to business. I could do no less. *I believe in you.*

"I need some silver," I said, not really directing my words to anyone in particular. "A case that's perfectly forged to hold a vial of blood would be ideal, but since I'm guessing none of you are metalsmiths, I'll take what I can get."

Unfortunately, there was none in the house. Not even the girls had any jewelry on. Rose dispatched one of the other guardians as though she were a general on the battlefield. "Find a store that sells jewelry," she told him. "And bring us some silver."

"Large men's rings, if you can find them," I added. "Five or six will probably work for a vial."

"Just one vial?" asked Olive. That earlier fierceness returned. "You can take as much as you need from me. I'll do whatever it takes to stop this."

"Easy there, champ," I told her. "We're not going to drain you when you're still recovering from literally having your life changed. Besides, I don't even know yet if your blood will keep holding the magic once it's out of you." Seeing everyone's blank looks, I realized I hadn't shared my idea with them. "Her body's brimming with spirit. I don't know if that's what creates the immunity, but it's the best lead we've had. But it's leaking out fast, which is why we need to hurry."

Rose's errand boy scurried away. With nothing to do but wait, Rose leaned against Dimitri and sighed. Neil, surprisingly, began lauding Olive for her determination and bravery. I was too restless to simply stand around, so I wandered out to the porch, wishing for the first time in a while that I had a cigarette, both because it was a nervous habit and because it could take the edge off spirit. Instead, I contented myself with pacing and obsessively checking for messages from Sydney.

"Expecting a call?" Nina appeared in the doorway, wrapped in the blanket again.

I put the phone away. "Just hoping I might hear from someone."

"Girlfriend?"

"A friend who's a girl," I said smugly. "I have a few 'friends' like that."

She leaned against the porch's wall, the inside lights illuminating her in the night's darkness. "So I've heard. I didn't realize who you were at first."

"Should you have?"

She shrugged. "You and your family are kind of well known."

I didn't ask her to elaborate. She could've been talking about Aunt Tatiana—or my mom, who was locked away in prison somewhere. No one would tell me where, and when I had tried to dream visit, she'd ordered me away with such vehemence that I had uncharacteristically obeyed. I wasn't sure if she was freaked out about spirit dreams or just embarrassed at me seeing her in that state. I held on to the hope that I'd get a better reception if I showed up in person, but that didn't seem to be a possibility anytime soon. With all the other complications in my life, I kept her on the far edges of my mind and contented myself with writing letters to her that were never sent. Not even Sydney knew that.

"Well," I said, putting on the arrogant role everyone expected of me, "I'm not surprised about that. My charm and good looks are legendary—especially with women."

"I'm sure," Nina said with a rueful smile. "But you aren't what I expected. Thank you . . . for helping Olive."

"Thank yourself for that. I'm not doing anything."

"You're helping her get over this—mentally. I mean, we haven't had a chance to talk much, but I can tell. I know her and realize how traumatic this was for her."

I shook my head. "I don't know her, and even I can see how traumatic it was. That, and I know enough people who've gone through it."

Nina was silent for a long time. "Do they ever get over it?" she asked quietly.

I thought about the haunted look I still sometimes saw in Dimitri's and Sonya's eyes. "No. But they learn to go on with their lives. Olive will too."

"Do you know how it happened?" Nina wrapped the blanket around her more tightly as a cool breeze ruffled her curly hair. "She was protecting our dad. He never even considered not letting us grow up together, you know. He and my mom split up, and then he married Olive's mom. She's a dhampir, obviously. Or was. She passed away a few years ago."

"Brave guy," I said. Moroi men usually kept their dhampir mistresses in the shadows.

"Amazing guy. But not royal. When Olive was in school, she found out there'd never be any way she could protect him when she was a guardian. They told her she'd have to go wherever she was assigned when she graduated—which would be some royal." Nina chuckled at the memory. "She didn't take that quietly."

I thought back to Olive's face, determined even in her weakened state. "I can see that."

"So she left the school and made herself Dad's unofficial guardian. He wasn't happy about that—dropping out of school.

But he respected the reasons and let her do it, so long as she took human GED classes. Everything was great, until . . ." Her words choked off.

"Strigoi?" I guessed.

"He was attacked on a business trip. She threw herself in their path, so Dad could get away. He did. She didn't. I thought she was dead for a long time, and when I found out she wasn't, I read everything I could about Dimitri Belikov and Sonya Karp. I got my friend James to help me . . . and here we are."

"It was very brave," I said. It was also incredibly dangerous, but who was I to fault her? I knew without a doubt I'd do something equally risky to save someone I loved. Hell, I'd brought Jill back from the dead.

The silver-seeking guardian arrived later, just before the nurse. No one bothered telling the nurse what was going on, mostly because we were all too keyed up. She glanced around nervously as she entered Olive's bedroom and silently set to work. For all the fuss, it was pretty simple. Less than a minute to draw the blood, and it was all done. She put a stopper on the vial and held it out uncertainly. I took it from her and peered at it intently. There it was, spirit still humming inside—but also still gradually fading.

I swore and quickly took hold of the silver rings. Our courier had done a good job. The rings were thick and plain and large enough to go around the vial. But I'd never charmed silver and had only a vague understanding of it, based on Lissa's explanations. Feeling everyone's eyes on me only made things worse. The metal was cool against my skin, and the rush of spirit filled me as I tried to send it into the ring. My plan was to create a type of compulsion that would trap the spirit within the blood. It would require making the two variants of magic butt heads, something I wasn't even sure was possible. I glanced up at the nurse.

"You aren't an earth user, are you?"

"No," she said. "Air."

Pretty much the opposite of what I needed. Spirit users exceled at compulsion more than other kinds of Moroi, but earth users had an affinity to metals and other things that dwelt in the ground. Silver readily accepted magic, but I wouldn't have minded an edge and wished I'd thought to have them rustle up an earth user. Too late now.

"Here." Nina walked up beside me and rested her hand over the ring in my palm. I felt her magic rise—only a trickle compared with mine—and help guide my spell into the ring. My hold faltered as I stared at her in surprise.

"You've made charms before."

"A few."

Once I saw how she did it, I was able to successfully meld spirit into the silver. I did it four more times with the other rings, and although I kept repeating to myself how Sydney believed in me, I also had a brief reminder of that concern in her eyes, her warnings about how continuing to use spirit would harm my mind. And I wasn't just using spirit today. I was drowning in it. Between using it to "peer" into Olive's blood and now this charm making, I felt as though *I* were made of spirit. It was overwhelming, but what I could do? Everyone was counting on me, and by the time I finished, I could barely stand. I rested my hand on the back of a chair to steady myself and handed the rings to Dimitri. "Put them around the vial."

The rings were a little larger around, and so he ended up

setting the vial in a small box stuffed with cotton so that the rings wouldn't slip off. Palpable silence filled the room, and he handed the box back to me. I used the last of my strength to study the spirit in the blood. The magic was still in there, and I was pretty sure it wasn't trickling out. I glanced at Nina for confirmation, but she shook her head.

"I can't see what you see."

"Then this is as good as it gets." I gave the box back to Dimitri. "Get it back to Court for Sonya as soon as possible. She's your best bet for figuring it out now. I think I've got it stabilized, but I don't know for how long." As the others scurried to make travel plans, I felt the room sway. I needed to get out of here but couldn't stand to show weakness in front of these people who'd placed so many hopes on me. I finally sought help from the person least likely to judge me and touched Nina's arm. "Can we talk in private about, uh, spirit stuff?"

"Sure." She gave Olive a few soothing words and then left Neil to keep the younger girl company. Nina walked out of the room with me and looked up in concern. "What'd you want to talk about?"

"Nothing," I said through gritted teeth. "I actually just need you to find me some place to lie down because I'll be damned if I faint in front of Rose and Belikov."

Her eyes widened, but she wasted no time and took me to her room. Under other circumstances, I might have had the nobility to tell her I couldn't take her bed away from her. But exhaustion trumped chivalry. I collapsed onto the narrow bed, and for once in my life, I had no trouble falling asleep.

I awoke to morning sunlight pouring through the window.

Jerking upright, I looked around, not sure where I was. Then, everything came back to me. Some of my strength had returned, but I still felt tired. Nearby, Rose sat with a human woman who bore the neck bites and telltale daze of a feeder.

"Breakfast," said Rose.

I wasted no time on pleasantries and sank my teeth into the woman's neck. The rush it gave me caught me by surprise. I'd been so sated on Dorothy recently that I'd almost come to take blood in stride, the way I would a glass of milk. Now, burned out and weak, I was hit with the full impact of how much my body needed the blood of others. It was as essential as air and water for Moroi, and as I drank greedily, I was certain I'd never tasted anything so sweet and pure.

The feeder relaxed happily into her chair when I finished, lost in a world of endorphins. "Glad it was good for you too," I told her, settling back against the pillows. I exhaled in satisfaction as the blood's energy continued working its way through me. "So what's the word, little dhampir?"

Rose's dark eyes regarded me with amusement. "You slept for ten hours. Dimitri left with Nina and Olive and the other guardians. Sonya's on her way back to Court, so hopefully they'll all meet up soon. It's just you, me, and Neil."

"You think Nina and Olive are ready to travel?" I asked.

"They were a lot better this morning too. And we didn't want to waste any time getting them back, just in case Sonya's still able to see something."

I swung my legs over the bed's edge and stood up, pleased to see the world was stable again. "I don't want to waste time either. I need to get back to Palm Springs." Back to Sydney. "Thanks for sticking around."

Rose nodded and stood as well. "Thanks for all you did. I don't understand a lot of it, but Nina did, and she was pretty impressed."

"All in a day's work," I said, hoping she believed me. I was fully aware that the spirit I'd used was off the charts. And I was also fully aware that there'd be a price.

A sly smile crossed Rose's lips. "I think Nina likes you. Maybe you could look her up the next time you're at Court. Would do you good to settle down." It was a dangerous comment, considering our past, but it no longer bothered me.

"What, and disappoint all the women of the world? How cruel do you think I am?"

She caught hold of my arm as I was about to go into the living room and join Neil. "Adrian, in all seriousness . . . I mean it, thank you for this. I'm sorry for what I said last night. You have changed. And . . . it looks good on you."

"Most things do," I told her.

That broke her serious mien. "Always a joke with you. I guess I shouldn't expect that to go away."

Then, astonishingly, she hugged me. Again, I was floored at how immune I was to it. That wasn't to say I felt nothing, but it wasn't the pain or longing for an ex. The hug was just a kind gesture from a friend.

We all went to the airport together; Rose was off to Pennsylvania, while Neil and I headed back to Palm Springs. A check of my cell phone at the gate found a number of messages from Sydney, excited that she'd made a breakthrough in her charm. Warmth flooded me as I imagined her face and that glint that shone in her eyes when she made some sort of intellectual discovery.

146

I wrote: *I never doubted. Would you believe I made a breakthrough with charms too?*

Her response came fast. *Of course I believe it. When do you get back?*

Early evening. Can you come over?

I'll try. We need to celebrate.

Should I get champagne and cake ready?

Get your bed ready.

Wear the black bra.

I didn't plan on wearing one.

"God help me," I murmured, earning a surprised glance from Neil.

I sincerely doubted we would cross the line into sex during a furtive visit like this, but just the hint of her touch made everything else in the world fade to unimportance. I felt my pulse quicken as I thought of *that look* she got in her eyes sometimes, the animal one that had no interest in books and was usually followed by the urgency of her lips against mine and her hands tightening against my back. Everyone thought Sydney had passion only for intellectual pursuits. That was their loss.

Daydreams of Sydney kept me on a high for the flight home, even making Neil's conversation bearable. He'd become uncharacteristically chatty, wanting to talk about how to help with the "Strigoi vaccine." He also kept going on and on about how brave the Sinclair sisters were—especially Olive. I could spot infatuation a mile away and put on my gravest look for him. "I've never seen courage like hers. I can't even begin to relate to it. You're probably the only one who understands that sort of awesome bravery. She can tell too. It was obvious from the way she was talking to you."

Neil's breath caught. "You think so?"

"Absolutely. It was in her eyes. You should keep in touch. I'll get her contact info when we're back home. It'd probably help her, having someone else to talk to."

That, at least, kept him dazed and happy. I was going to get in trouble with Jill for this, but I was still subscribing to the idea that she'd eventually thank me when she ran off with some Moroi prince. Or Eddie. I'd take either one.

When we landed in Palm Springs, I kind of hoped Sydney might be there to give us a ride from the airport, but we instead received messages to catch cabs to our respective homes. I also had a text from Jill waiting: *I know what you're doing with Neil. You're mean. How will I ever have a healthy relationship?*

By being with someone else, I wrote back.

Once I'd dropped off my suitcase and was in control of my own car, I headed out to a nearby grocery store. I felt like I was walking on air, buzzed with what I'd accomplished in Dallas and excited to see Sydney again. Being with her was about more than bras (or lack thereof). I also just wanted to be near her. I felt lonely inside my own head. Even with Jill or countless other friends, there was no one except Sydney that I truly felt comfortable with. She was the only one who truly saw me or heard me.

Inspiration hit, and I decided to make something for her tonight. Why wait for her birthday? Like she'd said, this was a special occasion. We were both celebrating our triumphs. Somehow, I became obsessed with the idea of making crème brûlée, even though I never had before. In fact, I'd never really made any sort of dessert, short of opening a carton of ice cream. But crème brûlée sounded classy, I was in love, and

I felt unstoppable after doing what few others could do with spirit. How hard could one dessert be?

Before I could even answer that question, an internet search on my phone told me I needed a lot more equipment than my sparse kitchen had. By the time I hit the checkout line with my mini-blowtorch, ramekins, cream, egg separator, double boiler, and organic vanilla beans, I'd racked up a surprisingly high bill—more than my bank account held. Or my credit card permitted, for that matter.

"Sorry," said the cashier, handing it back to me. "Declined."

An uneasy feeling welled up in my stomach. "Can we try it again?"

She shrugged and ran it once more, only to get the same result. "Declined," she repeated.

I nearly asked again but knew in my gut that nothing would change. Feeling like a total idiot, I abandoned my goods and left the store, unsure what I was going to do now. Panic began to rise up within me. I kept telling myself that neither my bank account nor my credit card were actually at zero. They just didn't have enough to cover a crème brûlée cooking kit. But just how much *was* left? That was something I needed to go find out. I only had to survive two weeks until my next payday, and as I made the agonizing drive home, I tried to add up what expenses I had to juggle. Gas. Groceries—unless I could get Dorothy to feed me. Had I paid electricity yet? I couldn't remember, but I knew cable was taken care of—not that it'd do me much good if they turned the power off.

Relax, Adrian, I told myself. *You've still got money. And they won't cut the electricity if you're a little late on a bill.*

But when I got home and checked my balances, I saw that

even though I wasn't at empty yet, I was pretty damned close. What was I going to do? I could barely scrape by with my living expenses, let alone the ever-looming task of Sydney's birthday. I sank down on the floor near the still-packed boxes of records and glared at them.

"Stupid, stupid," I muttered. "I am so stupid."

The high I'd been riding from my triumph in Texas crashed to the ground. Despair settled around me, its dark tendrils slowly creeping under my skin. After what I'd done yesterday, it was expected that I'd be susceptible to the magic's ups and downs. I'd had the up earlier today . . . now the down would try to come, seizing on annoyances like this and making them bigger than they were. And then, on cue, I heard *her* voice.

Why are you so sad? You aren't stupid. You're my brilliant, beautiful boy. You'll figure a way out of this.

I could hear Aunt Tatiana's voice as clearly as if she stood beside me. I buried my face in my hands. "Go away, Aunt Tatiana. I don't need to add hallucinations to my growing list of problems."

Since when was I problem?

"Since you died and I started imagining I could hear you."

Are you saying you can't, sweetling?

"Yes! I mean, no. This is a trick. This is all in my head." It was another secret I'd kept from Sydney, how in my darkest moments lately, I imagined conversations with my dead aunt. It was one of the most terrifying things that had ever happened to me because while certain actions might be jokingly called crazy, there was no question that ghostly imaginings actually were crazy. "I don't want to talk to you."

Why? Haven't I always been there for you? Didn't I always look after you?

"Yes," I said through gritted teeth. "But you're dead now, and I have to help my—"

I suddenly jerked my head up as an idea hit me. I sprang to my feet and hurried over to my dresser, where Aunt Tatiana's cuff links glittered up at me. Sydney had said I'd have a fortune if I sold them—but I didn't need to sell them. Not technically. I could take them to a pawnshop and get a loan. In two weeks, I'd go buy them out. Thrilled at my revelation, I scooped them up and started to turn away—then halted. Some inner voice of wisdom made me reconsider the logistics. After a moment's thought, I set one of them down and sought out a pair of tweezers in the jumble of various other items piled nearby. After a little maneuvering, I plucked out one of the rubies and held it up to the light. No need to risk the others. This was all I needed. More than enough to get me through the next two weeks. Inside my head, Aunt Tatiana's laughter echoed.

See? I always look after you.

"You aren't real," I said, striding toward the front door. "You're just part of spirit messing with my head. All of this is a mental rebound after everything I did with Olive."

If I'm not real, then how come you answer me out loud?

I'd known it would happen, that I couldn't walk away unscathed from all that spirit. I just hadn't expected it to bounce around these highs and lows or to escalate to this long of a conversation with my dead aunt. I had to nix this right now. I didn't want Aunt Tatiana talking to me while I was negotiating with a pawnbroker, and I certainly didn't want her around while Sydney was here. A check of the time told me I had a while before she showed up, giving me ample opportunity to fix my finances and blot out my aunt.

I hadn't had my daily drink and decided it was worth doing it early in order to get a grip. The agreement's terms referred only to "a drink," with no qualifiers on strength. So, when I found an old bottle of Bacardi 151—the strongest stuff I owned—I didn't really feel like I was cheating, even though it had enough kick for two drinks. After a shot of that, I was out the door. And once again, a bolt of wisdom struck me. The shot hadn't hit me yet, but I prudently chose to walk downtown rather than drive. It was less than fifteen minutes, and by the time I reached the pawnshop I'd passed a dozen times in the past, I was happily buzzed from the rum. The store owner's assessment soon put a damper on that, though.

"Two hundred," he said.

"That's bullshit," I said, taking the ruby back. "It's worth at least twice that." It occurred to me then that if I hadn't had the rum, I'd have full spirit to try to compel a higher price. Immediately, I regretted the thought. Even I had some morals. There was a reason the Moroi forbade the use of compulsion.

The guy shrugged. "Then run an ad. Sell it on the internet. You want fast cash? This is what you get."

I nearly walked out the door, but desperation made me stay. Two hundred was less to pay back, and really, did I need much more than that to get by in the next two weeks?

"You won't sell it?" I asked.

"Not if you can keep paying interest or come pay off the loan." There was a look in his eyes that told me most people never came back to pay those loans. In some of my darker moments, I would wallow in self-pity over how hard my life was. But just then, I couldn't help but think it must be pretty depressing to see the desperate dregs of the world coming in to sell off their prized possessions.

"I'll pay it back," I told him. "I'll be back in two weeks, so take good care of it."

"Whatever you say," he said.

I gave him the ruby and filled out some paperwork. He gave me the cash. And like that, I was out the door, suddenly feeling a weight lifted off my chest. I'd dealt with the problem. I was in control of my life again. Thinking of Aunt Tatiana's ruby in that grubby man's hands *did* give me a moment's pause, and I half expected her to protest. But the rum kept her quiet, and I told myself again that there was no harm done.

I made no attempts to repeat the crème brûlée experiment, but I did pick up some *pain au chocolat* on the walk home so that I'd have something nice for when Sydney came over. We could eat it by candlelight and catch up on what had happened over the last day or so. It cost me only seven dollars, so no one could question my fiscal responsibility.

My phone rang when I was nearly to my door, and to my surprise, the display showed Rowena's name.

"Hey, Prince Charming! A bunch of us are going to the Matchbox tonight. Eighteen and over, so you can bring your fictitious girlfriend."

"I'm bringing her to my apartment tonight for some very not-fictitious activities," I said. "I haven't seen her in almost two days."

"Boo-hoo. It's a wonder you haven't fallen to pieces. You know where we are if you change your mind."

My energy was running strong, and I started off doing some rapid-fire painting. After a while, I lost interest and decided to spend the rest of the day cleaning my apartment from top to bottom. I felt a burning need to prove myself, not just to Sydney, but to me. I didn't want to feel like I was drifting through life. I wanted to be responsible and in control. I wanted to be a worthy partner to her and threw myself into my cleaning more than I had in . . . well, I really couldn't remember the last time, seeing as I hated cleaning. But tonight, I was fired up. I was unstoppable, even going so far as to scrub my kitchen backsplash with a toothbrush. I was high and excited, and the earlier glum mood was banished to the winds . . . at least until I was dusting my dresser and I saw the cuff links with the missing ruby. My dust rag faltered, and I stared at the gaping hole in the platinum setting. I suddenly felt like I had a matching hole in my soul.

"No," I told Hopper, who was sitting on the bed, undoubtedly weirded out by my frenetic activity. "It's not gone. I'll get it back."

I could've sworn I heard Aunt Tatiana laughing again, and I rushed to the liquor cabinet, intending to take another shot. Sure, it was violating the agreement, but these were unusual circumstances. I was entitled to some leeway to fight against this spirit backlash . . . right?

No. That was just an excuse, and I'd hold true to Sydney. I wouldn't lose control. I couldn't. Everything was fine. I'd told her I'd be strong, that I wouldn't lapse again. In fact, to prove it to myself, I seized on an impulsive and questionably noble idea: I began emptying my liquor collection down the drain. Part of me winced at the waste, but the rest of me was proud. Now there'd be no temptation.

Sydney called when I was nearly finished. "Good timing, Sage. I'm just taking care of some housecleaning."

She sighed. "I can't come over. Zoe's got it into her head that she wants me to help her with this Alchemist database, and she overheard Ms. Terwilliger mention a date—with Wolfe, if you can believe it—so I can't use her as an excuse. I'm sorry."

I was glad she couldn't see my face. "No need to. You've got to do what you've got to do. And hey, this just gives me extra time to think of more ways to celebrate."

Her laughter was tinged with relief. "How many ways have you thought of already?"

"Who can count the number of stars in the sky or grains of sand upon the beach? It's futile."

"Oh, Adrian." The warmth in her voice stirred both my blood and my heart—and made the pain of her absence that much worse. "Tomorrow I'll come over. I promise."

"I'd say I'd count the seconds, but that's a pretty big number for me."

"I'll count for both of us. I love you."

The words were a dagger to my heart, sweet and cruel at the same time. We disconnected, and I stared around at my immaculate apartment with its latest freestyle paintings. On the kitchen counter, Hopper seemed to watch me judgmentally with his golden eyes. What was I going to do with myself now? It was embarrassing that I even had to ask that kind of question, like I was some child who required others to entertain him. But the canvas held no more interest for me, and I suddenly felt awake and wired. I had another night of insomnia ahead of me.

I put Supertramp on the record player and flounced onto my bed to read *The Great Gatsby*. I couldn't focus, though. I was too restless, too keyed up over Sydney and the usual questions about where my life was going. She and I were caught up in this dangerous game that had no end in sight. There was no clear direction on anything else either. What would happen after Jill left Palm Springs? Would I follow her? Would I stay to finish my art degree? And then what? Rowena always joked about limited career options, but she wasn't that far off from the truth. Tossing aside the book, I draped a hand over my eyes and tried to still the hamster wheel in my mind. Aunt Tatiana returned.

Why are you worrying about such things? It doesn't suit you. Just live in the moment.

"Go away," I said aloud. "You're not here, and I'm not engaging with a figment of my imagination. I'm not that far gone. Besides . . . I have a future to think about with Sydney. I have my own future to think about."

You'll get by, that damned voice said. *You always do. Your smile and charm will get you out of any situation. Forget all this brooding.*

Some reasonable part reminded me that this conversation was only imagined, brought on by a rebound of spirit. And yet, I found myself arguing back. "No. I'm not going to keep going moment to moment without any regard for the consequences. No more impulsive decisions. I'm done with that phase in my life."

Then why did you sell my ruby?

I opened my eyes. Undefinable emotions churned within me, and I didn't know what I was going to do, only that I had to do something or else I'd explode. I had to get out of my own head. I had to get out of here. "No more. I'm done with this. I'm done with you."

Scrambling out of bed, I went back to the living room to find where I'd discarded my cell phone. It was lying next to my uncapped oil paints. I scooped it up and dialed Rowena back.

"Yo," I said. "You guys still there?"

CHAPTER 10
SYDNEY

I'D JUST GOTTEN INTO BED WHEN SOMEONE showed up at our door, knocking as furiously as one dared at a time of the night when the dorm was supposed to be asleep. Zoe, who had just drifted off, sat bolt upright and stifled a small scream, no doubt expecting a swarm of bat-winged vampires to come swooping in. I stalked across the room in trepidation, unsure of what madness I'd find.

It was Jill.

"Hey," she said, strolling in like it wasn't almost midnight. "I need a favor."

The presumption in her voice was so like Angeline's, I had to blink a couple of times to make sure I had the right person. "Do you know what time it is?"

"It's not that late. Well, not for *our kind*. We're just getting started." Her sly tone and the small laugh that followed made Zoe clench the covers tighter. It made me raise an eyebrow in disbelief. "And that's the problem," Jill continued with a pout. "I know we were just at Clarence's yesterday . . . but you wouldn't believe how much I'm craving blood. Like, I can't stop thinking about it. You have to take me over there *right now,* or I don't think I can handle it!"

I studied her for a long moment, running a number of scenarios through my head, each one increasingly crazy. Before I had a chance to respond, Zoe spoke up. "It's after-hours. You can't leave the dorm."

"Sydney could get me out," Jill said. "Just call your teacher and tell her you want to do some late night studying off campus. She'll do anything for you. Come *on.* Please?"

Zoe gulped, indignation warring with fear. "We can't just jump on your whims. And Ms. Terwilliger's busy tonight. We heard her earlier."

"This isn't a whim! It's a necessity. I wouldn't bother you guys if it wasn't serious." Jill put her hands on her hips for emphasis. "Things are worse because I'm trapped in a building filled with humans. Do you know what kind of temptation that is?" She glanced meaningfully between the two of us.

"She's right, Zoe," I said, deadpan. "Abandoning her in this state could be dangerous to other humans. It's part of our job to prevent that. Besides, Ms. Terwilliger's probably back." Provided she wasn't staying the night at Wolfe's. Ew. "Even if she's not, she'll still call me in a favor to the front desk."

"She would?" asked Zoe, momentarily forgetting vampire threats.

Jill grinned, giving us a full-on view of her fangs. "See? No problem. Let's do this." She turned toward the door. "You guys should get moving."

I put on a stern look. "I'm the only one coming with you.

Aside from the fact that Ms. Terwilliger can't get everyone out of school, I just don't think . . ." I paused as long and melodramatically as I could stomach. "Well, Zoe, I'd just feel better if you stayed here. I mean, we still need an Alchemist on campus, right?" I tried to make that last statement sound upbeat while simultaneously shooting her a *It's for your own protection* look. She gulped.

"Sydney, you'll be at Clarence's *in the middle of the night—*"

"Everything'll be fine," I assured her, hoping I looked both terrified and brave. It wasn't that hard to pull off, considering my anxiety was growing by leaps and bounds. What was going on? Whatever progress Eddie had made with reassuring Zoe in her driving lessons had probably been undone by Jill acting like the bride of Dracula. I reached for my coat and purse. "I'll text you when I get there."

Jill cleared her throat and nodded at my clothes. "You might want to change. I mean, you know, Clarence is a formal guy."

I wasn't in full-fledged pajamas, but I'd figured my oversized shirt and flannel pants would be fine for whatever ulterior plan Jill had—because I knew there must be one. "What exactly do you suggest I wear?" I asked carefully.

She shrugged. "Jeans and a T-shirt should be fine."

I made a quick change, uttered more courageous proclamations to Zoe, and then followed Jill down to the end of my hall, near the stairwell. I lowered my voice once I was certain we had privacy.

"Okay. What's with the act? I've got two prevailing theories. One is that the bond has overridden you and made you act out some crazy impulse of Adrian's. The other is that you're helping him get me to sneak off on some romantic escapade—but I'm guessing you would have had me put on a dress for that one."

Jill made no attempts at a smile. "I wish it were either of those. Sorry if I was over the top back there. I figured me rampaging for blood would be serious enough for Zoe to let you go without too many questions—and that she wouldn't want to go with you. I feel kind of bad for freaking her out, though."

"It worked. But seriously . . . what's going on?" My chest tightened. "Is Adrian okay?"

"I don't know," she said morosely. "But probably not, since the bond numbed out when they started doing Jäger shots a half hour ago."

"When they—wait. What?"

"Adrian's at some bar by Carlton. He went out after you canceled tonight—but don't feel bad about that," she added quickly. "I know you didn't have a choice."

"I don't feel bad. I feel . . ." How did you pick only one emotion for this sort of situation? My mind reeled. Adrian. Out at a bar, so drunk he'd shorted out the spirit in the bond. I wanted to crumple to the floor and bury my face in my hands as a million sensations ran through me. Sadness. Anger. Disappointment. They were just the beginning of the feelings threatening to burst from my heart. I put on a stoic face. "Well. It doesn't matter what I feel. That's his choice, and I don't need to do anything about it. He can deal with the consequences tomorrow."

I started to turn around, but Jill caught my arm. "Sydney, please. Things are usually pretty bad if I lose him like this. And he had a rough time in Dallas yesterday. Really rough. You wouldn't believe how much power he used." She shuddered at the memory.

161

"Don't say 'it's not his fault,'" I warned.

"I won't . . . but I'm not surprised this happened after all that spirit. Look, you have every right to be upset. I know he broke your deal, but please go to him. Just to help. I'm so worried about him."

It was hard. The reason I was having so much trouble identifying an emotion was that I was just starting to freeze up all over, refusing to feel anything. Because if I did, I was going to have to accept that Adrian had betrayed me. Well, maybe "betrayal" wasn't the right word. But he'd definitely let me down. If anyone but Jill had told me Adrian had lapsed, I wouldn't have believed it. He'd seemed so adamant that night I'd dumped out his liquor, and I'd put all my faith in him.

"Okay," I said. The pleading look in her eyes nearly made me cry then and there. "Where's he at?"

She gave me the name of the bar and then returned to her room. Downstairs, I found one of the night clerks working the lobby. She was familiar with me and Ms. Terwilliger's errands and barely listened as I explained how I'd get retroactive permission to leave. Waving me on, she returned to her copy of *Vogue* and smothered a yawn with her hand.

The Matchbox wasn't exactly divey, but it also wasn't the kind of pretty, trendy place I knew Adrian liked to frequent. Still, it served alcohol and was chock-full of college kids, which were probably his only criteria. A bouncer let me in at the door, stamping my hand in red to show I was under twenty-one, and then nodded me inside. Music from some local band blasted through the air, and for a moment, there were just too many people and too much movement for me to focus on anything.

When I was finally able to get my bearings, I didn't see any sign of Adrian. What I did see, however, was a table of laughing people that had "art students" written all over them. Taking a chance, I walked over and waited for someone to notice me. Empty glasses and pitchers filled the table. When someone finally saw me, I asked, "Do you guys by chance know Adrian?"

A guy laughed. "Sure do. He's the life of the party. Bought us two rounds."

While surprising, that was the least of my worries right now. "Where's he at?"

A lavender-haired girl, much more serious than the rest of them, answered me. "He just left. He said he had to go pick up something."

"Did he say where he was going?" I asked.

She shook her head, and a blond girl cuddled up to her said, "He said something about 'un-pawning.' Is that even a word?"

"No," I murmured, feeling baffled. A pawnshop? Why would Adrian go there? And which one? There had to be a dozen in the area.

"He took a cab," added the first girl. "Then he said he'd walk home."

Ah. That was something I could go on. I took out my phone and did a search for pawnshops within walking distance of his apartment. There were two. I then texted Adrian, asking, *Where are you?* I didn't know if I could expect an answer, but in the meantime, it wouldn't be hard to check out both shops.

"Thanks," I told the girls. I was halfway to the door when the lavender-haired one caught up with me.

"Hey, wait," she said. "You're her, right? Sydney? The girlfriend?"

I hesitated. We weren't supposed to acknowledge our

relationship in public, but clearly, he'd been divulging a little. "Yes."

"I'm Rowena." Her face grew grave, and from the clear look in her blue eyes, I realized she wasn't as drunk as the others. "I'm sorry. I had no idea."

"No idea what?"

"No idea that he had a problem. He almost always turns down going out, and the few times he has, he hardly has anything. I was kind of blown away when he jumped in tonight, and then . . . the more I watched, the more I got it. He had this look my stepdad used to get whenever he fell off the wagon. Like he'd been living in a desert and suddenly stumbled across an Evian machine. Then the more it went on tonight . . ." She sighed. "I knew. I'm sorry. I should've gone with him, but he seemed so confident."

The earnestness and concern in her words nearly made me choke up. "You have nothing to apologize for. It's not your job to look after him." *It's mine.*

"Yeah, I know . . . I just . . ." She faltered, and I understood why Adrian spoke so highly of her.

I gave her the best smile I could muster, despite how dead I felt inside. "Thank you."

"I hope he's okay," she added. "He drank a lot."

"I'm sure he will be," I said, trying not to wince.

The first pawnshop I drove to was empty, and the guy working said no one had been by in an hour. I hoped my pawnshop deductions would actually prove right. Otherwise, I was out of luck since Adrian hadn't answered my text. But then, sure enough, when I arrived at the other shop, I found him. He stood just inside their entryway, blocked by a metal grating that they worked behind at night. I could understand it, since night probably brought out sketchy people. And studying Adrian, he certainly seemed like one.

"I need it back!" he exclaimed. "I need it back. She needs it back. It's a royal heirloom!"

The scruffy-looking guy behind the grating met him with a level look. "Sure it is. If you can't buy it out, I can't give it back." I had the distinct impression he'd told Adrian this many times.

"Adrian," I said. He spun around, and I flinched at the wild look in his bloodshot eyes. His normally perfect hair was disheveled, his clothes wrinkled. If I didn't know him, I'd want a grating between us too.

"What are you doing here?" he asked.

"Looking for you." I forced calm, trying to still the panic rising within me. "Come on. We need to go. I'll drive you home."

"You can't! Not until we get it back." He pointed an accusing finger at the pawnbroker. "He stole it!"

The man sighed. "Kid, you hocked it for cash."

"What?" I demanded. "What did you sell?"

Adrian raked a hand through his hair, messing it up further. "I didn't sell anything. I would never sell it. I just lent it to him. And now I need it back." He reached into his pocket and pulled out ten dollars. "Look, just give it back, and you can have this. It's all I've got, but I'll get you the rest in two weeks. I promise. That's a perfectly reasonable deal."

"That's not how it works," the guy said.

"What did you—lend?" I asked.

"The ruby. One of the rubies from Aunt Tatiana's cuff links. I shouldn't have left it here. Not in a place like this. It's . . .

sacrilege! Something like that has no business here. She told me to do it, but I know she doesn't mean it."

A chill ran over me. "Who told you to do it?"

"Her. Aunt Tatiana."

"Adrian, she can't tell you anything. She's . . . gone."

He tapped his head. "No, she's here. I mean, not right now, but I know she's waiting. And when I'm sober, she'll be back and give me hell for this! I have to get the ruby back!" He turned with startling speed and pounded on the grating.

The shopkeeper took a step back. "I'm going to call the police."

"No, wait," I said, hurrying forward. "How much does he owe?"

"Two fifty."

"It was two hundred!" cried Adrian.

"Plus fees and interest," said the man, with far more patience than I probably would've had.

I reached for my wallet. "What credit cards do you take?"

"All of them," he replied.

I paid for the ruby, and while the man went to get it, Adrian called after him, "There better not be a scratch on it!" When he got the ruby back, he held it up and scrutinized it with narrowed eyes, as though he were a master jeweler.

"Come on," I said, taking hold of his arm. "Let's go."

He stayed where he was, clutching the ruby in his fist and bringing it to his lips. His eyes closed briefly, and then, with a deep breath, he followed me to my car.

He chatted a lot on the way home, relating antics and stories from the night, and going on and on about how he'd been wronged by the pawnbroker. I said nothing and barely heard a word he said. My hands clenched the steering wheel with white knuckles, and all I kept thinking about was that frantic look in his eyes when he'd pounded against the grating.

He began to quiet as I hunted for parking in his neighborhood. When we got inside, I saw that the full effect of what had happened was sinking into him. I didn't know whether to be relieved or feel bad for him.

"Sydney, wait," he said, when he realized I was about to turn right around and leave. "We need to talk."

I sighed. "No. Not tonight. I'm tired, and I want to go to bed. And I don't want to talk to you when you're like this. There'll be plenty of time tomorrow."

"Will there?" he asked. "Or will you have to keep your distance and stay with Zoe?"

"Don't start with that," I warned. "You know we can't help that. You knew it when this started, so don't try blaming me for us tiptoeing around."

"I'm not," he said. "But why do we have to keep doing it? Let's make a real escape plan. Let's leave. We'll go to the Keepers or something and be together without all this bullshit."

"Adrian," I said wearily.

"Don't 'Adrian' me," he snapped, a surprising glint of anger in his eyes. "I don't know how you manage to do it, but just by saying my name like that, you make me feel like I'm five years old."

I nearly said he was acting like it but managed to bite back the comment at the last minute. "Okay. We can't go to the Keepers because the Alchemists visit there all the time. And you wouldn't last one hour in those conditions. Besides, could you abandon Jill?"

The pained look on his face answered for him.

"Exactly. We're stuck here and just have to manage as best we can until . . . I don't know. Something changes. You know that. You've always known that."

"I do," he said. He ran a hand through his hair again, and by this time, it was beyond hope. "I do . . . and I hate it. And I don't have to be drunk to feel this way. How long, Sydney? Where is this all going? At what point do we get out? When you and Marcus pull off your revolution against the Alchemists?"

"It's not that easy." I averted my eyes for a moment. "We're also pulling off a revolution against the taboos both our races enforce."

"What's going to happen to us?" He leaned against the back of his kitchen and stared off at the dark window, lost in his own thoughts. "What *is* our escape plan?"

Silence fell. I had no answer, and I did the cowardly thing by shifting the topic back to him. "Is that why you did this tonight? Because of us? Or was it because of spirit? Jill mentioned that you used a lot of it."

"No, Sydney." It was a little disconcerting that he kept using my first name. It made it hard to stay angry. He walked back to me and caught hold of my hands, a haunted look in his eyes. "I didn't just use spirit. It was like . . . I *was* spirit. It filled me up. I had to look into that girl—Olive—to find out what had happened to her. Spirit infused every part of her, and I had to summon so much to see it. Then I had to confine it. Do you know what that's like? Do you have any idea? The only thing I've ever done that required more was saving Jill."

"Hence your backlash," I said.

He shook his head. "I tried. I tried to hold out. But when

I swing up like that . . . well, eventually the pendulum swings back. It's hard to explain."

"I've been down before."

"Not like this," he said. "And I'm not saying that to be a smart-ass. The way I feel . . . it's like the world starts crumbling around me. Every doubt, every fear . . . it eats me. It weighs me down until I'm swallowed in darkness and can't tell what's real or not. And even when I know something's not real . . . like Aunt Tatiana . . . well, it's still hard . . ."

I went cold all over, recalling his words from the shop. "How often do you hear her?"

His voice was barely whisper. "Not often. Although, once is too much. It's so weird. I know she's not there. I know she's gone. But I can imagine what she'd say, and it's just so real . . . it's like I can practically see her. I haven't yet, though, but someday . . . someday, I'm afraid I really will, and then I know I'll really be lost . . ."

I was so floored, I didn't know what to say. There'd been lots of talk about madness and spirit, but I'd rarely thought it was more than his moodiness. I drew him to me and finally found words.

"Adrian, you have to get help."

His laugh was harsh. "What help is there? This is my life. Jäger shots are about as good as it gets. At least they take the edge off."

"That's not a solution. You need real help. Get a prescription like Lissa did."

He abruptly pulled away from me. "What, and kill it altogether?"

"Stop spirit, you stop the depression and . . . other things.

169

Like needing to drink until you're yelling at a pawn dealer."

"But then I don't have spirit."

"Yes, that's the point."

"I can't. I can't cut myself off from it." Lines of pain were etched on his face.

"You can do anything you want," I said firmly. There was a pain welling up inside of me, and I summoned as much steel as I could to keep it hidden. A concerned Hopper was sitting nearby, and I picked him up as a distraction, stroking the golden scales. "Do it, and you'll save yourself. And Jill. You know the darkness can bleed into her."

"I did save her!" he exclaimed. A bit of that desperate, frantic gleam returned to his eyes. "She was dead, and I saved her. With spirit. I saved Rowena's hand. I saved Olive's blood. Do you know how much effort that was? It wasn't just the amount—the magic was so intricate, Sydney. I don't know if anyone else could've done it. But *I* did. With spirit. With spirit, I can actually do great things for a change!"

"You can do plenty of other great things."

"Yeah? Like that?" He pointed at his latest self-portrait attempt, which even I had to admit was pretty bad.

"You're more than the magic," I insisted. "I don't love you because of the magic."

He faltered a moment at that. "But how can I just let go of the ability to help others? I asked you this before. Should I have let Jill die? Let Rowena ruin her career? Lose our chance at saving people from becoming Strigoi?"

My control finally snapped, and I set Hopper back down. "There's a line! At some point, there's a line you can't cross! Yes, you've done amazing things, but you're reaching a point where you'll have to pay a big price. Are you ready to pay it? Because I'm not! There comes a time when you have to step back and balance yourself with the needs of others. What happens if you do some major feat of spirit that pushes you over the edge? That gets you locked away? Or dead? Then what? How much else will you accomplish? Nothing. You don't know what the future holds. You don't know what you can do if you break free of spirit's influence."

He moved forward and clasped my hands again. "But I'm not going to be able to. You think I can stand aside the next time I have to heal someone? Let them suffer? That's a temptation I can't fight."

"Then remove it. Talk to a doctor. Take the decision away, and see what wondrous things you can do when you're in control of yourself again."

Those green, green eyes held me for what felt like an eternity. At last he swallowed and shook his head again. "I can't, Sydney. I can't give it up."

And at that point, I couldn't hold it in any longer. The tears started as just a few trickles and before I knew it, I was consumed by full-fledged sobbing. I buried my face in my hands, and all the grief, all the fear I'd held inside me for him came bursting out. I almost never cried. I certainly didn't do it in front of others. And although I considered most of my dad's lessons completely useless these days, I'd still clung to the idea that breaking down like this and showing so much emotion was a sign of weakness. But I couldn't help it. I couldn't stop.

I was scared. So, so scared for him. I dealt with logic and reason, and this was too hard for me, having to manage the unreasonable. And I'd meant what I said. I was afraid that one day, he'd go past frenetic painting and drunken antics. What if the pawnbroker had called the police before I got there? What if his aunt told him to walk off a building?

I felt Adrian's arms go around me, and although they were strong, his voice wavered. "Sydney . . . are you . . . are we . . . are we breaking up?"

It took me almost a minute to speak without choking. I looked up at him in shock, unable to believe he'd think I would leave him because he was suffering. "What? No! Why would you think that?"

The alcohol was wearing off, and his earlier frustration and sadness were now completely trumped by fear and confusion. "Then why are you crying?"

"Because of you!" I beat my fists on his chest. "Because I love you, and I don't know what to do! I can solve almost any problem, but I can't solve this. I don't know how to deal with that. And I'm afraid! Afraid for you! Do you know what it'd do to me if something happens to you?" I stopped hitting him and clasped my hands over my own chest, as though there was a danger my heart might fall out. "This! This would break. Shatter. Crumble. Crumble until it was dust." I dropped my hands. "Blown away on the wind until there was nothing left."

Silence fell between us, broken occasionally by my gasps as I tried to get over my sobs. It was so quiet that I heard my cell phone buzz in my purse. Zoe, I realized. In the wake of what had happened with Adrian, she seemed like something from another life. Slowly, reality seeped into me. She was very much a part of this life, and she was probably afraid that Jill was going to turn me into a snack.

I broke from Adrian and read the text, which was about

what I expected. I told her I was fine and was on my way home. When I looked back up, Adrian was watching me with a longing and despair that made me want to rush back to him. But I knew I'd never leave then, and it was time to go. The rest of the world was marching on.

"We'll talk later," I whispered, not that I had any clue what else to say. I found my wallet and set some cash on the back of the couch. "To get you by."

"Sydney . . ." He took a step forward and reached toward me.

"Later," I reiterated. "Go get some sleep. And remember, I love you. No matter what else comes, I love you."

It seemed like a paltry thing in the face of all that plagued him, but for now, it would have to be enough.

CHAPTER 11

ADRIAN

IT WAS THE TEARS THAT BROKE ME.

Maybe I could've stayed obstinate and argued against her, making excuses about why I was trapped by spirit. I could've probably done a decent job, even against her superior logic. But as I began sobering up after she left, the image of those tears haunted me. I'd always rejoiced in those rare moments of passion I saw in her eyes, that deeper emotional side she kept guarded. She wasn't someone who showed her feelings easily to others, yet I alone was special enough to see the full wealth of her emotions when she was full of joy and desire. And tonight, I'd apparently been special enough to witness her sorrow too.

It ate me up, especially because the next time I saw her, she acted as though nothing had happened. She was good to her word. She wasn't going to leave me. But despite her smiles and her cool countenance, I knew she must be frustrated. I had a problem—no, I *was* a problem. One she couldn't solve. It had to be driving her crazy, and the more I thought about it, the more

I realized she shouldn't have to solve it. I needed to step up. No one had ever cried for me before. Honestly, I didn't think I was worth anyone's tears.

"But I have to be," I told Jill one day. "If she cares that much and can hurt so much for me . . . how can I let her feelings go to waste? She thinks I'm important. I have to prove that I can be."

"You *are* important," Jill assured me.

We were sitting outside her dorm, enjoying a surge of winter warmth. The shadow of the sprawling stucco building kept the worst of the light away from us.

I shook my head. "I don't know. I don't know what I can offer her or the world. I thought it was spirit. I thought the things I can do with it would be my contribution to the world. Like you and Olive." I'd heard nothing about Olive since she'd gone to Court, and for all I knew, my efforts might have actually failed.

Jill squeezed my hand and smiled. "Well, it's certainly a contribution as far as I'm concerned, but Sydney was right— you don't know what else you might be capable of. Most people don't leave their mark on the world through big miracles. Some do," she added quickly. "But sometimes the biggest impact is made by a series of small, quiet things. You won't be able to do anything like that if you're—"

"—locked away or dead?" I finished, echoing Sydney's words.

Jill winced. "Let's not think about anything like that. No point stressing over what hasn't happened. Just work on what you can control now."

I slung an arm around her. "There you go again, Jailbait. Being all wise beyond your years."

"Your wisdom must be rubbing off on me. You're already doing great things without even trying." She leaned into me. "But seriously, Adrian. Try it. Try to stop spirit and see what happens."

"I haven't used it since then. Not even to look at auras." I also hadn't had a single drink, not even my daily allotted one.

"It's only been a few days. Not to say your sacrifice isn't noble. But are you going to be able to resist using spirit if . . . I don't know . . . if, say, Sydney cuts her leg shaving? Are you going to be able to resist, or are you going to think, 'Oh, a little spirit healing on that cut won't hurt'?"

"She does have great legs," I admitted. "I'd hate to see them marred."

"Exactly. And you'd think that a teeny, tiny bit of spirit wouldn't hurt anything. And then you'd think that the next time. And the next time—"

I held my hands up. "Okay, okay. I get it. Thank God Sydney's too careful for this shaving fiasco to even be a possibility." We both laughed at that, and then the severity of the situation settled back on me. "You win. I'll try . . . but I just can't shake the feeling I'm being selfish if I do this. I've been selfish my whole life. It'd be nice if I'd overcome that."

Jill met me squarely in the eye. "Every time you use spirit . . . is it just to do good?"

I took a long time to answer. "You're asking me something you already know the answer to," I said. I used spirit for the rush because I felt blissful and godly. At times, I got the same high I would from drinking or smoking.

"Then there you go," she said. "See what happens. If it doesn't work, you stop. It's a pill, not a lifelong commitment."

"Why does that sound familiar?"

She grinned mischievously. "It's what you told Sydney about birth control pills."

Hard to believe I'd nearly forgotten about that. "Ah, yes. A conversation you're best left out of. We need to preserve your innocence for as long as possible."

Jill's wry expression was another of those that looked too wise for her age. "That ended the moment we were bonded."

Just then, Sydney and Zoe stepped out of the dorm's front door. They didn't see us, sitting on our far bench, and Jill called out to them. Zoe stiffened. Sydney smiled, though it was a polite Alchemist smile.

I leaned back and crossed my legs, hoping I looked as insolent as possible. "Well, well. The Sisters Sage. Where are you guys off to? Volunteer work at the library? Liquidation sale at the Container Store?"

Incredibly, Sydney managed to keep a straight face. Aside from reinforcing my love for her, it also made me want to take her to a poker game sometime. Between that and my aura reading, we'd make a killing. "Close. Zoe needs some graphing paper for her math class."

"Ah," I said. "Office supplies. That was going to be my next guess. I only held off because I figured you guys kept reams of that stuff under your beds."

And still, Sydney managed that amazing control, though her lips *did* twitch ever so slightly. She glanced at Jill. "Need anything?"

Jill shook her head, but I piped in, "I could use a new sketchbook and some pigment sticks and—"

Sydney sighed and put on a tormented expression. "Adrian,

177

I wasn't talking to you. Come on, Zoe. We'll see you guys later."
They started to walk away, and then Sydney abruptly halted.
"Oh! I have to talk to Jill about something real quick. Here." She
tossed Zoe her keys. "You can bring it out of the parking garage."

Zoe's eyes widened like Sydney had just said Christmas
was coming early. It was actually kind of sweet, and I had to
remember that Zoe was a perpetual scourge upon my love life.
"Really? Oh! Thank you!" She snatched the keys without a
second thought and trotted away.

Sydney watched her fondly. "Really?" she asked me. "A
Container Store liquidation?"

"Come on," I said. "Don't act like you wouldn't be all over
that."

She grinned and turned back to us. The sunlight made her
hair turn to molten gold, and it took my breath away. "Maybe,"
she agreed. "Depends on how tasteful the colors were."

"I'm guessing you don't actually have to talk to me?" Jill
asked, with a sly smile.

Sydney shrugged and tucked some of that marvelous hair
behind her ear. "Not specifically. Mostly I just wanted some
breathing space. It's nice to talk to both of you." But her eyes
fell on me, and I could've cut the tension between us. I knew
that she, like me, was having a mental struggle in staying apart.
I would've given anything to hold her just then, to trace the
edge of her cheek or feel the strands of her hair between my
fingers. Clearing her throat, she looked away and seemed to
be groping for a safe subject. Well, a semi-safe one. Her voice
dropped as her eyes turned back up with a gleam.

"I did it." She cast a quick glance around before continuing.
"The salt. I got all four elements into it."

Jill caught her breath, just as consumed by the quest as Sydney and me. "You think you can use it to replicate Marcus's ink?"

Sydney nodded eagerly. "The hard work's done. It just needs to be ground up and suspended in any ink solution to use for tattooing. Then, I need a guinea pig. I guess the brave thing would be to try it on myself."

"I have absolute faith in your abilities," I told her, "but maybe you should wait and experiment with one of Marcus's starry-eyed recruits."

"I suppose I could. I mean, I don't think it'll cause any harm. The biggest problem will be whether it works or not. And the only way we can find out is if the Alchemists try to re-ink the guinea pig—which none of us want." Her small, thoughtful frown was adorable. "Unless I could get a hold of Alchemist ink and do more experiments . . . but, ugh. That won't be easy without sanctioning. And I don't have an earth user around either."

I scoffed. "I'm sure Abe would love to help."

"Oh, yes," said Sydney. "I'm sure he would. I'm sure he'd love to know *all* about my side project."

Zoe pulled up just then in that beast of a car. She didn't drive over the curb or crash into the building, so I supposed that was promising. Nonetheless, I saw Sydney's sharp eyes studying the exterior for even the tiniest ding. Satisfied, she took the driver's seat from Zoe and waved goodbye to us. Her eyes held mine, and for a few moments, I was suspended in that amber gaze. I sighed as she drove off, and when I glanced down, I saw Jill watching me knowingly.

"Fine," I said. "I'll make an appointment." She hugged me.

I called a psychiatrist recommended by Carlton's health center and kind of hoped it would take a while to get in. After all, specialists were always busy, right? This one apparently was—but had just had a cancellation for tomorrow. The receptionist told me I was incredibly lucky, so what I could do? I accepted and then skipped mixed media the next day, earning "slacker" name-calling when I asked Rowena to let me know what I missed.

The doctor's name was Ronald Mikoski, but I promptly forgot that because he looked exactly like Albert Einstein, complete with disheveled white hair and mustache. I'd thought there'd be a couch where I'd lie back and talk about my mother, but instead, he directed me to a plush armchair while he settled behind a desk. Instead of a notebook, he had a laptop.

"Well, Adrian," Einstein began. "Tell me what brings you in here today."

I started to say, "My girlfriend made me," but that sounded petulant.

"My girlfriend thought it'd be a good idea," I amended. "I want to get some antidepressants."

The bushy eyebrows rose. "Do you? Well, we don't just hand out prescriptions around here, but let's get to the bottom of things first. Are you depressed?"

"Not at the moment."

"But you get that way sometimes?"

"Sure. I mean, well, everyone does, right?"

He met my gaze levelly. "Yes, of course, but is yours worse than the average person's?"

"Who can say?" I shrugged. "It's all subjective, right?"

"Does your girlfriend think it's worse than the average person's?"

I hesitated. "Yes."

"Why?"

That made me falter. I didn't know if I was ready to talk about that. I hadn't expected to. I knew enough about mental health from Lissa to understand that psychiatrists prescribed medicine and therapists talked you through your problems. I'd thought I could just come in here, say I needed pills, and get them.

"Because . . . I drink when I get down."

Einstein's fingers tapped away. "A lot?"

I was ready with another "subjective" quip but chose to answer bluntly. "Yes."

"When you're happy too?"

"I guess . . . but what's wrong with letting loose?"

"Tell me how you feel when you 'get down.'"

Again, it was another opening for a joke. Like, I should've said something about getting down at a dance club. After all, how could I describe what I felt in those dark moments when spirit's shadow seized hold of my soul? And even if I could find the words, how could he understand? How could anyone truly, truly understand? No one could, and that was part of what made things so bad. I always felt alone. Even another spirit user couldn't completely understand my experience. We were all in our own personal hells, and of course, I couldn't actually mention spirit specifically.

Yet, I found myself talking to Einstein anyway, describing everything as best I could. After a while, he stopped typing and just listened, occasionally asking me to clarify my feelings. Soon, he shifted from how I felt when depressed and wanted to know how I felt when I was happy. He seemed especially interested in my spending habits and any "unusual behaviors." When we'd exhausted that, he gave me a bunch of questionnaires that asked variations of the same questions.

"Man," I said, handing them back. "I had no idea it was this hard to qualify as crazy."

I saw a glint of amusement in his eyes. "'Crazy' is a term that's used incorrectly and far too often. It's also used with stigma and finality." He tapped his head. "We're all chemicals, Adrian. Our bodies, our brains. It's a simple yet vastly sophisticated system, and every so often, something goes awry. A cell mutation. A neuron misfiring. A lack of a neurotransmitter."

"My girlfriend would love this," I said. I nodded at the paperwork. "So, if I'm not crazy, do I still get the pills?"

Einstein skimmed through the pages, nodding as though he was seeing exactly what he expected. "If you like, but not the ones you came in for. Your situation is more complex than just depression. You exhibit a lot of the classic symptoms of bipolar disorder."

There was something sinister about the word "disorder." "What's that mean? In words that don't begin with 'neuro'?"

That actually got a smile from him, though it looked a little sad. "It means, in very simple terms, that your brain makes your lows too low and your highs too high."

"Are you saying it's possible to be too happy?" I was starting to get very uneasy about this. Maybe the fact that his patients canceled on short notice should've been a warning sign that he wasn't a very good doctor.

"It depends on what you do." He opened up the packet of papers I'd filled out. "You spent eight hundred dollars on a record set recently?"

"Yeah, so? It's the purest form of music."

"Was it something you'd been wanting for a while? Something you've been searching for?"

I thought back to when I'd walked past the handwritten sign on campus. "Um, no. The opportunity just came up, and I thought it was a good idea."

"Do you have a history of other impulse purchases?"

"No. Well, I mean, I once sent a girl flowers every day for a month. And I also had a giant box of perfumes sent to her. And then I bought my current girlfriend some custom perfume that kind of cost a lot. And I technically bought a car for her. But you can't judge those," I added quickly, seeing his wry look. "I was in love. We all do things like that in pursuit of the fairer sex, right?" Silence answered. "Maybe I should just take a money management class."

He gave a small, nondescript grunt. "Adrian, it's normal to be happy and sad. That's human life." I definitely didn't correct him there. "What's not normal is to be so drastically sad that you can't go on with typical activities or to be so happy that you impulsively engage in grandiose activities without thinking through the consequences—like excessive spending. And it's definitely not normal to switch so quickly between these drastic moods with little or no provocation."

I wanted to tell him that there *was* provocation, that spirit did these things to me. And yet, did the cause matter? If fire users burned themselves with their magic, it didn't change the fact that they needed first aid. If spirit was causing this bipolar thing, then didn't I still need treatment? My mind spun, and I suddenly found myself caught up in a chicken-and-egg dilemma. Maybe spirit didn't cause mental illness. Maybe people like Lissa and me were already "off" chemically and that's what made us gravitate to spirit.

"So what do you do about it?" I asked at last.

He took out a small notebook and scribbled something onto it. When he finished, he tore off the top sheet and handed it to me. "You get this prescription filled and take it."

"It's an antidepressant?"

"It's a mood stabilizer."

I stared at the paper like it might bite me. "That doesn't sound right. Is it going to 'stabilize' me so that I don't feel happy or sad? So that I don't feel anything?" I stood up abruptly. "No! I don't care if they're dangerous. I'm not giving up my emotions."

"Sit down," he said calmly. "No one's taking away your emotions. It's what I said before: We're all chemicals. You've got a couple that aren't at the right levels. This will adjust them, just as a diabetic would correct their insulin. You'll still feel things. You'll be happy. You'll be sad. You'll be angry. You just won't swing unpredictably into such wild directions. There's nothing wrong with this—and it's a hell of a lot safer than self-medicating with alcohol."

I sat back down and stared bleakly at the prescription. "This is going to kill my creativity, won't it? Without all my feelings, I won't be able to paint like I used to."

"That's the cry of artists everywhere," said Einstein, his expression hardening. "Will it affect certain things? Maybe, but you know what'll really interfere with your ability to paint? Being too depressed to get out of bed. Waking up in jail after a night of drunken debauchery. Killing yourself. Those things will hurt your creativity."

It was surprisingly similar to what Sydney had said about how I'd be able to accomplish things. "I'll be ordinary," I protested.

"You'll be healthy," he corrected. "And from there, you can become extraordinary."

"I like my art the way it is." I knew I sounded childish.

Einstein shrugged and sat back in his chair. "Then I guess you have to decide what's most important to you."

That required no thought at all. "She is."

He stayed quiet, but his expression said it all.

I sighed and stood up again. "I'll get it filled."

He gave me some information on side effects and warned that it could take trial and error to get things right. Walking out of that office and going to a pharmacy, rather than a liquor store, took more self-control than I'd had to muster in a while. I forced myself to listen as the pharmacist talked about dosing—and warned me against alcohol while on the prescription.

But when I got home, I didn't have the courage to open the bottle. I put on a record at random and sat on my couch, staring at the bottle in my hand, more confused than I'd ever expected to be. This mood stabilizer was a mystery. I'd thought I'd go in and take something like Lissa had, and even if I wasn't a huge fan of pills, at least I had her as a reference. But this? What would happen? What if Einstein was wrong, and I stopped feeling any emotions? What if it didn't do anything except cause the ghastly side effects he'd said were extremely rare?

On the other hand . . . what if it didn't stop spirit but *did* curb the darkness? That would be a dream come true. That was what Lissa had originally hoped the antidepressant would do. The complete numbing of spirit had been a surprise. It was impossible to think I might still keep the magic yet stay in control of my life. The idea was so tempting, I opened the bottle and put one of the pills in the palm of my hand.

But I couldn't take it. I was too afraid—afraid of losing control and afraid of gaining it. I tried to think of Sydney but couldn't get a clear grip on her in my mind. One moment, she was laughing and golden in the sun. Another, she was crying. I wanted what was best for her . . . and yet, I knew what she actually wanted was what was best for me. It was so hard to know what that was, though. On a nearby table, Hopper—in statue form—seemed to watch me judgmentally, and I turned him so he faced away from me.

The music drifted over me, and I realized with a start I'd put on Jefferson Airplane. I laughed, but it soon turned into a sigh.

"'One pill makes you larger, and one pill makes you small.'" I squeezed the pill tightly in my hand. "'And the ones that Mother gives you don't do anything at all.'"

Take the damn pill, Adrian. The chastising voice in my head was my own, not Aunt Tatiana's, thankfully. I opened my hand and studied the edges of the pill. *Just take it.* I had a glass of water and everything.

But I still held off.

The chiming of the Love Phone made me jump. Still holding the pill in one hand, I found the phone with the other and read a text from Sydney:

Told Z I left my phone in the store, so I went back and got a sketchpad and some pigments. Know any starving artist who could use them?

My heart swelled, so full of love I didn't know how any physical body could possibly contain such power. I felt like my chest would burst.

"Okay, Alice," I said, eyeing the pill. "Let's see what you can do."

I put the pill in my mouth and swallowed.

CHAPTER 12

SYDNEY

I DIDN'T BLINK AN EYE when my AP chemistry teacher told us we had a pop quiz. But when Zoe told me our dad was about to be in Palm Springs, I nearly had a meltdown.

"What? When's he getting here?" I exclaimed. We'd just sat down for lunch in the cafeteria.

"Tonight. He wants to have dinner." She picked up a french fry and scrutinized it as though it held more interest than the news she'd just delivered. "They burned these today."

Food was the last thing on my mind, and it had nothing to do with concerns about weight. "How long have you known he was coming today?"

She shrugged. "I told you last week."

"Yeah, but you didn't exactly fine-tune the date and time! Couldn't you have given me a little more warning?"

At last, I warranted more attention than her lunch. "What's the problem? It's Dad! You should be excited. It's not like you have to prepare or anything."

Well, I wouldn't have minded preparing mentally. Even though I'd known he was coming, not having a fixed date had allowed me to relax about it. The rest of our gang was sitting with us—Jill, Eddie, Angeline, and Neil—and I could see them watching the exchange with interest. Only Jill really knew the full scope of my parental drama, and when it was clear neither Zoe nor I was going to say anything more on the subject, Jill helpfully shifted the conversation and began talking about some expo her sewing club was doing.

I robotically began eating my stir-fry without really tasting it. If I pretended to be interested in my food, maybe no one would notice I was on the verge of a panic attack. My dad would be here tonight! *Calm down,* I ordered myself. It was only dinner, and since we'd presumably be in public, he'd have to limit his ranting. It wasn't like he was going to search my room or follow me around.

And yet, no matter how hard I tried to soothe myself with logic, I couldn't shake my unease. Palm Springs had become a sanctuary for me, in which I tucked away all my secrets—not just my romance with Adrian, but also my true friendship with the others. And, of course, my illicit magic use. I kept all those things well guarded, but just knowing he would be here, in my territory, made me feel as though my entire life had just been exposed.

"Hey, Neil," said Angeline abruptly. "You ever staked a Strigoi?"

Considering Jill had just been talking about catwalk lighting, it was kind of a weird subject change. From Neil's expression, he thought so too.

"Er, well, not a real one."

"But you've had lots of practice on fake ones."

"Yes, of course." He relaxed a little, now that he was in familiar territory. "It was a requisite part of our curriculum."

She brightened. "You think you could give me some pointers after school today?"

Eddie frowned. "We went over that a couple months ago."

"Well, yeah," she said, "but I mean, it can't hurt to get different opinions on it, right?"

"How can there be different opinions on driving a stake through a monster's heart?" asked Jill. Her face declared she wasn't a fan of Neil and Angeline spending time together.

"I'm sure Neil and Eddie have different skills," Angeline insisted.

It was a dangerous comment, suggesting one might be more skilled than the other. The guys' faces confirmed as much. "I'd be happy to show you," said Neil, puffing with pride. "You're right that you might benefit from a different style."

"I'd be interested in seeing this," remarked Eddie.

"Me too," said Jill.

"No." Angeline shook her head adamantly. "You'd just be a distraction, and this is serious business. Just me and Neil." From the way she looked at him through her lashes, I wondered what business she had in mind. I grabbed hold of her arm as we were all dispersing for our classes later.

"Why the aggressive move on Neil?" I asked. "You were moping about Trey a couple weeks ago."

Her face fell. "Still am. Can't get him out of my mind. So I figure I have to get serious about Neil."

I didn't really know how to immediately respond to that. "But you said you didn't think you could really get into him."

190

"That's why I have to try," she explained, with a look that said I might not be as smart as everyone claimed. "Because then I won't think about Trey."

There was no point in fighting it anymore, and while I was dubious about her romantic methods, I knew her and Trey staying apart was a sound plan. "Well, good luck with that."

Anxiety about my dad continued to eat me up all day. Although I knew I should stay far away from Adrian today, I couldn't help myself. As soon as I stepped into Ms. Terwilliger's room for my independent study, she took one look at my face and smiled. "Go," she said. "Whatever it is you need to do, go."

"Thank you, ma'am!" I was moving before I finished speaking.

I headed over to his place and let myself in with my key. He was sitting in his living room, working on an unexpected project. A number of his paintings lay on the ground, and he was carefully cutting them up into pieces. It was enough to momentarily allay the panic over my dad.

"What's this?" I asked. "Did you hate them all that much?"

He smiled up at me. "Not exactly. I got an idea for the self-portrait. I realized all of these rejects are technically part of me, so I'm going to combine all of them into a collage there." He nodded up to a canvas on an easel, which already held the remnants of a painting he'd done of his aura.

"You're bending the assignment a little," I said, sitting down beside him.

He returned to his cutting. "I'm sure my professor will be so amazed by my brilliance and ingenuity that she'll want to keep it for herself and hang it above her fireplace. Or maybe her bedroom. Would you be cool with that? Or would that be weird?"

"I guess I could learn to share you," I said.

"You're a trooper, Sage." Setting down the scissors, he turned his full attention on me and raised an eyebrow. "What's wrong?"

I almost smiled at that. Everyone said I concealed my feelings, but he always seemed to know how I felt. "You read my aura?"

I kept my tone light. We'd spoken very little about spirit in the last two weeks, ever since his breakdown at the pawnshop. Thinking about him and the way the magic drove him to such extremes still ate me up inside, but I'd been careful not to nag. He already knew I was worried, and I wasn't going to bring it up again, unless he did first or I saw a reason. And recently, he'd seemed to be on good behavior. I'd seen no signs of excessive drinking or spirit use. That didn't mean the problem was gone, of course, but it was a relief to be in calm waters while I tried to puzzle out a way to help him.

"Didn't need to see your aura." He tapped my forehead. "You get a cute little frown there when you've got something bothering you."

"Not everything about me is cute."

"That's true. Some things are cute. The rest are sexy." His voice was low as he leaned toward me. "So amazingly, agonizingly sexy that it's a wonder I can get anything done when all I ever think about is the taste of your lips and the touch of your fingertips on my skin and the way your legs feel when I—"

"Adrian," I interrupted.

His eyes smoldered. "Yes?"

"Shut up."

We reached for each other at the same time, and all

thoughts of my dad melted away at the crush of Adrian's mouth on mine. Until him, I had always believed discussions of the periodic table or Latin declension would turn me on. Nope. When I touched Adrian, it was all about him. I came alive in a way I didn't know was possible and became obsessed with the feel of our bodies wrapped together. I think sometimes he thought I was holding back on sex because I wasn't ready to cross that physical threshold. But I actually was ready. Believe me, I was. It was the mental threshold that still held me up—the knowledge that once you crossed that line, there was no going back.

And in moments like this, when he laid me back on the floor and leaned over me, I wasn't sure why I'd ever want to go back. He slid his hand over my leg and hip, then up and under my shirt. There was a confidence in every single move he made, an assurance in knowing exactly how each touch would take me to the edge. His eyes, burning with both desire and urgency, held me as he took in my response, and then he brought his hungry lips back to mine. Meanwhile, my fingers fumbled to undo his buttons, though I didn't take his shirt off yet. It was just enough to run my hands over his bare chest and feel that warm skin under my fingertips. One day, I'd know what it felt like to have all my skin against his, but when he finally broke off our frantic kissing, I knew today wasn't the day—especially when he pointed out the obvious.

"Not saying I don't want to go on," he told me, voice husky, "but by my count, we've got ten minutes until you need to hightail it back to school. Unless . . ." He brightened. "Your sister got transferred?" When I laughed and shook my head, he sighed and eased off me. "Well then, as hard as it is to believe, your mind takes precedence over your body. Tell me what's wrong."

I didn't have to imagine how that concession felt for him, but I was pretty sure I felt the same. Reluctantly, I sat up and leaned against the couch.

"So, Zoe told me today that—"

"Wait. Are you going to talk like that?"

I glanced down and realized he was referring to the fact that my shirt was sitting on the floor beside me. "My bra's still on. What's the problem?"

"The problem is that I'm distracted. Very distracted. If you want my undivided attention and wisdom, you'd better put the shirt back on."

I smiled and scooted over to him. "Why, Adrian Ivashkov, are you admitting weakness?" I reached out to touch his cheek, and he caught my wrist with a fierceness that was surprisingly provocative.

"Of course. I never claimed strength in the face of your charms, Sage. I'm just an ordinary man. Now put the shirt back on."

I leaned forward, testing the strength of his hold. "Or what?" With my free hand, I caught hold of one of my bra straps and started to pull it down . . .

. . . which is how we ended up kissing and rolling around the floor again.

"Damn it," he said a little while later, breaking free again. "Don't make me be the responsible one here. We're down to five minutes."

"Okay, okay." I made myself decent and gave him an extra-abbreviated rundown of the news about my dad. "The whole

194

time I've been in Palm Springs, I've felt like I'm in control. With him here . . . I don't know. I suddenly feel like there'll be a power shift."

Adrian was all business now. "You aren't going to lose any power. He can't take your life away. He can't take away this." He gestured around us. "It's just dinner. He's probably going to talk about the divorce."

"I know, I know. It's just been so hard keeping secrets from Zoe, but I've pulled it off. He plays in a whole other league."

"You're smarter than him. You're a better person than him." He clasped my hands and kissed them, but it was a gesture of support and affection, not raging passion. "There's nothing to worry about. Be your clever Sage self and tell me about it later tonight."

"If you're awake," I teased. Adrian's dream visits had been few and far between the last week or so. He'd been sleeping better than usual and had apparently listened to me about the importance of avoiding excessive spirit use. "And we still need to get in touch with Marcus again, so you'll have to be ready for that soon."

"I guess I'll just have to drink more coffee to stay awake." There was a sly glint in his eye.

"Watch it," I warned. Taunting me with caffeine was a low blow. "You better stay on good behavior if you want some indecency again."

"Really? And here I thought it was bad behavior that earned me that."

We kissed goodbye, and I headed back to Amberwood a little later than intended. It was worth it, though. That short talk with Adrian—and the longer physical contact—had strengthened me. I felt confident, filled with both love for Adrian and readiness for my battles. I could handle my dad.

Mentioning Marcus made me think of my charmed salt. So far, I hadn't done anything with it. Maybe Adrian was right, and Marcus would want to test it on a new recruit. Ms. Terwilliger was keeping it at her house for me, and although I was familiar enough with Alchemist tattooing ink, I wanted her advice on the magical properties of certain substances that might go into the blend. But when I walked into her classroom, I saw I'd have no chance for magical discussion. Zoe was there, waiting impatiently. Despite being a little late, I'd made it back only a few minutes after classes had ended. She must have run straight from her last one here.

"There you are," she said.

Ms. Terwilliger glanced up from her desk and gave me a knowing look. "Thank you for taking those papers to the office for me. I was just explaining to your cousin how helpful you've been to me."

I smiled stiffly. "Happy to help, ma'am. Am I excused?"

"Yes, yes, of course." She returned to her paperwork without a second glance.

"What's the urgency?" I asked as Zoe and I left the classroom.

"We have to go meet Dad now," she said.

"Now? It's not dinnertime. It's not even senior-citizen dinnertime."

"Dad got into town early and didn't want to waste time."

I tried not to scowl. "And once again, I'm the last to know."

She shot me a wounded look. "You seem to have *other things* you think are more important. Figured you wouldn't care."

"Don't start," I warned. We reached the parking garage, and

I did my usual scan of Quicksilver to make sure no idiot parker had scratched the paint.

To my surprise, Zoe backed down. "You're right. We shouldn't be fighting with each other. Today we're sisters, not just Alchemists. We need to unite against our common enemy."

"You mean Mom?" I asked incredulously. Zoe nodded in confirmation, and I had to bite my lip on a retort, lest I really did get a fight going.

The restaurant my dad had chosen was exactly what I would've expected from him. He had no patience for what he saw as frills and excesses, so any fancy restaurant that played on mystery or romance was out. Yet, despite his pragmatism, he also couldn't handle a bare-bones café that would be loud and have questionable cleaning and food standards. So, he'd managed to find a Japanese fine-dining place adjacent to a hotel that prided itself on minimalism. The decor was stark, with lots of clean lines, but the food and reputation were outstanding.

"Hello, Dad," I said. He was already at the table when we arrived and didn't stand up to hug us. Not even Zoe expected that.

"Sydney, Zoe," he said. Naming me first wasn't a sign of preference, so much as respecting the birth order. If Carly had been here, he would have named her first. For double efficiency, that was also alphabetical order. A waiter came by to offer us water and tea just then, and my dad handed over the menu. "This is a dinner menu. Please bring us the lunch menu."

"Lunchtime is over, sir," the waiter said politely. "We've switched menus."

My dad met him squarely in the eye. "Are you trying to tell me three thirty is dinnertime?"

"No . . ." The waiter glanced helplessly around at the empty restaurant, save for two businessmen drinking at the bar. "It's not really anytime."

"Well, in that case, I see no reason I should have to pay dinner prices. Bring me the lunch menu."

"But lunch ended at two."

"Then bring me a manager."

The waiter left and returned quickly—with a lunch menu. I tried not to sink into my seat.

"Now then," said my dad, supremely proud of himself. "Let's get food out of the way and get down to business."

My stomach lurched as I wondered what kind of business he had to take care of exactly. Even without that anxiety, I wasn't really hungry but made a good faith effort and ordered sushi.

"That's a small plate," my dad noted.

The correct words flowed right off my tongue. "It's also the cheapest. Even on the lunch menu, this place is overpriced. No point in going overboard when eating during business is a social convention anyway. Besides, we're getting free food at our dorm tonight as part of our tuition."

He nodded in approval. "Very true. You look like you've gained some weight too, so it's smart to back off."

I gave him a stiff smile, swallowing the urge to tell him I still fit firmly in a size four. I was just a much healthier-looking four, rather than a slightly malnourished one. Meanwhile, Zoe—who'd been about to set the menu down—quickly opened it again when she heard him rebuke me. She'd probably planned on ordering tempura, one of her favorite dishes, and now feared my dad's ire over fried food. I could stomach him making comments about my weight, but if he said anything to her, I was going to have to resist the urge to throw my tea at him. In the end, she ordered what I did, even though I knew she didn't really like sushi.

Once the waiter left with our orders, my dad took out two manila envelopes and handed us each one. "No point in wasting time. As you can see, I've gathered information to help you in your testimony against your mother."

I had to shut my jaw as I flipped through pages of my mother's life. College transcripts, job history. There were a number of photographs, including one taken during what looked like a yoga class. I held it up. It showed several students, including my mom, walking out of the studio and carrying their mats.

"What is this?" I asked.

"See that man there?" My dad pointed at one of the guys talking to my mother. "That's her instructor. She talked to him a lot during her sessions."

"Well, wouldn't she if he's her instructor?"

There was an ugly sneer on my dad's lips. "Unless there were other reasons."

"What?" The picture slipped from my hand. "No. No way. Mom would never have an affair."

He shrugged. "She wants a divorce, doesn't she?"

I could've named a dozen reasons she wanted one, but I instead opted for neutrality. "Do you have any other proof?"

"No," he admitted. "But it doesn't matter. The insinuation is enough. We just need to make her look unreliable. Dropping out of college helps, as does her sketchy employment history. She's never held a full-time job."

"Because she was taking care of us," I said. My dad had

looked out for our education, but she was the one who handled our day-to-day lives, managing the house and hugging us through our injuries.

"Again—not important. There's enough documentation here to demonstrate what a fickle parental figure she'd be. At the very least, it'll ensure joint custody, though I'd be surprised if I didn't get full."

"Do you have any ins on the legal side?" I asked, again with a forced smile.

He scowled. "No, though not for lack of trying."

"So they'll just have to base the case on facts," I remarked, deadpan.

"Yes. We'll be fine if you girls do your part." He paused as the waiter delivered hot towels. "I know I don't have to tell you how important this is. Zoe is a valuable asset in our cause, which is growing more and more critical each day. The reintroduction of vampire hunters has gotten a lot of attention. We can't let their chaotic nature ruin what we've worked for."

That was a relief, at least. Most Alchemists found the Warriors of Light to be a primitive group of trigger-happy rebels, though Marcus had discovered recent evidence that some Alchemists were working with the Warriors. There was also evidence that the Warriors knew about Jill. I was glad my dad was on the side of reason and mainstream Alchemist thought here.

To my surprise, he looked directly at me. "A lot of what we know is a result of your efforts." It was as close as he could get to a compliment.

"I just did what I had to do," I told him.

"Between that, uncovering Keith's crimes, and stomaching

that wedding, you've caught the attention of many of our higher-ups."

Awkward silence fell. Condemnation was more our status quo than praise, and I certainly wasn't sure how to handle it. Zoe cleared her throat. "I supervised a feeding by myself," she said proudly. "I mean, not the actual blood drinking part. But Sydney couldn't make it when the Moroi had to go to Clarence Donahue's house for a feeding. So I took over."

My dad jerked his gaze back to me. "Why couldn't you make it?"

"I had to work on a school project," I explained.

"I see." But there was a small frown on his face.

"Sydney's always working on school projects," Zoe added. I think she was hurt that her "supervising" role hadn't received more acknowledgment. "Always gone after school. Always running errands and hanging out with her history teacher."

"We don't hang out," I countered.

"You have coffee together, don't you?" asked Zoe triumphantly.

"Well, yeah, but that's not—"

"What subject is this for?" my dad interrupted. "Chemistry?"

Zoe and I answered in unison. "History."

His frown deepened. "That's a nonessential subject. All of them are, actually. You've already received a superior education."

"Yes, but keeping my cover is essential," I pointed out. "Being an exemplary student has a lot of advantages. They give me a lot of freedom, and being able to leave campus after hours to run errands for Ms. Terwilliger means I'm able to get away and help the Moroi if needed without drawing attention. We can't risk them doing something stupid and creating a scene."

That seemed to mollify our dad, but Zoe was on the offensive now. "It's more than that. You and her are friends. You talk about vacations to Greece and Rome."

Where had this come from? I'd expected to face interrogation from my dad, not her. "So what if we talk sometimes? She's human. No harm."

"The harm is you can't give your full attention to the mission." There was a hard look on Zoe's face I didn't like. "And maybe she's human, but you certainly have Moroi and dhampir friends."

Our dad's eyebrows shot up, but the food arrived just then, giving me time to build a response. He jumped before I could. "What does that mean—Moroi and dhampir friends?"

"Sydney hangs out with them," Zoe declared. "Does favors for them."

I fixed her with a hard glare that made her flinch. "It's my job to oversee them. There's a fine line of learning how to socialize with them in order to earn their trust and get them to do what I need—something you haven't picked up on yet. Good God, I had to *live* with one! I was ordered to, something you'd never be able to handle, seeing as you freaked out 'supervising' that dinner. So don't judge my style, seeing as you aren't the one who uncovered Keith, the Warriors, and everything else."

"Now, now, girls. Don't fight." Yet I couldn't help but notice my dad looked delighted by it. I think he thought competition made us stronger. "You both make excellent points. Zoe, Sydney has demonstrated time and again how loyal she is and how outstandingly she can perform her job. Sydney, Zoe's right that you shouldn't get too caught up in this teacher or the Moroi, even if it is part of your cover. There are certain lines that must never, ever be crossed. You saw that with Keith, when he succumbed to making deals with Moroi."

Zoe and I were cowed for several moments. "Do you know how Keith is?" I asked.

My dad's features smoothed out. "Yes, he's been released."

I was so surprised, I dropped the sushi I'd carefully lifted with my chopsticks. "He has?"

"Yes. He was successfully re-educated and is now working in Charleston. In an office, of course. He's certainly not ready for the field. But it's a relief to all of us that the education took. It doesn't always, unfortunately. Not even when they reinforce the tattoo."

The hair stood up on the back of my neck. "Reinforce the tattoo? You mean re-inking?"

"Somewhat." He was very careful with his words. "Let's just say, there are certain modifications to the ink that can help troubled souls like Keith."

Until Marcus had told me about this, I'd never heard anyone give voice to it. "Ink with stronger compulsion for obedience and group loyalty?"

My dad's eyes narrowed. "How do you know about that?" he demanded.

"I've heard rumors." I prayed he wouldn't demand details but was fully prepared to lie. His gaze weighed me for several long moments before he finally decided not to press me for more.

"It's an ugly step," he said at last. "And it relies on getting help from *them*. But it's necessary. People like Keith are a danger not just to us, but to all of humanity. Maybe the Moroi aren't as bad as the Strigoi, but they aren't natural. They aren't part of the order of this world, and we must keep their influence away from our fellow man. It's our duty. Our divine duty. Anyone who can't understand the balance we maintain with these monsters hurts the cause. Yes, it took a lot of intervention, but Keith has been reclaimed. We've saved his soul. You did, Sydney." Inspiration lit my dad's face. "You should talk to him sometime. You should see the good you've done."

I shifted uncomfortably. "Oh, I—"

"After dinner," my dad said decisively. "We'll call him then."

A rebellious part of me wanted to ask, "Aren't we having lunch?" But I bit my tongue. I didn't really feel like talking anymore. Thankfully, Zoe was still gung ho to get his attention and talked enough for both of us. And as the meal wound down, it drifted back to the court hearing. I nodded along mechanically.

"I'm glad I can count on you two," he said as we stood up to leave. "Not that I doubted—but after Carly, well. It's hard to say."

"What about Carly?" I asked quickly. I noticed he hadn't left a tip, and I discreetly tossed cash on the table as we walked away.

He scowled. "She's going to speak on behalf of your mother. But don't worry. It won't be enough."

Joy filled me, and I struggled to keep it off my face. Carly was standing up to our dad! Admittedly, she didn't face the same pressures Zoe and I did, but I was so proud of my older sister. She was usually the timid one in the family. For her to make this stand for our mother meant she'd come a long way. I wondered if she'd ever have the courage to tell how Keith had raped her. This was a start.

Speaking of Keith . . . my father was determined to show me the "good" I'd done, no matter how much I assured him it

204

wasn't necessary. When we got to the parking lot, he made a couple of calls to get him through to Keith, and—worst of all—used the video feature. I silently begged for Keith to be doing something, anything, that would keep him away. No luck. After a minute or so, my dad finally got through, and Keith's face appeared on the phone's screen. Zoe and I crowded on each side of my dad.

"Mr. Sage," said Keith. His voice was flat. "It's so nice to hear from you."

I gasped in spite of myself. Keith had once been arrogant and obnoxious. In re-education, he'd been frantic and terrified. Now . . . there was nothing. He was blank. An automaton. One of his eyes was glass, but if I hadn't known which one, I never would have been able to tell now.

"I have Sydney and Zoe here," my dad explained. "Sydney's been worried about you."

"Hello, Sydney." I think he smiled, but it was hard to tell. "I've been wanting to thank you. I was sick, and now I'm better. I let myself get deceived by those creatures of evil. If not for you, I'd have lost my soul."

My tongue felt thick. "That . . . that's great, Keith. How is everything else? Outside Alchemist work?"

He frowned. "What do you mean?"

"Um, I don't know. Seen any good movies? Girlfriend?" I knew this was probably frivolous to my dad. "Are you happy?"

Keith barely even blinked. "My happiness doesn't matter. Only the work does. That and continuing to do penance."

"For . . . for what? For your moneymaking scheme with Clarence? I mean, it was bad . . . but it could've been worse." I had no idea why I was trying to defend him to himself, but there was just something deeply unsettling about all this talk of souls and penance—especially when I knew the Alchemists' real problem wasn't the side effects of Keith's scheme so much as the fact that he'd simply worked with a Moroi. "And you just said you were better."

"Better, but not cured." The tone of his voice sent chills through me. "Those who collaborate with those creatures for anything but the greater good have a long path to redemption, one I'm ready to walk. I have sinned against my own kind and let my soul become corrupted. I am ready to have the darkness purged."

"You sound legitimately sorry," I said weakly. "I mean, that's good, right? That's got to mean something."

"I am ready to have the darkness purged," he repeated. It was hard to say if he knew he was even talking to me. He sounded like he was reciting something. Something he'd recited many, many times, in fact.

Those who collaborate with those creatures for anything but the greater good have a long path to redemption. The impact of those words wasn't lost on me. I was doing a lot more than collaborating with Adrian. Was this what I risked? This . . . deadness? The last time I'd seen Keith, he'd been screaming for release from the Alchemists. It had been terrible, yet at the same time, there'd been something *real* to it. A fight. A fire within him. There was nothing now. Keith had been obnoxious and selfish, but he had also always been outgoing and full of personality—even if it was an annoying one. How did he go from cocky to . . . this? What had to be done to him to strip him of all that he was, to get him to agree to whatever he was told?

206

The tattoo, I realized. They must have re-inked him with some pretty serious compulsion. And yet . . . some gut instinct told me there was more. The Alchemist ink could make you obey simple commands and make you susceptible to suggestions. This complete personality reversal? That required greater intervention. I was seeing what had to be a combination of a reinforced tattoo and whatever they did in re-education.

I was also seeing what my fate might be if caught.

"Keith," I managed at last. "How exactly are you purging that darkness?"

"It's time to go," my father suddenly interrupted. "We're very happy to see you doing well, Keith, and will talk to you later."

Keith told us goodbye, and we headed out toward our respective cars. Zoe dared a quick, controlled hug to our dad before getting in Quicksilver. I turned to the driver's door, but he caught hold of my hand. I didn't resist because I was still numbed by what I'd just witnessed.

"Sydney," he said, eyes cold. "You truly have done outstanding work. I'm glad Zoe's here to learn from you. She's headstrong and untried but will eventually learn. And she's right about one thing—don't get distracted. Even if it's just this teacher of yours. There may be a time you can be allowed some recreation. It'd certainly be nice for you to continue talking to that young and upstanding Ian Jansen. But now, even a seemingly innocent social interaction—with a human—is dangerous. You must stay focused on your task. And I know I don't have to tell you about friendships with the Moroi and dhampirs."

"Of course not, sir." I wanted to gag.

He gave me what passed for a smile with him and then

turned without another word. I drove Zoe back to Amberwood, and awkwardness left over from our earlier spat lingered. As much I'd disliked her selling me out to our dad, I still loved her . . . and couldn't entirely blame her. He was an intimidating person, one who excelled at making you feel inadequate. I'd had plenty of experience with it.

"Hey," I said, noticing we were passing the ice cream place she and I had gone to last week. "You up for some praline pecan?"

Zoe stared straight ahead without even looking at it. "There's a lot of fat and sugar in that, Sydney." Silence fell for a few moments. "Maybe I should stop having driving lessons with Eddie."

"Is he a bad teacher? Has he done anything, um, sinister?"

"No . . ." The conflict in her voice was nearly palpable. "But he's still one of them. You heard what Dad said . . . what Keith said. No collaboration."

"It's not collaboration. It's business," I said pragmatically. "What if there's an emergency, and you have to drive? We need you prepared. It's for the greater good."

Her face relaxed. "I suppose you're right."

She was quiet again after that, giving my thoughts ample opportunity to spiral around as I contemplated possible consequences of today's meal. Maybe my sterling record still kept me untouchable, but Zoe had tattled on some of my other activities. Were my dad's suspicions raised? It was hard to say, but I would've preferred he had no reason to think twice about me.

And of course, I was still troubled by Keith. His face haunted me. What had they done to him? What had he endured in re-education? And how big a role had re-inking played? Those questions tumbled in my mind over and over, and when we reached the school, I made a decision. It was a difficult one, and one that wouldn't necessarily solve all my problems. But I had to act. Seeing Keith had driven home the desperation of my situation.

I had to make the ink. And I had to inject myself with it.

There was no other way. I had to start making preparations to find out if the ink would protect against Alchemist mental manipulation. One of Marcus's recruits would've been a better guinea pig, but there was no time to get one. Inez had said my magic use might muddle the results, but what else could I do? I had no clean test subject, and doing nothing was unacceptable. If there was a way to prevent others—and myself—from turning into Keith, I had to find it. This was my starting point, and I refused to waste another moment.

After the dorm's dinner, when Zoe went off to a study group, I prepared to go to Ms. Terwilliger's house after first calling her with a very surprising request. Maybe it was dangerous running out on Zoe after the earlier lecture, but I would claim it was a mandatory assignment if she questioned me later. As I was walking toward the student parking lot, I ran into Trey. He looked like he was on his way to work.

"Yo, Melbourne," he said, coming to a stop beside me. "I have to ask you something. Angeline's been hanging out with that dhampir. I just saw them walking off together. Is something going on with them?"

"Which dhampir?" I asked.

"The one with the fake British accent."

"I don't think it's fake."

"Well, whatever." Even I could read the jealousy in Trey's features. "What's up with them?"

"Pretty sure there's nothing."

"Then why are they always together?"

Because she's trying to get over you, I thought. "I think they're practicing or something. You know. Dhampir stuff." He didn't look convinced. "Maybe instead of stalking her, you should go out with someone else."

He sighed. "You don't think I've tried? How can anyone compare? You might not believe this, but there is *no one* like her at this school."

"Oh, I believe it," I said, thinking back to the time Angeline had forgotten her locker's combination and tried to get into it with an axe. No one was really sure where she'd gotten it from.

"Is she going to the dance with anyone?"

"What dance?"

He pointed to a sign hanging in the dorm's window that read VALENTINE'S DANCE. "Honestly, how do you miss this stuff?"

"I've got a lot on my mind."

"You don't think she'll go with Neil, do you?"

I thought about Neil's indifference and focus on duty. "No. I'm pretty sure that won't happen."

He put his hands in his pockets and stared off morosely. I waited for some further comment, but when none came, I felt my eyes widen in surprise. "Is it really that big a deal? Her going to do the dance with someone?"

"She's the big deal," he said, turning back to face me. "I think . . . I think I may have made a mistake with her. I thought I wanted the Warriors to accept me. But do I? What I really want is to wipe out evil vampires and right wrongs. That kind of thing. I don't need them to do that. I can think for myself and find a way to do that, maybe a way that involves Angeline."

I found myself unexpectedly riveted, mostly because what he was suggesting echoed some of my own desires so closely. "So, what then? You're going to get back together?"

"I don't know. I need time to think about how I can make this all work. And I need her not to go out with Neil or any other guy in the meantime." He shot me a wry look. "I know, I know. That sounds incredibly sexist, wanting her to put her life on hold so *I* can figure out what I want. But this isn't exactly a typical situation we're in."

"Isn't that the truth," I muttered. More silence fell between us, and two revelations hit me. One was that as crazy as Trey and Angeline seemed together, I wanted them to work. The second was that I suddenly had an opportunity before me. "I'll help you. I'll help Angeline stay single."

"What?" He scrutinized me closely. "You can do that?"

"Sure," I said. It was an easy thing to promise, seeing as she was still hung up on him and her alleged rebound was completely disinterested, but Trey didn't know that. A smile broke out over his face—then faltered.

"What do you want in return?" he asked cautiously.

"What makes you think I want anything?"

"You're an Alchemist." Again, he couldn't quite manage the smile. "Alchemists don't give things away."

"Friends do," I said, wondering if I should feel hurt at the insinuation or ashamed that he was right in this case. "I'll help you with Angeline. But I need a favor—a big one and one that you, as a friend, are going to have to trust me on."

He considered for several moments. "Go on."

Excitement fluttered in my chest, and I attempted to sound calm and trustworthy. "How would you like another tattoo? One that no one can see?"

He stared in astonishment. "Are you feeling okay?"

"I'm serious. There's something I'm trying to do, kind of a side project, that could help a lot of people. Human people. If you could do this, it would be *huge*."

More than huge. Trey would be the perfect test subject.

"When you and tattoos are involved, they aren't just decorative," he reminded me. It was true. When I'd first come to Amberwood, I'd discovered that Keith was running an illicit ring of magical, performance-enhancing tattoos. It was what had landed him in trouble with the Alchemists. Trey had seen the dire side effects of Keith's handiwork.

"No, but this one's not going to control you. If it works, it'll actually protect you from mind control."

His eyebrows rose. "I didn't even know I was in danger of that. And if it doesn't work?"

"Then nothing will happen. You'll just have had the chance to prove how tough you are by enduring another tattoo." Well, I was pretty sure that nothing would happen. Ninety-nine percent sure. No need to mention the one percent. "Although . . . you'll eventually need another tattoo to prove it works."

"Sydney—"

"Trey, please." I caught hold of his arm. "I can't tell you everything, but trust me when I say this is really important. I hope you know me well enough to know I wouldn't ask something like this casually." His face confirmed that. "You said you wanted to right wrongs? Believe me, this'll do it. And you'll get help with Angeline."

"So you won't help me if I don't do this for you?"

I hesitated, and some of my vigor faded. There was no way I could blackmail him. "No. I wouldn't do that to you. I'll still help keep her single, no matter what you decide."

He weighed me with his dark eyes for several long moments. "I may regret this, but okay. We don't always share the same philosophies, but when you say you're going to help people, you mean it. When is this going down?"

"I guess after you get off work. Isn't that where you're going?" I disliked the delay but would take what I could get to have a solid test subject.

"Nah. Just picking up my paycheck."

Luckier and luckier. "Can you go to Ms. Terwilliger's after that? I'll text you her address, and she'll take care of curfew."

"This is going down at Ms. T's?"

"Yeah. You can meet her boyfriend. He has an eye patch."

Trey mulled this over. "Why didn't you just tell me that in the first place? I'm so there."

I sent him her address and then headed off to my own car. Once I was on the road, I called Adrian.

"How'd it go with the old man?" he asked.

"Not great," I said. "I'm heading over to Ms. Terwilliger's place and need you to meet me there."

"Okay," he said unhesitatingly. "Do I get a heads-up why?"

"I found a guinea pig."

CHAPTER 13

ADRIAN

JACKIE'S FACE TOLD ME THAT THIS WAS NO JOKE.

"Come in," she said, opening her front door and waving me forward. "I hope to God you understand what's going on."

"A little," I said, not entirely sure if that was an exaggeration. Sydney had been clear enough on the phone that it was time to test out her ink, but it was hard for me to imagine her having jumped to this extreme. The last I'd known, she'd been content to wait for Marcus and let him find a guinea pig. If she was suddenly ready to do some home tattooing—and I could only assume it was on herself—something pretty serious must have happened.

Although Jackie had traded up to a modern house when her bungalow burned down, the inside of her new home looked pretty much identical to the old one. I stepped past a pile of books on crystal healing and bent down to pat a fluffy white cat rubbing against my ankle in greeting. A few moments later, Sydney emerged from a hallway, wringing her hands. When she saw me, she ran forward and threw herself into my arms. Jackie politely averted her eyes and pretended to be interested in straightening some candles. We'd never explicitly said anything about our relationship around her, but we did tend to relax in her presence, and I'd learned two important things about Jaclyn Terwilliger. One was that she wasn't stupid. The other was that she didn't judge.

"What happened?" I asked Sydney. "Your dad?" It was the only thing that could have brought about this change of heart.

She nodded. "Him. And Keith."

"Keith? He was there?"

"No. Not exactly. Dad called him. Video call." She pulled away and began pacing around. "It was awful. What they did to him. He wasn't even human. He was a robot. No feelings. No free thought. They did it to him in re-education—and not with just whatever training or counseling they do. They had to have also used the ink Marcus was talking about that had stronger compulsion, the kind that encourages loyalty. Dad says it doesn't always work that strongly on everyone . . . but God. It worked on him. On Keith."

She was rambling, and Sydney wasn't the kind of person who rambled, which made all of this that much more disturbing. There was a haunted look in her eyes, and I wanted to draw her to me again. Reluctantly, I held back. Jackie might have a neutral attitude about our relationship, but I wasn't going to flaunt things.

"What then?" I demanded. "Did they threaten to do the same thing to you?" Something told me that if they had, she wouldn't be free to be standing here right now.

She shook her head. "No, my dad was actually going on and

on about how awesome I am—well, in his way. He didn't exactly use the word 'awesome.' It's not in his vocabulary. Zoe was the one who kept calling me out! Making a big deal out of how well I get along with everyone and how I spend so much time with you." She nodded toward Jackie, who arched an eyebrow.

"I wasn't aware you'd shared our goings-on with your, uh, associates."

Sydney gave a harsh laugh. "What, the magic? No. Of course not. But it doesn't even take that to set them off. I got scolded just for being a dedicated academic assistant because it might distract me from Alchemist priorities."

Now I was incredulous. "They'd send you to re-education for that?"

"No. But it's all bread crumbs, as Marcus would say. It draws attention to me, and if they ever find out what I've done . . . they could try to re-ink me too, and I can't let them. I *won't* let them. I won't become like Keith."

There were golden glints of anger in the depth of her brown eyes, but despite that fierceness and passion, I had a feeling she was terrified. How could she not be? The itch to look at her aura stirred within me, and I squashed it, both because of sheer willpower and . . . well, I wasn't entirely sure I *could* look at her aura.

It had been almost two weeks since I went on Einstein's prescription. The first week, I'd noticed almost no difference in anything—with one exception. My sleep. I was actually getting it. I no longer stared at my bedroom ceiling for hours, trying to settle down. I would get into bed, lie there for fifteen minutes or so, and eventually drift off. It wasn't like being sedated either. Mostly, it was as though the hamster wheel in my head no longer spun out of control. My thoughts simply calmed for the night, letting me do what normal people must do all the time.

In the last week, I'd noticed more gradual changes in me. I was a little more patient. I thought things through a little more. That wasn't to say I'd become some upstanding, perfectly controlled person whose feelings ran an even keel. Not by a long shot. I still had plenty of what Sydney would probably call "Adrian Ivashkov moments." Listening to Pink Floyd's *The Dark Side of the Moon* one night had left me moody and speculative over the meaning of life, eventually triggering the purchase of some black-light paints to help express my metaphysical musings. And when I'd finally turned in that goddamned self-portrait, I'd helpfully told my professor that if she wanted to keep it for her private boudoir, I'd understand. Her response had not been positive.

That had probably been my stupidest act in the last two weeks, and really, compared with past history, it wasn't *that* bad. Most importantly, I hadn't felt out of control. There'd been none of the debilitating darkness. And Aunt Tatiana had remained quiet.

I thought I'd hit the jackpot until, the day after the boudoir comment, I'd seen my professor on campus and had wanted to know if I was still in trouble for the remark. I'd summoned spirit to sneak a peek at her aura—and nothing had happened. It was kind of like trying to turn over a car engine on a cold day. Finally, on the third attempt, the magic took, and her aura had flared in my sight.

That had been four days ago, and I was too afraid to try to use spirit again. I didn't know if I could handle what I'd find. Had that day been a fluke? Was spirit still functioning normally? Or was it fading away, maybe even gone? I didn't know how to feel about that. Relieved? Devastated?

That panic threatened to overwhelm me, and I had to take a moment to push those thoughts out of my mind and stay calm. Spirit wasn't the issue right now. Sydney was. I had to be there for her.

The thing was, I hadn't told her about the mood stabilizer. I hadn't even told her about Einstein. Part of me wanted her to know I really was trying to change—that I would do anything for her—but on the other hand, I was still too nervous about what the prescription's ultimate results would be. I was embarrassed at the thought of hyping the pills up to her only for them to fail. And I was equally wary of them working—and me stopping because I couldn't handle the changes. Until I knew what was going on, I didn't want Sydney to know about it. I'd rather have her think I hadn't tried at all than have her know I'd failed.

"What do you need from me?" I asked.

"From us," corrected Jackie.

I couldn't help shooting her a smile. Putting on charm and a happy face for everyone wasn't that difficult for me. Actually liking and respecting people was rarer, but Jackie had reached both of those bars in my esteem. A large part of it was that she cared about Sydney so much and would do anything for her. I loved Jackie for that. And I also loved that she needed to know only half of what was going on to want to help. That was one of the perks of her already being involved in supernatural affairs. She had an excellent ability to roll with new and unexplainable complications.

"I'm going to have to use the compound I made," Sydney said. She clasped her hands together, and I realized it was to stop them from shaking. "I just mixed the salt into some binding solution and ink. It all seems stable, so now the trick is to finally tattoo our subject."

"You actually have a subject?" I looked around to see if I'd missed somebody, but it was just the three of us. "One of the cats?" I asked.

There was a knock at the door, and a moment later, Jackie let in Trey Juarez, which was a surprise. I'd only ever talked to him a couple of times. Aside from having been born into the group that had tried to kill Sonya Karp, Trey seemed like a reasonably decent guy. I knew Sydney considered him a friend, despite everything that had happened, and her opinion went a long way. The fact that she'd invited him here spoke legions.

"Mr. Juarez, what a pleasant surprise." It was clear Jackie was, indeed, very surprised.

"I'm surprised you haven't invited me over sooner, Ms. T. I was your TA first! And here you let Melbourne over all the time."

He gave her a grin that could've been out of my playbook and probably worked wonders with women. Unlike Neil, who seemed to charm them haphazardly, Trey was a pro. I was glad he was stuck in a weird dysfunctional hang-up over Angeline because, let's face it, some might argue a good-looking athletic human scholar was a better match for Sydney than a mentally unstable vampire artist.

Jackie rolled her eyes, showing the smile had no effect on her. "Oversight noted. I presume Mr. Juarez is the subject you'll be tattooing?"

When Sydney nodded, I asked, "How are you going to pull that off exactly? Are you doing a fresh design? Or are you just using a syringe to touch it up?"

Marcus had only needed a syringe when he "broke" her tattoo. It was one of the useful things he'd done for her before he left town: injecting her lily tattoo with small amounts of ink derived from vampire blood. It had cracked all the tattoo's powers but had still left her susceptible to re-inking by the Alchemists if she didn't seal it.

"No syringe," she said. "I think we need a substantial amount in there, plus we have to make sure it gets into the dermis. That's the next layer of skin below the surface one."

"Okay," I said, thinking I understood. I had a feeling the "dermis" definition had been for me alone. "You need more ink in there. How are you going to pull it off?"

Another knock at the door startled us, and Jackie moved toward it. "Ah, that would be Malachi."

I did a double take. "Did she just say—"

There was no need to finish because she flung open the door, revealing our unstable former self-defense teacher in all his eye-patch glory. He jerked his thumb behind him. "Hey, darling. I got the tattoo apparatus in my van. Where do you want me to set up?" He squinted inside at us. "Oh. Hey, kids."

Jackie took him to the garage, and I tried to pick my jaw up off the floor as I turned to face Sydney. "He's your tattooist?"

She shrugged. "When I told Ms. Terwilliger I needed to do a tattoo, she told me he had his own machine. I guess he does all his own tattoos."

"I've never seen any."

"Maybe they're in places most people don't see," she said.

I winced. "Thank you for sending my imagination to a place it can never return from."

"Whoa, hold on here." Trey pointed down the hall, where I could hear Wolfe regaling Jackie with some crackpot tale of daring. "That guy's going to be using a high-powered needle on me? He has one eye! Do the words 'depth perception' mean anything to you?"

"Ms. Terwilliger swears he knows what he's doing," said Sydney. "And since the ink doesn't have any color, it's not going to show. So as long as everything's sterile, and he has some competence, the artistry won't matter. We just need the gun to deliver it. But if you're interested . . ." A small smile played at her lips. "It'd be easy enough to add some dye to it. I bet Wolfe could do a Chihuahua on you."

Trey shuddered. "No thanks."

Sydney suddenly frowned. "Your Warrior tattoo is just a tattoo, right? No powers?"

"Nope. Tattoos don't have to have amazing abilities for us. Decoration is enough."

"Okay," she said. "That'll give me a good cover story for Wolfe. Don't worry—whatever I say, nothing will happen to your current tattoo." Trey didn't look reassured.

I pondered that. "Doesn't he need a special tattoo, though?" I asked. I didn't elaborate in front of Trey, but the whole point of this experiment was to see if her ink could deactivate Alchemist ink.

She nodded, catching my unspoken question. "Yes, but we'll worry about that after this, once I get some of those materials. Then we'll do a second tattoo."

Trey's mouth dropped, but he didn't get a chance to

comment. Jackie and Wolfe returned just then, and he rubbed his hands together eagerly. "Okay, so what's the late-night emergency? You two getting your names tattooed on each other? I can do a pretty nice Courier font."

Sydney had been about to speak but faltered a moment. Wolfe had no evidence of our relationship, but he'd always assumed there was one, even before there was. She quickly recovered herself and laughed off his comment, like it was a funny joke. Trey, understandably, seemed too transfixed by the idea of a one-eyed man tattooing him to have really noticed.

"The opposite," Sydney told Wolfe. "We actually want to remove my friend's tattoo, and we've got some special ink that'll eventually make the old one fade over time."

He grunted. "Really? Never heard of that. I thought laser removal was really the only way to get rid of one."

"It's a new technique," she explained easily, giving a small nod to Trey. "His parents are visiting soon, and they'll kill him if they see it."

I blinked in surprise. She was so convincing, I nearly believed her story, and I knew the truth. Wolfe certainly bought it. It was something I tended to forget about: Alchemists were excellent liars. If Sydney ever wanted to lie to me, I'd probably be none the wiser.

"Where is it?" Wolfe asked.

Trey didn't react right away. I think he almost believed Sydney too. Turning away from us, he pulled off his shirt and revealed a sun tattoo on the back of his shoulder.

Wolfe leaned forward to study it. "So, what? Your parents see you shirtless a lot?"

Sydney winced at the flaw in her logic. "It's just better if it's gone when they visit, sir."

"Yeah," agreed Trey. "Sometimes we do family trips to the beach." I had to give him points for playing along.

Sydney explained how Wolfe only needed to deliver the ink into the existing tattoo. He looked disappointed that there'd be no chance to test his artistic skills, but I think he was happy enough about a late-night visit to Jackie to not be too put out about the time and effort.

Although Wolfe's equipment looked professional enough, the garage setup gave the whole operation a kind of sketchy feel. I didn't know the fine details of tattooing, but Sydney examined everything with a critical eye, asking about sterilization and seeming pleased that Wolfe used new parts on some of the equipment each time. Jackie looked as helpless as I felt and stood near me and a wide-eyed Trey, whose tanned skin had paled at the approaching feat. Even Sydney looked a little uneasy, however, when Trey lay facedown on a bench so that Wolfe could get to his shoulder with the needle.

"I'm sure he's very skilled," she said. It was hard to say which of us she was trying to convince.

"Damn boy," said Wolfe, poking one of Trey's huge triceps. "What sport do you play?"

"All of them."

"Oh yeah? You ever done speed-skating-javelin-throwing?"

"Speed-skating what?" asked Trey.

All of us could tell Wolfe was on the verge of a story, and Sydney cleared her throat. "Um, sir? We should really get moving." She went over her instructions one last time, and then Wolfe set to his task.

I'd never seen tattooing before. It sounded like a dentist's drill, and although I was no stranger to blood, seeing that high-powered needle go to work made me squeamish. It had to hurt, but Trey took it stoically, never twitching a muscle. Sydney supervised everything with a sharp eye, and I had a feeling that if Wolfe did anything even remotely irresponsible, she'd throw herself in there to stop him. She was literally and figuratively watching Trey's back.

I moved closer to her, careful not to touch but also not really leaving any space between us. "Okay. Presuming Wolfe doesn't accidentally impale Trey, what's the next step? I get your logic about giving him a tattoo with Alchemist ink later to see if this one will protect him, but how exactly are you going to get their ink? Doesn't that require vampire blood and earth compulsion? Those aren't things you have lying around your room."

A faint smile played at her lips. "No, nor are some of the other ingredients. And they're not exactly things I can order off the internet either or use regular Alchemist channels for. I'll have to think of some other way to get them."

"But you still wanted to do this first?" I nodded toward Trey.

Whatever fleeting smile she might have had vanished on the wind. "Yes. I had to, after seeing Keith today. Maybe this is preemptive. Maybe I should've held off until I had Alchemist ink, but when I think about Keith . . . I have to do something *now*, Adrian. I can't let them do that to other people. I've been talking about replicating this stuff in hypothetical terms for a while now, and I couldn't stand the thought of waiting for Marcus or the ideal procedure. This puts us one step closer. Trey'll be ready for when I get some Alchemist ink, and once we prove this works, Marcus will disperse it."

I resisted the urge to cup her face in my hands. What she was suggesting wasn't a bad plan. Would it have been better if she and Marcus had managed to tattoo one of his disciples with an Alchemist compulsion tattoo and *then* see if this stuff worked like Marcus's indigo ink? Sure, that would've been the ideal plan. And that was the thing. Sydney usually went with ideal. She was meticulous. She wasn't the type to rush stuff or settle for the second-best option. But she'd rushed now. She'd let the optimal order for her experiment be altered in order to speed things up. It was something anyone might do. I would. The fact that Sydney had done it, however, told me something crucial. She'd acted on impulse and emotion, which was out of character for her. Sydney was scared.

What the hell had she seen in Keith?

"You should have Wolfe tattoo you too," I said gently. "If you're worried, that is. Just in case Inez was wrong about magic use undoing yours."

A pained look crossed her face. "I thought about it, believe me. The problem is, I can't easily do it with Zoe around. This process irritates the skin, and even though the most obvious effects are gone in a few days, it's still not something I can hide while living with her. I've just got to take my chances and wait."

"You going to tell Marcus about this?"

"If he ever calls," she said, rolling her eyes. "He's probably passed out at some cantina."

"We can dream visit him, you know," I said.

"Adrian." Her voice was stern. "You know we can't."

"I know no such thing," I declared. "I haven't used spirit in a long time. Not really since—well. You know. That night. A little burst like this for the greater good? No problem." I made the boast without thinking, mostly because it was a gut instinct to help her. It occurred to me too late that I might not actually be capable of it with the pills.

"It's dangerous," she said. But I could see indecision in her eyes. She wanted to talk to Marcus in theory but didn't want to put me at risk.

"What's dangerous is not doing what we can to protect others. And if that means talking to my favorite outlaw, we should do it. I should do it." I had to try. Maybe it'd end in failure, but I was powerless against helping her.

She hesitated and then gave me the best answer I could expect: "We'll discuss it later."

Whatever his other flaws, Wolfe proved surprisingly competent. The tattoo process seemed to take forever, but he didn't gouge any holes in Trey's back. When they finally finished an hour later, Trey's skin was pink and irritated, dotted with a little blood. Both Sydney and Wolfe assured us that was normal. He nodded in satisfaction and allowed Trey to sit up for cleaning and bandaging.

"I covered the whole thing," said Wolfe. "How long until it fades?"

"It can take a while," Sydney said smoothly. "Sometimes you need a few more applications, but I've got a good feeling about this. Thanks for your help." Again, she spoke so easily that I could almost believe we were just doing a cosmetic removal and not protecting against mind-controlling magic.

"Wish they'd had that kind of thing back when I was younger," Wolfe said wistfully. "If I'd known what I knew now, I never would've gotten Tocllul tattooed on my thigh. But, hey,

I was practically a kid myself and thought Tocllul and I would be together forever."

"Toc—what?" I asked.

"Tocllul. This Aztec princess I met while I was backpacking around Mexico."

Trey leaned forward. "Did you say Aztec?"

"Yup. The last of her people. Her family had fallen on hard times, though, and had to sell souvenirs to make ends meet. I competed in several death-defying games of honor to prove my worthiness. I finally won the right to be her royal consort, but after a couple months, I got restless. I wasn't ready to settle down. It broke her heart when I left, but what could I do? I was young, filled with wanderlust. I had to be free. Free as a bird."

"'And this bird you cannot change,'" I said solemnly. Sydney shot me a wry look. "So you've still got her name on you?"

"Nah." He pushed up one leg of his Bermuda shorts, revealing a hairy thigh and *Tactful* written in slightly faded navy ink. "I got back to the States and found a guy to modify it. This was the best we could come up with the letters available."

"It's a very noble trait," said Jackie. I studied her and couldn't tell if she was lying either. It made the temptation to switch to aura vision that much stronger. She watched as Sydney helped patch Trey up. "Do you need anything else? Any of you? I admit, I feel rather useless."

"You were the hostess," said Sydney, stepping back as Trey put his shirt back on. "You've done plenty."

"Well, I'm happy to do more if you guys want to stay for a while."

Judging from the way Wolfe's eyebrow rose over his eye patch, the only person he envisioned staying longer was himself.

"We need to get going," I said, speaking for all of us. If Jackie gave Sydney permission to be out, I supposed we could theoretically use the time to sneak a bit to eat. Even Trey could come. I really didn't care, so long as it gave me a few more precious moments with Sydney. A buzz on her cell phone told me that wasn't an option. She checked the display and sighed.

"Yikes. This is the fourth one Zoe's sent. I didn't hear them over the needle." She put the phone away. "I'm sure I'll get an earful for being out this late."

"Don't go home," I said impulsively. Trey was asking Wolfe a question, and I leaned close to Sydney's ear. "Escape plan number thirty-one: We'll get in my car and won't stop until we're somewhere safe."

The love that answered me in her eyes had an almost tangible quality, and I had to fight the urge to hold her. "We'd have to stop a dozen times. Your car gets terrible gas mileage."

We walked out with Trey, who was handling all this surprisingly well for someone who got roped into an experiment he knew very little about. At first, I assumed it was just because he had that kind of faith in Sydney. Then I realized there was more to it.

"You've made my day letting me meet that guy," Trey told her. "Maybe my year. He's unreal. And he and Ms. T. . . . they're really . . .?"

Sydney winced. "I think so."

She walked out with Trey, giving me one last look, and I waited inside a couple of minutes, just so we wouldn't be seen leaving together. Even in a strange neighborhood like this, we couldn't take any chances. I knew I'd see her soon if I was able to pull off the dream, but that sense of melancholy clung to me over the frustrating state of our relationship. I didn't want a dream. I wanted reality, and having it beyond my grasp bit at me deeply. Einstein had been right. The prescription might take the edge off, but there was no getting rid of your emotions. They were part of being alive.

Back at my place, I kept an eye on the clock, trying to gauge how long it would take Sydney to get to her room and go to sleep. She'd said we'd talk about the spirit dream later, but since we hadn't, I was reading that as a go-ahead. I was tired myself—a new experience—yet insanely anxious and curious about whether or not I'd be able to create the dream. I knew there'd be no shame in telling Sydney the truth. She'd understand and even be proud of what I'd done. But it was a reminder of my own initial fears about taking the mood stabilizer: that in freeing myself of spirit's darkness, I'd also lose the ability to help those I cared about.

When enough time had passed, I relaxed into the meditative state necessary for dream walking. Reaching within myself, I pulled on the magic that slept inside me, the spirit tied into my life essence. I didn't come up empty, not exactly, but it was like trying to grasp water in your palm. It kept slipping through my fingers. Panic began to move through me, and I staunchly refused to let it get the best of me. Just like with my professor and the aura, I kept trying and trying to grip the magic. There was even less of it than I'd had then, and a spirit dream required far more than viewing an aura. Nonetheless, I was finally able to spin enough into the foundation of a dream. My bedroom vanished, and I found myself standing in the Getty Villa's courtyard. Only, it looked nothing like it. The world around me flickered and faded, like bad TV reception. And it took every ounce of my energy to maintain even that shoddy of an effort. Wasting no more time, I pulled Sydney into it.

"What's going on?" she asked, looking around in surprise.

"I'm tired," I said. "Downside of my new and improved sleeping habits."

I saw the slightest glimmer of doubt in her eyes, and I could guess her thoughts. "I haven't been drinking, Sage. I swear it. I really am just worn out. Let's get Robin Hood in here fast because I don't know how long I can do this."

She looked concerned but nodded in agreement. Reaching out to another person proved even more difficult, and it again took a few false starts, earning more surprise from Sydney. Eventually, Marcus appeared, and although his form was slightly insubstantial, his smirk was as annoying as ever.

"I wondered when you guys would come calling again." He frowned at the flickering surroundings. "What's going on?"

"It's not important," I said preemptively. "And we're short on time."

Sydney took the cue and quickly told Marcus the new developments. Seeing him gape almost made the effort I was exerting worthwhile. "You actually did it? And used it? Did it work?"

"I don't know yet," Sydney admitted. "So far, everything's gone as planned—and it doesn't show up on the skin. It's more or less invisible." Marcus lit up at that. One drawback of the indigo ink was that it made Alchemist rebels pretty conspicuous. "I've got a few other . . . experiments to do on my friend. But I feel pretty good about it, and as long as I can make the time, producing more ink for you shouldn't be a problem. When will you be back?"

"We expect to cross back in El Paso this week," he said. "We've got a new person to 'rescue,' and then I should be able to make my way to you. Maybe a week and a half? Two at most? You think you'd have something by then?"

She nodded. "Should be able to have the Alchemist ink for sure." I could tell by a catch in her voice that she was still trying to figure out how to make the original compulsion ink. "We can set up a drop at Adrian's. Do you remember where he lives?"

"How could I forget?" Marcus rolled his eyes. "Such fond memories of throwing him around there."

"Hey," I said warningly. "I threw *you* around."

Sydney shot us both chastising looks. "I'll make sure it's there. Do you have cell phones yet?"

"No, but we will when we're back in the States, and Sabrina still has your contact information, so I can get it from her. We'll get in touch and finalize things."

"Are we good then?" I asked. I was actually sweating. "I need to get some sleep."

"We should be," said Sydney, eyes worried as she looked me over. "Get in touch as soon as you can, Marcus."

"I will," he promised.

I took that as a dismissal and let him fade away. I could see from Sydney's face that she wanted to talk to me, but something was buzzing in my head, and I lost my remaining control on the dream. It fell to pieces around us, and I was just barely able to tell her, "We'll talk tomorrow." She grew translucent and disappeared.

When I came to in the real world, I discovered the buzzing I'd heard was from my cell phone, which I'd left on vibrate on my bedside table. I was surprised to see Lissa's name on the display and answered with shaking hands, astonished at how exhausted I felt.

"Kind of late for you, isn't it, Your Majesty?"

"You're on a human schedule," she reminded me, amusement in her voice.

"Ah. Right. It all starts to run together after a while. To what do I owe this pleasure?"

"Nothing social, I'm afraid. You're not going to like this, but I've got to play the queen card and summon you to Court. I know it's a pain. I know, and I'm sorry. Really."

"What's going on?" Dread built in my stomach.

"Sonya wants your help on what to do with Olive and the blood. She says the magic is starting to fade out from it, and no one knows how to stop it."

"She couldn't just call me?"

"She says it's too complicated and that you should be there firsthand since you helped contain it."

"I see." Spirit dreams and auras were problematic enough . . . how in the world was I supposed to even come close to replicating what I'd done before? And yet I wasn't ready to tell Lissa about the pills either.

"Sonya was also wondering if . . ." Lissa's voice grew hesitant. "Well, do you think Sydney would come? If we got permission from the Alchemists?"

My heart sped up. "Why her?"

"Sonya thought we could make some kind of binding tattoo out of the blood and says Sydney's had experience with that kind of thing." It was true. Keith had been busted for masterminding a performance-enhancing tattoo ring that

Sydney had uncovered. And if they really just did need me as an advisor on an experiment, then maybe I could hide my fading spirit. "And let's face it, Sydney's probably the only Alchemist who'd be able to handle time here at Court. It may be a few days. Do you think she'd do it? Travel with you? Or . . . well, maybe separately to hide your connection to Jill."

Holy shit. I could scarcely believe what I was hearing. Lissa was offering the chance for me to get away with Sydney. True, it wasn't exactly a romantic escapade, but the Moroi Royal Court was pretty much the last place we'd have to worry about Alchemist eyes. We'd just have to worry about my kind.

"If the Alchemists tell her to, she will." I played it as cool as I could. "Orders trump fear with them. She'd probably be able to handle traveling with me too, if you want to have us meet up on a connection like last time."

Lissa's relief poured through the phone. "I'm so glad. That'll make things a lot easier if we bring you guys and Neil together."

"Neil?"

"Well, yeah. You should travel with protection. Unless you want Eddie this time?"

So much for my alone time with Sydney. Hopefully we'd find some at Court. "No, send Buckingham Palace. He'll do less damage this way."

"Huh?"

"Nothing."

She promised I'd have flight details in the morning, and when we disconnected, I collapsed onto the bed and fell almost instantly into asleep.

More buzzing woke me up, but it took me longer to find my phone since it was lost in the covers. I just barely answered in time and squinted at the bright morning sunlight coming in from the window I'd forgotten to cover last night.

"Adrian?" It was Jill, sounding anxious. "I just heard you're going to Court."

"Yup. Royal directives and all. Don't worry, Jailbait. I'll bring you a T-shirt."

"Adrian." The sternness in my name was a remarkable match for what Sydney used sometimes. "I had to hear it from Neil."

I groaned. "Don't start this. Lissa said it'd be only a few days. You can live that long without him."

"No," she said impatiently. "You missed the point. *I had to hear it from him. Because I didn't read it from you.*"

My brain was still groggy with sleep and fatigue, though a prickling along my skin warned me that I was teetering on the edge of something. "What are you saying?"

"I'm saying, I don't know what's going on with you anymore. The bond's gone dark."

CHAPTER 14

SYDNEY

IT'S AMAZING HOW NICE PEOPLE CAN BE when they think you're going to die.

"Sydney, I'm sorry. I really am."

"And I told you to forget about it." I didn't even look at Zoe as I perused my sweater selection. My clothes were kept in a complex system organized by temperature and occasion. Pennsylvania in December was going to require some of my heaviest clothing.

"I just got upset that Dad didn't even seem to notice me," she continued.

Welcome to my world, I thought. It was ironic that I was now in a phase of my life where I finally had his attention and didn't want it. I was at least glad we were having this discussion, though. We'd talked little about our dinner with Dad, and if she was second-guessing criticizing me, that was good both for me personally and perhaps for her progress in lightening up in Alchemist beliefs. I felt a little bad that this was coming out

235

because she thought my Court trip would endanger my life, but no way would I correct her.

"He was right about you being so good at your job," she added. "If you hadn't gotten so comfortable with *them*, you'd never be able to go to their Court now. I know it's a big deal that you got chosen. Not many people could handle it. I couldn't." She sighed. "But I wish you weren't going. I'm so worried about you."

I finally looked over at her, sitting cross-legged on her bed. A pang stirred in my heart. Despite all the jealousy and suspicion, she was still my sister, and she loved me. She was just confused and insecure about her life right now, which was totally understandable. I was pretty sure she didn't want this strife between us any more than I did. It was just the lot we'd been given.

"I'll be fine. The Moroi are safe, and they want my help. Nothing's going to happen to me."

She still looked skeptical. "But you're staying overnight with them. *Surrounded by them.* Couldn't you have gotten a hotel in a nearby town? Isn't that what we usually do for trips there? It would keep you away from them."

It would also keep me away from Adrian. "Staying on-site means I can finish my work faster and get home faster," I said reasonably. That was hard logic to beat. "And I survived staying with them when they were all partying and drinking champagne at that wedding. This has to be better."

"Text me all the time so that I know you're okay."

I couldn't help a smile. "I'll see what I can do. And you text me too on how everything's going."

"I will," she assured me, nodding eagerly. "I'll be just like you."

236

"I know you'll do a great job." I actually meant it. She was smart and competent—and now motivated.

"And I'll make sure they get dinner at Clarence's and that Angeline doesn't do anything crazy. Too crazy." Her lips turned up in a mischievous smile. "Did you hear that she threatened to sue the school for misrepresentation when her history teacher explained that the War of 1812 lasted until 1815?"

"No, I hadn't heard that." I shook my head in exasperation yet was secretly thrilled to hear Zoe laughing over someone she thought of as a wacky acquaintance—and not as a creature of evil.

"I'll keep her in line, don't worry." Zoe grew a little more serious. "I don't suppose . . . well, could I drive them? You know I can do it. And it's not that far."

"It's not legal," I rebuked gently, hating to see the longing in her. "If you got pulled over—"

"I wouldn't! I'd be careful."

"It's the other drivers you have to worry about," I said, knowing I sounded like a driving instructor. "Just keep practicing with Eddie. You'll get your license at some point."

She sighed. "But when?"

"The next time you're back in Utah, I guess."

A moment of silence descended between us. From her face, I had a good guess at what she was thinking. When would she be back in Utah? I knew my dad wouldn't let her stay license-less forever. It was something she needed for the job. It wasn't a priority for him right now, though, so she'd have to wait. If she went back there to live with our mom, however . . .

"I guess . . . I guess I'll just be patient." Her mournful look intensified. "Anyway. I'll worry about you until you get back."

I patted her on the shoulder. "Don't. This is one of those times you can't think of me as your sister. Treat me like I'm another Alchemist, off to do a job."

"It's hard," she said, in a voice that made my heart break. "I don't know if I can."

"You'll learn to," I said.

My flight was leaving soon, and I spent the rest of our time together trying to look stoic and resigned about this unpleasant mission. But after a while, I had to admit that I was secretly elated. Adrian and I were getting away from here! True, it was no free-for-all, but it'd be a relief to be away from suspicious eyes—and to actually have reason to be together.

Just like the last time Adrian and I had flown to Court, we rendezvoused in Los Angeles for our connection to Philadelphia. He and Neil were already waiting at our gate when I arrived, and I paused in my approach to study them. Neil was reading a martial arts book. Adrian had the poetry book I'd given him open on his lap and was staring out the window. The light illuminated his fair skin and sculpted features, and even from here, I wanted to run my fingers through his dark hair. There was a pensive expression on his face, and I wondered if he was worried about our upcoming task. Things had been calm and steady for the last couple of weeks, which had me on edge that we were due for another episode of spirit's revenge.

"Sage," he said, when I resumed my approach. The brooding look vanished, replaced by his sly, lazy one. "Ready for an arctic expedition?" He nodded at the parka I carried. Faux fur, of course. "I bet you've gotten a lot of strange looks hauling that around here."

"Didn't you check the weather for where we're going? Never

mind. Of course you didn't." Neil at least had on a sturdy ski jacket, but Adrian's peacoat didn't reassure me. I supposed it was promising that he had anything at all. "Is that all you brought?"

"It's my best-looking coat," he said.

"So I take it that's a yes."

"Style over substance, Sage. I've got a lot of adoring fans back there that'll expect me to look my best. Can't weigh myself down in . . . well, down."

I put on my best look of disdain. "Well, don't come crying to me when you're out in twenty-degree weather. I'm here to do real work, not babysit you."

Neil shook his head at Adrian and gave me a sympathetic look before returning to his book. As soon as his attention was off us, I caught Adrian's eye. Neither of us dared to smile, but the knowing glint in those green depths made my heart rate pick up.

And . . . it continued to beat pretty fast for the rest of our travels. The three of us sat together in coach (earning no end of melodrama from Adrian), with me in between them. Neil was content to read about attack techniques and barely said two words to us. Adrian and I were each theoretically preoccupied with our own reading material, but I knew both of us were more fixated on each other's proximity. Our legs pressed together, and I was as guilty as he was about stolen touches. When the flight attendant came by with beverages, I practically ended up in his lap while reaching for my Diet Coke. And when Adrian wanted new reading material, he decided to search the pocket in front of me for magazines first, leaning so that his hand brushed my thigh. Even through my jeans, that touch was provocative and made me think of all the times he'd run his hands over my legs.

It was agonizing . . . and exquisite.

It was also frustrating. I spent most of the flight obsessing over each touch and when we'd touch again. These casual brushes set me aflame, but by the time we neared our destination, all I could think about was when we'd get a chance to be alone so that we could be done with this subterfuge. Judging from Adrian's growing silence and the way his breath caught when our eyes locked, I had a feeling I wasn't the only one thinking indecent thoughts. *Get a grip, Sydney,* I thought. *Or at least a cold shower. Aren't you supposed to be turning your mind to higher pursuits of knowledge?*

I was so consumed by my turbulent feelings that Neil totally caught me by surprise when our flight was descending. "Do you think I'll have a chance to see Olive?"

Adrian glanced up from his poetry book. "Probably. This whole thing is because of her blood, so I'm sure she'll be around."

"That's not what I—" Neil bit his lip and looked out the window. "Never mind."

"Ohhh," said Adrian, with a wink that was lost on Neil. "There's see and *see*. You mean *see*. I'm sure there'll be time between our breathtaking discoveries for you to take each other's breath away in a different kind of way."

Neil turned back, blushing bright red. "It's not that like that. We've been e-mailing since we met, and we really connect."

"Well, there's connect and—"

"Adrian, stop helping." To Neil, I said, "I don't know her, but whatever we have to do isn't going to be solved in five

240

minutes. You'll have time and won't even be on constant duty."
That brightened him up immensely.

Once we were in Philadelphia, we rented a car for the rest
of the trip. Normal trips to the Court's location on the edge of
the Pocono Mountains usually relied on puddle jumper planes
to a rural airport thirty minutes away, but those flights were
infrequent, hence the car. The trip took us about two and a half
hours, a drive that would've been scenic in the middle of the
day. But between the flights and the time changes, darkness
had long since overtaken us, something that put Neil on high
alert. He sat beside me as I drove, barely blinking as he scanned
around us. I'd talked a good talk to Zoe about my safety, but
that had been regarding Moroi. I'd forgotten that where Moroi
grouped, Strigoi often followed, and dark roads leading to Court
were fraught with danger at night. I didn't *think* any Strigoi
would come leaping onto the car as we drove at sixty miles per
hour, but I was grateful for Neil's painstaking diligence. Despite
his teasing, I think Adrian was as well.

It was midnight when we finally crossed the Court's borders.
Neil was as stiff and rigid as ever, but Adrian had sprawled out
and fallen asleep in the backseat. He yawned and stretched his
arms as I slowed down to talk to the guards at the gate. As far as
most humans were concerned, the Court was a very specialized
and private college. It certainly looked like one, with venerable
ivy-covered buildings and broad, beautiful courtyards. But as
sharp-eyed dhampirs peered into the car, I was reminded of
Zoe's warnings. I was about to enter a compound of supernatural
creatures.

"Lord Ivashkov," said one of the guards, noticing Adrian.
"Welcome back."

Adrian smothered another yawn and nodded. Lord Ivashkov. I forgot sometimes that Adrian was part of a royal family and that even minor members could use "lord" and "lady" when they were adults. It was unreal to think I was dating royalty. Even more unreal that these days his title weirded me out more than the fact that he was a vampire did.

The dhampir gestured to a narrow dirt road leading around outskirts of the Court's central grounds. "Follow that around and park behind the palace," he said. "You're expected."

"The palace," I muttered, once he'd waved us on. "We aren't in Palm Springs anymore."

"It's just what they call where the queen lives," said Adrian. He leaned forward and stuck his head between Neil and me. "Looks just like any other academic building. You'll feel right at home."

That wasn't entirely true. Once we'd parked and been admitted through a back door, a guide led us down grand corridors illuminated by crystal chandeliers and lined with portraits depicting centuries of Moroi monarchs. Those delicate, pale faces watched me, reminding me that I truly was in another world—a world where I was the outsider. The old Alchemist anxiety began to bubble up, and I told myself over and over that I was a guest here. No one would try to hurt me. And if they did, Adrian wouldn't let them.

I knew the queen's residence had an actual throne room and other areas for state functions, but tonight we were taken to a more casual setting: a media room. Definitely not something I imagined when I thought of palaces. A giant TV screen hung on the wall and displayed some show in which people appeared to be competing in teams on a muddy obstacle course. Large plush sofas were arranged around the screen and held various Moroi and dhampirs who didn't notice our entrance. A couple of guardians standing watch on opposite sides of the room saw us instantly, of course. I turned my attention to the spectators on the couch, one of whom I recognized right away.

"Come *on!*" Rose leapt to her feet and held her hands out beseechingly to the screen. "It was right in front of you, you idiot! Are you blind? You just gave them the win!"

"Actually," said Adrian, coming to stand beside me. "The green team wins. This is a rerun."

Everyone turned toward us, and someone shut off the sound. I heard a small shriek, and then a lithe blond figure darted up and threw her arms around Adrian. "You made it!"

He grinned and patted her back. "What'd I tell you, cousin? I'm your subject, and a subject serves his queen."

Lissa Dragomir didn't look particularly queenly just then. She was my age, and her long platinum hair was tied into a ponytail that hung sloppily down the back of her Lehigh sweatshirt. I hardly knew her, but her resemblance to Jill—mostly in the form of their light green eyes and high cheekbones—made her feel familiar. She broke from Adrian and turned to Neil and me. The gleeful smile she'd given Adrian turned to one a bit more formal, but still just as genuine.

"Sydney, I'm so happy to see you again. If there's anything I can do for you, please let me know. And you must be Neil."

"Your majesty." Neil swept her a bow so low that his forehead touched the ground. Above him, Adrian rolled his eyes.

"Easy there, Lancelot," Adrian said. "I don't think bowing is required when she's in jeans and bunny slippers."

Neil rose gracefully to his feet. "A queen's regality is not diminished by her attire."

Adrian glanced at the others for sympathy. "We've been together for almost ten hours today."

Lissa's eyes sparkled with amusement. "It's very nice to meet you."

Introductions were made to those who needed them. I knew most of the major players in the room. Dimitri and Sonya were there, full of smiles for me, and Rose went so far as to give me a hug. I'd met Lissa's boyfriend, Christian Ozera, briefly before, and although I didn't know him well, he gave me a nod of greeting. He and Adrian regarded each other warily, and I recalled something Adrian had once told me about him: *"His aunt's in prison for killing my aunt. I don't blame him for it. He doesn't blame me. We still like each other. But that doesn't mean things aren't weird, you know?"*

Two girls sat together on a loveseat, keeping their distance and watching the reunion quietly. One was a dhampir with black hair and coppery skin. The other, a Moroi, had a multitude of dark curls and beautiful gray eyes. Judging from the way Neil couldn't take his eyes off the dhampir, I could guess who the girls were. Adrian gave them one of his most charismatic grins.

"Well, well. Looks like you guys survived the trip, huh? I hope they've been showing you a good time. The royal treatment, if you will. Golden faucets. Velvet robes. Champagne for breakfast. And for lunch. And dinner. In fact, why isn't there a bottle in here now?"

Olive and Nina Sinclair responded with smiles, especially Nina. "You didn't bring it?" she asked, with a bit more warmth than I liked.

"I can send for some," said Lissa. She started to turn toward one of the guards at the door, but Adrian waved her off.

"Nah, we've got to be all responsible and stuff to deal with the spirit problem, right? We can celebrate later. Besides, Belikov can't hold his liquor."

Dimitri looked startled at that, and I had to repress a laugh at Adrian's deflection. When he was here, "Lord Ivashkov" could probably get anything he wanted, and I was proud of Adrian for holding true to his promise to steer clear of his vices. It was just as well he was facing away from me at the time because my face probably would've betrayed my affection.

Formal introductions were made between the Sinclair sisters and me. They murmured polite greetings and regarded me with curiosity before they dismissed me, turning their attention back to the others. An Alchemist was a novelty but nothing particularly exciting.

I assumed we'd all be reconvening in the morning, but as Sonya began discussing what she'd learned about Olive's blood sample, I realized we were doing business here and now. I nearly groaned as the obvious hit me. *It's the middle of their day. They're all bright-eyed and ready to get going.* That was probably why Adrian had power napped. Neil, as a dhampir, would have extra stamina and be able to go longer without sleep. But me? I was merely human, and it was past my bedtime in Palm Springs. But, if they were ready to do this, then so was I. A yawn started to well up in me, and I staunchly put it down.

"There's no question about it," Sonya was saying. "That blood sample is brimming with a kind of spirit we've never seen. And that charm you put on the silver is ingenious, but—"

The door burst open, and a Moroi man came striding

forward with a guardian on his heels. "The gang's all here, I see. You must have forgotten to send for me."

Rose rolled her eyes. "You weren't invited, old man."

Abe Mazur, her flamboyantly dressed father, clucked his tongue in disapproval. "Yes, because it makes perfect sense that one of the biggest breakthroughs in our world should be left in the hands of kids."

"I'm almost thirty," protested Sonya.

"Exactly my point." Abe took in his surroundings and brightened when he saw me. "My favorite Alchemist. So nice of you to lend your expertise."

I gave him a tight smile. "Happy to help."

Through some unspoken command, a servant appeared with drinks and snacks—though no champagne. Once everyone had reconciled themselves to Abe's uninvited presence, Sonya returned to her presentation and handed Adrian a small box. Curious, I walked over to study it, very conscious of the scant inches between us. The box held a small vial of blood with silver rings around it. After a few moments of scrutiny, I glanced up and saw Sonya watching Adrian and me with a frown. Her features smoothed when she noticed me looking at her.

"What do you think?" she asked. "Is there any way to reinforce the seals around it?"

Adrian looked distinctly uncomfortable. "Um, I don't think so. I used up all my tricks doing this the first time."

"But you can feel the way the spirit's intertwined with the blood's substance," she pointed out. Again, he seemed troubled.

"Yeah, I noticed. That's nothing I can replicate."

"Me either," Sonya said.

"Me either," added Lissa.

Sonya sighed. "And that's the key, I think. Even if we can't sense it in Olive's blood anymore, I'm certain it altered her in a way that now prevents Strigoi conversion. If we could do that for others . . ."

He nodded in agreement. "Yup. But I don't know how. Unless . . ."

I noticed then how everyone in the room was watching him, faces expectant. They were deferring to his expertise. Adrian had been right about one thing when defending his use of spirit: He'd done what no one else could. I wondered if anyone—including him—had ever expected they'd reach a point where he would be a respected authority, not just a joke. That kind of responsibility and prestige suited him. Lord Ivashkov.

He looked at Lissa. "You'd mentioned making this into some kind of tattoo maybe, right? I wonder if it's as easy as injecting it into someone else? I mean, isn't that how a vaccine works? When someone fights off a disease, you get . . ." He groped for the word and looked to me for confirmation. "Antibodies?" I nodded. "Would this be the same? The magic spreads to someone else?"

"I can't even begin to guess if there's an equivalency between those two," I admitted. "But when vampire blood is suspended in an Alchemist tattoo, some of that Moroi quick healing and resistance to sickness spreads to us." If magic use really had negated my tattoo, I wondered if I'd lost my immunity too. I hated colds.

Adrian lit up. "Could you make a similar tattoo with this blood?"

I hesitated. "Theoretically. We don't know that it'd work. And I've never made that kind of ink before."

"That'd be remedial work for you," he said confidently. "And there are always guardian tattooists around here. What else do you need?"

"I can get you whatever it is," Abe assured me.

"I'd need—"

I stopped, and the world reeled. *I can get you whatever it is.* Yes, he probably could. Abe Mazur was a man who could get all sorts of things, even the ingredients to a potential Strigoi-protection tattoo.

Ingredients that would be nearly identical to the ones used in a regular Alchemist tattoo.

They were out of my reach but not Abe's. He probably wouldn't even need to use any illicit channels. He'd once smuggled C4 into Court, after all. I knew he had Alchemist contacts and could make a good case for why the Moroi needed to do this experiment. The Alchemists would certainly support it. Really, though, it didn't matter if Abe got the ingredients through legitimate or shady means. What mattered was that he could get what I needed without it actually being linked to me and a personal project to crack Alchemist compulsion.

"I can get you a list of things," I said as casually as I could. "We should double it, though. In case I make a mistake." Adrian met my eyes, and I could tell he'd picked up on what I was thinking.

Rose scoffed. "Have you ever made a mistake in your life?"

"Remains to be seen," I murmured. I stifled a yawn. "Get me some paper, and I'll write you a list." I couldn't hide my next yawn.

Sonya looked at me in sympathy. "Let poor Sydney go to bed. She's not on our schedule. We can't expect her to do this on no sleep, and we don't even have what we need yet."

Lissa looked mortified. "You're right. I'm sorry, Sydney. I wasn't thinking."

I logged into an Alchemist database on my phone in order to find the ingredient list. Lissa called for another servant while I wrote out what I'd need. As we waited, Christian asked, "Who are you going to give the tattoo to?"

Silence fell. "Me," said Rose at last. "It should be a dhampir. We've got the strongest bodies to handle something like that, and besides, if it works, we're more likely to run into Strigoi."

"You're too valuable to the queen," said Neil. "I'll do it, in case something goes wrong."

"Nothing's going to go wrong," said Adrian hotly.

Rose ignored him and glared at Neil. "*I'll* do it. No one else is going to risk themselves for this."

"What's your blood type?" I asked, looking between them. I turned to Olive. "And yours?"

"Don't get her involved," warned Neil.

"O positive," said Olive defiantly.

"B negative," said Rose.

Neil shot frustrated glances to both of them. "A positive."

"You win," I told Neil. I honestly thought a Moroi receiver would be best, but I had a feeling none of them would budge on that. Standard blood-typing rules seemed like a safe bet, though.

Rose's hurt expression implied I'd purposely betrayed her. Olive, excited for Neil, hurried over to his side. He puffed up with pride at her attention, and the scientist in Sonya decided she had no more patience for drama. "Fine. Neil gets it. Now for God's sake, get Sydney over to guest housing."

"I'll go too," said Adrian. He yawned, and I was pretty sure it was faked. "I've been around humans too long."

"You aren't staying at your parents' place?" asked Lissa.

Adrian scoffed. "Not if my dad's there. I actually want peace and quiet."

Lissa's servant arrived, and Rose decided to accompany us, thinking she was the only one I was truly comfortable with. As we were walking out, Nina hurried up and caught Adrian's sleeve. I was close enough that I could hear her, despite her lowered voice.

"I was hoping we could talk some more," she told him. "Do you think you'll have time tomorrow?"

Adrian put on the gallant smile most women received. "Sounds great, but I don't know if I'll have a chance. I think they expect me to work. It's such a pain being responsible."

Rose overheard. "Oh, yeah. So inconvenient, helping with a major breakthrough in Moroi life. Poor, poor Adrian."

Adrian winked at Nina. "I'll let you know."

We left, but not before I saw the longing in Nina's eyes. Even I could guess her intentions.

Guest housing was in one of the other venerable buildings, and we cut through a courtyard to get there. Light snow was falling, and I tugged my coat around me tightly. Adrian didn't complain, but he looked a little blue when we reached the building's lobby. It was run like a hotel, and Rose took it upon herself to arrange our rooms. I lingered on the far side of the lobby, and Adrian strolled over.

"You have no idea how cute you look with all those snowflakes in your hair," he murmured.

"And you look cute with hypothermia. I hope to God you can get a real coat while you're here."

He grinned. "You'll have to warm me up later. You know I was just playing it up for Nina, right? There's only one girl for me, but around here, I have to act like there's a dozen."

"Only one dozen?" I asked.

"Hey," Rose called to us. "You've got a room with a view on the second floor, Adrian. Sydney—what's going to make you feel better about creatures of the night? Easy escape on the first floor or distance on the second?"

"Second," I said, face neutral. "I'll climb out the window if I need to."

She led us upstairs and wished Adrian a good night. I received a personal escort to my room, and she looked around it with approval. "Same thing they'd give a royal. Is it okay?"

I wandered around, taking in the enormous suite with its sleek furniture and state-of-the-art entertainment center. "Uh, yeah. I'd say so."

"I know how weird this must be," she said kindly. "But we're doing big things here. At least that's what everyone says."

"They're right," I said. "And after rooming with Jill and fleeing authorities with you, this is kind of a non-event."

That got me one of her brilliant smiles. I was struck by how beautiful she was and couldn't help a pang of insecurity as I recalled that Adrian had once been so close to her— romantically and physically. Quickly, I pushed those worries aside. The past was done. I had no doubts about Adrian. Rose left with more assurances and urged me to let her know if I needed anything. When she finally took off, I settled into unpacking. Five minutes later, Adrian showed up at my door.

"Damn," he said, kicking it shut. He grabbed hold of me

and pushed me against the wall. "You have no idea what I've gone through today."

I put my arms around his neck and pulled him even closer. "Actually, I have a pretty good idea," I said, just before I met his lips in a crushing kiss.

There was an urgency in him that answered my own, and all the tightly wound tension I'd carried today exploded between us. He ran his hands over my body and then caught hold of one of my legs and hiked it up beside his hip. My blood burned within me, and I no longer felt even the least bit tired.

As sexy as an against-the-wall make-out session was, we eventually retired to my bed, which gave us both easier access to clothes, skin . . .

I sat beside him on the bed and helped him take off my sweater. "Who knew that escape plan number seventy-one would end up being 'Vacation at Moroi Court.'"

He laughed and then brought his lips to the nape of my neck, making me shiver. "Well, why not? No Zoe . . . no Alchemists . . . no time constraints." He trailed his lips to my shoulder and gently pushed the bra strap down. "We have a lot of freedom, Sage, and a lot of privacy."

I couldn't help a small gasp as his skilled lips continued their exploration. I closed my eyes and sank down into the bed, drawing him to me. This could be it, I realized. What I'd been preparing for. We finally had a very real chance to have sex without detection or interruption. It was heady. When were we going to get a chance to do this again?

And yet, as his touch continued to drive me wild, some old, frightened instinct held me back. What was I waiting for? Why was I still afraid? I wanted him, and I loved him, yet some

252

part of me still kept hesitating. It was maddening, especially since my body was screaming for Adrian to rip my clothes off. I opened my eyes and found him looking at me.

"It's okay," he said, guessing my thoughts.

"I'm sorry. I don't know what's wrong with me."

He placed a kiss on the tip of my nose. "Nothing's wrong with you."

"I want this. I really do. I just feel like I'm waiting for something."

"Then wait." The kindness and patience in his green eyes—mingled with unquestionable desire—made my heart ache.

"I just hate to waste this room and this night," I admitted.

He pulled off his shirt and tossed it on the floor. "Who said we're wasting anything?" He stretched his body out alongside mine and leaned in for another kiss. "Maybe we're not doing *it*, but believe me, Sage, there are plenty of other ways to pass the time."

CHAPTER 15

ADRIAN

I SLEPT WITH SYDNEY THAT NIGHT—in the literal sense, not the sexual one.

And it was glorious. I hadn't thought I could feel such joy over something so simple. For so long, I'd wished we could have more time together, that I could just drink her in and not be pressured by everything conspiring against us. Here it was.

It was also a little torturous at times. It made yesterday's travel tension seem downright easy. Even in a T-shirt and flannel pajama pants, she was agonizingly sexy. As she lay wrapped in my arms, sleeping with her head against my chest, I found myself thinking a lot about the thin fabric of her shirt and how there was nothing on underneath it. I thought a lot about what it'd be like to remove those clothes. I thought a lot about what I'd do after that. I loved her for her beautiful soul and desired her for her beautiful body. There was nothing sordid about it. It was nature.

As a result, sleep didn't come easy for me. My earlier

nap probably didn't help matters. When I wasn't fantasizing about Sydney, my mind wandered to our mission here and the potentially crackpot idea of using Olive's blood to make an Alchemist-like tattoo for Neil. Everyone was looking to Sydney and me to pull it off. I was *pretty* sure the spirit-infused blood wouldn't hurt Neil, so, much like Sydney's own experimental tattoo, there'd probably be no harm done in trying. After all, we were out of options for the blood. It was as good an idea as any and really didn't bother me.

What did bother me was my rapidly decreasing grasp of spirit. When Sonya had asked me about sensing what was in the vial, I'd had to lie. She was one of the best spirit users at reading truth but had thankfully been too distracted to notice. Because the thing was, I hadn't been able to read *anything* off of it. I knew there had to be spirit in the blood, based on her and Lissa's observations, but I could no longer sense it. I could no longer see auras either, and although I'd made no healing attempts, I could guess those results too.

Jill's revelation about the bond had been a slap in the face. Spirit's disappearance had always hovered as a real possibility, but I'd never thought too much about the consequences with her. She'd explained that although she still sensed we were connected, it felt as though there was a curtain between us that blocked my mind coming through to her. That wasn't exactly a bad thing. It meant my life was private again and that she would be protected from any of spirit's darkness seeping into her.

And I couldn't deny the most obvious truth: I now appeared to be protected from spirit too. I felt . . . good. My world was calm. I didn't have that frantic need to paint a whole gallery in one night, but I was still full of ideas, ideas that I could actually develop because my focus was stronger. Brooding about Pink Floyd didn't lead to outright depression. My love for Sydney burned just as strongly.

Life was good.

Waking up with her drove that home. I'd finally fallen asleep but came to when I felt her stirring. We'd both changed positions throughout the night but had never lost our hold on each other. With her sleepy eyes and tousled hair, I was pretty sure she'd never been more adorable. I leaned in to kiss her, and she turned her face away.

"I need to brush my teeth," she grumbled.

"Practical as soon as you wake up. I shouldn't be surprised."

"That's just common sense." She rolled to her side, and I pressed up to her back, wrapping my arms around her waist.

"You want to get breakfast?" I asked.

"We can't go out together. It's going to be bad enough if someone sees you leaving my room."

I glanced at a clock. "Nah. They're all going to bed right around now."

"Then how are we going to get breakfast?"

"There are a couple of twenty-four-hour places since there are always some people coming in and out from human schedules." I kissed her neck. "I'll lift your coffee restriction since this is a special occasion."

"Hey, I'm sticking to my word."

"We'll see what you say if it's a late Moroi work night."

She was quiet for several moments. "You haven't had a drop of alcohol in a while, have you? Not even your daily one."

"Easier that way. No point dancing on the line."

Her response was simple and perfect: "I love you."

She eventually sent me on my way so that we could both get ready on our own, despite my well-thought-out argument for why sharing a shower would be effective. I kept my shower uncharacteristically brief so that I could run over to the building next door for a quick visit with the feeders. Sydney and I met up a half hour later in the lobby of guest housing, just like any proper Moroi and Alchemist would do. The guy working the desk didn't pay much attention to us, but we still put on an Oscar-worthy show of formal greetings and safe distance.

Outside, the watery sunlight did little to warm the winter morning. Sydney looked snug and cute in her furry coat, and I cursed the idiocy that had driven me to wear my thin one. No way would I complain, though. I had to stand by my fashion choice.

The grounds were as deserted as I expected, the only people out being occasional guardians still on diligent patrol, despite the wards that protected Court from Strigoi. Of course, these days, with people still opposed to Lissa's rule, we faced as much danger from our own kind. One of the restaurants I remembered was still in business, and Sydney chuckled as we entered.

"Incredible," she said. "There's a whole civilization tucked inside these buildings."

"Yup. This, and a whole lot more. A club, a spa, a bowling alley. Not that I'm stupid enough to take you to that last one." Sydney seemed to be ridiculously good at most sports. It wasn't even because of any special athletic powers. Half the time, she just used logic and mathematical calculations to size up her moves.

The restaurant was actually more of a diner. We ordered at the counter and then relaxed at a table with coffee while the cook made our food. Both of us were still a little tired, and I was again struck by how much I loved this normality.

"Someday, Sage," I told her. "Every morning in our apartment in Rome. Us in bed, breakfast together . . . I don't know how we'll make it work, but we will."

She turned from where she'd been examining the menu on the wall and smiled. "Rome, huh? Which escape plan is this?"

"Number one," I said promptly, knowing that Rome was a dream of hers.

Her smile grew. "Are you going to learn Italian?"

"Don't need to. I can communicate with my eyes."

"You'll have to learn the numbers at least, so you can haggle with people when you sell your art on the street," she teased.

I put my hand over my heart. "You wound me, Sage. In this fantasy, I give you credit for attending some top university, but you put me on the streets."

"Hey, we all have to start somewhere. I start with classes. You start on the street. Eventually, I get my doctorate and you're doing world-famous gallery shows."

I nodded, mollified. "Okay, I can roll with that. And then after that, I suppose it's just a matter of time until we're taking the kids to soccer practice."

Her eyebrows rose. "Kids?"

"Relax, it's years away. But can you imagine? Your brains, my charm, our collective good looks . . . then add in the usual physical abilities dhampirs get." She looked more amused than appalled at the speculation, which was something I'd never thought I'd see. "It's really not even fair to everyone else. Good thing you're on birth control, since the world obviously isn't ready for our perfect offspring."

"Obviously," she laughed.

Our gazes locked, and as usual, my mind jumped from birth control to the inevitable. This trip could be it, I realized. There was no Jill, and last night had proven we could have plenty of time together. From the way she went still as we stared at each other, I knew she was thinking exactly the same thing. Was she ready yet? That was still the big question, the one I'd wait on forever, if need be. It'd just be a lot easier waiting if she didn't obviously want it so badly too.

"Holy shit! Ivashkov, is that you?"

A jarring voice startled me out of my daze. My stomach sank. Slowly, putting on that damned smile everyone expected from me, I turned toward the diner's entrance. There he was, Wesley Drozdov, one of the most obnoxious people I knew. Worse, he had a couple other royal assholes in tow: Lars Zeklos and Brent Badica.

They used to be my drinking buddies.

They were obviously drunk now, judging from the way they staggered over to our table. The overpowering reek of alcohol radiating from them was another tip-off. Wesley slapped me on the back, making my teeth rattle.

"When did you get back?" he demanded. "Why didn't you call?"

"Just got back last night. Barely enough time," I said.

"Are you kidding? You could've gone out with us! We've been partying for, like . . ." Brent turned to the others, probably because the math was too hard. "Six hours. This new club just opened, and then Monique Szelsky threw this crazy party we just closed out. Time for some power food now, and then we're going to crash."

It was then that they noticed I wasn't alone. Lars straightened up and put on the pseudo-responsible look he'd try to pull off if his parents came home early while he was throwing a party. "Hello." He held out his hand. "I'm Lars."

Sydney hesitated before taking it, less from fear of Moroi than disdain for drunken idiots. "Sydney Sage."

The others crowded to shake her hand, and I knew that the icy "I'm tolerating you" Alchemist smile she sometimes faked when we were in public was completely real for them.

"I heard there might be humans here." Brent peered at her cheek. "You're one of those? Those Alch—Alchemists?" The Alchemists actually weren't widely known to all Moroi.

"That's right," she said coolly.

"She's here on top secret business for the queen. Or something." I laughed and leaned back in my chair. "I don't know. They don't tell me that kind of important stuff. They just asked me to be a tour guide. I think they'll comp my food and drink, so hey, bonus."

Wesley couldn't take his eyes off Sydney. "We're going out again after sunset. You want to come with us? Ivashkov's not really showing you Moroi life unless you hit some parties. There are a couple good ones planned."

Sydney was so stiff, she could've broken in half. "No thanks. I have to meet with the queen."

"See?" I said. "I told you. These Alchemists are all business."

Lars nudged me. "Well, I know *you* aren't. Why don't you come out with us? There's some girls, man, that if they knew you were back, they'd—" He bit off his words and shot an apologetic look at Sydney.

Just then, the cook called out that our order was ready. Sydney stood up so quickly, her chair nearly fell over. "I'll get it." She strode off without another word or glance. All three of the guys stared after her, making no attempt to hide their lascivious looks. Sydney and I had experienced many things in our relationship, but this was the first time I'd ever felt such consuming hostility toward other guys. I wanted to punch them all.

"Goddamn," said Wesley. "I never knew an ass could look so hot in khakis."

"How the *hell* can you sit there so calmly?" Lars demanded of me.

I put my feet on an empty chair, clasping my hands behind my head. If they were restrained, maybe I wouldn't try to choke anyone. "What do you mean?"

"You know what I mean." Lars shook his head. "God, we were just at the feeders, and there is nothing, *nothing* like that there. They're like week-old leftovers compared with her. We never get anything that good."

"Not a mark on her neck," breathed Brent, eyes wide. "You know she's never done it. Can you imagine what it'd be like, burying your teeth in that? Ambrosia, man. And you know she'd love it. Those prim and proper ones always do."

I clenched my hands together so tightly that my nails practically pierced my skin. Even to jerks like these, sex with a human wasn't a consideration. But drinking from one? A beautiful one who'd never been touched before? That was as mind-blowing as sex to them, driving them into a frenzy with lust of a different kind.

"Hose yourself down," I laughed. "Do you even know anything about Alchemists? She can barely stand being in the same room as us. You'd never get near her neck."

Wesley leaned toward me. "Get her to go out with us later! The queen can't keep her all night."

I was pretty sure the nails digging into my palms were drawing blood now. "Did you even hear what I said? She's out of our league."

Brent's lips were parted, showing his fangs as he watched Sydney turn around with her tray. "Not if we go dabbling."

"You're still drunk, man." I managed the painful smile but couldn't laugh this time.

"It'd be easy," he hissed. "Tell her you're going to take her on some cultural experience. I can score something for her, and we can each get a turn. God, I'd love to see her face when—"

"No," I said.

Lars scowled. "You've gone soft, Ivashkov. You never minded dabbling before."

But Sydney had reached us by then, and the three of them at least had the sense to shut up. "It's getting late," I said. "You better get your food and rest up for later."

They took the hint and wandered off laughing and whispering toward the counter, but not before telling me to get in touch if I changed my mind. I took a deep breath to steady myself and be interested in my French toast so that Sydney wouldn't pick up on my mood.

"Sorry," I said. "Friends from another time."

"What's dabbling?" she asked.

I winced. So. She'd heard that last part. She obviously hadn't heard the rest, or she wouldn't be nearly so calm. I had to choose my next words very carefully. If I gave her a total lie, there could be trouble if she ever found out the truth. And yet, I couldn't answer with full honesty either, so I opted for something that skirted the truth.

"It's stupid." I rolled my eyes and munched on my side of bacon to buy me more time. "Jerks like that think it's hilarious to try to recruit new humans as feeders. They take a human out and talk a bunch of crap to try to win them over."

She actually dropped her fork. "Are you serious?" She glanced over her shoulder and studied them in disbelief. "They . . . they wanted to talk me into being a feeder?" She was so shocked at the idea of *her* being a feeder that she didn't even think about the implications of them openly discussing vampires with outsiders. Feeders were usually recruited from the fringes of human society, often from those who were already addicted to something and had little promise in their lives. Living with the Moroi was an upgrade. Normal, active members of human society were never approached.

"It's okay," I assured her. "I blew them off. They're not going to try anything. They think you're pretty—which is true—but they're just a bunch of talk. They won't even remember it when they sober up."

Sydney still looked worried and tore her muffin into pieces without eating or speaking.

"I'm serious," I said, wishing I could touch her hand. "They're assholes. They're nobodies. I'd never let them do anything like that."

She eventually nodded and then gave me a smile of such warmth and trust that I wanted to die for my lie. "I know," she said.

I swallowed and tried not to pay attention to where Wesley and his friends sat, still casting covert looks back at us. "Let's hurry up and do some sightseeing. Best time to do it, with everyone in bed. Maybe, *maybe,* we should look for another coat for me."

As I hoped, the satisfaction of being right perked her up. "I knew it! I knew you had to be freezing."

"Yeah, yeah, you're a genius, Sage. We'll get the coat, bum around, and then maybe visit bed like everyone else for a while."

Before long, those drunken idiots were a distant memory. We sneaked into my parents' town house and found an old winter coat of mine. My dad was there, sound asleep, and never knew we came by. After that, I did my best to point out all the old architecture I thought she'd be into. I didn't know any of the technicalities, but as I'd hoped, she did, and she loved it. We wrapped up back in her room afterward, cuddling in bed until our appointed meeting time. It was an amazing day.

Back at the palace, Lissa had arranged for a vast breakfast buffet for all of us. It was dinnertime for Sydney and me, but we didn't mind the repeat, and she certainly didn't mind the ready supply of decaf coffee. People chatted in clusters throughout the room as we ate, and Nina beckoned me over from the opposite side, where she stood with Neil and Olive. I smiled and mouthed "maybe later" to her.

Rose strolled over to us, carrying a plate with five donuts on it. Dhampir metabolism was nuts, and I could almost understand Sydney's weird body hang-ups when she spent time around people who could eat so much and still keep decent figures.

"Did you have a good day?" Rose asked. "I assume you weren't sleeping it away like the rest of us."

Sydney laughed. "No. Neither was Adrian. He's been

converted to our Palm Springs schedule, so he took me around and showed me all the wonders of the Moroi Court."

Rose shot me a pleased and proud look, like she could barely believe I'd do anything so thoughtful. "Well, good. Hopefully it's another step in convincing you we aren't all bloodthirsty minions of hell."

Sydney started to laugh again and then grew pensive. "Well . . . not all of you."

"What do you mean?" Rose asked, her words muffled in a chocolate donut.

"It's nothing," said Sydney. "Just some drunk guys we met who wanted to . . . what'd you say it was, Adrian? Dabbling?"

Rose nearly choked on her donut. "They did *what*?"

"They didn't *do* anything," I said carefully. An uneasy feeling spread over me, and I prayed we'd either abruptly change topic or that Lissa would start this operation.

"Who the hell would even suggest that?" I recognized that look on Rose's face, the one that said her fist had an appointment with someone. "Tell me who they are."

Sydney seemed touched by the concern. "It's nothing, and Adrian's right. They didn't do anything. He scared them off. Besides, it's not like they could've talked me into doing it."

I was feeling ill. I glanced around the room. "Hey, where's Honest Abe? Wasn't he supposed to get Sydney's goods?"

Rose didn't even hear me. Her gaze was fixed firmly on Sydney. "Do you know what dabbling is?"

"Yeah," said Sydney uncertainly. "It's when they try to convince you to be a feeder."

"I wouldn't say 'convince' is the right word," growled Rose. "It's when Moroi go out and drug a random human so that they can drink from him or her. Usually her, since it's usually guys behind it. The human's kind of out of it from the drug and doesn't remember anything later, just that they somehow ended up with bruises on their neck. It's essentially date rape for blood drinking."

Sydney looked so pale, she could've been one of the Moroi. "What . . ."

Rose seemed to realize just how traumatizing that might be to an Alchemist and tried to backpedal. "It doesn't happen very often," she said quickly. "And it'd never happen here—especially if you've got Adrian as your noble defender. And me."

Sydney couldn't formulate a response.

Someone called for Rose, and she bit her lip, glancing worriedly between Sydney and me. "Look, I'm sorry. I shouldn't have said anything. Don't freak out. There's nothing to worry about." She gently touched Sydney's arm. Sydney flinched and pulled back. Rose heard her name again and glanced up at me. "Talk to her. I'll be back."

She scurried away, and I took a step closer to Sydney, who thankfully didn't jerk away. "She's right, it's—"

Sydney's eyes sharpened. "Why did you lie to me?"

I pointed at her. "Exactly because of this. I didn't want to scare you."

"You shouldn't have sugarcoated it," she said. "I'm tough enough to handle it."

"I know you are," I said softly. "I'm just not tough enough to tell you ugly things. I figured the point was the same: It's a bunch of bastards taking advantage of someone."

She nodded, and I held my breath, hoping we were done with this. Then, that cursed memory of hers came into play.

"One of them said you used to not mind. Did you go along with it?" Her breath suddenly caught. "Did you ever do it?"

The world swayed around me. I wished to God I had my spirit back so that I could compel her into discussing *The Great Gatsby*. Instead, I manned up and answered as concisely as I could: "Sort of."

CHAPTER 16

SYDNEY

"SORT OF?" I DEMANDED. "How can you sort of do . . . something like that?"

I couldn't bring myself to go into detail. What Rose had just described was horrible. It was the kind of thing Alchemists had nightmares about, the kind of thing that confirmed every allegation of dark, twisted creatures.

Adrian glanced around, but everyone else was preoccupied with their own conversations. "It wasn't like that. I never drugged anyone. It was a long time ago, just one time, when I was a lot younger and a lot stupider. We were out at a club, and we ended up hanging out with some human girls. They were all drinking a lot—we all were—and there was one who liked me. She got pretty wasted, one thing led to another . . ."

"And you drank from her," I finished. "When she really didn't know what was going on."

"I didn't drink very much." I could tell from his expression that even he knew it was a lame excuse. "And technically, she drugged herself."

I swallowed and tried to address it in an objective Alchemist way. "That was beyond careless. You could've exposed the vampire world! Our whole job is covering you guys up, and then you just show everyone."

"I don't think she remembered."

"That almost makes it worse." My objectivity crumbled. "What you did . . . how could you? It doesn't matter if it wasn't a drug! No, it *was*. Alcohol's as bad as anything you could've slipped her. You took advantage of someone who wasn't in control of herself. It was a violation."

Pain crossed his features. "Hell, Sydney. *I* wasn't in control of myself."

"You think that justifies it?" I hissed. "And even if it was 'just one time,' how many other times did you look the other way while those friends of yours did a lot worse things?"

"They aren't my friends anymore. And do you think I could've really stopped them?"

"Did you even try?" I demanded.

"I was a different person then!" Realizing how loud he'd gotten, Adrian stepped forward and lowered his voice. "You of all people should understand that. Not even a year ago, you were making the sign against evil around us and wouldn't shake hands because you thought we were the spawn of Satan."

"Yeah, well, maybe I was right. And don't even try to compare superstition to . . . to . . . blood rape."

He winced. "I'm not saying it's in the same class. I'm saying people change. We grow up, we learn. You know the kind of person I am. You know I wouldn't even dream of something like that now."

"Do I?" I tried to summon up as much outrage as I could

because if I didn't, I might start crying. No way would I crack in a room full of Moroi. "Are you saying you wouldn't drink my blood if you had the chance? That you don't think about it?"

"No." He spoke with such certainty that I almost believed him. "The only thing I want from your body is—well, it's not that. And you should know that."

I didn't know that I did. I turned away, trying to come to terms with something that had just knocked my world off-kilter. I had long ago accepted that he had an extensive romantic past. Surprisingly, it didn't bother me so much anymore. It was before my time. Those girls were gone. He didn't love them. He'd been free, and if he'd wanted to fool around with girls who wanted to as well, then that was his right.

And yet . . . here he was, admitting to fooling around with a girl who hadn't wanted to. "Fooling around" was being kind, considering what he'd done. Drinking blood was probably the biggest sin Moroi committed, in Alchemist eyes. I'd made my peace with it, that it was their way of life, but it still made me squeamish. It was nothing I could watch, and I was always relieved when Jill and Adrian finished at Clarence's. Now, I couldn't shake the image of him doing that terrible thing. He embodied every fear Alchemists had about monsters stalking unwitting victims.

"Sydney . . ."

The pain in his voice made my heart ache, but I had no words of comfort to offer. I couldn't even comfort myself. He said he'd changed, but was that enough? Could that make up for something so horrific?

"Sorry I'm late." Abe strolled in with a dhampir man I didn't know, giving me something to look at besides Adrian's grief-stricken face. Abe was carrying a crate and wore a bright teal silk scarf. He probably loved that it was winter. "Some of these things aren't so easy to get a hold of."

"But you got everything?" asked Lissa eagerly.

"Of course." Abe gestured grandly to the dhampir beside him. "Including our tattooist, Horace. We're ready to start when you are."

It wasn't until all eyes in the room swiveled in my direction that I realized he was talking to me. For a moment, my mind was blank. Why on earth were they staring at me? What was I supposed to do? The only thing I could think about was Adrian and that dark confession. Then, slowly, the scientist in me stirred. Right. The ink. Measurements, chemicals. I could do that. There was no moral ambiguity there.

Throwing my shoulders back, I strode up to Abe and spoke in a cold voice I hadn't used in a very long time. "Let's see what you've got."

He set out the supplies on a wide table. I examined each one critically and then nodded in satisfaction. "It's all here."

"What do you need us to do?" he asked.

"Stay out of my way."

I pulled up a wooden stool and then took out my cell phone, which contained the exact formula and directions for making the Alchemist ink. A heavy silence fell on us, and I tried to ignore the fact that I had an audience. It had been a long time since I worked with Alchemist substances, though the concentration and diligence weren't that different from creating spell components. I was simply facilitating chemical reactions instead of magical ones.

It was straightforward Alchemist work, but my hands

271

trembled as I measured and mixed. I had to keep forcing my mind back to the task, away from my broken heart. When they realized the procedure wasn't going to take five minutes, the group dispersed and talked quietly among themselves, finally giving me some privacy. Rose and Dimitri, thinking I was upset about helping Moroi, stopped by once to tell me what a great thing I was doing. I took their praise with a curt nod.

Sonya came up as I was finishing and offered similar sentiments. "This could be so useful to us, Sydney."

I glanced up briefly. "I know. I'm glad to help."

Whatever she saw in my face took her aback. "What's wrong?"

"Nothing." I looked back down. "Just being at Court and on a weird schedule."

"It's more than that. Don't you think I can tell?"

Yes, of course she could, I thought bitterly. She could probably read the distress in my aura because that's what she did: peer into others whether they wanted it or not. Boundaries, I was learning, were a negotiable thing among Moroi.

"I saw you talking to Adrian," she continued. "What did he say to you?" Her voice faltered. "Sydney, I've seen things with you two . . ."

I looked back up, and my earlier anger returned. "If you want to help, let me work and forget whatever it is you think you've seen."

She flinched, and I experienced a small pang of regret. Sonya was my friend and probably did have good intentions. I just didn't want them right now, and after a few more seconds, she backed off.

I completed the suspension and sat back to admire the

vial I'd created. It was as perfect as it could get. The others returned, making me feel oppressed and trapped.

"That's it?" asked Neil. "You can tattoo me now?"

"No." I pointed to the untouched vial of blood, still in its silver-bound box. "My suspension needs to sit for a while before we can mix them together."

Clearly, they hadn't expected that. "How long?" asked Abe.

"A couple hours should do it."

Sonya sighed in dismay. "Each hour, the spirit weakens." She turned to Adrian. "Do you think there's still enough in it to be useful?"

"There has to be," he said enigmatically.

"There's nothing I can do to speed it up," I explained. "Unless you want to deviate from what we've done for hundreds of years." I was being snippy but couldn't help it. "I'm going to go back to my room and rest. I'll come back when it's time for the next step."

"Do you want me to walk you?" asked Dimitri. My bad mood was coming through to all of them.

I stood up and carefully placed the duplicate ingredients back in the crate. "Thanks, but I know the way." I preferred to take my chances walking through Court at night than deal with more good-intentioned counseling. "Although . . . Abe, if you've got a minute, I have a question . . ."

My soliciting Abe caught a few people by surprise, especially Abe. He hid it quickly, though, and his natural sense of curiosity immediately took over. "But of course. Here, let me carry that for you. Or, actually, if you just want to leave it, I'll take care of them since you didn't need the duplicate set."

I held my chin up in an imperious Alchemist way. "These

are ingredients used for one of our most important purposes. I can't leave these behind."

We walked out, passing Adrian and Nina near the doorway. His heart was in his eyes as he watched me, and he barely seemed to hear Nina worriedly telling him about how Olive and Neil had stayed out late together. I quickly averted my eyes from him, afraid of what I might betray.

The night was crisp and cold and dotted with stars as Abe and I walked out toward guest housing. "So," he said. "To what do I owe the pleasure of your company?"

"The ingredients you got me. One of them was Moroi blood."

"It was on your list, though it seemed strange," he replied. "I mean, I understand that's normally in Alchemist tattooing ink, but in our case tonight, we already had a specific blood sample to use. In fact, that was kind of the point."

Clever Abe. Nothing slipped past him.

"Is it charmed?" I asked.

"No. You didn't leave any other directions, so I simply obtained a plain sample. Again, since we weren't making standard ink, I didn't think it was necessary. I wouldn't have known what kind of compulsion you wanted anyway."

"Have you ever done it?" Here it was. No way would Abe think this was a hypothetical. "Done a compulsion charm for the Alchemists?"

Silence. Yes, he knew something was up, but he hadn't put it together. "No, I haven't. I understand the principles, though. A fairly straightforward compulsion spell encouraging discretion and group loyalty."

"Fairly straightforward," I repeated. That was an understatement.

He chuckled. "For an earth user, yes."

"So you could do it, even though you haven't? You could do it to these samples?"

"I could . . ." My building was in sight, and he came to a halt. "Miss Sage, let me make sure I'm following correctly. You're asking me to put a compulsion spell on the blood samples you have. And what you *aren't* explicitly asking—but are wishing—is that I not tell the other Alchemists."

I kicked at a tree branch with my boot. A recent storm must have knocked a number of them down because they were strewn about the quads and walkways. "You're too smart for your own good."

"So are you. Which is what makes this completely and utterly fascinating. And let me guess. You aren't carting off the extra ingredients simply to make sure they return to righteous Alchemist hands." His eyes were dark and foreboding in the dim lighting. "Who are you trying to compel? Some boy? Love compulsions almost never work."

"No! It's nothing like that. I just need an all-purpose, off-the-rack compulsion charm on it like you'd do for standard ink. I'll take care of the rest."

"You'll take care of 'the rest,'" he said, clearly amused. "The rest being where you activate the magic as it's injected and are able to imprint your command on someone."

"Can you do it or not?" I asked. The wind stirred, lightly scattering snowflakes down upon us from a nearby tree.

"Oh, I can do it right now," he said cheerfully. "The question is, what do I get in return?"

I sighed. "I knew it'd come to this. Does there *always* have to be something? Can't you do things just to be nice?"

"My dear, I do plenty of things to be nice. What I don't do is let an advantage slip through my fingers. Do you think I've gotten where I am today by heedlessly giving away things that can result in power and knowledge?"

"Power and knowledge?" I shook my head. "You might be asking for more than I'm capable of giving you."

"Explain to me why you're interested in an off-the-record tattoo, and that'll be knowledge. More than enough payment."

I hesitated. Abe wasn't going to sell me out to the Alchemists, but no way was I going to get into the backstory of Marcus's rebel movement. This was a tightly guarded secret. "I'm not trying to control anyone. This is part of an experiment—purely scientific. That's the truth. Beyond that, though, I can't tell you. That's the extent of the knowledge you can have. But if you want to haggle for some other payment, be my guest. Let's just do it somewhere warmer."

I shivered and tugged my coat around me as Abe deliberated. At last, he said quietly, "I've already gotten more knowledge than you might think. I know that Sydney Sage, do-gooder and darling of the Alchemists, is working on clandestine affairs that go against her order's directives. That's more than payment enough. Give me your blood. The samples, I mean."

I knelt down on the ground and opened the crate. "What are you going to do with that knowledge?"

"I'm not going to announce it to the world, if that's what you're worried about." He paused and laughed to himself. "But of course you aren't. You never would've asked for this charm if you thought I'd give you away."

I found the two capped vials of Moroi blood and handed

them over. I needed only one but didn't want the other to go to waste.

"No," I agreed. "I didn't think you'd tell on me. I didn't even think you'd be shocked."

"I'm not. Surprised, but not shocked." He held up one of the vials, and I could see lines of concentration deepening on his face as he focused on it. I sensed nothing with my human skills, and this type of earth magic spoke directly to the substance of the blood, meaning there was no flashy burst of fire or water like you'd get with one of the other elements. "There." He handed it back to me and focused on the other.

"You didn't answer my question," I reminded him.

"Because I don't know," he said several moments later. I accepted the second vial from him. "Ultimately, I imagine it'll go toward serving the same thing it always does."

"Yourself?"

"My loved ones."

I fell speechless. That certainly wasn't the answer I'd expected from Abe "Zmey" Mazur. He took a step closer so that he could look me more squarely in the eye.

"You think I'm so manipulative and scheming, Miss Sage? It's all for them. For my loved ones first. My people second. And yes, I suppose I'm in the mix there too, but don't think for an instant I wouldn't sacrifice myself if it could save someone I love. And don't think for an instant that I wouldn't do terrible, unspeakable things if it could save someone I love." When he backed up, I noticed I'd been holding my breath. "Good luck with your experiment. Let me know if I can be of any more assistance."

I watched him walk off into the night, his words replaying in my mind. When he'd disappeared into the darkness, I returned to my room with the crate. And there, the ominous meeting with Abe vanished from my mind because I amazingly had bigger problems that came crashing back down on me.

Adrian.

Adrian, who'd withheld the knowledge that he'd taken advantage of a human girl.

Adrian, whom I'd trusted.

I threw myself on my bed and waited for the tears to come. They didn't. The storm of emotions I'd felt earlier had simply gone numb. I was left with a cold, empty hole inside my heart and the gears of reason turning in my brain. Was Adrian right? Was it wrong to hold him responsible for something he'd done so long ago? We both were different people, and who was I to judge others when I'd orchestrated an act of revenge that had cost Keith his eye? I was no saint.

But Keith had committed a terrible crime, and the girl Adrian had drank from had done nothing except be in the wrong place at the wrong time. Why did it have to be that? Why the blood? The thing that played the most upon my fears?

He texted me three times on the Love Phone, asking me if he could come over and talk. I didn't answer. At least he had the sense not to barge on in. I spent my entire break lying on the bed like that, with Hopper curled to my chest in statue form.

When I returned to the palace later, I felt more in control, mostly because I'd shut down almost all my feelings. The scene I walked into was similar, though a few people had left for the break. Adrian and Nina were sitting and talking together. She looked radiant, and although he was smiling, I knew him well enough to recognize when he was faking it. Our eyes locked for a few brief moments and then I marched back up to my table.

The rest of the procedure was simple: adding the blood to the suspension I'd created. The liquid turned silver, earning a surprised grunt from Abe.

"Shouldn't it be gold?"

I hesitated. "That's the one part I changed. Silver's more in tune with Moroi magic. I thought it'd be better."

Sonya's eyes widened in alarm. "The spirit's leaking out now that it's out of the case! Help me!"

Nina and Lissa hurried beside her, looks of concentration on their faces. They were using their magic to try to protect the vial, I realized. I didn't know how successful they were, but I knew enough to realize we couldn't waste time. "Hurry up," I told Horace the tattooist.

He had a machine similar to Wolfe's and loaded the ink into his needle. Neil sat down beside it, and Olive hovered near him. "Does it have to be the face?" he asked.

I shook my head. "No. We just do that to identify ourselves."

After a moment's hesitation, Neil pulled off his T-shirt, revealing a well-muscled physique. He pointed to his upper left arm. "Here."

Horace brought the needle down and then turned, puzzled. "What am I drawing?"

There were a few moments of comical silence. "Whatever's fastest," I said.

"I kind of wanted a cross," said Neil wistfully. His stoic mask fell into place. "But do whatever you need to."

"Do a cross with simple lines," Adrian said unexpectedly. "I'll design more art to go around it later, and you can just get regular ink to embellish it."

279

Even I was surprised at the offer, considering how much Neil usually irritated Adrian. Horace was already at work. Even with a simple design, tattooing wasn't something that could be done in a hurry. He was obviously moving as fast as he could, but I could tell by the spirit users' strained faces that they were still losing ground. I grew so caught up in the drama that I actually forgot about Adrian. My world narrowed down to each drop of ink that went into Neil's skin.

When Horace finished, everyone looked ready to faint from the exhaustion of stress. Lissa rested her head on Christian's shoulder, and a paler-than-usual Sonya sank into a chair. "There was still magic in the ink when you finished," she said. "But I don't sense it anymore. I have no way of knowing if it worked—aside from the obvious."

I was struck by the parallels between Neil and Trey. Both were now marked with experimental ink to protect them from insidious powers . . . but nobody truly knew if the procedures had been effective. The potential to solve Trey's mystery was in a crate back in my room. The answer to Neil's, unfortunately, was in the teeth of a Strigoi.

Sonya closed her eyes and rested her hand on her forehead. I could only imagine what she was feeling. Protecting Moroi from Strigoi had become an obsession for her, a project with very personal implications. This had to be monumental for her, the potential conclusion to her work. Suddenly, she opened her eyes and fixed them on Adrian as a revelation seemed to hit her.

"Why didn't you help us? We might have saved more magic. You did nothing."

"She's right," Lissa said, clearly surprised. "I didn't realize it until now. It was just the three of us."

We all looked at Adrian, and even I was astonished. This had become a personal mission for him too, especially considering his monumental role in saving Olive's blood. Why would he shirk helping now? Indecision warred on his face. At last, he sighed with resignation.

"I didn't help . . . because I can't."

Lissa straightened up from where she was resting against Christian. "What does that mean exactly?"

He gave her a rueful smile. "It means, cousin, that I'm going on my third week of mood stabilizers and no longer have access to spirit."

My heart stopped.

"Why . . . why would you do that?" Lissa asked.

"You tell me," he replied. "You did it once. Or something like it. I wanted my life back. I didn't want spirit to control me anymore. You know what it can do." He looked at Lissa, Sonya, and Nina in turn. "You all know."

From their chagrined expressions, they did know. But it was clear they were also confused.

"Why would you do it now of all times?" exclaimed Sonya. "When you knew we still needed you?"

He focused back on her, holding his ground. "Did I know that? I did my part—a big part. I had no idea it'd come to this. Besides, what time should I have waited for? When I was about to jump off a bridge?"

The words hit Sonya like a slap in the face. "Of course not. But . . . there are other ways to cope . . ."

Adrian laughed. "Yeah? Alcohol poisoning? Cutting? Turning Strigoi?"

It was a cruel thing to say to Lissa and Sonya, but neither of them could muster an argument. Nina was the one who spoke up, confusion in her gray eyes. "But how can you stand to be away from the magic? The rush? Don't you miss it?"

"Yes," he said bluntly. "But other things in my life are more important."

My legs grew weak, and I backed up, settling down into a plush armchair. I clasped my hands together to stop them from shaking.

"I'm sorry I couldn't help this time, but none of you have the right to judge me," Adrian added. There was a strength and conviction in his voice that I doubt any of them had seen before. "This is my life, and there's nothing you can say to change my mind—unless Her Majesty wants to give a royal command for me to stop."

Lissa blanched. "Of course not."

Everything was kind of weird after that.

I kept my distance from the others, and this time, no one seemed to notice or care. Adrian became the new attraction. Sonya and Lissa apologized, and Nina tried to engage him about what it was like. He shot me another pained look from across the room, and I had to glance away because my confusion was too great.

And as the night progressed, it became clear to me they weren't going to give him up anytime soon. The spirit users wanted to know more about Adrian and the pills. Everyone else wanted to know what the next step with Neil was. My role was done, and when exhaustion began weighing me down, I quietly slipped out of the room to go get some sleep. I knew travel arrangements were being made for later tomorrow, so no one would need me right away. The nice thing about being forced onto this schedule was that I was so legitimately tired that my body wasn't going to let my mind keep me awake with questions. And believe me, I had plenty. I needed to understand the Adrian of long ago. I needed to understand the Adrian I loved. And I needed to understand why he hadn't told me he was facing one of his greatest fears by taking a prescription.

Tears sprang to the corner of my eyes and then began to freeze. I stopped in the middle of a walkway leading through some ornamental trees and tried to wipe my face as best as I could.

"Hey, are you okay?"

I jerked my head up at the unfamiliar voice. Well, not entirely unfamiliar. A young man materialized from the trees, and a moment later, a second joined him. Tired and emotionally frayed, I didn't recognize them at first. Then, I realized they were Adrian's friends—or, well, ex-friends—from the café. I stiffened, suddenly wide awake and alert.

And terrified.

"Sydney, right?" It was the guy who'd first spoken. "I'm—"

"Wesley," I said. "I remember."

"You do? That's great. Then you must remember Lars too."

The faint light of a lamppost a little ways away filtered through the branches of a tree above us, lighting up his face as he grinned in what he probably thought was a friendly manner. I didn't need him to get any closer to know he was drunk—just like he had been yesterday. Was that what Adrian used to be like? Waking up and going from one state of intoxication to another? It was a pathetic, dismal life.

"Where are you headed?" asked Lars. "You need directions?"

"I'm just going back to my room to get some sleep." I

pointed at the building, which suddenly seemed very far away. "Right over there."

"Sleep?" Lars laughed. "That's right. You're on a flipped schedule. Look, why don't you come out with us? Live it up while you're here. We'll get you some caffeine and hit some parties."

"Or if you want something quieter, we could just go back to my place and talk." That was Wesley, and he seemed to be having a difficult time sounding serious and responsible.

"No, thank you," I said, shifting a little. It put me two steps closer to my building. Unfortunately, I probably had about two hundred more to go. "I'm really tired."

Lars nudged Wesley. "See, this is what happens when you get stuck with Adrian as a tour guide. It makes you feel satisfied with boredom."

"Adrian's not boring," I said. "Especially—from what I hear—the way he used to be."

Wesley scoffed. "Even then, he never let loose like the rest of us."

"We can tell you everything about him if you want," exclaimed Lars, apparently feeling inspired. He glanced past me briefly and then fixed his eyes back on mine. "We'll tell you all you need to know. Let's go back to Wesley's."

"No, thank you," I said. I already knew all I needed to know about Adrian, primarily that he was nothing like these losers. "I have to go." I made no attempts at subtlety and began hurrying toward the building.

"Hey, wait," offered Lars. He moved with remarkable speed for someone so intoxicated. He caught hold of my arm, just as two startling thoughts came to me. *Why do they keep looking behind me? And weren't there three of them before?*

I started to turn around, just as that third person came up behind me and clamped a hand over my mouth. That split second of anticipation was enough to trigger some instinctual Wolfe training. I kicked backward into Brent and had the satisfaction of hearing, "Oof!" His hand slipped on my mouth, giving me a chance at another Wolfe tactic: screaming for help.

Old Alchemist fears, bred into me since birth, reared up. Here it was, the evil we'd always been warned about: vampires coming after me in the night. Creatures of hell, intent on drinking my blood when I was alone and vulnerable. For a moment, fear and panic crippled me. Then, a strong voice inside me spoke up: *You are not vulnerable. You are not out of options. Now, RUN!* But when I tried to run away, I discovered that Lars had a surprisingly strong grip on me. Wesley appeared on my other side and attempted to help his friend in restraining me. "We have to get out of here," gasped Brent.

"No," said Wesley. "It's not too late. We can get her back to my place and make sure she doesn't remem—"

You are not vulnerable.

Magic stirred within me, surging out and upward to the tree above us. A limb, already heavy with snow, gave way easily to my power and came crashing down on Lars. It was enough to grant my freedom, and I broke away. Wesley stood between me and my building, so I ran the opposite direction, knowing I only had to stay away long enough for some patrolling guardian to come. Surely someone had heard me.

As it turned out, someone had heard me. Adrian emerged near the path I was running on, wielding a limb similar to the one I'd just summoned. I came to a halt as he put himself between me and the other three, who also slowed their pursuit.

"What are you doing?" demanded Wesley.

"Practicing my treejitsu skills. You've probably never heard of it, but believe me, it's enough to knock you on your ass and wipe that smug look off your face."

A typical Adrian remark, even in a dire situation. Yet, despite his flippant tone, there was a hard look on his face that I rarely saw, a look that said even if there was an army standing in front of us, he would still defy them with a tree branch if they tried to lay a hand on me. Tension filled the air around us as our adversaries contemplated their next move. Even drunk and uncoordinated, they might still have an advantage if they decided to rush us with brute force. Adrian and I probably had enough collective Wolfe training—and his "treejitsu"—to fend them off, but it might still be an ugly altercation. I pulled more magic into me but restrained myself from using it yet. The falling limb might be written off as a natural phenomenon. A fireball wouldn't.

"I'm out of here," said Lars, staggering to his feet. Without further delay, he turned and ran, leaving Wesley and Brent behind.

"Are you seriously threatening me with a branch?" exclaimed Brent. "Aren't you supposed to be some big, bad spirit user? Shouldn't you be making my head spin? God, I knew you'd changed, but I never expected this."

"He hasn't changed," said Wesley, getting his courage back. "Adrian Ivashkov doesn't get dirty. This is a bluff. Grab her."

"Don't touch her," said Adrian, as Brent took a step toward me. Some terrified part of me was screaming at me to use this chance to run, but there was no way I'd abandon Adrian.

"Come on, Adrian," Wesley coaxed. "Put down your tree and come back with us. We'll let you have her first."

Brent shot him a startled look. "We will?"

"He can use some hard-core spirit compulsion to make her forget everything later." From the pleased tone in Wesley's voice, you'd think he'd just made some space-age discovery. "We won't need any drugs."

"Oh, yeah." Wonder filled Brent, and he moved toward me again. "Tastes so much better that way. Of course, she'll probably scream more, but after a while—ah!"

Adrian slammed the limb into Brent's head so quickly, I almost could've believed I'd imagined it. Brent keeling over and collapsing to the ground proved it was all very real.

"Looks like I made your head spin after all," observed Adrian, standing menacingly over Brent.

Wesley looked like he might go join Lars but never got the chance. Shouts sounded nearby, and two guardians suddenly raced up to us. I recognized one of them: Mikhail Tanner, Sonya's husband. He looked back and forth between us all, a comic expression of shock on his face. "What's going on?" he exclaimed.

The guardians were efficient in their work, taking all of us (including Lars) to their headquarters and ferreting out the night's events. In the end, it was obvious that the threesome had made a drunken advance on me but had succeeded in nothing more. They were branded with the Moroi equivalent of disorderly conduct, which Mikhail—apologetically—explained would only result in jail time tonight and fines. A cold lump formed in my stomach each time I thought about what they'd wanted to do, and I thought they were getting off easy.

I was practically asleep on my feet when Adrian walked me out to the guardians' building's main entrance. We hovered near the door, clinging to the warmth before we headed outside.

"I'm sorry," he told me. "I'm sorry for everything tonight."

The encounter had barely lasted a minute, but that surge of panic and adrenaline had torn me open, spilling out the emotions I'd been so carefully trying to keep in check. The full force of my love for Adrian consumed me, and I nearly reached for him until I remembered there was a desk clerk across the room. He couldn't hear us, but he'd certainly be able to see us if I threw Adrian up against a wall and started kissing him.

"There's nothing to apologize for," I said, looking straight into his eyes.

"I should've told you what I did to that girl." A small frown crossed his face. "I shouldn't have done what I did."

"It's not even in the same league as what those other guys do. And you weren't really yourself."

He shook his head. "I was myself—getting that wasted. Maybe I wasn't in a rational frame of mind, but I chose to get that way. I'm responsible for that."

"It's done. You're not the same person now as you were then. It could've been bad, yes, but you got lucky and had minimal consequences. Most importantly: You learned from it. That's more than can be said for those other guys."

There was a tension crackling through Adrian's body, and I had a feeling he too was fighting the urge to grab hold of me. "I'm not a violent person, Sydney. Not at all. I'll make love over war any day. But I swear, if they'd hurt you—"

"They didn't," I said firmly. I refused to let him know how scared I'd been because I was afraid he might go after them. "I'm fine. You came to the rescue."

A smile played at his lips. "Something tells me you would've rescued yourself." And like that, the smile vanished. "But spirit would've been a lot more effective than a branch."

"Your treejitsu was very effective." The clerk was typing away on a computer, and I dared to give Adrian's hand a small squeeze. "Why didn't you tell me? Why didn't you tell me about the mood stabilizers?"

He took a moment to answer. "Because I couldn't have faced you if I failed. If I was too weak to stay on them. Even now, I don't know. After those guys and then what happened back at the palace—"

"Stop," I interrupted. "You're doing the right thing. And what's crazy is that you have no idea how strong and how brave you are. I'm so proud of you, and I'm going to help you through this. I love you so much."

Loving him wasn't a surprise. What was, however, was the realization that ultimately, that was all that mattered between us. I'd been trying to figure out what it was that was holding me back from sex. It wasn't Jill. It wasn't some physical threshold I was afraid to cross. There was nothing, nothing except an anxiety my love had banished to the winds. And standing there, in that improbable location, the full force of how much I wanted him nearly knocked me over. A desire that was as much spiritual as physical burned through me, and I suddenly felt as though there was no way I could go a moment longer without having all of him.

"Come on," I said in a low voice. "Come back to my room."

A fire in his eyes told me there was no need to spell things out. "You're exhausted."

"Says who?"

A voice shattered the spell weaving itself around us. "Ah, you're still here," exclaimed Mikhail, hurrying into the room. "Good. I hate to detain you further, but this stuff spreads, and the queen heard about what happened. She wants to talk to you, Adrian." He gave me a kind look. "But you're off the hook. I'll walk you back so you can get some rest."

I swallowed, momentarily unable to focus on anything except the electricity flaring between Adrian and me. I wanted to tell Mikhail to leave us alone because I needed to taste Adrian's lips and run my hands over his skin. Instead, I said, "Thanks. That's nice of you."

Adrian gave me a rueful smile. "We'll continue this conversation another time. When you're wide awake."

"I'll be awake when you finish talking to the queen," I told him. I didn't trust myself to add anymore, but as Mikhail led me away, I gave Adrian a parting look that told him all the things I wanted to "talk" about.

CHAPTER 17

ADRIAN

I WAS THIS CLOSE TO IGNORING MY QUEEN and marching straight back to Sydney's room. I'd read Sydney as clearly as if her aura had lit up in front of me. I knew what she wanted, and dear God, did I want it too.

But Mikhail's stern face was kind of a buzzkill, and no matter how friendly we were, I was still Lissa's subject. So I practically sprinted back to the palace, eager to give her a report and then run back to Sydney's arms.

Unfortunately, Lissa had other plans.

"You're leaving," she said as soon as I walked in. Christian stood beside her, arms crossed over his chest, looking furious. "I heard what happened. The Alchemists will flip out when she reports back, and we're going to do damage control now by getting her out of here as soon as possible—which means you and Neil have to go too."

"Don't worry," said Christian. "I'll finish what you started with those guys tomorrow."

291

"Christian," groaned Lissa, remarkably similar to how Sydney said my name when she was exasperated.

He threw up his hands. "What? Those guys deserve a hell of a lot more than they're getting, and you know it, Liss."

"I know that we have laws," she said patiently. "And I have to uphold them."

Christian said nothing, but our eyes met in a brief moment of solidarity. He might not know that I'd been driven by romantic feelings to defend Sydney, but I knew he was driven to fight against those who bullied others. He and I still had a lot to sort out between us, but just then, I took comfort in knowing Wesley and his asshole friends might find their clothing a little singed tomorrow.

"We got you a morning flight in Philly," Lissa continued. "If you guys leave now, you'll make it."

All thoughts of fiery retribution vanished. Leave now? And abandon the privacy of Sydney's room and a rare night together? I wanted to laugh and cry at the same time. Sydney and I were so close! So close to finally making that leap in our relationship. And there was no point of logic I could argue because what Lissa was suggesting was absolutely correct for an Alchemist in this situation—had Sydney been any other Alchemist.

"Neil won't want to leave Olive," I said lamely.

"Neil's the least important piece in this right now," said Lissa firmly. "Besides, he's with Sonya. She's monitoring him for side effects."

And so, within an hour, we were on the road. Sydney drove again, and this time, I got to ride shotgun. Every once in a while, I'd dare a covert touch to her leg or arm when I thought Neil wasn't looking. It'd make her smile, though she always kept her eyes on the road. I enjoyed those smiles, though none of us was thrilled about the abrupt departure. Neil truly hadn't wanted to leave Olive. And Sydney and I hadn't want to leave our sanctuary.

"It's darker than I'd expect," she remarked at one point. We'd left in evening, but heavy clouds had brought the night early.

"What'd the weather report say?" I asked. There'd only been light flurries at Court, but snow was steadily increasing the further we drove.

"I don't know," she admitted. "I forgot to check."

I put my hand to my heart in mock horror. All joking aside, it was pretty out of character for her. "Sydney Sage not prepared? What is this world coming to?"

She smiled again. "I wasn't the one who made these travel plans."

"Good thing you've got me as a sidekick." I took out my phone and felt my levity fade when I checked my weather app. "Shit. Blizzard warning for the mountains."

"What? Why didn't anyone tell us?" she exclaimed.

"They probably didn't check either. Whoever booked the flight probably just made sure it was on time. I bet Philadelphia's not getting this mess."

Sydney's face grew grave, and for the first time, I truly paid attention to the conditions we were in. I could barely see the road through the thick curtain of white coming down. She sighed. "One hour into a nearly three-hour drive. Maybe we should turn around and wait this out. Any idea which direction the storm's going?"

"Court's at a lower elevation," said Neil from the backseat.

He probably wanted to get back to Olive. "Less snow and less twisty roads—"

Maybe it was ice on the road; maybe it was just all the snow. Maybe she was more tired than I'd thought. Whatever it was, she took a turn on the winding mountain road, and the car's tires caught and slid, spinning us off toward the side. She screamed, and I just barely processed the pine tree before the car slammed into it and the air bags blocked my vision.

Time stopped having meaning. It seemed like both an eternity and a heartbeat before I was cognizant of my surroundings again.

It was my nightmare coming to life.

And in those seconds after the air bags deflated, when everything was still, all I could think was, *Sydney is dead, and there's nothing I can do.*

I turned to her, my heart beating out of my chest, and saw her trying to unfasten the seat belt. "Thank God," I breathed, reaching out to catch her hand. She squeezed mine, strong and confident. Remembering Neil, I was about to check on him when I heard him stirring in the back.

"Everyone okay?" he asked.

"Fine, I think," Sydney said. "Maybe a little whiplash. Can't say the same for the car."

We got out to survey the damage. My legs felt weak, but it was mostly from the shock of what had just happened. I could see similar feelings on their faces, but thankfully, that was the worst of it. No real injuries. The car had hit a pine tree, crushing the front, but obviously not severely enough to crush us as well. I didn't spend a lot of time thinking about higher powers, but if one had had a hand in this, I was grateful.

Neil knelt down to look at the smashed fender. "Could've been a lot worse. Whatever you did, you minimized it."

"You just have to turn into the slide," said Sydney, like the driving prodigy she was. "No brakes."

"And no signal," I said, looking at my phone. "I just lost mine."

She took out hers. "I've got one." Of course she did. Alchemist phones were probably wired into some high-tech antenna on the moon. Not that we had any view of that tonight. It was all darkness and snow out here—and bitter cold. Even in my heavier coat, the cold seeped into my bones as I waited for her to call for help.

She grimaced when she disconnected. "There's a tow truck coming, but it may take at least an hour."

"Then let's get back in," I said.

We did, only to discover the car wouldn't start. The best we could do was hope enough warmth from earlier would linger inside. I wanted to draw Sydney into my arms, but we kept a respectful distance in the front seat. Nonetheless, out of Neil's sight, she rested her hand on my leg.

Time wore on, and the car grew colder and colder. Sydney huddled in her parka, and I could hear Neil rubbing his hands together in the backseat. I was on the verge of saying to hell with propriety and cuddling with Sydney—maybe even Neil too—when she put her hand on the door's handle and said, "Enough."

To my astonishment, she walked over to the side of road, vanishing in that curtain of snow. As one, Neil and I scurried out after her. "Sydney?" I called.

We found her kneeling on a flat patch of ground that was

already covered in almost a foot of snow. I was about to ask what she was doing when fire suddenly flared from her fingertips. An orb of flame soon appeared between both of her hands, about the size of a beach ball. Carefully, as though she were holding fine china, she set it down on the ground where it impossibly blazed against the snow. After studying it a few moments longer, she slowly removed her hands and rested them on her knees.

I caught my breath. I'd seen her perform this fire spell a number of times, but the progress she'd made had grown by leaps and bounds. Jackie had originally taught the fireball to her as a weapon, meant to be thrown, and had said that sustaining it in one place consumed energy. Sydney, however, seemed perfectly at ease. It was Neil whose eyes were enormous in the flickering light.

"How did you do that?" he exclaimed.

"Don't," she said, not looking at him. "Don't talk." There was a command in her voice that got through to him, and wordlessly, he joined her on the ground to take in the fire's warmth. We sat like that for a long time, until headlights gleamed through the snow. Sydney let the fire burn until the headlights came to a halt, and then she quickly extinguished it and walked to the road.

A tow truck had pulled up to the side, and the driver stepped out, peering in the direction we'd come from. "What was that light?" he asked.

"We had a flare," Sydney said.

The car hadn't gone into a ditch and took only a little finagling to hook up to his tow. We helped the driver as best we could and then crowded into the truck's cab.

"No clue how long this'll take," he told us, slowly pulling

back to the road. "I have a feeling it's going to be a rough night. There's a place you can stay a few miles from here, and then I'll take this back to our shop, which is a little past that. We'll figure out the details in the morning."

A few miles took a long time when driving at twenty, but at last, we could make out the lights of a small building. He took the exit and pulled up in front of a cozy establishment whose sign read POCONOS VALLEY BED AND BREAKFAST. Sydney exchanged info with the driver, and we all thanked him for coming to the rescue. He pulled away, off to save other stranded drivers.

Inside, an older woman looked up in surprise from a desk as we entered. "My goodness," she said, getting to her feet. "I didn't expect to see anyone tonight."

"We didn't expect to be here," I told her. "Our car went off the road a few miles back."

"You poor things. Well, we're pretty empty tonight, so there's no problem staying here."

There was a kind grandmotherly air to her that made me think she would've let us stay for free, but her eyes certainly lit up as Sydney took out a credit card. I glanced around as they filled out the paperwork, taking in the scene. Sydney and I had recently done some investigating at a bed and breakfast that had redefined tacky. This place was its opposite, and though it was certainly rocking the antique look, everything was ornate and well decorated, showing off art in a way that wasn't cluttered.

The innkeeper handed over three keys and gave us a brief tour of the main floor, showing us where we'd eat breakfast in the morning and where she kept snacks for guests. When we finally headed upstairs, I drew Neil back and let the women go on.

"Listen to me," I said quietly. "Sydney may have just saved you from losing a finger from frostbite. If you really live by the code of honor you claim, you will not breathe a single word about what you saw. If you do, you will ruin her life, which would be a shitty thing to do, seeing as you owe her yours. Do we understand each other?"

Neil met my eyes for several heavy moments. "Perfectly."

I wouldn't have minded being able to use a little compulsion to ensure his silence, but there was something in that steady gaze that made me believe him.

Upstairs, I wanted to go to Sydney but decided to settle into my own room first. We'd retrieved our luggage before the driver left, and I tossed my suitcase heedlessly into a corner. Like the rest of the inn, the room was well done. The bed was canopied, and there were fresh flowers in vases. I ran my fingers over the soft petals of the blue hydrangeas, amazed that the innkeeper had gone that extra mile when she hadn't even expected guests. In the bathroom, I found a large marble tub and equally impressive glass shower. Suddenly feeling grimy from the road, I took off my clothes and turned the water on high. It scalded my skin but felt wonderful after that searing cold.

When I got out, I heard the Love Phone ring with a text message. I hurried to it. *Did you get it?* asked Sydney.

Get what?

Look under your door.

I did and found that a room key had been slid inside. Not even bothering to respond to her, I quickly dressed and headed out into the hall, turning toward the room number on the key. I nearly knocked but then decided I must have an open invitation and unlocked the door.

I stepped inside, shutting the door behind me, and found the room was even nicer than mine. Most of the lights were off, and a blazing fire crackled in the wood-burning fireplace. Sydney sat on the bed and rose as I approached.

And she was naked.

I came to a halt, the key slipping from my hand to clang on the wood floor. My heart stopped for a few seconds and then beat faster than it ever had in my life.

"Come here," she said in a voice that offered no arguments.

My feet moved me forward, but all I could see was her. No skill of mine, no artist anywhere, could've immortalized how gorgeous she was. It was impossible to believe she'd ever had any doubts about her body. The firelight shone on her skin, golden and perfect, making her look like some radiant goddess of legend. I wanted to kneel before her and offer eternal obedience.

When I reached her, she took my hands and rested them on her bare hips. I was surprised to find myself trembling. Those long-lashed eyes, brown and amber and every shade of gold, met mine with a certainty that made me feel like the novice here.

"I'm wide awake now," she added.

I had to swallow twice before I could find my voice. We were so close. There were only a few breaths between me and the glorious body that had haunted my dreams—dreams, which it turned out, were paltry things compared with reality.

"I don't deserve this," I whispered. I lifted my hands so that I could cup her face. "Not after what I've done with my life."

"I told you before: That chapter's done and gone," she said. "We aren't the same people. We're always changing, always becoming better. What you did with the pills . . . well, it's not just about what they can do. It's about the courage it took to take that step. I always believed in you, but . . ."

"I made you cry," I said. That memory would always be a wound in my heart.

"I cried because I loved you, and I didn't know how to fix you." She reached up and brushed my lips with her fingertips. The world swayed around me. "And that was my mistake. You fixed yourself. You didn't need me."

"No, Sydney." My voice was ragged. "I do need you. You have no idea how much I need you."

I brought my lips down to hers, and it was like everything that had ever happened to me had simply been a warm-up for this moment, that this was where my life truly began. I pulled her to me, and if she'd ever had any doubts about whether I wanted to taste her blood, I knew they vanished then and there. It was the taste of her mouth, the taste of her skin . . . those were what I craved, the things that drove me wild. Her hands caught the edge of my shirt, and we broke the kiss briefly so that she could pull it over my head. She splayed her fingers on my chest, and this time, she was the one who shook. I looked into her eyes, and although they burned with passion and longing and that primal need that had fueled both our races since the beginning of time, I could see nervousness in them too.

She had no experience with this, and that wasn't a situation she found herself in very often. It was up to me to lead this, but the thing was, I was inexperienced here too: I'd never been with a virgin. I'd never had that pressure on me before. It had been mindless with other girls, but I knew with Sydney, whether we were together forever or ended up parting ways, this would be the time she judged all others by.

But as I guided her to my belt and then laid her down on the bed, I knew which way our path would go. We *would* be together forever. We had to be. There was no way that all these feelings between us could ever dim or be defeated. Her breath came fast, and she tangled her hands in my hair as I kissed her neck and then began moving down to her chest. I could tell that she expected us to just jump right into it, into something fast and furious, but I'd waited too long to have full access to her body and wasn't about to take it for granted by rushing forward. And so I took my time, exploring all that beauty she didn't even know she had. It was agonizing for me but also sweet, and for the first time in my life, I was thinking more about the person I was with than myself.

When I brought my mouth back to hers, my body lying over hers, she clung to me with an urgency that held no more fear. And then it happened, what I'd dreamed of for so long. I lost myself in her arms, in her touch, in everything. Sonya often said she didn't believe in soul mates, but in that union, I believed there was something in my soul that spoke to Sydney's, that this connection between our bodies called to something greater than us, something preordained.

And when it was over, I was reluctant to let her go. I looked down at her face, with her flushed cheeks and damp strands of hair, and thought, *Whether it's simply some fierce animal joining of mates or a sublime merging of souls, she is mine, and I am hers.*

We curled up on our sides, arms still tightly around each other, and there was so much emotion building inside me, I thought I would burst. I wanted to tell her a hundred times that I loved her, but when I looked in her eyes, I knew I didn't have to.

"What are you thinking?" I asked.

"That we should've been doing this a long time ago."

I brushed my lips over her forehead. "No, this was the moment. The moment it was meant to be." I knew how she felt about destiny and fate, and under other circumstances, she probably would've given me a lecture about free will. Instead, she trailed her fingers along my neck and smiled.

"What are you thinking?" she asked.

"About Rudyard Kipling."

Her hand froze. "Are you serious?"

"What, you don't think I'm capable of poetry after sex?"

That made her laugh. "Adrian, I learned a long time ago that you're capable of anything. I just would've expected Keats or Shakespeare."

"I like the book of poems you got me. They're short, and the crazier ones sort of speak to me." I rolled to my back, throwing an arm over my head and gazing up at the gauzy canopy. "I was thinking about 'The Female of the Species.'"

"Okay, I *really* didn't expect that."

"It's not about cruel women, even though it sounds like it."

"I know." Of course she did.

"'She knows, because She warns him, and Her instincts never fail, That the Female of Her Species is more deadly than the Male.'" I closed my eyes for a moment, adrift on love and exhaustion and bodily bliss. "We're suckers for this, Sydney. Men. You've got me completely helpless right now. You're so beautiful and alluring, and we guys can't help ourselves. We fight wars for you, cajole you . . . and you put up with us. We have it easy here in bed."

She turned my face toward hers. "This wasn't exactly difficult for me."

"But we still have it easy. You're the strength, the pillars . . . our defenders, our children's defenders."

"You're selling yourself short," she said. "You're just as strong. I wouldn't be with you otherwise. We're equals in this, in whatever comes."

I didn't feel equal. I still had that dizzying sense that she was some goddess come to earth whom I wasn't worthy of. At the same time, I didn't want to depend solely on her strength or use it to hold my life together. I didn't want a mother—well, not for me. I wanted a partnership, a union just like we'd had, except spreading to every part of our lives. We would march forward, hand and hand, and I would spend the rest of my days making our love greater and greater.

"I'm messing this up," I told her. "I should've stuck to Keats."

"No, it's nice to know that pensive, metaphysical Adrian is still around."

"He's hard to get rid of, even with pills."

Her expression softened. "Is it terrible? Being cut off from spirit's high?"

"No, because being with you is a greater high than spirit, drinking, or anything else could ever conjure."

Her eyes glistened, and she blinked rapidly to clear them. "You didn't mess it up—the Kipling. I know what you meant. And I hope you know I feel exactly the same way about you. I feel weak around you. But strong at the same time."

I had no more doubts about being worthy. We were each

other's strength but still possessed our own. I sighed and gathered her to me. "I don't think I'll ever be able to express enough how much I love you."

"Well," she said, with a heated look I knew well, "you can certainly try."

So, I did, for a lot of the night. And as we'd often pointed out, she was a quick study.

I woke in the morning, happier than I'd been in a long time, and saw she was standing at the window in nothing but my T-shirt. It was so mind-blowingly sexy that all coherent thought stopped for a moment. Finally, I managed to drag myself up. I walked over to join her, standing behind her and wrapping my arms around her. She leaned into me.

"Look at it out there," she breathed.

I only wanted to look at her, but I lifted my gaze to the window. Everything was covered in a thick blanket of snow. Fences, cars, anything else . . . it was all hidden. The tree branches were coated in ice. Pale winter sunlight shone down on it all, turning everything into a glittering array.

"It's unreal," she said. "Like everything's been carved out of diamonds. It's hard to believe the world can ever go back to normal after this."

I tightened my hold on her. "I know," I said. "I know."

CHAPTER 18

SYDNEY

IT TOOK TWO DAYS FOR THE ROADS to get cleared and for our transportation to be figured out. Both the Alchemists and the Moroi told us not to worry about the follow-up on the rental and that we'd just get a new one since we couldn't wait out the time for a body repair. I told them I wouldn't feel right about abandoning the original car, since it was my fault it was wrecked, so I managed to drag out our stay while the shop sorted out the many vehicles it had retrieved that night. We were invited back to Court, but I also fought against that, telling the Alchemists I felt better in a human-run inn. Naturally, they backed me.

Those two days were spent in a dream. Adrian and I might as well have been on our honeymoon. We saw Neil for breakfast, but he otherwise kept to himself in his room, leaving us to our own activities.

It wasn't *all* sex. Just mostly.

Adrian teased me that I was making up for lost time. Maybe I was, but I didn't think so because I honestly couldn't imagine having done it with anyone before him. There was nothing to make up for. I also couldn't imagine how one-night stands or any sort of emotionless sex worked. I knew people did it all the time, but it seemed like such a waste. With Adrian, every touch . . . every action between us . . . well, it was all enhanced by our love. How did people have sex without that? That was a question I had no interest in exploring.

Even when not having sex, we spent a lot of time in bed. I'd read or work on my laptop. He'd watch TV or sleep. He claimed I was exhausting, though he certainly never seemed to lack for energy during the act. As for me, I actually found sex invigorating. I was wired afterward. I felt like I could take on a hundred projects. I wanted to eat.

Reality finally called, however, and we had to return to our responsibilities in Palm Springs. Too many people needed us. Unlike that tension-filled flight to Pennsylvania, our trip home was filled with contentment. It was a six-hour afterglow. Adrian and I sat next to each other, burning with the bond between us, and even if we wanted to touch, we didn't need to.

When we stepped outside the Palm Springs airport, warm desert air hit us, confirming once and for all that our winter paradise was gone. And within hours, I found myself slipping back into my former role. I was no longer the storm-tossed heroine lost in her lover's arms. I was Sydney Sage, Alchemist and caretaker, and I was back in business.

Adrian had to go back to his place and find out what he'd missed at Carlton, leaving Neil and me to return to Amberwood. Neil was quiet in the taxi, and I was finally able to give him my full attention. During our snowy interlude, I'd been far too distracted by Adrian and had written off Neil's solitude as some personality quirk. Now, I could tell there was something troubling him.

"Everything okay?"

He dragged his gaze from the window. "Yeah, just thinking about a lot of stuff."

"Olive?"

"Sometimes." He started to smile, but it faltered. "Among other things."

A panicked thought hit me. "Do you feel okay? You're not having any side effects?"

"No. I've just got a lot to think about." This time he did smile. "Don't worry. You've already got plenty to keep you busy."

For a moment, I wondered if he knew about Adrian. Was that why he was so pensive? He didn't know what to do about us? But no, that was my own selfishness. My romantic escapade with Adrian had been the biggest thing in my life back there, but Neil had barely known we were in the inn with him. He had his own concerns, and after everything he'd been through, I could understand.

The taxi stopped at his dorm first, and he started to get out of the car. "Sydney . . ." He hesitated. "I know you'll have to catch up on whatever's going on, but there is something I want to talk to you about alone if you get a chance. Doesn't have to be today. Just soon."

"Sure," I said. "We'll make it work."

It wasn't until I was on my way to my dorm that I realized he might very well want to discuss how I'd created a blazing inferno in a blizzard. I'd known even then that it was foolish and dangerous, but those things had been trumped by the prospect of us freezing to death.

"Sydney!"

Zoe ran into my arms when I entered our room. For a moment, I worried something had gone wrong, but then I saw her face was radiant. "Things were great while you were gone! I mean, I missed you, but there were no problems. I made all the arrangements for Clarence's, and Eddie even let me drive. Like, not just in parking lots."

I'd started to open my suitcase and let the lid fall back down. "He did what?"

"It was only on the back roads between the highway and Clarence's, so there was no problem."

"Police can be anywhere," I protested. "Accidents can happen anywhere." Didn't I know it.

"Everything was fine," she said. "He even said I did a really good job. That I was a pro."

Maybe I should've been pleased she was getting friendly with a dhampir, but I couldn't. "I can't believe Eddie of all people would do that. It's irresponsible."

She nodded. "He said you'd say that and that I should tell you, 'At least it wasn't Angeline.'"

I couldn't help it. I laughed at that. "That's true. He does have limits."

Seeing me relax perked her back up. "Speaking of Angeline . . . can you believe she'd never had praline ice cream? I showed them that place you and I went to, and it was so funny. We were all trying not to stare, but it was impossible not to when her eyes were so big. She had three bowls and probably would've gone for four if we didn't have to get back for curfew."

I stared at Zoe's sparkling eyes in amazement, overjoyed to

hear her talking about hanging out with Jill and the dhampirs like she would ordinary human friends.

"Sorry," Zoe said, mistaking my silence. "I haven't even let you talk. How was everything? Anything big happen?"

Yes, most definitely.

"We're waiting to see how it goes," I said, returning to unpacking. "They injected Olive's blood into Neil and have high hopes it'll protect him from becoming Strigoi."

"That was very brave of him," she admitted.

I looked up from a shirt. "Why, Zoe, I think you just said nice things about dhampirs twice in the last five minutes."

"Don't get any ideas." But she was smiling. "But . . . yeah, maybe they aren't that bad. I mean, they're not *us*, but they aren't so bad to be around. It actually makes things easier, not hating them."

"It certainly does," I agreed. A spot of hope blossomed in me. Living with Zoe and her harsh Alchemist attitudes had been agonizing this last month or so. But could I blame her? Hadn't I been the same? It had taken me a long time to come around . . . could she? Maybe in time, she'd get over trying to impress our dad and realize Moroi and dhampirs were just ordinary people. It was a heady thought, that we could actually be like sisters again and share the same rebel Alchemist philosophy. Maybe Marcus would eventually break her tattoo.

I kept those thoughts to myself, knowing I couldn't jump ahead of myself. But it was hard not to be hopeful later when we ate dinner with the others and I saw that she no longer looked like she wanted to jump up and run away. Everyone was in good spirits until Jill's eyes focused on something behind me, and she sighed heavily. I turned and saw two girls hanging a sign for the Valentine's Dance.

"I wish I could go," she said mournfully.

"Me too," said Angeline.

"Well, why don't you?" I asked.

Jill gave Neil a sidelong look. He was off in his own world. "There's no one to go with," she said. Angeline nodded in agreement.

"I'm sure you can find someone." I glanced at Zoe. "So could you."

Her eyes widened. "What? A dance?"

"Sure. It's what the rest of the world does. You should try it."

"Would *you* try it?" she asked. "Seems frivolous in our line of work."

"I have tried it." For a few seconds, I couldn't continue, as the memory of my one and only dance sucked me in. Adrian had shown up, drunk, and I'd ended up taking him back to his place, where we'd been caught in a blackout. "Sometimes frivolity isn't a bad thing."

Eddie, who didn't seem put out about the dance, grinned. "Sydney, when we first met, I never would've thought those words could come out of your mouth. What happened to you?"

Everything, I thought.

I met his grin with one of my own. "We all need some fun. We should forget that dance and go out and see a movie that night. When was the last time we all did that?"

"I think the answer is 'never,'" said Jill.

"Well, there we go. We'll get tickets and bring Adrian along." I gave Angeline a scrutinizing look she didn't notice. "Maybe some other people too." I was feeling a little guilty about having promised Trey to keep Angeline away from Neil, seeing as Neil himself was taking care of that. I felt I owed Trey more for being my test subject, and maybe bringing him along on a group movie outing would help speed along his "figuring things out" process.

Life soon fell into its normal rhythm. I resumed my pattern of quick visits to Adrian after school, though the level of what we did now had definitely been kicked up. I missed those long, languid stretches of time from the inn, but we certainly made the most of what we had. I continued "making up for lost time" and even went so far as to start reading sex how-to books. I felt nerdy until the day I earned an impressed "Where did you learn *that*, Sage?"

The new developments with Adrian gave me even more motivation to protect us, meaning I went out of my way to pacify Zoe. We still didn't spend enough time together to make her happy, but I did other things she liked, like letting her drive the car once in a while. I also encouraged non-threatening activities with the rest of the gang and continued to watch as she grew more comfortable with them.

The only thing marring our relationship was the threat of our parents' divorce. Zoe continued to assume I was on our dad's side. Whatever uncertainty I'd possessed about the matter had vanished after that lunch/dinner with him. I intended to testify in favor of my mom, even though I knew that could have serious ramifications for the comfortable life I was carving out. The hearing was still a month away, and I did my best to keep reminding Zoe about how much our mom loved us and that she really wasn't a bad person. I even once suggested that if the court granted joint custody, Zoe might truly be able to split her time between our parents, rather than be one hundred percent committed to Alchemist work, as my mom had feared. Zoe had momentarily brightened at that idea and then shook her head. "Dad wouldn't like it," she'd said. Her fear of him was too great.

One of the stranger things to happen to me was that I learned to use a tattooing apparatus. My triumph at returning with bona fide Alchemist ink had vanished when I realized I couldn't have Wolfe tattoo Trey with it. Not only would it blow our cover story about tattoo removal, it would also mean Wolfe would witness the activation of the charm. So I got Ms. Terwilliger to convince Wolfe to leave the machine at her place, in case we needed him again. In the meantime, I looked up the model and read everything I could about how to use it. When I told Trey the news, he wasn't thrilled.

"How am I scarier than a one-eyed man?" I demanded, when we met up at Ms. Terwilliger's place.

"At least he's been doing tattoos for years. How many have you done?"

"None," I said. "But I bet I know more about it than he does."

One thing I did feel bad about, though, was that, unlike the salt ink, the blood ink had color. It was going to leave a mark. Since my understanding was that the two tattoos had to be done pretty much on top of each other, I had to do this one on top of the one Wolfe had done—which was in turn over Trey's Warrior sun. My hope was that I could just trace the sun's lines, but I didn't know how skilled my hands would be.

"If I mess it up, I'll pay for you to get it redone," I assured him.

That mollified him, but as he lay down on the workbench, I heard him grumble, "Remind me why I agreed to do this."

"Because I'm keeping Angeline away from other people. Although . . . I don't suppose you want to, uh, go to a movie with her on Valentine's Day. With all of us, that is."

He groaned. "I'm supposed to stay away from her."

"Well, you don't have to sit by her. And it's not like you'll be alone."

"I'll think about it," he said reluctantly.

I didn't know if this movie plan would result in anything. I didn't have much practice at matchmaking, but Trey and Angeline obviously weren't having success getting over each other. And it occurred to me that if they started going out again, surely he'd have to break his ties to the Warriors. Wouldn't that be an accomplishment for the greater good? Or was I just complicating things?

Regardless, it was a problem for later. For now, my focus was on being an amateur tattooist—which I actually pulled off pretty well. I reinforced the sun design and didn't stray from the lines too badly. Trey wanted to check it in a mirror, but before he could, I had to finish the spell. Earth compulsion charms could be time delayed, triggered by a certain event. Abe had put an urge to obey in the blood, but it didn't have a specific focus. That was where I came in. Once the blood was delivered into the subject, the magic was unlocked and ready to be directed. Trey sat up, and I leaned forward, looking him in the eye.

In the Alchemist ritual, after the blood was delivered, a hierophant would give the new recruit a standard set of instructions: "Our words are your words, our goals are your goals, our beliefs are your beliefs." I'd never thought much about those words. They had a ritualistic feel, and until recently, I hadn't realized how literally the charm worked them into the person. After that, the hierophant would add, "Never shall you speak of the supernatural to those who aren't part of it. You will guard its secrets." That was about all the charm could handle. You couldn't give infinite commands. The Moroi had enough hang-ups about compulsion that they'd give the blood only a low level of magic. Or, well, at least most Moroi would. Apparently, since some Alchemists were being programmed with stronger commands, there were Moroi willing to bend the rules and power up the blood.

I didn't bother with any of that with Trey. All I needed to do was give him a command while the charm was active in the blood and ready to receive.

"You will not speak of your feelings for Angeline to anyone," I told him sternly.

Trey met my gaze, and I saw his dark eyes start to glaze over in obeisance. My heart sank. I'd seen this in other Alchemists being tattooed. I'd experienced it myself. It was the compulsion taking hold. We'd failed. The magic was still able to work and—

He suddenly blinked rapidly, as though he were shaking off a dream. "Why not?" he asked.

"Why not what?"

"Why can't I talk about Angeline?"

"Do you want to?"

"I don't know. Sometimes."

"You know, the other day at lunch, we were all talking about spring break plans, and she suddenly started going off about how meerkats aren't cats at all and how zoologists should really rename them because it could cause a lot of trouble if someone took one home as a pet." I eyed Trey carefully. "What do you think of that?"

His expression softened as a smile filled his face. "It cracks me up. No, I love it. I know this stuff sounds so crazy, but it's just because everything is so new to her, you know? We take everything for granted, but when I'm with her, I see the world through new eyes. She makes my world better. It's why she's so great." He suddenly snapped to attention. "Why do you have such a big grin on your face?"

"Because you're talking about how you feel about Angeline."

"So?" he asked suspiciously.

"I asked you not to."

"You did?"

The door to the garage opened, and Adrian appeared. He'd had to stay on campus late and was only just now able to join us. "You still giving out tattoos, Sage? You up for my skeleton pirate?" He glanced between our faces. "What's going on?"

I laughed and clasped my hands together in front of my chest. "It worked. The salt ink negated the other ink. It undid the compulsion! The human magic triumphed."

Trey arched an eyebrow. "Do I really want to know the details here?"

I surprised him with a quick hug. "The details are that you just helped prove a major discovery. One that's going to help a lot of people."

He still looked understandably puzzled. "Just as long as you didn't do any lasting damage."

"You're free and clear to go to the movie with us," I said.

"We're all friends, though," said Trey quickly.

"Absolutely," I said.

He had a shift soon and was able to talk to us only a little while longer. Once he was gone, I threw myself into Adrian's arms and he spun me around.

"My brilliant girl," he said. "You did it."

I brushed my lips against his cheek. "I couldn't have done it without you."

"Me? I'm not the one who conned her way into getting illicit ingredients, scored a test subject, and learned to use a tattoo machine in a week."

"You were moral support," I said. "The most important job of all. And now that I know it works, I've got to go make more ink for when Marcus shows up. Keep me company."

Marcus had sent word to Adrian via Sabrina that he'd be in town next week. I'd been making extra ink whenever I could get a free moment and wasn't going to waste this one. I had to give Marcus his best fighting chance. Ms. Terwilliger was working in her kitchen when we came back into the house. She waved and assured me I could use her workroom. Although she didn't understand my project exactly, she had no problem sharing her space and letting me store things. Adrian had come by a number of times in the past, and like tonight, he sat near me and quietly did his own work while I did mine. It was warm and comfortable and *almost* normal.

"Isn't it weird?" he said, glancing up as I measured salt. "All the variety that life offers? Here we sit, me reading expressions of creativity." He held up the poetry book, which to my dismay, was now worn and dog-eared. "And you doing scientific and magical calculations. We're thinking, cerebral beings one minute . . . and the next, completely given over to physical acts of passion.

316

How do we do that? Back and forth, mind and body? How can creatures like us go from extreme to extreme?"

"Because that's what we do," I said, smiling. I was really glad the pills hadn't muted philosopher Adrian. I loved listening to him go off on these flights of fancy. "And it's not necessarily extreme. I mean, what we did yesterday at your place . . . well, maybe it was a 'physical act of passion', but it was also *very* creative. Who says mind and body can't work together?"

He unfolded himself from his chair and walked over to me. "Fair point. And if memory serves, it was my genius that came up with that."

I set down my materials. "It was not. That was all me."

"There's only one way to settle this." His arms encircled my waist, and he pressed me against the table. "We need to surpass that creativity. Are you thinking what I am?"

"That Ms. Terwilliger's in the next room?" But my pulse had quickened at the feel of him against me, and I was already figuring out how to clear the table.

He pulled away and shut the workroom's door. "She's discreet," he said. "And smart. She'll knock first."

I almost thought he was joking until he grabbed hold of me again and seated me on the table, wrapping my legs around him. Our lips met hungrily as his deft artist's fingers began working at the buttons on my shirt. A sudden buzz from my regular cell phone startled me from the kissing.

"Don't," said Adrian, his eyes ablaze and breathing ragged.

"What if there's a crisis at school?" I asked. "What if Angeline 'accidentally' stole one of the campus shuttle buses and drove it into the library?"

"Why would she do that?"

"Are you saying she wouldn't?"

He sighed. "Go check it."

I hopped off the table, clothes askew, and found the message was actually from Neil, of all people. *We still need to talk. Can you meet tonight? Somewhere private? It's important.*

"Huh," I said. I showed Adrian the message.

He was equally puzzled. "Do you know what it's about?"

"No, he mentioned it when we first got back to town." The heat between us was cooling, and I began buttoning my shirt back up. "What if it's about me using magic?"

Adrian had grown serious. "No, I don't think so. I could tell. He's not going to talk about it to anyone."

"I should find out, though. If something's wrong . . . well, I'm the one who ultimately deals with it." I knelt down to put my supplies away on the shelves Ms. Terwilliger had allotted to me. "This could be important. Besides, it *is* getting late."

"You know what else is important? Your birthday in a few days. Are you going to get shore leave?"

I smiled as I straightened up. "I don't know. Zoe's going to want to do something with me. We might be able to manage a group outing you could go on."

He put his arms around me. "Not good enough. I want you—just you—over at my place, where I'm going to cook you the most amazing dinner you've ever had by someone who can't really cook. And then . . . we're going to get in my car."

I waited for him to elaborate on a destination. "And?"

He gently kissed the nape of my neck. "What do you think?"

I couldn't help a small gasp of delight. "Oh, wow."

"I know, right? I was racking my brain for the best present ever, and then I realized that nothing was going to rock your world more than you and me in your favorite place in the entire world."

I swallowed. "I'm kind of embarrassed at how excited I am about that." Never had I guessed my love of cars would play a role in my sex life. Eddie was right. Something had happened to me.

"It's okay, Sage. We've all got our turn-ons."

"You kind of ruined the surprise, though."

"Nah. It's part of the gift: you getting to think about it for the next three days. Figure it's incentive for you to escape Zoe too."

"Excellent incentive."

We kissed goodbye, and I set up Neil's meeting. The private place he wanted to meet was a cluster of trees near the library. They were technically off-limits, especially this time of night, but if we were caught, we could claim we were cutting through to the library. With my studious reputation, no one would question it.

Surprisingly, he was late, which didn't seem in character. When he finally arrived, he looked chagrined. "Sorry. Angeline kept following me around, and I had a hard time shaking her."

"She likes you, you know." I didn't feel bad pointing it out because he had to know. "Or, well, she likes the idea of you. She wants you as a theoretical rebound."

"What in the world is that? Never mind." He shook his head. "I don't have time for anything like that."

I wondered if he'd have time for something "like that" with Olive if she lived closer.

"So what's going on?" I braced myself for some sort of interrogation about the magic. What came instead nearly knocked me over.

"I need you to help me go after a Strigoi."

Silence fell between us for several strained moments. "You're going to need to elaborate on that."

Neil pointed at his arm, where the tattoo was. "Everyone's so excited about this, but what does it mean? Is it worth anything? We're never going to find out unless we test it with a Strigoi."

I was aghast. I'd known that, of course, but proactively pursuing it wasn't something I'd really expected to happen. "You want to be turned?"

"No, no. Of course not. Here's the thing. I was looking through some guardian reports, and there have been sightings of Strigoi in this neighborhood in Los Angeles."

I wasn't surprised by that. There were always Strigoi in Los Angeles.

"One Strigoi, actually," Neil continued. "I want to find him and lure him out before others go after him. They know his patterns enough now that it's going to happen sooner or later. Usually, he just drinks and kills, but there've been reports that he sometimes turns victims. Either way, if we use me as bait, he'll have to taste my blood, and we can find out what kind of reaction he has."

It was one of those things that seemed so logical on the surface, I was almost on board. There were just a few flaws. "If the tattoo doesn't work, you end up dead or Strigoi."

"That's where you come in," he said excitedly. "That thing you did with the fire—"

"Neil—"

He held up his hand. "No, no. I'm not telling anyone. I'm not even going to ask you how you did it. But if you could hide somewhere nearby and make that fire again, you could incinerate him before he does anything to me." A little of Neil's enthusiasm dimmed. "And if he does manage to turn me, then you can kill us both."

"Neil! Do you hear yourself? This is insane. You're literally talking about suicide."

His gaze met mine through the shadows. "Yes, and my life would be a small thing to give in order to obtain these answers. And that's not melodrama. I know some of you—especially Adrian—think I'm ridiculous and over the top, but I swear, service to the Moroi is my highest goal. I want what's best for our people. All we're doing now is waiting . . . which is the same as doing nothing. If we could pull this off, it could be the breakthrough everyone keeps talking about."

I had to look away. It was all crazy . . . but there was some sense to it. "I understand your point, but if you want to toy with Strigoi, go get it sanctioned by the guardians. Let them arrange something."

"Do you think they'd let me do this?" I didn't answer because I doubted they would. "Exactly. That was a lot of fire you summoned that night. Do you think you could engulf a Strigoi with it?"

"Yes," I said without hesitation. "But I'm really not comfortable being all that stands between you and damnation."

"You won't be." Neil pointed behind me. "Right on time."

I turned and saw a very puzzled-looking Eddie striding toward us. "Hey, I got your message," he said. "What's going on?"

Incredibly, Neil began the same sales pitch to Eddie about sacrificing for the greater good of the Moroi. Neil didn't mention me and magic, but his offer to Eddie was the same, how there'd be need for someone to stop the Strigoi if things got out of hand. Actually, there was no "if," I decided. "When" was a better word.

I think Eddie was even more shocked than I was. "No!"

"Eddie," said Neil in a calm voice. "I know we have our differences, but the truth is, I respect you. I think you're one of the greatest guardians I've ever met, and you've done more in your life so far than most seasoned guardians ever will. You and Sydney are the ideal team to have at my back. You have to understand how important this is. It's true I've never fought a Strigoi, but I've seen them kill. When I was young." His expression darkened. "I still dream about it, and if there's even a tiny thing we can do to stop those monsters, we have to. Just think if we could prevent the conversion of more!"

Eddie wasn't swayed, and there was a look on his face I'd never seen before. "I'm not denying the principles, but it's too dangerous. And not just to you. I did something like this once . . ." A pain so intense that it tore at my heart crossed Eddie's features. "Me and some friends. We thought we could take on Strigoi . . . and my best friend ended up dead. No matter how prepared you think you are, even against only one, the unexpected can happen. You and I may not be enough. Certainly Sydney isn't—no offense. We'd need more to tip the odds in our favor."

Neil suddenly looked at me expectantly. It took me a few seconds to realize what he wanted. "You said you wouldn't tell!"

"I won't," he agreed. "But I thought you might want to. If you don't, I'll let it go. Do you think Eddie will betray you?"

Both of them were watching me intently, and I kind of wanted to smack Neil. He'd been true to his honor . . . in a loose sense. After hearing his speech twice, I was almost swayed by it. Maybe it was because I was high on the triumph of Trey's tattoo working. How great would it be to accomplish another feat so many people were depending on? And if Eddie was involved, one Strigoi seemed feasible.

But it'd mean telling Eddie my secret, and too many already knew. The old saying came back to me: *Two can keep a secret if one of them is dead.* The more this got out, the more trouble I was in.

And yet, as I looked into Eddie's steady gaze, I was reminded of our friendship and all we'd been through. In a world of secrets and lies, there were few I could thoroughly trust anymore, but I knew then, without a doubt, that Eddie was one I could.

Taking a deep breath, hoping I wasn't being a fool, I held out my hand. A nervous glance around confirmed we were alone, and I brought forth a spark of fire in my palm that soon grew into the size of a tennis ball.

Eddie leaned over and gasped, the orange flames reflecting off his face. "Maybe . . . maybe our odds have gotten better," he said.

CHAPTER 19

ADRIAN

IT WAS SYDNEY'S BIRTHDAY, and my car wouldn't start.

"You have got to be kidding me," I said, turning the key for what felt like the hundredth time. The engine churned and churned but wouldn't turn over. I groaned and rested my forehead against the steering wheel. "This is not happening."

"Problems?"

I looked up and saw Rowena standing outside the driver's side door, which I'd left ajar. I threw my hands up. "As you can see."

She tilted her head to study the car, causing some of her lavender braids to slip forward. "How old is this piece of junk?"

"Bite your tongue, woman. Sydney loves this car. Maybe more than she loves me. Besides, you're an artist. Figured you'd appreciate a vintage piece. You know, the history, the craftsmanship . . ."

She shook her head. "I drive a Prius."

I tried to start the Mustang again. No luck. "Damn it, not today of all days. It's Sydney's birthday. We had plans."

"Call a tow, and I'll give you a ride back home." She patted my shoulder in sympathy. "I know a guy who works at a shop. He'll give you a good deal."

"Not that good," I said, getting out my cell phone. "Unless it's free. I'm pretty much broke for the next week and a half."

"I assume because you got her some sort of extravagant gift?"

"Not exactly. It's a long story."

I'd actually come to terms with not being able to shower Sydney with gifts. I was no longer depressed over it or worried I'd have to sell Aunt Tatiana's cuff links. The pills probably helped with that, but I knew there was more. Between Jill's pep talk and what had happened in Pennsylvania, excessive material goods no longer held the appeal they had. Would I have loved to drape Sydney in diamonds? Sure, but I didn't need to. There were far more important things between us. I was content to make her dinner and just savor time alone with her. That was what mattered now. Just us.

Of course, I'd planned on some of this aforementioned alone time taking place in my car, which now seemed to be out of commission. Maybe I no longer plunged to not-getting-out-of-bed levels of despair, but I could get as down as anyone about a failed plan. I said little as Rowena waited with me in the campus parking lot and mostly just let my dark mood simmer around me.

"You're a poster boy for a brooding artist," she teased me. "You take classes to learn to do that?"

"Nah, it's a gift I was born with."

She grinned and elbowed me. "Cheer up. I'll take you wherever you need to go. We'll salvage this day, kiddo."

It was hard to stay too glum in the face of her sunny

disposition. More than that, I could hardly have Sydney come over tonight just to find me pouting. She'd had to pull off a miracle to escape Zoe tonight and postpone a sisterly celebration. She probably could've saved herself a lot of stress by just postponing her festivities with me, but it meant something to me to celebrate on the actual day. I had pushed for this night, and now I had to make it work.

A tow truck hauled the Ivashkinator away, and Rowena and I were able to head back to town. I'd scraped the last of my money together to buy food for tonight's dinner, and Rowena nearly had a heart attack when we arrived at a grocery store and she heard what I was buying.

"Frozen lasagna? And store-bought cake? I thought you loved this girl!"

"I do, but I'm no culinary student."

"Cassie is."

"Well, she's not here."

Rowena sighed and got out her phone. "Honestly, it's a wonder you got by before me."

An hour later, Cassie met Rowena and me at my apartment, carrying a bag of groceries. I watched as they unloaded all sorts of ingredients I'd never dream of using, like andouille and okra. There was also a bottle of white wine.

"Sydney doesn't drink," I told them.

"Whatever," said Cassie, getting out a corkscrew. "This is for me while I cook."

Rowena winced. After our outing to that bar, I was pretty sure Rowena thought I should be in a recovery group. Maybe she was right. I could tell she was about to chastise Cassie for drinking, and I waved it off.

"I'm fine." To my surprise, I realized it was true. "Far be it from me to do anything that would interfere with a cook's genius."

Cassie glanced up from her glass. "Hey, you're going to help. I'm not making this gumbo alone."

"When I think romantic birthday dinners, I don't think soup."

"Soup?" She nearly choked on her wine. "You think this is mere soup? I needed something you can't mess up while you're waiting for her to get here. This is going to get better and better the more it simmers, and when she does arrive and taste it, she'll be yours forever. You're welcome."

Despite her claims, Cassie didn't actually make me do that much. I think she was afraid I'd mess it up, though I really did try to pay attention in the hopes of improving myself. Peeling prawns was a mystery to me, and I'd never even heard of roux. Cooking was actually kind of fun when you were with someone who knew how to do it. Once the gumbo was covered and on its way, Cassie began mixing up ingredients for chocolate-peppermint cupcakes. She had just handed me a spoon to stir when I heard my phone ring. Usually, I kept it on vibrate, but today, Queen's "Under Pressure" played in full effect. Rowena and Cassie made no effort to hide their laughter.

I yielded the spoon and ran off to the living room, where I saw an unfamiliar number on the phone.

"Adrian? It's Marcus. I'm in back in the country."

For a horrifying moment, I had visions of Marcus crashing my awesome birthday celebration with Sydney. I could practically see him slurping gumbo.

"We're still in Arizona finishing some stuff," he continued.

"But I'm planning to be in Palm Springs on Sunday. I figured we should set things up—and that I shouldn't contact Sydney directly."

"Good idea." The Love Phone was just for us, and her other phone could be too easily tracked by the Alchemists. Sydney always worried about getting in trouble with them, but Marcus actually risked a lot more. "What'd you have in mind?"

"Do you know how much ink she made?"

I'd been around for a lot of the process. "About enough to fill a standard-sized paint bucket."

"Hmm. Maybe we could meet in the parking lot of a home-improvement store. We'd look like ordinary customers."

"Pulling up beside each other and exchanging a paint bucket? Yeah, that's not suspicious at all."

"You got a better idea? You never know where the Alchemists are watching."

"Pretty sure they won't be watching a teacher of hers," I said. "The ink's at her house anyway. Meet up there, and you'll at least have a chance to talk. I'm sure Sydney'll want to give you some instructions."

"That's a good idea," Marcus said reluctantly. "As long as you think this teacher's safe."

"Perfectly."

I gave him the address, and we set up a time. When we disconnected, Cassie and Rowena were giggling as they leaned together and worked on the cupcakes, so I decided to let them be. I dug out the Love Phone and texted Sydney.

Robin Hood called. He's going to meet you at JT's, Sunday at 8 p.m. Will that work?

Her response came quickly. *I'll make it work. Thanks for setting it up.*

He figured everything should go through me to be safe. Think you can still come over tonight?

I could practically hear her sigh. *Yes, but it was hard-won, and there'll be hell to pay tomorrow. Plus we had another fight about the divorce. Tell you later.*

Did you just use the H-word? Nineteen, and you're a whole different woman.

As I started to put the phone away, I noticed I'd missed two calls from Angeline a couple hours ago. I debated over whether I should call her back. After all, there was always the stealing-a-shuttle-bus possibility. But surely if something was wrong, Sydney would know before me. Angeline hadn't left voice mail, so I decided to take it on faith that everything was fine and she just had some random question.

The cupcakes were in the oven when I returned to the kitchen, and Cassie was finishing stirring a bowl of frosting.

"Wait, you can make that stuff?" I asked. "I thought it just came in cans."

She tapped the spoon on the bowl to shake off the excess. "You sure you vouch for this guy, Ro?"

Rowena grinned. "Not for cooking. But for art and romantic good intentions, he's a sound investment."

"Don't forget life advice," I said. "I'm pretty good at that too."

"I assure you, I didn't forget that," Rowena said drily. Glancing around, she frowned. "This is a nice place, but I'd never guess you had a girlfriend. There are no pictures. Doesn't she ever leave anything? A coat or a stuffed animal?"

Her words caused a pang in my heart because she was right. Normal people let relationships fill their homes. At the very least, I should have had a picture of Sydney and me together taped on my refrigerator. My apartment showed no signs that I had a girlfriend because as far as most of the world was concerned, I didn't.

"If you knew her, you'd know she never leaves stuff behind." I didn't acknowledge the lack of pictures. "She's too organized. I'm the one you can't trust to remember things."

Cassie pointed at the stove's timer. "Think you can be trusted to take them out and frost them? You've got to wait for them to cool. Most people don't."

"Sure thing. And just to prove it, I'll write it down and—"

A knock sounded at my door, and for half a second, I worried Sydney had shown up early. Even if Rowena and Cassie were friends, finding two girls at your boyfriend's apartment probably wasn't an awesome birthday surprise. But when I looked out the door's peephole, I was blown away to see Angeline.

She sashayed in when I opened the door and flipped her red hair over one shoulder. "We need to talk, and you wouldn't answer your phone. Oh." Her eyes focused on the kitchen. "You got a date?"

Rowena snorted. "In his dreams."

I made introductions, passing Angeline off as my cousin, per our usual procedure in Palm Springs. Since there was no telling what might come out of her mouth, I decided it was best to get rid of Rowena and Cassie as soon as possible.

"You guys saved my life," I told them. "For real. This is a lot better than frozen lasagna."

Rowena winked at me. "Something tells me you and your charm could've sold it."

"Well, now I can save that charm up for something else."

Even Cassie smiled at that. "Don't forget to add the crushed peppermint candy. And when you frost—"

"—make sure they're completely cool," I finished.

I walked them out, and she kept giving me last-minute instructions until the door actually shut between us. When I returned inside, I found Angeline poking around in the kitchen. "Do *not* touch anything," I warned, seeing her reach for the gumbo lid.

She pulled back. "How'd they save your life? What's all this for?"

"A friend."

"Like a friend you sleep with?"

"Like a friend who's none of your business."

"These cupcakes look good." She peered into the oven door. "You know, it's Sydney's birthday. If you were nice, you'd send me back with some."

"I don't even know why you're here to begin with. Or how."

"I took the bus." Angeline abandoned her kitchen inspection and trudged out to the living room. "Something weird is going on."

I nearly laughed, except her face looked so serious. "Which, uh, particular weird thing are you referring to?"

"Sydney, Neil, and Eddie. They're up to something. They're always talking and then stop whenever I come around."

After what had happened at Court, I wasn't surprised to hear that Sydney and Neil were talking a lot. I had no doubt she'd want to find out if everything was going okay with the tattoo—

which, I reminded myself, I needed to help him embellish.

"A lot of stuff went down at Court," I told Angeline. "Stuff that Sydney and Neil had a big part of. They're probably just debriefing over it."

"Then why's Eddie involved?"

Good question. His role was a bit harder to understand, but maybe Sydney just wanted someone else to bounce ideas off of. I could understand why she'd prefer Eddie to Angeline. It was also possible that Angeline was exaggerating how clandestine the conversations were. Regardless, I trusted whatever Sydney was doing, and if she didn't want Angeline involved, I'd support that.

"She probably doesn't want to bother you since you're so busy," I said. "Aren't you failing English?"

Angeline flushed. "It's not my fault."

"Even I know you can't write an entry on Wikipedia and then use it as a source in your essay." Sydney had been torn between horror and hysterics when she told me.

"I took 'primary source' to a whole new level!"

Honestly, it was a wonder we'd gotten by for so long without Angeline. Life must have been so boring before her.

"You better work on taking your grade to a whole new level." I sounded nearly as responsible as Sydney. The oven timer went off, and I hurried to take the cupcakes out. "So get back on the bus, stop dreaming up conspiracy theories, and—God. You're not supposed to leave campus alone!"

Her face showed that was the least of her problems. "I figured you'd give me a ride back and could cover if anyone said anything."

"My car's in the shop. You've got to get yourself back." I

carefully set the cupcakes on the counter. "Please, *please*, don't get caught. Sydney doesn't need that kind of trouble."

"Her? I'll be the one who's in trouble," Angeline argued.

"No, because you'll just get to sit around and wait while she bails you out." I would've preferred Marcus coming to eat Sydney's birthday gumbo than Sydney sitting in the Amberwood principal's office tonight, trying to keep Angeline from getting expelled. "Now get back. You're sneaky. You can get in without them noticing."

"I still think there's something going on." When I refused to play along with that, she nodded to the cupcakes. "Sure I can't take some back?"

"They're not ready. They need to be frosted."

"Frost 'em now. I'll help. That waiting-until-they're-cool stuff is a bunch of crap."

It was another moment I wished I still had full control of spirit so that I could compel her away. Finally—after I rustled up some change for the bus—she left me in peace so that I could finish the rest of my birthday preparations. I cleaned up the apartment and set out candles and then changed into a dark green shirt I knew Sydney liked. By the time that was done, the cupcakes were ready to frost, and when I dared a taste of the gumbo, I discovered Cassie had been right. It was more than soup. It was sublime.

Sydney showed up around eight, coming to a halt as soon as she stepped inside. "It smells like . . . shrimp. And mint. And pineapple."

"Dinner, dessert, and these." I pointed to a bright yellow candle. "Just got them. They're called 'Hawaiian Siesta.'"

"That's not even—never mind." She shut the door and

hurried over to kiss me. It was one of those scorching kisses that made me lose track of my surroundings. "My best birthday present so far today."

"Withhold your judgment," I said, gesturing grandly to the kitchen.

She followed me in and stared openmouthed. "You actually made a roux?"

"If by 'made,' you mean 'supervised,' then yes."

We ate at the coffee table in the living room, sitting on the floor by candlelight like we had two months ago. I'd never imagined she could be more beautiful than she was in that dream of a red dress, but with each passing day, she proved me wrong. We let Hopper come out, and he curled up near Sydney, taking delicate bites of andouille.

I fessed up to my kitchen helpers, which actually seemed to endear me to her further. Jill had been right that imperfection would get me farther than perfection. Sydney's laughter died down when she recounted her day.

"Zoe was so mad. We'd been doing so well, Adrian! And now our relationship just totally regressed. I told her I was doing stuff for Ms. Terwilliger—like usual—and that it'd be better for us to go out on the weekend for my birthday anyway. More time and all that." She shook her head. "Zoe didn't buy it. All the work I've done to get in her good graces . . . gone. She went off about how I was neglecting the mission for personal reasons and that I just wanted to postpone the outing so that *those creatures* could come with us. But that wasn't even the worst part. I said something I shouldn't have."

"That you were already spending your birthday with one of those creatures?" I couldn't help but feel a little guilty. But surely if something too awful had happened, she wouldn't be here.

Sydney gave me a small smile. "I told her if she really cared about me, then she'd let me do whatever I wanted for my birthday, just like Mom did when I was twelve."

"What happened when you were twelve?"

"Oh, Mom offered to take us all out for dinner—us girls, Dad was out of town—to celebrate, but I didn't want to. This book I'd been waiting for had just come out, and the only thing I wanted to do was read it all night."

"My God," I said, touching the top of her nose. "You're adorable."

She swatted me away. "Anyway, Carly and Zoe really wanted to go out so that they could score a meal, but Mom just said, 'It's her birthday. Let her do whatever she wants.'"

"Your mom is cool."

"Very." Sydney stared off for several long moments, the candlelight reflecting in her eyes. "Well, mentioning her was the worst thing I could do to Zoe tonight. I've been trying to sell her on the idea of testifying for joint custody, in case she really can live both lives with Mom and Dad. I think she was considering it . . . then she asked Dad about it. And, well . . . he had plenty to say. One conversation, and she was completely brainwashed again, so when I brought up Mom, Zoe started going off on how we need to remember what a bad person she is. On and on." She sighed. "I think the only thing that got me out of our room was when I told Zoe I managed to get her permission to practice three-point turns by herself in the faculty parking lot."

"Ah, yes, nothing to get a young girl's heart racing like control of a car. I hear that's big in the Sage family."

Her smile was starting to return. "That's the thing, she's still so young in many ways. One minute, she wants her license. The next, she's got the power to call me in for breaking Alchemist rules. It's dangerous, especially since she thinks she knows everything."

I gathered our empty bowls and stood up. "And as we all know, only one Sage sister knows everything."

"Not everything. I don't know that recipe," she called. "But I might have to. That was amazing."

"Maybe we could go to New Orleans instead of Rome." I put some cupcakes on a plate and gathered up a tiny candle and my lighter. Hopper watched with interest, especially the cupcakes. "Escape plan number thirty-seven: Go to New Orleans and sell overpriced Mardi Gras beads to unsuspecting tourists. No language problems. And I bet it'd be sexy if I learned to talk with a Cajun accent."

"Sexier, you mean. You know, I bet Wolfe wrestled alligators down in the bayou."

"I bet he tamed them in order to facilitate his escape from pirates down there." I returned to the living room and sat beside her with the plate.

"I bet he did both," she said. We were both silent for a moment and then burst into laughter.

"Okay, birthday girl." I set one of the cupcakes in front of her and pushed in the little candle. My lighter, despite a month of neglect, lit the wick. "Make a wish."

Sydney gave me a smile brighter than the flame in front of her and then leaned forward. Our eyes locked briefly, and I felt a bittersweet tug at my heart. What was she wishing for? Rome? New Orleans? Anywhere? She kept the wish to herself, as she should have, and simply blew out the candle.

I clapped and whistled and then dove into my own cupcake, dying to know how my creations tasted. And seeing as I'd done the hard work—frosting and decorating—I felt like I *could* take credit and call them my creations. All Cassie had done was get the ingredients, come up with the recipe, and do all the measuring and mixing.

"I never would've thought following up gumbo with cupcakes like this would work so well." Sydney paused to lick frosting off her fingers, and I momentarily lost all higher cognitive functions.

"It was part of Cassie's master plan," I said at last. "She said making out is always better after peppermint."

"Wow. She really is a culinary genius." She finished off the frosting and then delicately wiped her hands with a napkin. "Speaking of making out . . . can I assume you got the Mustang detailed?"

"Ah. Well." I'd nearly forgotten about that. "Don't freak out but—"

"Oh no. What'd you do to it?"

I held up my hands. "Hold on, I didn't do anything."

I gave her a brief rundown of what had happened this afternoon and then watched as that earlier mischievous look turned to glumness. "That poor car. I'm going to have to call the shop in the morning and find out what's wrong. We might have to take it to a specialty place."

"Gah. I don't know if I can even afford this place."

She put her hand over mine. "I'll spot you."

I'd had a feeling that was coming and knew there'd be no way to fight it. "Coming to my rescue?"

"Of course. It's what we do." She scooted closer to me. Hopper tried to move in, and I pushed him out of the way. "I rescue you; you rescue me. We just take turns whenever the other needs it. And if it makes you feel better, think of it as me coming to the Ivashkinator's rescue, not yours."

I laughed and put an arm around her waist. "That totally fixes everything. Except, now that I don't have a car, I can't really make good on my birthday promise."

Sydney thought about it for several moments. "Well. I've got a car."

An hour later, I vowed I'd never make fun of that Mazda again.

It turned out to be one of our most intense encounters and certainly one of our most inventive, seeing as we had to deal with the space constraints of the backseat. As we lay together afterward, curled up under a blanket I'd had the foresight to bring, I tried to etch every detail into my mind. The smoothness of her skin, the curve of her hip. The exhilarating lightness that burned in my soul, even as the rest of me felt blissfully lethargic.

Sydney boldly sat up and reached for the moon roof. "How's that for a birthday?" she asked triumphantly. A partial silver moon gleamed down at us through some branches.

Before the clothes had come off, she'd driven around the block to ascertain that there was no tail lying in wait. Even though she had no reason to think the Alchemists were tracking her, she still erred on the side of caution. Satisfied, she'd ended up parking in a pretty strategic spot on my street, one that was overhung with trees and in front of a vacant house a block from my building. Someone could still obviously come by and spot us, but the odds were pretty low in this darkness.

She snuggled back under the blanket with me, turned toward me so that she could rest her head on my chest. "I hear your heart," she said.

"Do you check every once in a while, just to make sure I'm not undead?"

Her answer was a soft laugh, followed by a long, sensuous kiss at the side of my neck.

My hands tightened on her, and I again tried to memorize every part of this moment. There was such perfection in the way our bodies were wrapped together. It didn't seem possible that outside the sanctity of this moonlit car was a world we had to hide from, a world that wanted to tear us apart. The thought of what surrounded us made what was between us seem that much more fragile.

"'Things fall apart; the centre cannot hold . . .'" I murmured.

"Are you quoting Yeats now?" she asked incredulously, lifting her head slightly. "That poem's about apocalyptic visions and World War One."

"I know."

"You have some very strange post-sex poetic choices."

I smiled and ran my fingers through her hair. It looked neither gold nor silver in here, just some fey color in between. Even in the throes of love and joy, I could feel a little of the Adrian Ivashkov moodiness settling over me.

"Well . . . it's just sometimes I feel like this is too good to be true. I couldn't have created anything this perfect in one of my own spirit dreams." I pulled her closer and pressed my cheek against hers. "And I'm enough of a pessimist to know we eventually wake up from dreams."

"That's not going to happen," she said. "Because this isn't a dream. It's real. And we can handle whatever comes. You come across any William Morris in your poems?"

"Isn't that the guy who makes cigarettes?" And here she was accusing me of non-romantic poems.

"No. *William* Morris was an English writer." She rolled over and rummaged through the mess of clothes on the floor. A moment later, she lifted up a phone and did a search on it. "Here we go. 'Yet their hands shall not tremble, their feet shall not falter.'" She tossed the phone back into the pile and snuggled up to me again, resting her hands over my heart. "The poem's called 'Love Is Enough.' As long as we're together, that's how we'll be. No trembling. No faltering. We're unstoppable."

I caught hold of her hands and kissed them. "How did you become the starry-eyed romantic while I became the worrier?"

"I guess we rubbed off on each other. Don't make a joke out of that," she warned.

"Don't leave me such good setups, then."

I smiled at her, but that brooding cloud still hung over me, even as I lay there so full of happiness. I had never thought I could love another person this much. I also never thought I'd live in such fear of losing another person. Was that how everyone in love felt? Did they all cling tightly to their beloved and wake up terrified in the middle of the night, afraid of being alone? Was that an inevitable way of life when you loved so deeply? Or was it just those of us who walked on a precipice who lived in such a panic?

I brought my face a mere whisper from hers. "I love you so much."

She blinked in that way I'd come to recognize, when she was afraid she might cry. "I love you too. Hey." She slid one of

340

her hands up and rested it on my cheek. "Don't look like that.
Everything's going to be okay. The center *will* hold."

"How do you know?"

"Because we are the center."

CHAPTER 20

SYDNEY

I SAT BACK ON MY KNEES AND SURVEYED MY WORK. One gallon of the ink that could help free other Alchemists tired of being controlled by our superiors. It would change the way Marcus carried out his missions. It would change everything.

The power of that realization with Marcus was part of why I'd agreed to Neil's madness. It was another chance for a monumental discovery. I'd followed up on the Los Angeles Strigoi in question with Alchemist reports and found that Neil's assumptions were right. All signs indicated this Strigoi worked in a very specific territory and usually worked alone. The prevailing theory was that it must be a newly turned one. Although they weren't the best at organization, experienced Strigoi knew the power they had in groups. If this one was a beginner, so much the better for us. I just hoped two dhampirs and a fire-wielding witch were enough to take this one out.

But I was fully aware that something could go wrong, and that was why I hadn't told Adrian. I *hated* that. I knew relationships fell apart all the time because someone was stupid and withheld a vital piece of information. When I'd gotten involved with him, I'd sworn I'd never do that. And yet, I also knew a couple things would happen if Adrian knew our plans. One was that he'd want to come. The other was that if something went wrong, if one of us was hurt—or, God forbid, killed—he would never forgive himself for not being able to perform a healing. I'd seen it in his face, both before and after the pills. Maybe the rush of spirit had been addictive, but it was being powerless to help others that truly tormented him. I couldn't let him face that.

My last reason for keeping him out of it was purely selfish: I couldn't risk anything happening to him.

Things fall apart.

I knew Adrian's words were just part of his contemplative, metaphysical moods. They haunted me nonetheless, maybe because I understood what he was saying. There was a perfection to what we had, even if it was all in stolen moments, and at times, it did seem as though we were dancing on a razor's edge that we'd inevitably plummet over. As I contemplated my task with Neil and Eddie, I wondered bitterly if this would be what broke Adrian and me. We worried so much about getting caught by others. Maybe things would fall apart because I was running off on some foolish and noble task.

The center cannot hold.

I sighed and stood up. There was nothing to be done now. I was resolved to do this thing. Sydney Sage really was the reckless one.

Back in my dorm room, I found Zoe finishing up her homework. Things had eased up a little since our birthday fight last night, but tension still hung heavy between us. "Hey," I said, taking off my coat.

"Hey," she replied. "Finish your work for Ms. Terwilliger?"

I ignored the accusatory tone. "Yup. The big project's pretty much wrapped up, so I should have some more time." I thought that would please her, but she still looked sullen, so I tried another approach. "Want a cupcake?" I'd brought home leftovers and told her they were from Spencer's, which kept a well-stocked pastry cabinet.

Zoe shook her head. "Too many calories. Besides, it's almost dinnertime."

"Are you going to eat with us?" I asked hopefully. Like me, she'd made some human friends and sometimes preferred them to the Moroi gang.

I saw her hesitate and then finally give me a tentative smile that filled me with hope. "Sure." She wanted us to be sisters. But like me, she wasn't sure how to make it work.

Someday, I thought. Someday I'll fix everything. Adrian, Zoe. Life will be easy again.

She perked up a little when we went downstairs and I told her she could take the car out tonight to practice her turns. For the first time in a while, I was staying at school for the evening, so she might as well get her chance with the Mazda. Admittedly, it was a little hard to yield the car after what Adrian and I had done last night. The memories washed over me, and even now, my breath caught. The moonlight, his touch. I'd never look at that car the same way, but my sentimentality wasn't enough to keep it from Zoe.

In the cafeteria, we found a weird atmosphere settling around my friends' table. Jill was the only one semi-upbeat, largely because she'd found a date to the dance. A friend of her ex, Micah, was going to go with her. "It's just platonic," she said, giving Neil a meaningful gaze. "But it'll be fun to have a chance to get out of the uniform for a change. And it's here, so no real security problems."

Neil nodded, but it was obvious to me that he hadn't heard a word she'd said. Eddie also seemed checked out, which was surprising since even though he denied wanting Jill, he usually had some problem with the guys she went out with. Both he and Neil wore mirrored expressions of preoccupation now, and an alarm went off in my head that something had happened. When I'd seen them yesterday, both had certainly had our trip to LA on their minds, but they hadn't looked this glum. I wondered if maybe some enterprising guardian had taken out our "easy" Strigoi.

The last piece of this drama was Angeline. She was making no effort to hide her suspicion. Adrian had told me how she'd come over to his place yesterday, and I watched as she leveled glares at me and the guys. As distracted as she got, I never would've guessed she'd be the one to pick up on subtle clues. Even now, despite her watchfulness, she'd occasionally oscillate between random topics, like how shepherd's pie wasn't a pie at all and why it was pointless to take a class in typing when technology would eventually develop robot companions to do it for us.

When she started going off on the cafeteria's carrot cake and how cream-cheese frosting should be considered cheese spread instead of frosting, I couldn't take it anymore. I took my empty tray and stood up to get a water refill. It wasn't a surprise when Eddie joined me across the room.

"What happened?" I asked. "Is Angeline still critiquing the carrot cake?"

"No, she's moved on to baking in general and whether it's best to frost before or after something's cool." He sighed. "But I'm guessing you know there's more than that going on."

"Bring it."

"We just saw some guardian reports about a Strigoi gang that's been moving down the coast. Everyone's pretty sure they're going to end up in Los Angeles."

I immediately picked up on the subtext. "And you're worried they'll join up with your guy."

He nodded. "I mean, we don't know for *certain*, but it's a new variable to deal with. Part of what made this idea kind of not crazy was that other Strigoi activity had been low in the area."

"So what are we going to do?" His dismay began to spread to me.

"Neil and I think we should go tomorrow. The other Strigoi shouldn't be there yet, and it's a Friday. We know this guy likes club goers."

I groaned. "Zoe and I are supposed to celebrate my birthday. If I cancel . . . God, Eddie. It's going to be ugly. Things are bad between us."

His expression turned kind, but there was steel in his eyes. "This may be our only chance."

Turning from him, I stared across the cafeteria. Neil had left, and Zoe was standing up, no doubt off to take the car out. Angeline was already eagerly leaning toward Jill, and I wondered if there'd be more talk of conspiracy theories. Or maybe cake. Or robot companions.

"Okay," I told Eddie. "I'll make it happen."

I did, but as I'd warned him, it was ugly.

Zoe was in a bad mood when she got back from parking practice, and I prayed she hadn't hit something. When school got out the next day, her mood was still in full effect, killing any fleeting chance that I might get away unscathed. There was nothing to do but push forward and give her the bad news that my birthday was being postponed again. She was nearly in tears by the end of our "discussion."

"How can you keep doing this?" she yelled. "What's wrong with you? I thought when I came here . . . I thought things would be great. I thought we'd be a team."

"We are," I said. "We're getting so much done, and I thought . . . well, I thought you were making good progress in getting along with the Moroi and dhampirs."

"Yes, but they're not the ones I want to spend time with. You are, Sydney. My sister! Why is everything else more important than me?"

I walked over to put my arm around her, but she pushed me away. "Zoe, you are important. I love you. But there's just a lot I have to deal with. It's how our job works. Sometimes we get cut off from our families for a while."

"We aren't cut off! I'm right here." She wiped furiously at her eyes. "You said that thing for Ms. Terwilliger was done!" Once again, I'd relied on my old excuse, simply because it was one of the few things she couldn't fight against.

"It was supposed to be, but then we found out about a library in Pasadena that has something we need. Remember that crazy guy I told you she's dating?" I managed a hollow laugh. "They're going to a dog show during the day, so she isn't

347

free until tonight. Good thing the library's open until—"

"I don't care about your stupid library!" A coldness filled Zoe's eyes as she stared at me. There was an almost tangible quality to it. "I want to know something, Sydney. And don't lie or dodge the question. What are you going to say at the hearing?"

It hit me out of left field. A story was ready on my lips, but as I met the intensity of her gaze, I couldn't bring myself to lie. "I'm going to tell the truth," I said.

"What truth is that?"

"That both Mom and Dad have good things to offer. Mom's not an evil person, Zoe. You know that."

Zoe's face was impassive. "And if they ask you who you think should have me, who will you say?"

I stared into her eyes, so like my own. "Mom."

She sank back into her bed as though I'd punched her. "How could you do that to me?"

"Because Mom loves you," I said simply. "And you should have a normal life before swearing to this one."

"I've already sworn to this one," she reminded me, touching the tattoo on her cheek.

"It's not too late." I wished I could tell her about the salt ink, but obviously she wasn't ready for that. "Zoe, since coming here, I've had the first chance in my life to do what other people do. To have normal relationships."

"Yeah," she said bitterly. "I know."

"It's not frivolous. It's amazing. I love it. I want you to have that kind of life."

"That doesn't sound like any Alchemist belief I've ever heard."

"It's not—because I'm talking to you like a sister now, not just another Alchemist."

"You sure do flip between those pretty randomly. How do you know which one to be at any given time?"

I shrugged. "It's in my gut."

Zoe stood up, her hard expression showing me she was unmoved. "I'm going out. See you for Clarence's."

Her words reminded me that it was a feeding night, and as I collapsed onto my own bed, dejected, I wished we were already at Clarence's. I got out the Love Phone and texted Adrian. *Can't wait to see you tonight. I wish you were here. I need you right now.* No immediate answer came, probably because he was working on something for class. I kept writing anyway because it felt good to vent. *I love you. The center will hold, and someday, we'll get away from all this.*

When we picked him up for Clarence's later, I had to fight the urge to get out of the car and run into his arms. Too much was weighing on me. Zoe. The trip to Los Angeles. I didn't expect Adrian to fight my battles for me, but I just wished he could give me courage before them.

He did without even knowing it, when we got a brief moment alone later. I'd gone to put our leftovers away in the kitchen, and he followed me after a minute or so. "Hey," I said. My hand twitched with the need to touch him.

"Everything okay?" he asked. I could see the same longing in him. "You didn't look so great back there. I mean you always look great, but . . . you know what I mean."

"I do. Big fight with Zoe. Details don't matter. The short version is she hates me right now." I shrugged. "Welcome to my life. Did you get the car back? Did you get my texts?"

"Ah." He averted his eyes. "Yes to the first question. As for the second . . . I, uh, kind of lost the Love Phone."

"What?" My whole world reeled. "Adrian! That phone's a record of everything that's gone on between us. Please tell me you've been deleting everything after it comes in."

His guilty expression told me he hadn't. "Relax. I didn't lose it at Alchemist HQ or anything. I'm pretty sure I lost it at a coffee shop with Rowena yesterday. My name's not on it or anything. Clarence is going to let me borrow his car, so I'll go back and get it."

I still couldn't stop the sick feeling rising in my stomach. "This could be a disaster."

"How? If anyone even finds it—and it's not just sitting under a table right now—they'll just have a good laugh at our sappy talk. No one's going to be like, 'Aha! Proof of an illicit human-and-vampire affair.'"

He made me smile, just like always, but I was still worried. Jill came into the kitchen just then and grinned when she saw us. She no longer had the inside track into our relationship, but I was pretty sure she knew it had hit the next level.

"Good news," she said in a low voice. "You've probably thrown Angeline off your trail. She's been trying to get me on board about you, Neil, and Eddie doing covert things. She probably thinks you're dating one of them."

I laughed at the joke, glad that Jill was thrown off the trail of our LA trip too. "Yeah, because that totally wouldn't be a problem."

Whatever else she was going to say was interrupted as more people came in to put away their dishes. It also ended any further conversation between Adrian and me, and the most I could do was exchange a long, meaningful look with him when I prepared to leave. I hoped I'd survive this night and see him again.

Eddie, Neil, and I took my car to Los Angeles. The only time anyone spoke on the two-hour drive was to go over the plan, which we did about a hundred times. Both of them were armed with silver stakes, and I'd practiced my fire spell as much as I could. Once I'd needed physical materials and a lot of concentration to do it. Now, I could practically do it in my sleep.

We can do this, I kept telling myself. *It's as good a plan as any.*

We found the night club our Strigoi liked to frequent. Immediately, I understood its appeal. It was loud and crowded, and the bouncers didn't do a good job checking IDs, meaning lots of young and naive people showed up. The club was surrounded by dark, winding alleys, mostly deserted except for drunken clubbers stumbling home. There were a lot of corners and shadows to hide in.

"Here," said Eddie. We'd done a circuit of the club and found a blind alley beside a building in severe disrepair. Marcus would've felt right at home. A second-story window had been broken, and when Eddie climbed up to it via a dumpster, he found a trashed, empty apartment. "This is where we'll wait." He helped me get up there, and we took up a position that mostly hid us in darkness while giving us a vantage on the pavement below. Neil waited down there, hoping he could be the bait he'd proposed. He'd done a lot of vigorous exercise before we left, leaving him sweaty so that the Strigoi would have an easier time smelling him. Strigoi loved drinking from dhampirs more than humans, and they loved Moroi most of all—which was another reason I hadn't wanted Adrian to know about this. If our guy caught Neil's scent, it'd be an irresistible lure. Our assumption was that if the Strigoi smelled Eddie, he'd just blend in with Neil. I would blend with the other humans in the area.

After that, there was nothing to do but wait. Our Strigoi usually struck in a specific time frame, and we'd come in advance of it. I hoped that meant he hung out in his lair for a while and hadn't already been on the scene while we set up. I also hoped he'd actually come out tonight, or we'd have wasted a trip.

When it happened, it was so fast I thought I'd imagined it. The Strigoi leapt off the building opposite the one Eddie and I were in, landing effortlessly on the ground and knocking Neil down in one fluid motion. I stifled a gasp. If the Strigoi had looked around a little, our window hideout would've been spotted. He must have been too worked up over finding a lone dhampir.

Neil was completely pinned down, no chance of getting his stake. As the Strigoi leaned in, Neil did have a chance to gasp out, "Wait—turn me—make me one of you—awaken me—"

The Strigoi paused and then laughed. "Awaken you? Do you know how long it's been since I had a dhampir? I'm not wasting my own blood on you. I'm going to savor this."

"I can help you. I can serve you." I didn't doubt the terror in Neil's voice was real, and yet here he was, offering himself up for the greater good. I wanted to cry but had to stay strong and wait for my part. "I can help you find other dhampirs . . . and Moroi . . ."

As the Strigoi laughed again, Eddie leaned over to whisper in my ear, so close his lips nearly touched me. Strigoi had excellent hearing. "He's a strong one," Eddie breathed. "And old. Very old. We were wrong."

Neil screamed as the Strigoi bit into his neck. Eddie tensed, and I grabbed his arm. "Wait. We have to know."

I knew what agony Eddie had to be in because I shared it. We both wanted to help Neil. Doing nothing, even for a handful of seconds, went against every part of our beings. Neil's cries faded to moans, and as the Strigoi continued drinking, I knew the awful truth. The tattoo was a failure, and we—

The Strigoi suddenly jerked back. "What's wrong with you?" he snarled. "You taste . . . wrong!"

That was all Eddie needed to hear. In a flash, he was out the window, landing nearly—though not quite—as gracefully as the Strigoi. Eddie's silver stake was already in motion as his feet hit, but the Strigoi, incredibly, anticipated it. Eddie had been right. Old and powerful. Maybe too old and powerful for us.

Eddie and the Strigoi engaged in a deadly dance, and I looked for an opportunity. It had been obvious to us that if we were fighting in cramped quarters, a fireball could incinerate all of us. My instructions had been blunt and simple. Use the fire only if the Strigoi killed or turned my friends. I was supposed to be the last resort, yet I hoped there was a way I could help Eddie before then because it was clear he had his work cut out for him. Neil, though alive, was down for the count.

For his part, Eddie was magnificent. It had been a while since I'd seen him fight, and I'd nearly forgotten that the adopted brother I joked and ate lunch with was a lethal warrior. He made the Strigoi work for his kill, slipping only once when a glancing blow knocked Eddie into the brick wall. He recovered instantly, but I could see the inevitable. A series of small hits, small injuries . . . they'd take their toll. Combined with the Strigoi's superior strength and stamina, it would be only a matter of time.

I had to act. I couldn't just stand by and let Eddie be annihilated, not if there was anything I could do. Maybe sending a fireball down was out of the question, but I was pretty sure I could provide a good distraction. I jumped down from the window to the dumpster, using it to get down to the ground. I was a disgrace after Eddie's amazing exit earlier. My foot landed wrong, and I stumbled. I didn't even need to create a magical distraction, because the Strigoi noticed me right away. He shoved Eddie back and shot toward me.

Fear filled every part of me as that deathly white face leered down. Somehow, in spite of the overwhelming urge to just scream and scream, I held up my hand and summoned a small ball of fire. My hope was that it might startle him back enough for Eddie to get in for the kill. To my astonishment, the fire didn't scare the Strigoi. In fact, he grabbed my wrist and slammed me into the brick wall. The flame disappeared, and I let out a small scream.

"Don't try that game with me, witch," he growled. "I know your kind. I know your tricks. Maybe your blood is off-limits, but your neck snaps the same as anyone else's."

I could see my death in his eyes, and it wasn't terror I felt so much as sorrow—a great and overwhelming sorrow for all the things I would never do. I would never see Adrian again, never create a life with him, never have those perfect children he'd joked about. Even small things took on a terrible sense of loss.

I'd never have lunch with my friends again, never hear Angeline make one of her ludicrous comments. I'd never patch things up with Zoe.

It was amazing how so many things flew through my mind in a millisecond. And it was amazing how the smallest things in life became monumental when you were about to lose them.

Suddenly, the Strigoi spun around, anticipating an advance from Eddie. I was momentarily forgotten as the two engaged in battle again, and I wasted no time scurrying toward Neil's fallen form. I was trying to drag him away when two dark figures came tearing down the alley. At first, I thought partyers had stumbled on us. Then, I recognized them.

Angeline and Trey.

"No way," I said.

She was unarmed, but Trey carried a sword, the favorite weapon of the Warriors of Light. Their presence momentarily startled the Strigoi, enough for Eddie to slam into him and finally land a solid offensive blow. Trey approached from the other side, swinging the sword remarkably close to the Strigoi's neck. Angeline helped me pull Neil out of danger and then knelt beside him. His eyelids fluttered, and his hand moved toward his pocket, where I could see a gleam of silver. Angeline took the stake from him, gripping it in her hands and watching the combat unfold before us.

The Strigoi was trapped between Eddie and Trey but seemed undaunted. He sized them both up, and I could guess his deliberation. Even armed and trained, a human like Trey was the easier target. Was it better to take him out immediately or deal with the bigger threat? The Strigoi opted for the former, lunging for Trey and simultaneously dodging an attack from

Eddie. The impact knocked Trey to the ground, but it took enough of the Strigoi's attention that he left an opening for Eddie, who scored a swipe with his stake.

The Strigoi hissed in pain but didn't slow down. He managed both offense and defense with seemingly no effort. No one gained any ground, and my frustration grew. I felt helpless and began racking my brain for other spells I might use. I had a vast repertoire at my fingertips, but with the erratic way everyone was moving, I couldn't be sure I wouldn't hurt one of my friends.

Eddie made a desperate attack and actually knocked the Strigoi to the ground. Needing no communication, Trey advanced with the sword, going in for decapitation. But the Strigoi continued to thwart us. He sprang up, doing a spinning kick that knocked both guys away. Apparently deciding to change tactics, he went after Eddie this time, who even I could tell was getting up just a little too slowly.

That's when the unthinkable happened. A thick white mist suddenly appeared and rose from the puddle-covered ground, momentarily enveloping and blinding the Strigoi. That's when Angeline acted. Everyone had forgotten about her. Even I had. She leapt up from beside me, charging forward unhesitatingly as she plunged the silver stake into the Strigoi's back. He screamed. It wasn't enough to kill him, but it was enough for Eddie to recover and send his own stake through the creature's chest and into the heart. The Strigoi flailed a little, one last attempt to save himself, and then he collapsed and went still. Silence fell as we all held a collective breath.

"What are you doing here?" demanded Eddie.

"Saving your ass," said Angeline. "I knew there was something going on."

"I'm not talking to *you*," he snapped. He threw down the stake and strode past her, toward the entrance of the alley. I followed with my eyes and saw a tall, slim figure standing there, her hair glowing in the light of an overhead lamp. Jill. I remembered the water on the ground turning to mist, and it all made sense.

"You have no right being here!" exclaimed Eddie, coming to a halt in front of her. It was one of the few times I'd ever seen him angry. I'd certainly never seen him angry at her. He cast a glare back at Angeline before returning to Jill. "They shouldn't have brought you."

"I have every right to be here," she retorted. "When Angeline finally convinced us, I knew we had to help. And we did."

Eddie was undaunted. "I don't care what *they* do. If they want to endanger their lives, so be it. But a princess of her people has no business putting herself in danger."

"A princess of her people has no business sitting off to the side while said people are in danger," Jill returned.

"Do you have any idea what could have happened if—"

"Oh, shut up," she said, reaching for him. He flinched in surprise, but once she started kissing him, the tension left his body. I shook my head and looked away.

"Oh, man," I said to no one in particular. "This night is just full of surprises."

With the immediate danger gone, I was able to examine Neil more closely. He was weak and groggy from the blood loss and Strigoi endorphins, but he'd survive. "Hey," I said, gently touching his face. He looked up at me in a daze, not seeming to know me. "You did it. You proved that the tattoo worked. We have a way to keep Strigoi from drinking from us." Even if Olive's blood couldn't technically stop turning, it seemed pretty unlikely a Strigoi could stomach draining anyone in order to complete the process.

Neil gave me an addled smile and closed his eyes. "We need to get him fluids," said Eddie. Jill was standing a couple feet from him now, but he had a dazed, starstruck quality to him. "Back to the car."

As he and Trey helped Neil up, I took care of the Strigoi body, destroying it with Alchemist chemicals. As I watched that gruesome face dissolve into smoke, I had a surreal moment of clarity. I remembered those frantic seconds when I'd thought all I loved and knew, all that was Sydney Sage, would be lost from this world. My battered friends and I had just had a brush with death, dancing with this evil. We'd destroyed it, but it was terrifying how touch and go it all had been. At any moment, the Strigoi could have gained the advantage and killed one or all of us. Life and death were inextricably bound together, and we wavered between them. But we'd triumphed over death tonight. We were alive, and the world was beautiful. Life was beautiful, and I refused to waste mine.

As we returned to the cars, Angeline and Trey bragged how they'd been lying in wait to follow us. "I knew," she said. She was holding Trey's hand, which I didn't have the mental energy to ponder right now. "I knew something was going down tonight."

"You did good," I told her. "Really good." The widening of her eyes told me she'd been expecting a lecture. Maybe she deserved one, but I just didn't feel it. We treated her like a joke, but she was a fighter against evil, every bit as tough as Eddie and Neil. Glancing over at Trey, who was trying to keep his sword obscured under a coat, I realized he was one of us too. Even Jill was.

"I actually didn't believe it," Jill said with a small smile. "When Angeline told me she was taking off, I went to your room to let you know. Zoe said you were out for the night, and that's when I realized something might actually be happening, so I went and caught up."

Angeline gaped. "You were going to tell on me?"

Jill shrugged. "It all worked out."

"This time," I said. I wasn't up for any lectures, but one would be needed. Eddie was right. It was fine for the rest of us to do foolhardy things, but our sole purpose for being here in the first place was to protect Jill. If that Strigoi had broken loose . . .

At my car, we patched Neil's wound and plied him with water and orange juice. He gradually shook off the endorphins and grinned as the impact of what we'd accomplished hit him. I don't think he'd yet realized Jill was along, or he wouldn't have been so giddy. "It really worked. We did it." He gave a soft laugh, and I tried to remember if I'd ever heard him do it before. "We're going to get yelled at when we report this."

Eddie smiled back, and I saw genuine friendship between them. "I doubt it'll last for long when they get the results."

"What's the plan now?" asked Trey. "We're out way after curfew."

"Did you sign out?" asked Eddie. They shook their heads. "Neither did we. The plan was to stay out all night and then slink back tomorrow when things are busy so that they hopefully won't notice anything. None of our roommates is going to tell on us."

"We could go to Clarence's or Adrian's," said Angeline.

"I'm hungry," muttered Neil.

"I know a great twenty-four-hour place," said Trey. "We'll have a victory meal of fried food."

We made plans and headed back to Palm Springs in our respective cars. As soon as I was on the road with Eddie and Jill, I told them, "I need to see Adrian. Drop me off and take my car. He'll give me a ride back."

Eddie looked totally surprised by that. "Why do you need to see him?"

"I just do." I didn't feel like attempting an excuse, and Eddie wasn't the type to badger me. The most I got was a curious look when we reached the apartment. His curiosity turned to panic when he realized I'd be leaving him alone with Jill.

"Good luck," I said as I got out, not entirely sure who needed it the most. "Call me if anything goes wrong with Neil." He'd ridden back with Trey and Angeline, and I didn't expect him to have any issues. He'd been on his own two feet when we parted, and dhampirs were fast healers.

Eddie pulled away, and I strode up to Adrian's building, my heart racing. I still hadn't shaken that earlier exhilaration from having been so close to having my life snatched away.

I let myself into the apartment, which was dark and quiet. It was still amazing to me how well he slept. I crept to his bedroom and found him lying there in just boxers, the covers tangled up and one arm thrown over his head. A streetlight outside shone faintly on his face, illuminating a rare moment of peace. He was so breathtakingly gorgeous that I could almost buy into his earlier comments about us living in a dream.

But this was real. It was real, and we were alive. We were alive, and I desperately needed to be reminded of that. Without further hesitation, I stripped off my clothes and slid into bed with him.

CHAPTER 21
ADRIAN

"SYDNEY—"

The word came groggily to my lips as I felt her get into bed. My sleepy brain didn't have a chance to come up with anything more because my voice was lost as she leaned over and kissed me. I wrapped my arms around her and had the extremely pleasant surprise of finding her naked.

"What's going on?" I asked. "Not that I'm complaining. It's more of an intellectual curiosity."

"I did something potentially dangerous," she said nervously. "No, there's no 'potentially' about it. It was dangerous and actually pretty stupid."

She then proceeded to tell me an unbelievable story about how she and Eddie had thrust Neil into the path of a Strigoi. It was all I could do not to leap up and rage at her for risking herself like that. A terrible memory flashed through my mind of the time she and I had been trapped by two Strigoi, and one had bitten her. I couldn't even comprehend a repeat of that.

"Hold on." I sat straight up as I did a mental enumeration of the cast she'd described. "*Everyone* was there? *Jill* was there?"

"That wasn't part of the plan," she said quickly, sitting up beside me. "That was improvisation from her and Angeline. And Trey too, I suppose."

Imagining Sydney dying was beyond terrible. And in some ways, imagining Jill dying was even worse because I'd already seen it happen.

"Jill could've been killed," I said. "We're supposed to be keeping her safe!"

"I know, I know." Sydney leaned against my shoulder. "I really didn't want her to be there. Eddie was pretty upset too, though I'm not sure how he's feeling now after she kissed him."

"After she—what? Okay, we'll come back to that. God, Sydney. Why didn't you tell me any of this was going down?"

"Because you would've tried to stop me. Or tried to go yourself. Believe me . . . I'm sorry. I don't want to keep things from you. Ever. I want complete honesty between us. I just want . . . well, I wanted you to be safe even more." She snuggled closer. "Don't tell me you don't understand that logic."

"Of course I understand it! And yes, I would've tried to stop you. Damn it, Sydney!" I caught hold of her hands and was surprised to find I was shaking. Again, terrible, bloody images of her flashed through my mind. "This isn't the same as you running off to a witch's tea party! This is life and death. If you'd been killed—if you'd left me—"

"I know," she breathed. "I know."

And suddenly, her arms were around me, her mouth crushing mine in a demanding kiss that chased away all other thoughts as she pushed me down on the bed. There was an urgency and intensity burning between us that I'd never felt before, and that was saying something, in light of our recent active sex life. Maybe it was this brush with death that was driving us to furiously prove we were alive. All I really knew for sure was that I needed her, that I needed to lose myself in passion and get as close to her as possible . . . so that I'd never lose her again.

She continued kissing me with that ferocity, so much so that her lips lightly scraped my teeth. It was only a few drops, but as the sweet, metallic taste of her blood touched my tongue, a blinding ecstasy flooded my body. She pulled back with a small gasp, and looking up at her in the fickle light, I could see an answering rapture on her features as the barest flush of Moroi endorphins seized hold of her. Her lips parted; her eyes were wide with desire. I knew then, without a doubt, that I could've brought her throat back to my fangs and that she would've let me sink them into her. I could have her blood and her body tonight, if I wanted. And I *did* want it. The tease of her blood had me high and hungry, not just because it was blood—but because it was hers. Her essence. I yearned for that type of all-consuming union with her, to have no boundaries left between us, to see her lost in the pleasures of an endorphin wave. She would've let me do it all. She might even want me to—or at least, the Sydney who'd accidentally gotten a brief rush of endorphins might want me to. The thing was, I couldn't be sure that normal Sydney, no matter how much she loved me, wanted that. And until I was, it was a line we wouldn't cross, despite how frenzied the thought made me.

She hovered over me for several more tense seconds, as we each fought our own inner battles. Then, the moment of temptation passed, and we were suddenly back on each other as though nothing had happened, with a fierceness that shattered the memory of her blood. I was awash on a sea of desire, drowning in everything about her. Her passion answered mine as she murmured my name and clung to me so tightly that her nails dug into my skin, as though she feared she might lose me if she let go.

Afterward, she collapsed at my side, still clinging to me as her ragged breathing slowed to normal. I draped an arm over her, my own heart beating frantically from what had just passed. I was no longer angry. Mostly I still felt scared at how close she'd come to death. But she was alive. I told myself that over and over as I tightened my arms around her. She was alive and safe. She wasn't going anywhere.

And, to be honest, I had to admit I understood her reasoning for keeping me in the dark. I didn't like it, but I understood it. If our roles were reversed, I would've done the same thing to protect her. It was also hard to judge when I'd done my own share of withholding secrets upon starting the mood stabilizer.

The last critical piece in all this was that their risk had paid off. I couldn't deny the results. Olive's blood had worked. Somehow, through our fumbling and guesswork, we'd actually created a magical vaccine against Strigoi. If only there were a way to replicate it.

"You know," I mused, mulling over the story in my mind, "Angeline and Neil really put it all on the line tonight. I'll never make fun of them again."

"Never?" Sydney teased.

"Well, maybe not as much."

"Eddie 'put it all on the line' too," she reminded me.

"Yeah, I know, but that's normal for him." I then recalled her earlier words. "Wait. Did you say Jill kissed him?"

"Yup. It was actually very romantic, in a why-did-you-just-risk-yourself-you-fool kind of way." She paused. "Actually, it was kind of like what just happened with you and me."

"It better not've been," I growled.

"Okay. Let's just say the motivations were sort of the same," she corrected.

I sighed, making a mental note to have a talk with Jill tomorrow. "Seeing as everyone's alive, I can acknowledge what a big deal this fiasco was. It's going to blow their minds back at Court."

"And tomorrow night we see Marcus and get to deliver the *other* big deal," she said. "Maybe this is all crazy enough to work."

"It always is," I said. I trailed my fingers along on her shoulder, which was damp with perspiration. As I moved upward to her neck, my fingers touched a fine metal chain and I discovered she hadn't taken off everything. She still wore the wooden morning glory cross I'd made her, and somehow, that was sexier than if she'd been completely naked.

"Escape plan number forty-five," I said. "Join nudist colony in Fiji."

"Do they have those in Fiji?"

"Well, they've got to be somewhere warm, right?"

The panic of losing her still burned within me, almost enough to urge me toward sex again. But as we lay there, talking throughout the night, it was our minds and spirits that ended up connecting. There was peace and joy in each other's embrace, and the balance we brought to each other's lives allowed me to drift into a deeper sleep than I'd had in a long time.

I didn't know what questions she'd face the next day. The Ms. Terwilliger excuse went a long way, but surely Zoe would wonder what had kept Sydney out all night. Maybe Sydney could say they'd been up so late that she just stayed over on Jackie's couch. Whatever it was, I could see from Sydney's resolve the next morning that she would handle it. This was her battle, not mine.

She scoured the ingredients that Cassie had left behind and found enough to make us pancakes. I didn't actually have any syrup, but I did have raspberry jam. We slathered it on the pancakes, and it was the best thing I'd ever tasted. And as we sat there at the kitchen table with our pancakes and coffee, Sydney reading news on her phone while I leafed through the poetry book, I knew without a doubt that I could do this for the rest of my life.

"Escape plan number seventy-three," I said. "Open a pancake restaurant in Sweden."

"Why Sweden?"

"Because they don't have pancakes there."

"They do, actually."

"Well, then, it looks like we've got our market already in place."

Dropping her off at Amberwood was bittersweet, mostly because it ended the spell we'd been in since last night. We both had things to do, though, and I was going to see her later anyway.

"You know I love you, right?" The urge to kiss her goodbye was so strong that I almost broke our rules.

She smiled, beautiful and golden in the late morning light. "Not as much as I love you."

"Oh, man. This is my dream come true: having an 'I love you more' debate. Here, I'll start. I love you more. Your turn."

Sydney laughed and opened the door. "I've taken debate classes. You'd lose to my logic. See you tonight."

I watched her walk away and didn't leave until she disappeared inside the building.

A text chimed for me when I walked in the door of my apartment. For a moment, I thought it was the Love Phone, and then I remembered I was an idiot and had lost it. When I'd called the coffee shop I'd been to, they told me they had a couple phones in their lost and found, and I intended to go there later today. Meanwhile, on my regular phone, the message was from Lissa: *Get on your laptop. We need to talk face-to-face*.

I had a good idea what this was about, and when we connected, her radiant face confirmed it. "You heard?" she asked excitedly.

"About the dangerous and completely unauthorized field trip the kids went on last night? Yeah, I heard."

Lissa ignored my snark. "Adrian! This is monumental. It's amazing. It's a dream come true. I know they shouldn't have done it, but it's over, they're safe, and now we have a real answer."

"I know."

She gave me a puzzled look. "You're awfully calm about this."

"I found out last night. I've had a lot of time to process it." That, and the thought of how Sydney had endangered herself took away some of the awesomeness of the escapade for me.

"You realize how big a role you had in this, right?" Those jade green eyes were piercing. "You figured out what none of us could. What happened is because of you."

I shrugged. "Nah, one of you smart girls would've figured it out."

"But you were the one who did. Now we've just got to find a more efficient way to do this that doesn't involve restoring a Strigoi each time." Her enthusiasm faltered. "I wish . . ."

"I know," I said. I'd guessed this was coming. "But I can't, Lissa. I'm staying on the pills."

She nodded, resigned. "I figured. And it's wrong of me to ask. You look good, you know—and no jokes about how you always do. There's something different. A light. A happiness. I don't know."

"Hey, it's not all sunshine around here. I was listening to *The Wall* the other day. Man, let me tell you my opinions on that."

"Maybe some other time," she said with a grin. "And for now, maybe you can just help advise the rest of us. Nina and I have brought back Strigoi. Sonya was restored. You and I have brought back the dead."

"Impressive resume, Your Highness."

"You know what I'm saying. Between all of us, we've done enough and seen enough to figure out how to make this work. We won't let spirit beat us." Her earlier rapture returned. "I don't want glory and fame, Adrian, but I'd like to leave behind some kind of legacy. This could be it. I don't want to be one of those monarchs who 'just ruled.' I want to do something for my people."

"You're going to do a lot of things for us, cousin. You're going to get that age law fixed, right? And the family quorum?"

"Ah." She grew serious. "That's the thing . . . I was going to tell you later. The council's on the verge of voting about the

369

two-person family rule, and from what we can tell, we've got all the votes we need."

"Holy shit," I said, unable to help myself. "If that passes . . . Jill's safe. She can leave Palm Springs."

Which meant Sydney would also have to leave.

"I know. And it will pass. I'm certain."

The world as I knew it was suddenly altered. "What happens to her then?"

"She can come back to Court, go to school here, learn royal stuff. I know she'll want to see her mom too." Lissa hesitated. "And I wouldn't mind getting to know her better. I know you think I've treated her badly."

"You did what you had to do," I said, which was neither a confirmation nor a denial. Circumstances had put both sisters in very, very bad positions.

"Well, you can tell her the news, but otherwise, try to keep it quiet until the vote happens. Once it's secure, we can tell the world."

I saluted. "As you command." I could tell she was getting ready to end the call. "Hey, is your worse half around? I need to ask him something."

A flicker of surprise showed in her eyes. Christian and I hadn't been the best of friends lately. "Sure. He's actually right over here." I saw her get up and leave, and a moment later, Christian appeared with his trademark sarcastic smile.

"What's up?" he asked. "Need some hairstyling tips?"

I choked up for half a second. Maybe Aunt Tatiana didn't haunt my waking days anymore, but she lived forever in my memories. The Ozeras all had a strong resemblance, and looking at him, with his black hair and icy blue eyes, suddenly made me see his aunt, Tasha Ozera. The old panic and depression started to rear up in me, and I slowly, carefully urged it back down. What had happened wasn't Christian's fault. We were friends. I could handle this.

"Tips you stole from me? No thanks. But I hear you've got a really good bacon meatloaf recipe."

It was worth it then and there to see his complete and total surprise.

"Since when do you cook?" he finally managed to stammer.

"Oh, you know. I'm a Renaissance man. I do it all. Send it if you've got it, and I'll give it a try. I'll let you know if I make any improvements."

His smirk returned. "Are you trying to impress a girl?"

"With cooking?" I pointed at my face. "This is all it takes, Ozera."

Once I finished with royal shenanigans, I got in touch with Jill. I wanted to be the one to tell her the news about the law. I would've really liked to have taken her out somewhere, but one of the dhampirs would've insisted on going. I wasn't up for that, so she and I made arrangements to meet at her school for a "brother and sister" picnic. It was a nice day, and I still had two leftover cupcakes. Hopper had eaten most of them this morning before Sydney returned him to his inert form to bring him along with her for some togetherness time.

"I can't believe you made these," Jill said between bites, when we met up later. Another perk of the bond fading was that I could embellish my role in the baking.

"I can't believe you joined an impromptu Strigoi hunt without telling me," I said sharply.

She sighed. "I would have, but there wasn't time. It all

371

happened so fast. One minute it's a chase, the next, we're in the middle of the action."

"Yeah. I heard about that too—how you got some action."

Her cheeks turned pink. "It's not like that. It was just a kiss. And we talked about it later. Kind of. He says he 'has to think.' Whatever that means." She sighed again, this time in a lovelorn way. "He probably wasn't really into the kiss and is just trying to find a way to let me down gently."

"Did he kiss you back?" I asked.

"Yeah, but I think I caught him off guard."

"Jailbait, he's a guardian. They're never caught off guard." I watched with amusement as a smile slowly blossomed on her face. "It's about time you get your own romance," I added. "Instead of always looking in on mine."

Her smile turned into an outright grin. "I kind of miss not being part of that," she said. "That sounds creepy. I didn't like the voyeur part, but feeling all that love . . . it was amazing."

"Be patient. Your time will come." The sun was going strong, but we were in the shade, and I sprawled out on the blanket I'd brought. "Just try not to let it be in the midst of any more deadly Strigoi battles, okay?"

"Doing that was dangerous," she admitted. "Not just to my own life but also to Lissa's rule—and all the consequences that would follow if I died."

I sat back up. "Funny you mention that . . ."

I told Jill the news, about how she might no longer be on Lissa's enemies' most-wanted list. I told her how she might be able to live a normal life—as much as a princess whose half sister was queen of a nation could. Jill's eyes grew so wide, I thought her face would run out of room.

"I could see Mom . . ." She blinked back tears. "I've gotten used to being here . . . but I've missed her so much. I want to see her again."

I gave her a comforting pat on the hand, refusing to let her know she wasn't the only one wishing for a mother.

She brushed her emotions aside. "What'll happen to everyone if I leave? Everyone else will leave too, right? New assignments?"

"I suppose so. No reason to stay."

"Sydney will leave too," Jill realized.

I nodded.

"What will you do?"

"I don't know," I said honestly. "I came here for you. I still want to support you, you know that. But do we need to stay together so long as the bond is inactive? And how can I follow Sydney to her next assignment? We have the excuse of her job now for seeing each other. If I followed her halfway around the world . . . well, there'd be no explaining that."

"She could leave them. Marcus did." The sympathy in Jill's face almost made me want to cry. "You could go somewhere. Are you still making up escape plans?"

West Virginia. Rome. New Orleans. Fiji. Sweden.

"Those are just jokes," I said, feeling sad for reasons I couldn't understand. "I need to talk to her about it. She doesn't even know the news, and there's been no vote yet."

But first we had to get through Marcus and the ink delivery. I texted Sydney when I got home, careful in my wording since it wasn't the Love Phone. *Everything still a go?* Her answer came back swiftly: *As far as I know.*

The day dragged after that, mostly because I missed her and

wanted to see her. I took care of some assignments and went to the coffee shop, which had disappointing results when my phone didn't turn up. My only hope was that someone had found it in a classroom and turned it in to Carlton's security office. Otherwise, Sydney and I would have to get new Love Phones.

When I went to Jackie's later, Marcus actually answered the door with two guys behind him I didn't know. They both had golden lilies on their cheeks with no indigo seal. I wondered if these were his guinea pigs.

"Adrian," Marcus said, striding forward to shake my hand.

"Marcus," I returned. It was hard to believe we'd reached this point, since I'd tried to punch him sixty seconds after the first time we met.

"This is Jamie and Chad; just picked them up in New Mexico."

I shook their hands too, and Jackie strolled into the living room. I grinned, genuinely happy to see her. "Always a delight." She set down a tray of tea and lemonade and kissed me on the cheek.

"No hot date tonight?" I asked.

Her eyes sparkled with amusement. "Well, I could hardly go out when I was hosting some sort of clandestine meeting, could I? Rest easy, you'll have your privacy, and if you're worried about my relationship with Malachi, be assured that we're going out later and that things are still going wonderfully."

"Worried? No. Puzzled, slightly disturbed? Yes. But I'm not surprised things are going well. I'm sure you have him eating out of your hand, heartbreaker."

She chuckled. "Oh, Adrian, I'm glad Sydney keeps you around for entertainment."

"I supposed it'd have to be that," said Marcus, nodding in

thanks as he took some lemonade. "And speaking of her . . . I'm surprised she wasn't here an hour beforehand."

I glanced at a clock. It was actually five minutes before the designated time. "A month ago she would've been. But now her sister's been assigned here, and life's a little more . . . difficult."

Marcus's eyebrows knit together. "Yeah? Want to elaborate?"

Jackie scooped up a tabby cat. "I think this is my cue to go in my workshop. Come get me if you need anything, and make sure Sydney says hello before she leaves."

I sat down in the living room with Marcus and his Merry Men. I strategically took over a whole love seat so that no one else could sit there until Sydney came. Well, no one human, at least. As soon as I sat down, three cats jumped up with me and made themselves comfortable.

"They recruited Sydney's sister," I explained to Marcus. "And made her part of the Amberwood act. She's got a lot to prove and has been extra suspicious of Sydney's activities—like if she's gone too long or seems extra friendly with any Moroi."

Marcus's face darkened as I spoke. "I warned her. I told her this would happen. She should have come with me."

I pointed to the pail of ink that Jackie must have brought out. "If she had, she wouldn't have been able to do this. She may have changed the whole way you do business, Robin Hood. Ink that permanently breaks the Alchemist hold but that they can't see? You can put double agents everywhere."

"I know." He glanced over at Jamie and Chad, who were watching their leader with rapt eyes. "And believe me, I've thought about it. But it's so dangerous. The Alchemists are good at sniffing out traitors."

"Sydney's good too," I said staunchly.

"I know she is. But like I told her before, you can't be on your game all the time. Eventually, you slip up. Little things. Little bread crumbs."

I kept my own game face on and pretended to be very interested in a calico purring on my lap, but inside me, unease stirred. Little things. Like sex in a car. Or staying the night. Or picking me up from a pawnshop. Any one thing that some spy for the Alchemists could find out about. We'd gone in with good intentions, but Marcus was right. We'd grown careless. When I looked up, I saw him studying me with his bright blue eyes. He might not know about the specifics of Sydney and me, but he knew what I was thinking: that she'd slipped up.

"Would you be able to get her out of here?" I asked. "If she would go?"

He nodded. "I should be able to."

"Where would you take her?" West Virginia. Rome. New Orleans.

"I don't know yet. Somewhere she can still be useful but safe." Marcus grew silent for a few moments, and I could tell he really did care about her and all his other recruits. "*Would she go?*"

"She'll go," I said firmly, in no way letting on how difficult it would be to talk her into running away. *And I'll go with her.*

Marcus fell into his own thoughts for a bit and then checked his cell phone. "Where is she? I'm dying to know about this ink."

I looked at the time as well. She was fifteen minutes late. I couldn't remember Sydney ever being late in her life. Taking out my own phone, I tried to think of a neutral message and texted: *Everything right in the world?* When no answer came right away, I took that as a good sign.

"She's probably on her way," I explained to Marcus. "She won't text and drive."

He wanted to know about the ink, so I gave him a very vague overview that didn't mention Sydney using magic. I couldn't recall the geological specifics, but it was enough to intrigue him, as did the news about the spirit "Strigoi vaccine." I figured that wasn't going to stay a secret for long, and Marcus was no friend to the Strigoi.

When another fifteen minutes passed, I started to get uneasy. I actually called her, knowing the Bluetooth in her car would pull in the call. Instead, I went to voice mail. Marcus's eyes watched me sharply.

"Adrian, what's going on?" he asked.

"I don't—there."

We all listened as a car pulled up into the driveway. Almost immediately, its door slammed and was then followed by frantic and loud knocking at Jackie's door. I was a little surprised that Sydney wouldn't just come on in. Jackie appeared at the commotion, but I made it the door first . . .

. . . and found Eddie.

His clothes were dirty and torn, and the right side of his face was swollen and red. There was a wild, half-crazed look in his eyes I'd never seen before. A feeling of dread settled over me, and the darkness and despair and fear that had left me alone for so long began to rear their collective ugly head. I knew, even without Eddie saying a word, what had to have happened. I knew because of that terrible look of pain on his face, a pain similar to when he hadn't been able to save Mason. I knew because I had a feeling my face looked the same as Eddie's.

"What's wrong?" exclaimed Jackie.

But Eddie's eyes were on me alone. "Adrian," he gasped out. "I tried, I tried. There were too many. I couldn't stop them." He came forward and gripped my arm. "I tried, but they took her. It was a setup. I don't know where she is. She tricked me, damn it! I never would have left her if she hadn't tricked me!"

With his free hand, he reached into his coat pocket and pulled out a tiny golden dragon. He offered it to me, but I couldn't touch it.

Marcus had come over to join us. "What are you talking about? What happened?"

I closed my eyes briefly, trying to steady myself. I didn't know the details yet, but I knew the ultimate result.

"Things have fallen apart," I said, finally taking the dragon. "The center didn't hold."

CHAPTER 22

SYDNEY

ZOE WAS STILL IN BED when I got back from Adrian's, sullen and curled up with a book she didn't seem to be reading. For half a second, I thought maybe she just had some normal high school angst problem, like a bad grade or no date for the dance. But from the glare she shot me, it was obvious who was responsible for her bad mood. She hadn't liked me always being busy, but I realized that was nothing compared to me siding with Mom. To Zoe, that was unforgivable.

"Zoe," I said pleadingly. "Let's go out for lunch or something. Get away from cafeteria food."

"Don't you do plenty of that already?" she snapped. "Coffee breaks with Ms. Terwilliger. Cupcake runs." The animosity in her gaze made me wince.

"It's not about the food. It's about you. I want us to talk."

"I don't want to talk to you." She rolled over with her book, putting her back to me. "Go away. Go do whatever it is you do."

The thing was, I actually didn't have anything pressing for

a change, not until the meeting with Marcus later that night. My ink was done, and there was no magical work with Ms. Terwilliger that needed my attention. I really had hoped I might patch things up with Zoe, but that looked like it wouldn't be happening anytime soon. There was always homework to be done, I supposed, so I packed up my bag and headed to the library. I certainly wasn't going to stick around with all the hostility in my room.

I was halfway through an acid and base assignment when a shadow fell across my table. Looking up, I saw Trey and Angeline standing over me, hand in hand. I didn't know why, but I just started laughing. Maybe after all the tension and danger that had suddenly filled my days, their relationship had actually become something refreshing, no matter how complex.

"You okay there, Melbourne?" asked Trey. "You didn't get hit in the head last night, did you?"

I smiled and gestured for them to sit down. "No, no. Just a little slaphappy, that's all."

Angeline yawned. "We had a good time staying out all night. You should've come with us. Eddie said you saw Adrian or something?"

"Yeah, I had to go over something with him about Jill." Another beautiful lie, and from the way neither of them even blinked, I knew they didn't doubt me for a minute.

"Is everything okay with her?" The sudden seriousness in Angeline almost made me smile again. She really was in this for the long haul.

"Fine, fine," I said. "Aside from her running off on a dangerous Strigoi hunting trip last night."

"Crazy stuff last night," said Trey, a gleam in his eyes. "Crazy but awesome."

"I had no idea you were so good with a sword. You work on that between chemistry homework and football practice?"

He grinned at me. "Just part of the way I grew up."

"And how are you going to reconcile that with *that*?" I looked down meaningfully at where their hands were clasped together.

They both sobered, and Trey squeezed her hand. "This means more. I told you I needed time to figure out what I should do? Well, it turns out I already knew. I've known for a long time."

"It goes against how you were raised," I reminded him. "Against the beliefs of your group."

He seemed unconcerned. "Things change. They're not my beliefs anymore. They're not even my group anymore. They've made that clear."

I felt the need to keep playing devil's advocate. "It's that easy to break away?"

"Am I really breaking away *that* much? The Warriors' original purpose was to actively seek out and destroy Strigoi. The leaders just kind of went astray over the years." That earlier delight returned. "What we did last night . . . I mean, it was terrifying as *hell*. I was scared, especially when that one had me on the ground. But at the same time, it felt so right. Like that's what I was born to do, help smite evil from the world."

"Did you seriously just say 'smite'?" I asked.

He shook his head in amusement. "The way I see it, I'm not doing that much different from what I was taught. Strigoi are evil. We need to stop them. I can do that in my own way, without the Warriors. I can do it the way it should be done."

"And I can help," declared Angeline. They stared into each other's eyes, and I thought they might start making out then and there. "We'll start our own group."

"The guardians have strict rules about what dhampirs do," I warned.

"I'm not a guardian," she said simply. "I don't answer to them. And anyway, wasn't there talk with the Moroi about going after those monsters?"

"Yes."

The queen had so many problems right now that I think that one had slipped through. But there had indeed been growing interest in actually doing preemptive strikes against Strigoi— with both guardians and Moroi. For centuries, the Moroi had argued that it was immoral to use magic as a weapon. As time went on, it was becoming more apparent that magic might very well hold the key to their nation's safety.

"Okay," I continued, surprised to hear myself getting a little combative. "So the Warriors let you go all freelance. But what do you think they're going to do when they find out you're involved with a dhampir? You aren't really keeping it secret."

He shrugged. "No, but it's not like they have spies here. Even if they find out, all I have to do is put up with the ranting. They won't punish me or anything. Why are you so worked up about this? What's with the twenty questions? Weren't you helping us?"

"She's an Alchemist," said Angeline, looking uncharacteristically wise. "It's just how they are." Even more surprisingly, she suddenly grew hesitant and withdrew her hand from Trey. "Sorry. This is probably like . . . really gross to you. We should've been more considerate."

It was hard to say which was more ludicrous: Angeline actually being conscious of something like this or the fact that it was completely untrue.

Because honestly, the reason I was giving them such a hard time was that I was jealous. That wasn't an emotion I experienced very often, but here it was, alive and well in me. I was so, so envious that they could do this, be together so openly. No sneaking around. No fears of retribution. Trey had been so casual about being caught by the Warriors. A month ago, their rebuke would've been awful for him. Now, having come to terms with his feelings, he saw their wrath as a small thing. After all, it seemed they'd mostly berate and condemn him. For all their savagery, the Warriors weren't like the Alchemists, who felt a need to eliminate and sanitize their problems. I wanted to cry and scream to the world that this was unfair, but I knew I had no right. Life was unfair to a lot of people. I wasn't special, and this was the fate I'd been given.

"No," I said, trying to smile. "I'm happy for you guys. Really."

After a few moments, they decided to believe me and smile back. My phone buzzed with a text, and I saw it was from Adrian: *Everything still a go?* I wrote back: *As far as I know.* After Trey and Angeline left, I tried to use the knowledge that I'd see Adrian tonight as a way to bolster myself. Things could be worse, I supposed. Even if it wasn't unrestricted, we still got to see each other every day.

And yet . . . I was reaching a point where that wasn't enough. I wanted to go to bed with him each night, not just for sex, but so that I could wake up with him in the morning. I wanted to have pancakes together. I wanted to go out on double dates with his friends. I wanted a life with him. I wanted a life for myself.

When I returned to my room later, I saw that Zoe was gone. Things were still a mess between us, but I was at least relieved that she'd dragged herself up. I'd seen too much of that depressed behavior with Adrian and didn't want anyone else to go through it. *Zoe and I will fix this.* We had to.

About an hour before I was supposed to go to Ms. Terwilliger's, another text came in from Adrian: *Change of plan. We're meeting at that restaurant that went out of business on Indian Canyon.*

The news came as a shock. *Marcus got in touch?*

Adrian's answer was slow in coming. *Yes.*

Well. It wasn't that out of character. When I'd dealt with Marcus the last time he was in town, he'd constantly switched meeting spots on us, often deciding at the last minute. He believed it was safer. Maybe there was something to this.

That's a scary place at night, I wrote.

That's part of the reasoning. Don't worry. We'll all be there.

Okay. I need to stop and get the stuff first.

I'll get it for you.

A realization hit me. We were using the Love Phones. I'd picked mine up without even thinking about it. *You found the phone!*

Yup.

Happiness and relief flooded me. I should've known by now not to doubt Adrian.

I love you, I wrote. *See you soon.*

I waited for an answer, but when none came, I started getting ready to go. The restaurant was about twenty minutes away, in a pretty remote place off the main road. As I packed up, I began to think more and more about how sketchy the location was.

As I'd thought earlier, it was ideal for Marcus, but it wasn't the kind of place I'd normally go alone. I didn't fear him, but I did worry about other less noble people. One of Wolfe's lessons had been to avoid walking into uncertain situations, and although Adrian's comment about how they'd all be there reassured me, I decided to take an extra precaution for my own peace of mind.

I dialed Eddie.

"Hey," I said. "You want to run an errand with me?"

"The last time you asked that, we went and met with a bunch of rebel Alchemists."

"Well, I hope you had fun because that's what I'm doing tonight." I'd known him long enough to know exactly how to win him over. "I have to go to some remote place in the middle of nowhere. Neil and Angeline will be here for Jill."

A few seconds passed. "Okay. When are we going?"

"I'll be right over."

Eddie was relaxed and upbeat when I picked him up, so I knew that he must have gotten in touch with the other dhampirs in the short time it had taken me to come over. Eddie wasn't with Jill twenty-four hours a day, but he seemed to feel as though she were particularly vulnerable if he wasn't on campus. Despite their differences, I knew he felt better having Neil as extra protection.

"Hard to believe everyone's acting so laid-back after last night," I remarked, noting his good mood.

"Neil's not," said Eddie. "He seems overwhelmed. I mean, not down or anything. He's happy about the outcome. I think it's just a big thing to accept you hold the solution to a huge mystery. He was trying to explain it last night when we were out."

"Sorry I missed it," I said. I really wasn't, not when I looked back upon that heated, urgent night with Adrian.

"Sydney . . ." Eddie's light mood vanished, and even with my eyes on the road, his tone tipped me off that something serious was about to happen. "About that. About you going to Adrian's . . ."

I felt a tightening of my throat and couldn't answer immediately. "Don't talk about that," I said. "Please."

"No, we need to."

Eddie knew. Eddie knew, and if the subject wasn't so dire, I would've laughed. He was oblivious to his own social affairs, but guardians were trained to watch and observe. Eddie did that, and no doubt he'd picked up all sorts of little things between Adrian and me. We tried so hard to hide from the Alchemists, but hiding from our friends, who knew us and loved us, was impossible.

"Are you going to lecture me?" I asked stiffly. "Tell me I'm breaking taboos that have been in place for centuries to preserve the purity of our races?"

"What?" He was aghast. "No, of course not."

I dared a look. "What do you mean 'of course not'?"

"Sydney, I'm your friend. I'm his friend. I'd never judge you, and I'd certainly never condemn you."

"A lot of people think what we're doing is wrong." It felt strange and oddly relieving to acknowledge my relationship with Adrian to another person.

"Well, I'm not one of them. If you guys want it . . . that's your business."

"Everyone's suddenly very liberal about this," I said with wonder. "I just heard a similar thing from Trey and Angeline—

about their own relationship, that is. Not about . . . other people's."

"I think my ill-fated time with Angeline may be part of it," he said, with more humor than I expected, considering she'd cheated on him. "She talked enough about her people that after a while, it didn't seem that weird. And, well, my race exists because humans and Moroi got together and had kids way back when."

I felt a smile start to grow on my lips. "Adrian says it wouldn't be fair to the world if he and I had kids, what with the overwhelming power of our collective charm, brains, and good looks."

Eddie laughed outright, not something I heard very often, and I found myself laughing too. "Yeah, I can see him saying something like that. And that's the thing, I think . . . the real reason I'm not that weirded out by you two. It goes against all sound logic, but somehow, you two together . . . it just works."

"'Against all sound logic,'" I repeated. "Isn't that the truth."

A little of his amusement faded. "But that's not what worries me. Or the morality of it. It's your own people I'm worried about. How long are you going to be able to go on like this?"

I sighed as I took the exit for the meeting spot. "As long as the center holds."

The dilapidated restaurant, uncreatively called Bob's, was easily visible from the freeway in the daytime. Nighttime was a different matter. Large overhead lights had burned out long ago, and most of the gravel parking lot was buried in shadows. The only real light, once I turned off the car, came from a lightbulb near the back of the building. It was the kind of place serial killers, hobos, and Marcus Finch would hang around in, and those first two categories were the reason I had Eddie along.

Clarence's Porsche wasn't here yet, but there was a large gray van parked nearby. "Oh God," I said. "I wonder how many recruits Marcus has with him."

Eddie said nothing. All romantic musings were gone, and he'd snapped into guardian mode. This was the kind of place that triggered all his alarms, and I knew his training had seized hold and had him looking in every corner. He even walked ahead of me and tried the door first. The windows had been covered over for a while, but I thought I could see a hint of light within. The handle turned in Eddie's hand, and he pushed the door open and stepped inside—

—into an ambush.

I couldn't make out any identifying features. They were all in black and wore black ski masks. I think they were just expecting me because only one reached for Eddie, and the guy's eyes went wide when Eddie not only eluded him but also grabbed and threw him across the room, into someone else.

"Sydney, run!" Eddie yelled.

My immediate instinct was that I couldn't leave Eddie, but as he shoved me out the door, I realized he was coming with me. We tore out into the parking lot, only to see two more figures in black getting out of the van, cutting us off from my car. Eddie grabbed my hand and steered me in the opposite direction, behind the building and into a dark, sandy field that stretched as far as I could see.

I was a good runner, but I knew Eddie had to slow down for me. I also knew any attempts to tell him to go off without me would be foolish. The grass in the field was scraggly and scant, and there was only a handful of trees. For long moments, there was no sound except the thud of our feet and our heavy breathing. Then, from behind us, I heard shouts . . . and a gunshot.

Eddie managed to glance over his shoulder without breaking stride. "They're coming," he said. "About seven of them. With flashlights. And apparently guns."

"Look," I gasped out. In front of us, I could see two more flashlights approaching from the direction we were headed.

He said nothing and then suddenly jerked me to our right and down to the ground, into a ditch his superior eyes had seen. He threw me to my stomach and hovered protectively over me. The way the ditch was carved out offered partial coverage, and a thin, sad tree clinging to the side offered a little more. My heart was pounding, and I tried to calm down, lest my breathing give us away. Above me, Eddie was perfectly still, every muscle tense and ready to pounce if needed.

The shouts grew closer, mostly our attackers calling directions to one another and speculating over where Eddie and I were. As I lay there, hoping they'd walk by us, I wondered frantically who they were. Not Marcus and his Merry Men, obviously. But it was someone who cared enough about seizing us—or, well, me—to have set up a very organized trap, and there was only one group of people I could think of that fit that description.

The Alchemists.

It was what I'd lived in fear of so long; I just hadn't expected it to go down like this. A million questions raced through my head. How long had the Alchemists been here? Had they caught Adrian and Marcus too?

"Sydney!"

The familiar voice made my breath catch. My dad.

"Sydney, I know you're here somewhere. If you have any common sense or decency left, come out and surrender."

A skilled negotiator might have delivered that speech in a kind, beseeching way. Not my dad. He was as harsh and unfeeling as usual, managing to make every word sound like an insult.

"It'll be a lot easier on you if you do," my dad continued. "And as for that that . . . boy. We don't need him. He can just go if you come with us." In a lower voice, I heard him ask, "Is that *him*?"

A young female voice answered. "No, he's not the one."

I could tell from a slight stiffening in Eddie's posture that he recognized Zoe's voice too.

"This is for your own good," my dad growled, not sounding altruistic in the least. "It's for your soul. For your humanity. We know everything. We found the phone. Come with us so that we can save you from further damnation and defilement."

The phone. Adrian's missing phone. I'd been so afraid it would come back to haunt us, despite Adrian's flippant comment that it would mean nothing unless someone knew it was his. He was right because apparently, someone *had* known. Someone had known it wasn't a lovesick random stranger's phone. How? Had someone followed him at school and stolen it there? It was a mystery I had no time to ponder.

Silence fell as they all waited for me to give myself up. Eddie and I barely breathed. Suddenly, a light shone into our hideout. Eddie sprang up before the guy could even shout for help. Eddie punched him with a force that knocked him to the ground, and then seized hold of me without a moment's hesitation. Another guy was right there and actually managed to land a hit on Eddie's face. Eddie knocked him aside and kept going with almost no delay, dragging my stumbling self along. He must have assessed the least surrounded route because I saw no lights ahead of us. A gun went off again, and I heard my dad yell, "Hold on, or you might shoot her! Don't fire unless you have a clear shot on him."

My eyes weren't much use out here, and I had to trust in Eddie's. "I think this area just gives way to foothills and more wilderness," he said. "We'll lose them and hide out there as long as we need to." For Eddie, surviving off the land for a few days was probably easy work. "Then we'll go home and figure out something."

Figure out something. What exactly would that be? An attempt to negotiate with people trying to abduct me and kill Eddie? He made an abrupt turn left, and I understood why when I caught sight of a light in the direction we'd been headed. There was no telling how far their net extended. The next gunshot we heard was closer, far closer than I would have expected. It meant that someone had gotten a sight on Eddie and was catching up to us. That was remarkable, since it wasn't easy overtaking a dhampir on foot.

No, not a dhampir. Me. Eddie wasn't running at his normal pace. He was going at mine. Maybe on his own, he could have eluded them and run off to the wilderness, but not while I was with him. I was human, and one of my feet still ached from my ungraceful landing in the alley last night.

Eddie won't leave me, I thought frantically. He'll never leave me. They want me, but they don't care about him. He can live or die, and it won't matter to them. But if he's what's keeping them away, they'll shoot him and destroy his body.

391

"Eddie," I said, panting. "We need to split up."

"Never."

That answer wasn't a surprise. What was a surprise was that out of all the things rattling around in my mind, Abe Mazur's words popped up in the forefront: *Don't think for an instant that I wouldn't do terrible, unspeakable things if it could save someone I love.* Because it was Abe, I'd naturally assumed he was talking about doing terrible, unspeakable things to other people. But as Eddie and I held on to each other, the words took on a whole different meaning. In that moment, I knew I would do anything to save Eddie—my friend—whom I loved.

Even if it meant doing something terrible and unspeakable to myself.

I could hear shouts and feet pounding on the earth. They were getting closer. So were the guns. And even in the throes of terror, with my heart ready to explode in my chest, I managed an effortless Alchemist lie.

"You saw what I did with the fire? I can do another spell like that. Not the same but just as good. I have an object—a charm—but it has to be used from a distance. If we split up and I distract them, you can cast it. It's a sleep spell. It'll knock everyone out, except me because I'm protected."

"I can't cast a spell," he said. "Why don't you do it, and I'll distract them?"

"Because it'd knock you out too if you're in its path. You *can* do it. The magic's in the artifact. You just say the words to make it work."

With my free hand, I managed to fumble in my purse while still running. I pulled out Hopper, in inert form, and handed him to Eddie, along with my keys. "Take the keys since you can start the car faster when we escape. For the spell, hold up the dragon," I panted. "And say *centrum permanebit*."

"Cen—what?"

"*Centrum permanebit*," I said firmly. "Say it three times, and face toward us, but make sure you've got some distance. If someone catches you and interrupts, the spell will backfire."

"I can't! I can't leave you. We'll find a different way."

"No, we won't." I could feel myself tiring, and my foot ached even more. If Eddie found out, I knew he'd try to carry me, and it'd only make things worse. "This is our chance. There are too many, but we can take them out in one blow. Please, Eddie. You said you're my friend. I'm your friend. Trust me. I know what I'm doing."

Another gunshot, and dirt kicked up only a foot away where the bullet struck the earth. "I'll go over there," Eddie said, gesturing with Hopper. "You go left. None of them seem to be there. If you try to draw their attention, they won't have time to get to you before I cast the spell . . . right?"

"Right." I squeezed his hand and had to try not to choke up. "You can do this. And remember, I'm your friend."

"*Centrum permanebit*."

"*Centrum permanebit*," I repeated. He let go, and we split off. He ran at an angle to our right, but instead of heading in the opposite direction, I turned around and ran straight back the way I'd come from. I hit my captors almost immediately.

"I won't fight you," I said in a low voice as they grabbed me by the arms. "But you have to take me to my dad *right now*. Get me out of here. I'll only talk to him."

I prayed they'd listen and that we'd cover enough distance before Eddie realized I'd lied to him and walked right back into danger. My captors practically dragged me but listened to my request and ended up making good time. It was part of that Alchemist efficiency. They had a mission. They wanted to complete it quickly and thoroughly.

My dad and Zoe, unmasked, stood near where the field met the parking lot. I was so exhausted, I wanted to fall over, but I held myself straight, even when my escorts let go and pushed me forward. I met my dad squarely in the eye.

"Eddie's off calling for help," I said coolly. "If you want to avoid a major bloodbath with the guardians, you'll leave right now."

He grunted. "At least you have some sense." He jerked his head toward the van. "Take her there."

My captors hauled me over and shoved me inside, onto a long seat. The van had a weird orientation, and the back of my seat touched the back of the driver and passenger seats so that I faced the van's rear. Another Alchemist sat beside me, and two others took the front, out of my sight. Moments later, my dad and Zoe slid in and sat in the seats opposite me, allowing me to see their faces. I had the impression there were other vehicles for the other raiders hidden on the property. I'd barely fastened my seat belt when the Alchemist beside me grabbed my hands and zip-tied them behind my back. The van started, and we peeled away in a storm of gravel and dust. I prayed the other Alchemists would hightail it out of there before Eddie came calling. I wanted no confrontation that might endanger him.

Silence hung heavy in the van. Only my dad and Zoe kept their faces uncovered, and I turned my gaze on her. "You sold me out."

She hadn't been prepared for the hardness in my voice

and eyes. She swallowed. "Y-you sold yourself out. You've done horrible things. You've let them corrupt your mind."

"Is that what this is really about?" I asked. "Or is it because I was going to testify for Mom?"

My dad flinched. "This is about us showing you what family *really* means. I take responsibility, of course. I should've known when you ran off with that dhampir girl that this would happen. I should've intervened then, but I was blinded by sentiment."

I gave a harsh laugh. "Really? Sentiment? I can't believe you said that with a straight face." I turned back to Zoe. "Did you steal the phone?"

She shook her head. "I found it in the car when I was practicing those turns."

Any other laughter, mirthless or otherwise, withered inside of me. Of course. Adrian had noticed the phone was missing the day after my birthday. It must have fallen out of his pants when we'd strewn our clothes all over the backseat.

No, I realized with a start. It hadn't fallen out. It had been *taken* out. By me. When I read Adrian the William Morris quote, I grabbed the first phone I could find, which wasn't hard since we had four of them between us. I hadn't paid much attention to whose it was, and I certainly hadn't been careful when I tossed it back into the pile of clothes so that I could go back to being naked with Adrian.

"But there were other things too," Zoe was saying, her eyes glittering with tears. "Just the way you talked and laughed around them. The way you always disappeared. The cupcakes."

My defiance faltered, mostly due to confusion. "The cupcakes?"

"You said you bought them. But in the cafeteria that one

day, when Angeline was complaining about the cake, she started going off about the chocolate-peppermint cupcakes Adrian had made. Something about waiting until they're cool to frost them."

It was another horrible yet almost laughable moment. Cupcakes and birthday car-sex had been my undoing.

No, Sydney, I thought. *Don't think too highly of yourself. You slipped up long before this.*

Her voice was tremulous. "We're going to save you."

"I don't need saving," I said. "There's nothing wrong with me. You should've come to me first before unleashing all of this." I tried to wave my hand for effect, but it was stuck. "We could've talked. I'm your sister."

"No, Sydney." The hard, flat look on her face was frighteningly close to our dad's. "You're just another Alchemist, and I'm treating you like one—just like you told me to."

Her words struck me deeply, and my dad was quick to jump on my moment of weakness.

"You've been brainwashed, and we're going to undo it," he said. "This'll be a lot easier if you cooperate."

"I told you, there's nothing wrong with me!" Anger I hadn't known I held burst out, shoving aside my fear and sadness. "You're the ones deluded by centuries of bigotry and superstition. The Moroi and dhampirs are just like us—well, except they've got more honor and decency."

I didn't see the slap coming. For all his faults, my dad had never struck us, but the blow he delivered then made me painfully aware that he had no moral qualms about that kind of discipline. My head snapped back, and I bit my tongue.

"You don't know the sacrifices I'm making here for you," he

hissed, his eyes cold. Keith's glass one had more feeling. "You have no idea how lucky you are that we're doing this for you. The darkness has corrupted you so much that I don't know how long it'll take to fix. But we will. No matter how long or how difficult, we will undo whatever that Moroi boy has done to you."

I managed a wavering smile, tasting blood in my mouth. "You sure about that, Dad? Because he's done *everything* to me."

My dad's eyes flicked to someone in the seat behind me. I flinched as I felt the sting of a needle in my neck. The world spun, and I felt light and tingly all over. His and Zoe's faces swam in my vision for a few moments, and then I fell into darkness.

CHAPTER 23

ADRIAN

IF EDDIE WAS THE DRINKING TYPE, I'm pretty sure he would've joined me at a bar. I wouldn't go so far as to say he was as upset as me about the disaster we'd fallen into, but he probably took the next spot on the list.

After he'd burst into Jackie's with his story that night, we'd immediately tried the obvious things. We'd called Sydney's phone, multiple times. We'd driven out to the closed-down restaurant. There wasn't a trace of her there—or even at Amberwood. In barely two hours, her room had been completely cleaned out, and the administration had been notified that Sydney Melrose and Zoe Ardmore were withdrawing, effective immediately. No forwarding address. Our confusion was understandably perplexing to the staff, seeing as we were all supposed to be related.

Marcus had waited for us back at Jackie's, uneasy about showing his face at the dorm, just in case the Alchemists were still in the area. He stood up as we entered the living room, agitation all over him. Jackie had already been up, pacing around.

"Anything?" she asked. Eddie shook his head, and I strode over to Marcus.

"Where is she?" I demanded. "Where would they have taken her?"

"I don't know," he said, face drawn.

"Yes, you do! It's what you're all about." I had to resist the urge to shake him. "You know these things, damn it! You're supposed to be some great big mastermind! *Where is she?*"

Eddie came up and caught hold of my arm. I think he was afraid I really would attack Marcus. "Easy," Eddie warned.

Marcus looked pale. "I'm sorry. I really don't know where she's at. I can make guesses, I can make calls . . . but without anything to go on, it's the proverbial needle in a haystack."

Real people didn't use the word "proverbial." Only smart people like Alchemists did. Sydney would have. Groaning, I flounced back into an armchair.

"They said they were going to save her from damnation," said Eddie. He still looked like hell and hadn't made any attempts to clean himself up.

"Yeah," said Marcus darkly. "I'm sure that's what they think they're doing. And there's any number of places they could hide her—many, no, most of which not even my contacts know about. The places they take people like her to . . . well, they're not really on the public Alchemist grid."

People like her.

I felt ill and buried my face in my hands as I thought back to the frantic story Eddie had told us. "That phone. That goddamned phone." It was my fault. My fault she'd been caught.

If I hadn't been so careless, I wouldn't have lost it wherever I had. When I glanced up, I saw everyone looking at me, puzzled. Even Eddie, who'd related the story, didn't entirely understand the phone's role. Marcus suddenly sat straight up.

"Wait. We can find her. I know how."

I stopped breathing. "How?"

"You," said Marcus eagerly. "Your spirit dreams. She has to sleep sometime. Find her, and have her tell us where she is."

I sank back into the chair. I wanted to laugh. I wanted to cry. I wanted to punch something. "I can't. My spirit's kind of out of commission right now."

And there it was. The fear of being unable to heal Sydney if she got injured had haunted me from the first day I took the mood stabilizer. Never, ever, had I imagined that it was a dream I'd need. Even though I knew it was hopeless, I tried to reach out and touch spirit the way I used to. Nothing happened. It wasn't even like I could sense it and not reach it. It just wasn't there at all.

I had failed her. I'd been weak, too weak to handle spirit's dark side. I'd given in to the pills, and now I was useless. Would spirit come back if I stopped taking them? How long would it take? In this moment, the questions were pointless. Sydney was gone, and none of us could do anything when we most needed to.

Jackie cleared her throat. "I might be able to help. I can scry for her—the same kind of spell she did for your Moroi friend. I'd need a lock of her hair."

Wan hope surged in me. "I'm sure there's plenty at my place." Marcus's eyebrows rose at that.

"I might have some too . . ." Jackie turned and hurried toward her workroom. I followed and watched as she knelt down to the shelf where she'd let Sydney store things that couldn't go to her dorm room.

Most of it was magical paraphernalia, things Sydney couldn't risk Zoe finding. There were a few changes of clothes too, in case Sydney spilled anything on her while working, Jackie explained. It was the kind of precaution Sydney would take. There was also a velvet cloak and some spell books. We carefully unfolded the clothes, desperately searching for any stray hairs that might have fallen. I found one at last, as fine and brilliant as real gold, lying near the collar of a purple T-shirt. I handed the hair to Jackie and opened up the shirt fully. I had to stop myself from breaking down then and there.

It was the shirt I'd made her, dark purple with a flaming heart painted in silver. For the space of one breath, I saw us back in a crowded, smoky sorority house. We'd sat on the floor side by side, and when I'd looked into her eyes, I'd seen my own longing mirrored in them. Her kiss had unbalanced my world, and I'd known from that moment that no matter how hard she denied it, we were bound together.

I clenched the shirt and pulled it to me. It still held the fleeting scent of her perfume. "I'm taking this."

Jackie nodded. "Go join your friends. It's going to take me a while to set this up."

"You have to find her," I said, grabbing her arm. I knew I sounded crazed and desperate . . . but, well, that's kind of what I was in that moment. "You have to. If something happens to her . . . I can't . . . that is . . ."

Tears glittered in Jackie's eyes, and to my astonishment, she hugged me. "I'll do what I can. For now, you need to get a hold of yourself."

I didn't know if I'd achieved that by the time I came back to Eddie, Marcus, and the others, but they were all so lost in their own worries that no one really noticed mine. Eddie glanced up at my approach. His face was still lined with grief.

"I tried," he whispered. "Adrian, I tried. I never would have ever left her if I'd known. I would have stayed with her to the end. I would have laid down my life and—"

I had to forcibly hit the pause button on my own feelings as I dealt with his. Eddie had lost another person. It was bad luck, that was all. He was one of the most badass, capable guardians out there, but he couldn't believe that about himself, not when he kept seeing these failures laid at his feet. Looking into his eyes, I recognized the intense self-loathing consuming him. I knew the feeling well because I was carrying around a fair amount of it myself.

"I know you would have," I said. "There was nothing you could do."

He shook his head and stared off with a haunted look. "I was an idiot. I never should've bought into that spell stuff. After what I'd seen her do with fire, it just seemed so . . . well, real. I believed her. It made sense."

I smiled without humor. "Because that's what she does. She's trained to make people believe things. And outsmart them. You didn't have a chance." She also was willing to trade her own life to save her friend's, but no one had trained her to do that. It was just something within her.

Eddie wasn't going to be swayed so easily, and I left him to his grief as I huddled with mine. Einstein had said even with the mood stabilizer, sad things would make me sad and happy things would make me happy. He'd been right because as I sat there, with my world completely falling apart around me, I felt as though I'd never taken any of those pills. The dark, smothering despair that I thought I'd banished crashed down around me, seeping into every part of my being. I hated myself. I hated my life because Sydney wasn't in it.

My misery swirled around me, and it was just like the old days of spirit—except that I didn't *have* spirit. If I'd had it, I wouldn't have been so goddamned worthless. I had nothing to offer Sydney. I never had.

But Jackie does. If I couldn't pull myself out of that choking despair, I would at least look for light in someone else. Jackie would pull this off. She would find Sydney, and somehow, maybe with Marcus's voodoo and Eddie's fists, we would get Sydney back. I clung to that spark of hope, nurturing it into a small flame that chased some of the shadows in my heart away. The blame and self-hatred eased up, and I told myself to be strong. I had to for Sydney. She had believed in me.

But when Jackie returned, I could tell by her face that the spell hadn't worked.

"I tried," she said, her eyes red. "I thought I connected to her, but I couldn't grasp at anything substantial. No images. Just darkness."

"Is she alive?" I asked, barely recognizing my own voice.

"Yes," said Jackie and Marcus together. I glanced between them questioningly.

"If she were dead, I'd be able to tell in the spell." Jackie didn't elaborate.

"They won't kill her. It's not their style," said Marcus. "They prize their people too much. They'll just try to change her, make her think differently."

"Re-educate her," I said dully.

He spread his hands out in a helpless gesture. "Well, that is where the name comes from."

"How much can they really change her, though?" asked Eddie. "I mean . . . she's Sydney. She'll be the same . . . right? She can fight them."

Marcus took a long time in answering. "Sure." He wasn't nearly as good a liar as Sydney. To me, he asked, "She never gave herself the salt tattoo, did she?" I shook my head but could tell from his face he'd already known the answer. I didn't say anything about the possible but unproven protection Sydney could have from her magic use. We'd had nothing more to go on than Inez's word, but Sydney had remained optimistic about conducting some experiments on herself when she had time. Which we were now apparently out of. "Once everything's settled down," she had told me. "Then we'll have some time."

I stayed up all night, unable to find rest. The next day, our entourage was summoned to a meeting at Clarence's with an Alchemist named Maura. She was about Sydney's age, with her brown hair cut in a blunt style. She wore an Amberwood uniform. "I'm the new Alchemist assigned to Palm Springs," she said, her voice prim. "I will be your liaison to handle any Moroi friction that might rise. Since I understand you've mostly adjusted, Princess, I doubt there'll be any reason for us to have excessive interaction."

The rest of us stared morosely. Everyone else knew by now that Sydney had been taken, though all the reasons weren't widely known. Those who didn't know about Sydney and me believed they'd snatched her for getting too close to us—which, really, wasn't that far from the truth.

Maura handed us all business cards. "Here's my e-mail and phone number if you need to get in touch. Do you have any questions?"

"Yeah," I said. "Where are Sydney and Zoe Sage?"

Maura's smile was as polite as a politician's, but I could see that Alchemist ice in her eyes. I doubted she'd be able to stay in the same room as me if she knew Sydney's backstory, but it was obvious Maura still had the usual disdain and distrust for my kind.

"I'm sorry," she said coolly. "I just go where my orders send me. They don't share classified information with me. You'd have to check with my superiors to get any details about where the Sage sisters' new assignment is." From the tone of her voice, she didn't think anyone would tell me, and that, at least, we could agree on.

I hadn't taken the mood stabilizer that morning and had felt little change throughout the day. Jackie had told me she'd be able to try some other location spells during the dark moon in two weeks, and that and the hope I might recover spirit were all that kept me from a case of vodka. The biggest feat of all was going to class. I wanted to stay home and curl up in a ball. Or keep nagging Marcus for updates. It was only the thought of Sydney that got me to Carlton each day. She would want me to keep up with it, not just because of her educational convictions but because she'd hate to see me plunging into despair. I trudged around campus like a robot, and my palettes strayed to gray and black.

Three days after I'd stopped the pills, I was pretty sure the dark moods were here to stay. It was just like before.

Five days in, I woke up in the morning and felt the first glimmers of spirit.

I nearly cried. It had been so long, and as I extended my senses, brushing them against those glittering, brilliant strands of magic, I felt as though I'd been unable to breathe until now. It was an essential part of me that had been missing. How could I have given it up? I couldn't fully grasp or wield it yet, but the sweetness of that power was heady and restorative. It gave me my first surge of hope since Sydney's disappearance, as well as the initiative to call Lissa. I flipped the switch on my malaise and suddenly had enough energy to take on the world.

"You need to get in touch with the Alchemists and find out where Sydney is," I told Lissa when she answered.

"What . . . are you talking about?" she asked, understandably bewildered.

Apparently, no one had bothered to tell her about the regime change in Palm Springs. As long as Jill was safe, the Alchemists hadn't felt Lissa needed to know the logistics. I kept our relationship out of it and explained how the Alchemists had freaked out and carried Sydney away for getting too friendly with us. Again, it wasn't that far off from the truth.

"That's awful," she said. I could hear the compassion in her voice. "But there's not much I can do. That's their business, no matter how terrible it is. I can't go make demands of them, any more than one of them could come ask about one of my subjects. Alchemists and Moroi work together, but we don't have control over each other."

"Can you please just ask? Please?" I tried to keep my voice level and was glad this wasn't a video call. I couldn't even imagine what my face would reveal.

"I'll ask," she said reluctantly. "But I can't promise anything."

"I know. Thank you." A flash of inspiration hit. "You met

her . . . could you go to her in a spirit dream? I've been trying, but with the pills . . ."

"Ah." She paused. "I'd like to . . . I can try, but I'm not as good as you. I have to know someone *really* well to visit them. Maybe you can ask Sonya."

It was a good idea, and I followed up on it, once more clinging at whatever threads I could. Sonya and Sydney had become good friends, but Sonya was also a weak dreamer. When she called me a couple days later, the news wasn't uplifting. "I tried," she said. "I couldn't reach her. Maybe I don't have the skill after all. You're the best at this."

"Maybe she was awake," I said, not sure I believed it. My hopes plummeted down to endless depths once more, but they didn't stay down for long because the next morning, I was able to touch spirit.

There it was again, that sense of recovering some intrinsic part of myself. I gasped at the feel of it. The magic burned within me, euphoric and glorious, and I ran outside in boxers and a T-shirt. Not many people were out, but a man walking his dog across the street gave me a surprised look. Without hesitation, I drew on spirit's power, and the man's aura flared within my vision, orange and blue.

"My God," I breathed. I had my magic back. I could do this. I waved at my neighbor and then hurried back inside. Once I was in my bedroom, I settled down on the bed and tried to summon spirit's dreaming state. It required a fair amount of calmness, and my excitement and agitation made it hard to relax. When I finally managed the trance state, though, I couldn't reach her.

I shifted back to the waking world and tried to be

reasonable. If she was anywhere in the United States, it'd be daytime for her too. And there was also a chance I still had to strengthen my powers a little. But the darkness was temporarily cast aside, and I felt myself carried upward on wings of hope, possibly into the state that Einstein had warned was *too* up. I couldn't imagine that, though. For the first time in days, I felt as though all wasn't lost. I could save Sydney.

The rush of it gave me so much energy that I hardly slept at all for the next four days. I was too wired. That, and I didn't want to waste any opportunity to seize on when she might be asleep. My control of spirit was back to full strength, and I constantly flipped into dreaming mode, hoping I'd catch her. But it never came. Sometimes I made no connection at all. Sometimes I'd have the sense of darkness or a wall. Whatever it was, the result was always the same: no Sydney.

My mood was starting to fall again when Jackie finally called and said she could attempt her next spells. I dutifully went over, but my high had shattered, swinging me down to the other extreme. It wasn't so much our failures (though those weighed on me), as it was other things. I'd focused so much on my efforts that I'd had little time to spare for Sydney herself. What was happening to her right now? Marcus hadn't offered much illumination on what they'd do to her, and my imagination ran wild. That self-hatred returned. Sydney was suffering. She needed me, and I wasn't there for her.

A strange car was in Jackie's driveway, and when she let me in, I was surprised to see Jill and Eddie. "What are you doing here?" I asked.

"I wanted to see the spells," said Jill. She gave me a long, appraising look. "And I wanted to talk to you."

"How did you know we were—" I stopped. Of course. Along with everything else, the bond had been restored. Jill was in sync with me again, and judging from the haggard look on her face, she was being dragged along with my wild moods.

"Adrian," she said softly. "You need to sleep."

"I can't. And you know why. I can't risk missing her. She *has* to sleep, and I have to be awake to catch her."

"You've been trying for days. It's time to admit something's wrong. Something's blocking you."

She had a point, but I didn't want to admit to it. I wanted to believe that if I just tried a little harder or caught the right moment, I'd reach Sydney. I'd spoken to Lissa in a dream recently when she'd reported no luck with the Alchemists, so I knew I still possessed the ability.

"It doesn't matter," I said obstinately. "Jackie's going to find her. She'll pull this off. You've got two things you can do, right?"

Jackie nodded. "One can only be done at this time of the moon. The other can be done almost any time . . . it just requires an extensive expenditure of magic and some rare ingredients I was out of. It took time to get them again."

"Then let's do this."

The dark moon one had to be done outdoors. She'd set up an altar covered in incense and other components, and we kept our distance, waiting in tense silence. It was nothing but unintelligible words and gestures to us, and I found myself thinking of the times I'd been with Sydney when Jackie had worked magic. Sydney could sense it, and there'd always be a catch in her breath and wonder in her eyes as she watched her mentor. I felt nothing, only a war of hope and fear within me.

When Jackie finally rose and returned to us, she shook her head sadly. "Nothing. I'm sorry. Let's try the other."

She cast the other one inside, a spectacular feat that created a large spinning disc in midair. The power it required nearly made her pass out, and I caught her as she started to collapse. "Still nothing." It was only then, seeing her on the verge of tears, that I understood just how deeply she cared about Sydney. "I thought one of these would work. But all I get is a dark wall." We helped her back to the living room, and I dug through her kitchen for food. One thing I'd learned was that depleted magic users needed calories. "I had a similar experience when my sister was in a coma."

Jill flinched. "Do you think Sydney is? Would they have hurt her?"

"I don't know enough about it or their methods," said Jackie, gratefully taking a glass of apple juice from me. "I'm still certain she's alive, but that's it."

I sat back on the love seat and shifted into a dream trance. It seemed unlikely I'd reach anything if Jackie hadn't, but I had to try. As I'd feared, there was just more darkness. It was getting hard to tell where hers ended and mine began.

When I came back, the others were watching me with grim looks. "Go home, Adrian," said Jill. "Get some rest. You're of more use to her if you're at full strength."

"I'm no use to her," I said.

When I'd been with Sydney, whether it was in the heat of passion or simply sitting around and talking, I hadn't thought it was possible for my heart to hold any more love. Now, I didn't think it was possible for my heart to hold any more despair. No, not just my heart. Every part of me grieved so much. People used to tease me about alcohol poisoning, but this was the real stuff, the toxin that would finally win.

And speaking of alcohol . . . for the first time in a month, I wanted a drink. I wanted a lot of drinks. I wanted to drink until I passed out into my own darkness, until I was beyond feeling because I couldn't go on for another moment feeling like this. It would numb me from spirit and the ability to dream, but at this point, the dreams I had weren't helping Sydney anyway.

"Don't," said Jill, guessing my thoughts. She came over to sit beside me. "There's still hope."

"Is there?" I leaned against her shoulder, wondering how she could still feel that way—especially if she had a direct line into my heart.

Out of the corner of my eye, I noticed Hopper lying on an end table. I'd left him here after the night Sydney had been taken, which had been bad form on my part. "What'll happen to him?" I asked Jackie. "Is there any way you can bring him back?"

Her eyes fell on the glittering dragon. "No. She's the only one who can summon him. Keeping him around you, even in this form, might help, but if he ever comes out of this state, he'll be weak and sick. Of course, after the year is up, he'll fade back to his realm anyway . . . but it's a miserable, trapped state to be in for that long."

"I know how he feels," I muttered. Too bad I couldn't take Hopper out drinking with me. He could have become Bar Hopper.

Eddie stared at Hopper with contempt, but I suspected it was for himself, not the dragon. "I'm so stupid," he muttered. It was a refrain I'd heard from him a lot. "I never should have believed it. I shouted that 'spell' over and over in that field, and all I did was give them more time to get away with her."

"She was just protecting you," said Jill.

"It was my job to protect her," he growled.

Jackie finished off her juice and turned to a package of cookies. "What spell did she tell you to recite?"

Eddie's brow furrowed. "*Cent . . . centrum permanebit*. Is it even a real spell?"

"Not that I know of." Jackie gave him a sympathetic look he didn't even really notice. "But if it makes you feel better, it *is* Latin. A lot of spells use that language."

"What's it mean?" asked Jill. I was still leaning into her, but my mind was wandering to an analysis of nearby bars. Downtown's were nicer, but I might run into people I knew if I went to Carlton. Did I want to be alone or not?

"Well, *centrum* means center," said Jackie. "*Permanebit* is a future tense verb. 'Remains' is one translation. Or maybe 'endures.' Together it'd be something like, 'the center will endure.'"

I jerked my head up. "Hold," I whispered, my voice cracking. "The center will hold."

Sydney's last words. Not for Eddie, but for me.

The last of my self-control shattered, and I abruptly stood. Jill reached for me. "Adrian . . ."

"I'll see you guys later." I moved toward the door, pausing to scoop up Hopper and put him in my jacket.

The center will hold.

Will it, Sydney? I wondered. *Because I'm falling apart.*

"Where are you going?" asked Eddie.

"Out," I said. "Escape plan number eighty-two: Go somewhere where I don't have to feel anything for a while."

He exchanged a worried look with Jill and asked, "When are you coming back?"

Centrum permanebit.

I shook my head and turned away. "It doesn't matter."

CHAPTER 24

SYDNEY

IT WAS THE COLD THAT FINALLY WOKE ME UP. I'd been going in and out of a dark, dreamless haze for an indefinable amount of time, and I had no idea how long it had been since I was in the van with my family. Judging from my dry mouth and groggy mind, there was still some drug kicking around in my body, but they must have lifted it enough to let me finally grasp at consciousness.

The floor I was lying on was a rough, uneven concrete that held no warmth and was made even more uncomfortable because it was damp. It added to the chill seeping into my bones, and I slowly and awkwardly managed a sitting position, so that I could wrap my arms around myself in a weak attempt to hold in body heat. The damp cell couldn't be any more than fifty degrees, and the fact that I was naked wasn't helping matters.

The room was also black. Pitch-black. I'd been in darkness before, but this was impenetrable. There was nothing, not even a whisper of light, that my eyes could adjust to. That blackness was nearly tangible, heavy and smothering. I had to rely on my other senses to get any idea of my setting, and from the ominous silence, my hearing wasn't going to do me any favors.

My teeth began to chatter, and I drew my knees up to my body, wincing as the harsh floor scraped my skin. I huddled into a ball as best I could, scarcely able to believe I'd just been in a desert. How long ago had that been? I had no clue, nor did I know where I was now. The drug they'd given me had stopped the passage of time. It could've been days or minutes since my abduction.

"Hello, Sydney."

The voice came without warning, seemingly from every part of the cell, echoing off the walls. It was female, but there was a synthesized quality to it, like she was speaking through a filter. I said nothing but lifted my head up and stared straight ahead unflinchingly. If this room was equipped with a fancy sound system, then they probably had some sort of night vision cameras that let them view me. The Alchemists might try to cut off my senses, but they would certainly make sure they had every advantage for themselves.

"Do you know where you are?" the voice asked.

I had to swallow a few times before my tongue would form words again. "Being held by a bunch of sick voyeurs who get their kicks out of locking up a naked girl?"

"You're the one who's sick, Sydney." The voice had no emotion whatsoever. "The darkness that surrounds you is nothing compared to the darkness that's defiled your soul. We're here to help you expel it."

"I don't suppose you could help me to clothes and a blanket?"

"You're being reborn into the world, cold and naked, given a new chance to save yourself."

I rested my head on my knees again and didn't reply. They could dress it up with as many metaphors as they wanted, but I was perfectly aware that this sort of deprivation was a psychological technique to try to crack me. The voice's next words confirmed as much.

"The more cooperative you are in your salvation, the more comfortable we'll make your stay."

As though on cue, my stomach rumbled, again making me wonder how much time had passed. "Keep your comfort. I don't need to be saved."

"Everything you came in with has been destroyed, with one exception. It's a sign of our goodwill. We aren't doing this to be cruel. We want to help you."

I stayed silent.

"The item is in your cell if you want it," the voice added.

It was already starting: the Alchemist's mind games. I hadn't known what to expect from re-education. The reason it was kept so shrouded in mystery was undoubtedly to inspire fear. Mental and physical torture seemed like obvious conclusions, though. If you wanted to remold people, you had to break them down first.

The voice didn't say anything else, and I vowed not to play into this ploy. And yet, the longer I sat there, the more curious I became. What item were they trying to tempt me with? If there really was one. I knew I shouldn't indulge them. I knew defiance was the best course. But that curiosity continued to gnaw at me, and I really didn't know what else was in this room. Exploration wouldn't hurt.

I stood up, surprised to find how weak my legs were. I felt a little light-headed, but in the darkness, I at least had no sense of the room spinning. Cautiously, I moved forward, hands outstretched. It didn't take me long to hit a wall. The surface was as cold as everything else in here, but the texture was smoother, with lines etched into it as though they were bricks or tiles. Compartments for the speakers and cameras?

My survey was brief. The cell appeared to be about twelve by eight feet. There was no obvious door. A small toilet and sink sat openly in a corner, no doubt meant to increase the humiliation of this experiment. Groping around, I managed to turn on the faucet. The water that came out was one step away from ice, but it didn't smell or taste strange, and I cupped some in my hands to drink, suddenly feeling parched. Near the sink, embedded in the wall, was a small hand-soap dispenser that smelled antiseptic. I nearly smiled. Even amid prisons and torture, the Alchemists had to maintain their hygienic standards.

When I found nothing else, I returned to my original spot on the floor. "Well played," I said. "I guess you got me."

Nothing. After several seconds, I had the idea to start feeling around on the floor. I knew they were watching and I had to push my self-consciousness away as I crawled around, running my hands over every rough inch. In the end, though, the only thing it yielded me was painful knees.

"There's nothing here," I said. "Hope you at least enjoyed the show. I've been working out."

Brilliant light suddenly flared before me, and after all that blackness, I cried out and covered my eyes from the shock of it.

"It hurts, doesn't it?" the voice asked. "After living in darkness, it's hard to return to the light."

It took a long time for me to adjust. Even when I was able to remove my hands, I still had to squint. I peered ahead of me and saw that the light was coming from a square in the wall. As I'd suspected, there seemed to be several compartments embedded within the wall. This one's surface was made of glass, allowing me to look inside. It was small but still large enough to hold those blinding lights—

—and Adrian's cross.

The defiance I'd tried to maintain started to crumble, and I quickly caught myself, knowing I couldn't show my feelings on my face. Nonetheless, I couldn't hold back from trailing my fingertips along the glass surface as I stared achingly at the cross. They hadn't done anything to it. The small wooden cross was exactly the same, painted with delicate blue morning glories, strung onto its fine chain.

"You have no right to wear such a holy symbol," the voice said. "But we took it as an optimistic sign that you even carry an item like this at all. It tells us that no matter how far you've fallen, how corrupted you've become, some part of you longs to return to purity and the righteous path."

"I'm already on that path," I said, unable to take my eyes off the cross. "I've been on it for a long time."

"No. You've strayed from it and debased yourself. You've become enmeshed in an unholy, twisted world that runs contrary to all the rules of nature and salvation. When you can admit that, when you can confess your sins, you may have your cross back."

My hand, still pressed on the glass, twitched with the need to touch the cross, to have some piece of Adrian to cling to. The coldness that still tormented me momentarily lost its hold as thoughts of him flooded my mind and heart. Adrian, with his easy smile and his breathtaking green eyes. Adrian, his arms holding me tight and keeping me close to his heart. Adrian, fighting through the torment within him to do the right thing. Adrian, with his unfailing faith in me.

If I could have the cross, if I could have that connection . . . then surely the obstacles and distance between us would mean nothing. Surely I could endure whatever torturous challenges they threw at me.

This is one of them, I realized. *This carrot they're holding out.* They wanted me to take the cross. If I gave in, if I acknowledged their accusations, I wouldn't be closer to Adrian. No matter how much I wanted the cross, accepting it would mean I was going against him, turning my back on all I'd worked so hard for. Slowly, painfully, I withdrew my hand and clenched it into a fist. I needed no physical object to remind me of his love. I already carried it in my heart, and it would be enough to get through this.

"I have nothing to confess," I said through gritted teeth.

"You have everything to confess," said the voice. "But you only need to start small. Take one step on the path to redemption. Say, 'I have sinned against my own kind and let my soul become corrupted. I am ready to have the darkness purged.' Say those words, and things will become much easier for you. You can have your cross. You can have a blanket. You can have food. One way or another, we *will* purge that darkness, but if you are uncooperative, you will find the methods we must sadly resort to will be . . . unpleasant."

A bubble of fear rose in me, and I staunchly pushed it down. I gave the cross one last, hungry look and tried to focus not on the object itself but the love in Adrian's eyes when he'd given it to me. I turned away and walked to the other side of the room.

"I have nothing to confess," I repeated.

"Then you leave us no choice," said the voice. "That disappoints us and makes us very, very sad."

The light went out in the box, plunging the cross—and me—into darkness. My head started to feel fuzzy, and I realized they were somehow getting that drug into my system again, dragging me back into a dreamless world. Had it been the water?

One way or another, we will purge that darkness, but if you are uncooperative, you will find the methods we must sadly resort to will be . . . unpleasant.

"All right," I managed to say, just before I crumpled to the floor. "Let's see what you've got."

ACKNOWLEDGMENTS

The Fiery Heart is a new venture for me, seeing as it's the first time we've truly followed two characters in the Moroi world. It was an exciting project to work on, and I couldn't have done it without the support of many, many people. Thank you so much to my family and friends, particularly my wonderful husband and son, for their constant love and cheerleading. Many thanks are also due to the amazing publishing team who makes these books possible: my literary agent extraordinaire, Jim McCarthy of Dystel and Goderich, and my uber-patient Razorbill editor, Jessica Almon. Lastly, thank you to my wonderful readers, who constantly inspire me to write. We're in the middle of a series, so you know things are going to get rough for the characters, but hang in there! It'll be worth it.

GO BACK TO WHERE IT ALL BEGAN....

Vampire Academy

NOW A MAJOR MOTION PICTURE!

TURN THE PAGE TO READ THE

FIRST CHAPTER . . .

ONE

I FELT HER FEAR BEFORE I heard her screams.

Her nightmare pulsed into me, shaking me out of my own dream, which had had something to do with a beach and some hot guy rubbing suntan oil on me. Images—hers, not mine—tumbled through my mind: fire and blood, the smell of smoke, the twisted metal of a car. The pictures wrapped around me, suffocating me, until some rational part of my brain reminded me that this wasn't *my* dream.

I woke up, strands of long, dark hair sticking to my forehead.

Lissa lay in her bed, thrashing and screaming. I bolted out of mine, quickly crossing the few feet that separated us.

"Liss," I said, shaking her. "Liss, wake up."

Her screams dropped off, replaced by soft whimpers. "Andre," she moaned. "Oh God."

I helped her sit up. "Liss, you aren't there anymore. Wake up."

After a few moments, her eyes fluttered open, and in the dim lighting, I could see a flicker of consciousness start to take over. Her frantic breathing slowed, and she leaned into me, resting her head against my shoulder. I put an arm around her and ran a hand over her hair.

"It's okay," I told her gently. "Everything's okay."

"I had that dream."

"Yeah. I know."

We sat like that for several minutes, not saying anything else. When I felt her emotions calm down, I leaned over to the nightstand between our beds and turned on the lamp. It glowed dimly, but neither of us really needed much to see by. Attracted by the light, our housemate's cat, Oscar, leapt up onto the sill of the open window.

He gave me a wide berth—animals don't like dhampirs, for whatever reason—but jumped onto the bed and rubbed his head against Lissa, purring softly. Animals didn't have a problem with Moroi, and they all loved Lissa in particular. Smiling, she scratched his chin, and I felt her calm further.

"When did we last do a feeding?" I asked, studying her face. Her fair skin was paler than usual. Dark circles hung under her eyes, and there was an air of frailty about her. School had been hectic this week, and I couldn't remember the last time I'd given her blood. "It's been like . . . more than two days, hasn't it? Three? Why didn't you say anything?"

She shrugged and wouldn't meet my eyes. "You were busy. I didn't want to—"

"Screw that," I said, shifting into a better position. No wonder she seemed so weak. Oscar, not wanting me any closer, leapt down and returned to the window, where he could watch at a safe distance. "Come on. Let's do this."

"Rose—"

"Come *on*. It'll make you feel better."

I tilted my head and tossed my hair back, baring my neck. I saw her hesitate, but the sight of my neck and what it offered proved too powerful. A hungry expression crossed her face, and her lips parted slightly, exposing the fangs she normally kept hidden while living among humans. Those fangs contrasted oddly with the rest of her features. With her pretty face and pale blond hair, she looked more like an angel than a vampire.

As her teeth neared my bare skin, I felt my heart race with a mix of fear and anticipation. I always hated feeling the latter, but it was nothing I could help, a weakness I couldn't shake.

Her fangs bit into me, hard, and I cried out at the brief flare of pain. Then it faded, replaced by a wonderful, golden joy that spread through my body. It was better than any of the times I'd been drunk or high. Better than sex—or so I imagined, since I'd never done it. It was a blanket of pure, refined pleasure, wrapping me up and promising everything would be right in the world. On and on it went. The chemicals in her saliva triggered an endorphin rush, and I lost track of the world, lost track of who I was.

Then, regretfully, it was over. It had taken less than a minute.

She pulled back, wiping her hand across her lips as she studied me. "You okay?"

"I . . . yeah." I lay back on the bed, dizzy from the blood loss. "I just need to sleep it off. I'm fine."

Her pale, jade-green eyes watched me with concern. She stood up. "I'm going to get you something to eat."

My protests came awkwardly to my lips, and she left before I could get out a sentence. The buzz from her bite had lessened as soon as she broke the connection, but some of it still lingered in my veins, and I felt a goofy smile cross my lips. Turning my head, I glanced up at Oscar, still sitting in the window.

"You don't know what you're missing," I told him.

His attention was on something outside. Hunkering down into a crouch, he puffed out his jet-black fur. His tail started twitching.

My smile faded, and I forced myself to sit up. The world spun, and I waited for it to right itself before trying to stand. When I managed it, the dizziness set in again and this time refused to leave. Still, I felt okay enough to stumble to the window and peer out with Oscar. He eyed me warily, scooted over a little, and then returned to whatever had held his attention.

A warm breeze—unseasonably warm for a Portland fall—played with my hair as I leaned out. The street was dark and relatively quiet. It was three in the morning, just about the only time a college campus settled down, at least somewhat. The house in which we'd rented a room for the past eight months sat on a residential street with old, mismatched houses. Across the road, a streetlight flickered, nearly ready to burn out. It still cast enough light for me to make out the shapes of cars and buildings. In our own yard, I could see the silhouettes of trees and bushes.

And a man watching me.

I jerked back in surprise. A figure stood by a tree in the yard, about thirty feet away, where he could easily see through the window. He was close enough that I probably could have thrown something and hit him. He was certainly close enough that he could have seen what Lissa and I had just done.

The shadows covered him so well that even with my heightened sight, I couldn't make out any of his features, save for his height. He was tall. Really tall. He stood there for just a moment, barely discernible, and then stepped back, disappearing into the shadows cast by the trees on the far side of the yard. I was pretty sure I saw someone else move nearby and join him before the blackness swallowed them both.

Whoever these figures were, Oscar didn't like them. Not counting me, he usually got along with most people, growing upset only when someone posed an immediate danger. The guy outside hadn't done anything threatening to Oscar, but the cat had sensed something, something that put him on edge.

Something similar to what he always sensed in me.

Icy fear raced through me, almost—but not quite—eradicating the lovely bliss of Lissa's bite. Backing up from the window, I jerked on a pair of jeans that I found on the floor, nearly falling over in the process. Once they were on, I grabbed my coat and Lissa's, along with our wallets. Shoving my feet into the first shoes I saw, I headed out the door.

Downstairs, I found her in the cramped kitchen, rummaging through the refrigerator. One of our housemates, Jeremy, sat at the table, hand on his forehead as he stared sadly at a calculus book. Lissa regarded me with surprise.

"You shouldn't be up."

"We have to go. Now."

Her eyes widened, and then a moment later, understanding clicked in. "Are you . . . really? Are you sure?"

I nodded. I couldn't explain how I knew for sure. I just did.

Jeremy watched us curiously. "What's wrong?"

An idea came to mind. "Liss, get his car keys."

He looked back and forth between us. "What are you—"

Lissa unhesitatingly walked over to him. Her fear poured into me through our psychic bond, but there was something else too: her complete faith that I would take care of everything, that we would be safe. Like always, I hoped I was worthy of that kind of trust.

She smiled broadly and gazed directly into his eyes. For a moment, Jeremy just stared, still confused, and then I saw the thrall seize him. His eyes glazed over, and he regarded her adoringly.

"We need to borrow your car," she said in a gentle voice. "Where are your keys?"

He smiled, and I shivered. I had a high resistance to compulsion, but I could still feel its effects when it was directed at another person. That, and I'd been taught my entire life that using it was wrong. Reaching into his pocket, Jeremy handed over a set of keys hanging on a large red key chain.

"Thank you," said Lissa. "And where is it parked?"

"Down the street," he said dreamily. "At the corner. By Brown." Four blocks away.

"Thank you," she repeated, backing up. "As soon as we leave, I want you to go back to studying. Forget you ever saw us tonight."

He nodded obligingly. I got the impression he would have walked off a cliff for her right then if she'd asked. All humans were susceptible to compulsion, but Jeremy appeared weaker than most. That came in handy right now.

"Come on," I told her. "We've got to move."

We stepped outside, heading toward the corner he'd named. I was still dizzy from the bite and kept stumbling, unable to move as quickly as I wanted. Lissa had to catch hold of me a few times to stop me from falling. All the time, that anxiety rushed into me from her mind. I tried my best to ignore it; I had my own fears to deal with.

"Rose . . . what are we going to do if they catch us?" she whispered.

"They won't," I said fiercely. "I won't let them."

"But if they've found us—"

"They found us before. They didn't catch us then. We'll just drive over to the train station and go to L.A. They'll lose the trail."

I made it sound simple. I always did, even though there

was nothing simple about being on the run from the people we'd grown up with. We'd been doing it for two years, hiding wherever we could and just trying to finish high school. Our senior year had just started, and living on a college campus had seemed safe. We were so close to freedom.

She said nothing more, and I felt her faith in me surge up once more. This was the way it had always been between us. I was the one who took action, who made sure things happened—sometimes recklessly so. She was the more reasonable one, the one who thought things out and researched them extensively before acting. Both styles had their uses, but at the moment, recklessness was called for. We didn't have time to hesitate.

Lissa and I had been best friends ever since kindergarten, when our teacher had paired us together for writing lessons. Forcing five-year-olds to spell *Vasilisa Dragomir* and *Rosemarie Hathaway* was beyond cruel, and we'd—or rather, *I'd*—responded appropriately. I'd chucked my book at our teacher and called her a fascist bastard. I hadn't known what those words meant, but I'd known how to hit a moving target.

Lissa and I had been inseparable ever since.

"Do you hear that?" she asked suddenly.

It took me a few seconds to pick up what her sharper senses already had. Footsteps, moving fast. I grimaced. We had two more blocks to go.

"We've got to run for it," I said, catching hold of her arm.

"But you can't—"

"Run."

It took every ounce of my willpower not to pass out on the sidewalk. My body didn't want to run after losing blood or while still metabolizing the effects of her saliva. But I ordered my muscles to stop their bitching and clung to Lissa as our feet pounded against the concrete. Normally I could have outrun her without any extra effort—particularly since she was barefoot—but tonight, she was all that held me upright.

The pursuing footsteps grew louder, closer. Black stars danced before my eyes. Ahead of us, I could make out Jeremy's green Honda. Oh God, if we could just make it—

Ten feet from the car, a man stepped directly into our path. We came to a screeching halt, and I jerked Lissa back by her arm. It was *him*, the guy I'd seen across the street watching me. He was older than us, maybe mid-twenties, and as tall as I'd figured, probably six-six or six-seven. And under different circumstances—say, when he wasn't holding up our desperate escape—I would have thought he was hot. Shoulder-length brown hair, tied back in a short ponytail. Dark brown eyes. A long brown coat—a duster, I thought it was called.

But his hotness was irrelevant now. He was only an obstacle keeping Lissa and me away from the car and our freedom. The footsteps behind us slowed, and I knew our pursuers had caught up. Off to the sides, I detected more movement, more people closing in. God. They'd sent almost a dozen guardians to retrieve us. I couldn't believe it. The queen herself didn't travel with that many.

Panicked and not entirely in control of my higher reasoning, I acted out of instinct. I pressed up to Lissa, keeping her behind me and away from the man who appeared to be the leader.

"Leave her alone," I growled. "Don't touch her."

His face was unreadable, but he held out his hands in what was apparently supposed to be some sort of calming gesture, like I was a rabid animal he was planning to sedate.

"I'm not going to—"

He took a step forward. Too close.

I attacked him, leaping out in an offensive maneuver I hadn't used in two years, not since Lissa and I had run away. The move was stupid, another reaction born of instinct and fear. And it was hopeless. He was a skilled guardian, not a novice who hadn't finished his training. He also wasn't weak and on the verge of passing out.

And man, was he fast. I'd forgotten how fast guardians could be, how they could move and strike like cobras. He knocked me off as though brushing away a fly, and his hands slammed into me and sent me backwards. I don't think he meant to strike that hard—probably just intended to keep me away—but my lack of coordination interfered with my ability to respond. Unable to catch my footing, I started to fall, heading straight toward the sidewalk at a twisted angle, hip-first. It was going to hurt. A *lot*.

Only it didn't.

Just as quickly as he'd blocked me, the man reached out and caught my arm, keeping me upright. When I'd steadied myself, I noticed he was staring at me—or, more precisely, at my neck. Still disoriented, I didn't get it right away. Then, slowly, my free hand reached up to the side of my throat and lightly touched the wound Lissa had made earlier. When I pulled my fingers back, I saw slick, dark blood on my skin. Embarrassed, I shook my hair so that it fell forward around my face. My hair was thick and long and completely covered my neck. I'd grown it out for precisely this reason.

The guy's dark eyes lingered on the now-covered bite a moment longer and then met mine. I returned his look defiantly and quickly jerked out of his hold. He let me go, though I knew he could have restrained me all night if he'd wanted. Fighting the nauseating dizziness, I backed toward Lissa again, bracing myself for another attack. Suddenly, her hand caught hold of mine. "Rose," she said quietly. "Don't."

Her words had no effect on me at first, but calming thoughts gradually began to settle in my mind, coming across through the bond. It wasn't exactly compulsion—she wouldn't use that on me—but it was effectual, as was the fact that we were hopelessly outnumbered and outclassed. Even I knew struggling would be pointless. The tension left my body, and I sagged in defeat.

Sensing my resignation, the man stepped forward, turning his attention to Lissa. His face was calm. He swept her a bow and managed to look graceful doing it, which surprised me considering his height. "My name is Dimitri Belikov," he said. I could hear a faint Russian accent. "I've come to take you back to St. Vladimir's Academy, Princess."

He just wanted a decent book to read ...

Not too much to ask, is it? It was in 1935 when Allen Lane, Managing Director of Bodley Head Publishers, stood on a platform at Exeter railway station looking for something good to read on his journey back to London. His choice was limited to popular magazines and poor-quality paperbacks – the same choice faced every day by the vast majority of readers, few of whom could afford hardbacks. Lane's disappointment and subsequent anger at the range of books generally available led him to found a company – and change the world.

'We believed in the existence in this country of a vast reading public for intelligent books at a low price, and staked everything on it'
Sir Allen Lane, 1902–1970, founder of Penguin Books

The quality paperback had arrived – and not just in bookshops. Lane was adamant that his Penguins should appear in chain stores and tobacconists, and should cost no more than a packet of cigarettes.

Reading habits (and cigarette prices) have changed since 1935, but Penguin still believes in publishing the best books for everybody to enjoy. We still believe that good design costs no more than bad design, and we still believe that quality books published passionately and responsibly make the world a better place.

So wherever you see the little bird – whether it's on a piece of prize-winning literary fiction or a celebrity autobiography, political tour de force or historical masterpiece, a serial-killer thriller, reference book, world classic or a piece of pure escapism – you can bet that it represents the very best that the genre has to offer.

Whatever you like to read – trust Penguin.